Hearts of Ice & Stone

Martin Dukes

For Linda

Chapter One

The fire began in the oil room, so they said. And the warm wind that had blown from the south those last few days nourished the fury of the flames. Within hours the east wing of the great necropolis was ablaze, and nothing could be done to save it. The flames reached high for the night sky, and an oily pall of dark smoke trailed for miles across the constellations or was swept suddenly downwards by the whim of the wind to swirl and billow around the villages to the north-west. Some said that they smelled the spice with which the dead were anointed but intermingled with it was the familiar scent of burning timber and of more unwholesome things besides. Laura could see it from the window of her bedchamber more than three miles away, the long black blot on the night sky with the red fire at its core. At times, she fancied she could see the familiar stone pinnacles of the high central nave silhouetted against the angry red blaze. Even though she could hear nothing at this distance, she could readily imagine the roar of the flames, the crackle of tumbled black timbers caressed by the restless fingers of the flame.

'I can almost feel the heat of it,' she told her younger sister Emily, standing next to her at the window. 'Can't you feel it on your face?'

'You're crying,' said Emily, turning to her, running a small hand across Laura's cheek and wiping the tears away. 'That's what you can feel. Why are you crying? I'm excited. This is the most exciting thing that ever happened.'

'I'm crying for the dead people,' said Laura solemnly, 'because now they can't come back.'

I

And it was true. Darkharrow was a "sleep-hall", a house of the dead, the greatest necropolis in the Eastings, and whilst the living fought desperately to extinguish the blaze, the dead in their cool halls, their niches and their shadowed passages were at the mercy of the advancing flames. It was a night of great activity, even at Groomfield Hall. Before long there were riders on sweating, snorting horses in the courtyard, calling out for the girls' mother, the lady of Groomfield, in loud and insistent voices that carried none of the deference due to her status. It was clear that this was a night during which all normal expectations must be set aside.

'What's happening?' asked Laura, taking the stairs two at a time and running to the front door. Mary, the scullery maid, was standing there, a lamp in her hand, peering out into the darkness. The sharply uneven lamplight on her face made her pinched, anxious features seem grotesque, almost unearthly.

'You shouldn't be up!' hissed Mary, turning to Laura and to Emily as the two girls crossed to her side. Emily, genuinely alarmed by now, buried her face in Mary's pinafore, finding comfort in cool white cotton.

'You'll catch it if your mother sees you,' warned Mary, running her hand distractedly through Emily's hair. But her gaze and her attention had already returned to events outside. The girls' mother was in urgent conversation with two of the riders, her nightdress a lighter patch in the darkness, a shawl thrown around her shoulders. Laura could hear the urgency of their voices, but she could not make out any of the conversation.

'Where's Old Jonah?' asked Emily, peering past Mary.

'That's no way to speak of your father,' said Mary disapprovingly, giving her a nudge.

'He's not my father,' Emily told her, regarding the servant coldly. 'Father's dead.'

Mary might have been about to respond, but now a wagon was clattering and rumbling into the courtyard and Mama was coming up the steps with distinctly unladylike haste. She was crying, Laura noted, as the door swung open and she hurried through into the hall, already calling out instructions to Mary and to David, the steward, who was following at her heels.

'Mama!' exclaimed Laura, plucking at her sleeve.

'Not now, my sweet,' said Mama. 'There are things that we must do. And you must be abed this instant. Mary, will you...?'

But before Mama could complete her instruction for her daughters to be returned at once to bed, one of the two riders stomped in after her, asking her which way lay the cellar.

'David will show you,' she answered. And then, 'Will you get some more lamps, Mary? Take the ones from the parlour.'

Soon their visitors' purpose became clear. The canopy at the rear of the wagon was already pulled open and men were unloading its contents. Panting, stumbling on the uneven cobbles in the dark, they were bringing bodies into the house. Each corpse lay on a door that served as a makeshift bier; each was covered by a cloak or a sheet or even a few coarse strips of sacking. Sometimes a wizened arm hung loose. Sometimes pale feet disclosed themselves beneath a slipping cloth. Emily and Laura observed unseen from behind the staircase as the grim cavalcade continued. More wagons arrived. More bodies were carried in and down into the cellar amidst much irreverent cursing and ill humour.

'They are rescued from Darkharrow,' Laura told Emily when it became clear to her what she was witnessing. 'They are preserving the dead.'

'But why are they bringing them to Groomfield?' asked Emily in a small voice as two burly men came past with yet another corpse, head lolling beneath a scrap of canvas.

'I don't know,' shrugged Laura. 'Perhaps because the cellar is cool.'

'Your sister is correct,' interjected their mother's consort, Jonah, towering over them like a great black cliff as one last body was brought through the hall. He had appeared so suddenly that Laura felt her heart leap within her and drew her breath with a sharp, involuntary gasp. He had a way of doing that, the man that had shared their mother's bed since their father passed within the portals of Darkharrow. He was a tall man with features that were slow to disclose emotion, but they showed them now – a certain dark humour enlivened his face as if he rejoiced to have alarmed them so. There was triumph written in the set of his shoulders, too.

'All done,' said David, rubbing his hands together. 'We can accommodate no more unless we stack them two deep.'

'David!' scolded Mary, closing the cellar door. 'Such a thought.'

'You'd better tell them we can take no more,' said Jonah to one of the men. 'They could try up at Parry Garside. The church there has something of a crypt, I believe.'

'Indeed,' the man nodded, before tipping his hat respectfully and withdrawing.

Silence settled momentarily upon the hall, broken only by faint shouts from without and the sound of a wagon creaking into motion.

'To bed, this instant!' commanded Mama, as though seeing them for the first time. She smoothed a wisp of hair away from her face, and for a moment lamplight glinted on her tear-wet cheeks.

'Mama, what's the matter?' cried Emily.

'This instant!' reiterated Mama, taking a step towards them.

'Questions tomorrow,' said Jonah, taking off his hat and settling it on the newel post. 'Now your beds summon you.'

Reluctantly the sisters climbed the stair as Mary lit the way for them, maintaining a steady stream of admonishments as she led them to their room. Behind them, as voices drifted up from the hall, Laura could hear Mama talking to Jonah.

'Where were you?' she asked in a voice that carried with it suspicion as much as enquiry.

'I was at Darkharrow, of course,' she heard him say. 'The blaze had already taken hold. It was all we could do to...'

What Jonah had done was lost to Laura as the door clicked shut behind them. Mary was already pulling up the cold bedclothes over Emily and kissing her brow, more from habit than from any impulse of affection appropriate to the moment. And then it was Laura's turn, and the lamp was gone and the room quite dark except for what faint starlight crept in at the window.

'The dead are downstairs,' said Emily softly, when Mary's footsteps had faded away along the passage.

'Yes,' said Laura, her eyes fixed on the slit of night sky beyond the curtains.

'Do you think any of them awaken?'

'The dead do not awake in a single night, silly,' said Laura. 'It takes ages and ages. Edward Broadfoot was telling me.'

'How does he know?' asked Emily.

'He just knows, that's all,' said Laura, who could feel sleep reaching for her. 'Sleep now.'

'Sleep like the dead,' said Emily drowsily.

'Just sleep.'

The dead cast a long shadow over the living in the Eastings – and that shadow began at Darkharrow. They cast a long shadow, indeed, across the whole of Britannia and the whole of the wider world beyond. In most places that shadow crept forth from the hollow hearts of the hills in which the dead lay sleeping, but in the Eastings, there were no hills, only the endless salt marshes and the low reaches of cultivated land between. In the Eastings the soaring spires and honey-stone halls of Darkharrow marked the labours of twenty generations. The dead could not be buried in the cool earth here, for the low eminence on which the great mausoleum stood had 'wet feet.' so the local people said. Its foundations stood uneasily on the million wooden piles that long ago had been driven into the mud. Instead, the dead were housed in a vast maze of dark halls and corridors, lying on stone biers in cold cells or in narrow niches in the walls according to their wealth and status. But now the place was scarred by fire. The whole of the east wing lay in ruins, blackened pinnacles stark against the long eastern skies, crows wheeling raucously around the skeletons of tumbled roofs.

A week after the fire, Laura stood with Emily and her family at the southern portal of the abbey church that formed the publicly accessible part of the place. The dead that Groomfield's commodious cellars had briefly accommodated had been returned to their places in Darkharrow, if places for them could be found. There had been a great deal of difficulty in identifying many of them, since the carved plaques that named each one had not been brought with them in the hurry and the confusion, and large numbers had had to be squeezed into other, less crowded wings. Nevertheless, it was presumed, if any of these were resurrected, that they would know their own names. Laura was only ten years old then, but she was already conscious of the dignity of the dead, of the hushed tones that one should adopt in their presence, even within sight of the portals of this place. She glanced up to the high gothic arches, the niches with their statues, the complex encrustation of ancient carving that so amazed and baffled the visitor. Long ago, with Mama's help, they had unfolded their mysteries to her, and now she could name each of them in turn. There was Saint Barbara and Saint Eustachius with his flowering staff. There was the Blessed Saint Lydia and St Theobald with the flail that was the symbol of his martyrdom. There was Saint Philip and Saint Eulalia Martyr, who had come from these parts…

'What does the writing say?' asked six-year-old Emily in the loud tones of one who had not yet learned the decorum that was due in these environs. The disapproving glances of others who waited with them showed that they, at least, knew how to accord the departed the respect that was their due. Laura, stung by this unspoken criticism, pulled her sister close and placed a finger to her lips.

'But what does it say?' insisted Emily, somewhat more quietly.

'Blessed are the dead,' read Laura, tilting her face upwards to the cracked and time-worn scroll that surmounted the arch of the central portal. 'For they have gazed upon the face of the Lord, and they shall be awakened.'

'And will they?' asked Emily, awestruck. 'Will the dead be awakened?'

'Some of them will,' shrugged Laura. 'You know it. You know *them.*'

'Who do I know?' enquired Emily, her large blue eyes wide and her brow furrowed in perplexity. 'I wish you would talk sense.'

'Old Ma Catchpole, for one. She was dead once. Now she's alive. She went through that there door stone dead, and now she's as live as you and me.' Laura felt a smile tug at the corners of her mouth at the expression of awestruck incomprehension that transfigured her sister's small face.

'No,' she said.

'It is no more than the truth, I swear.'

'But how?'

How indeed? A thousand years or so had passed since the first mortal resurrection. All who knew their scripture and many besides knew that Saint Simeon was the first, emerging blinking from his stone-cut tomb fully twenty years after the funeral rites that had marked his passing. This miracle amazed the world. But soon there were others, and those whose powers of deduction and observation equipped them to see beyond the hand of God saw a pattern in these awakenings. In each case the miracle had taken place within the confines of an airy, stone-cut tomb. In each case the dead had been anointed with an unguent that contained the rare spice Sarconexine. In each case the tomb was entrusted to the care of the Camoldolite Order, whose prayers and rituals emphasised the preservation of the flesh so that the body might remain whole and intact in readiness for the day of judgement. But Judgement Day remained a vague and distant prospect, the last trump no more than a dream in the mind of angels when the dead came shambling from their halls to feel once more the breath of day upon their withered cheeks. It was not that all were awakened – far from it. Those uncounted millions buried in their churchyard graves did not shoulder the worms and the earth aside; mouldering to the white bone remained their fate. Even in the rock-cut tombs the oil-anointed dead lay still beneath the chanting of the monks and slumbered in their thousand and did not wake. But hardly a year had passed and there was not one such resurrection to bring hope and joy to the people of the Eastings.

'And that's why folks get taken here when they pass,' said Laura, running a hand through her sister's golden tresses. 'The Camoldolites know how to care for the dead. Sometimes, if it pleases the Lord, they come back. Sometimes they sleep until Judgement Day.'

'Mick, the miller's boy, didn't come here,' objected Emily. 'I saw them bury him in the ground, like they did with little Timmy when he died.'

Laura felt a hot tear spring in her eye at the thought of their dog that had died that Michaelmas just past.

'The poor must wait for judgement day for their bones to be clothed in flesh once more,' she told Emily, the prayer's familiar words coming easily to her tongue. 'Or else to be cast into the abyss if they have sinned. Only the rich can pay for the Camoldolites to look after their mortal remains and commend them to the Lord. Only the rich can dream of living twice.'

'Well, I don't think it's fair,' said Emily, pursing her lips. 'Poor Mick.'

'Life doesn't have to be fair,' said Laura piously. 'It's the will of the Lord, that's all.'

There was a commotion now at the portal as the crowd parted to admit a party of Laura's immediate family and their chief retainers. There was a murmur that rose to an unseemly level before subsiding as their mother approached, her face pale, eyes tear-reddened, supported on either side by Laura's aunts. Jonah, the man who now demanded to be regarded as their father but who was not, strode at their head. His face was grim, but his small eyes enlivened by a gleam that was quite at variance with the circumstances. His gaze fell upon the girls, who must consider themselves his daughters.

'What is it?' asked Laura as she felt Emily melt into her side, suddenly oppressed by some nameless fear. 'What is it?' she asked again as Jonah moved wordlessly aside and her mother stooped to enfold them in a tremulous embrace.

'It is your father,' came the words that Laura had dreaded must come. 'And it as we had feared. He is no more. His body is consumed in the fire, and he is beyond hope of resurrection.'

Mama drew away, and her cool grey eyes now held Laura's steadily.

'We must accept God's will, no matter how hard it seems. We must rise to his test. We must move on.'

'We must indeed,' said Jonah, placing a hard hand upon her shoulder. 'We must submit to the will of the Lord.'

And that submission had meant submission to the will of Jonah, it appeared. When Father died, fully six years ago, their mother had been cast adrift in a sea of troubles that her experience of life had not equipped her to navigate with any certainty of success. Her husband, George DeLacey, had been a proud and masterful man, a man for whom the running of a large estate ran deep in the blood of generations. The son of sons who had farmed Groomfield and its satellite estates for at least three hundred years knew every stile, every turn of the plough, every spreading oak with the intimacy of one whose roots reached far into the soil of those marsh girt acres. His wife, Margaret Strongbow, he loved with a passion that drew near to this first blood-borne abiding love. Rich clothes, rich foods and the society of her peers in the Eastings were to be her diversion and the estate no more than the backdrop for the elegant drama of her days. He was a fine judge of horseflesh and of the weather, so far as the harvest was concerned. He was a level-headed man when not in drink. But he was often in drink, and when he was in such a state, he was a poor judge of cards. All Mama's weeping and her earnest entreaties could not keep him from the game by which their wealth leached away, year by year until they could no longer keep a carriage and those days when she would shop for fine silks in Market Lavenshall seemed a glimpse of a golden age long gone.

'I cannot sustain the dignity of my station… our station,' Laura remembered her Mama say one night, when she was very small as she lay wakeful in her bed, 'if you insist on squandering your inheritance so.'

'We must endure the shifting squalls of fate with patience,' her father assured her, his voice muffled by the thickness of her bedchamber wall. 'Why, only last month I came away with fifty sovereigns.'

'And only this morning your steward assured me the chest was quite bare,' objected Mama. 'Are we to squeeze even more money from our poor tenants for you to pitch it all on a turn of cards? Are we to take the bread from their mouths for you to hand it all to a parcel of sharps and scoundrels? I swear that John Collyer sees you coming and his palms itch with the joy of the gold that soon thereafter passes over them, our gold, husband. Gold that comes by the honest sweat of brows. Gold that is your daughters' birth-right.'

'Our fortunes will revive, I do assure you,' said Father in a placatory, wheedling tone that was quite foreign to him and set Laura's heart racing with concern. At length their voices faded to silence along the corridor that led to their bedchamber. Laura pulled the bedclothes over her head, sighed deep and prayed with all her might that their fortunes might revive and that her Mama's peace of mind might revive in its turn.

But this did not come to pass. Instead, her father ventured all their estate on a single hand of cards, and a quartet of kings undid him. All would have been lost had Father not accidentally shot himself dead whilst cleaning his pistol soon afterwards, so Mama told her daughters. And a man's debts died with him, or so the law said.

Mama was already struggling to cope with Father's affairs on her own when Jonah Stephenson, their estate manager, came to the door a month or so later, offering to take care of her dealings in their entirety. Another month and Groomfield was restored to a semblance of order, a further month and he was in her bed.

'They do say that your daddy shot himself,' said shrew-eyed Tilly Mayhew one day, a year or so after the fire, when Father's body was no more. 'And self-murder is a mortal sin, so the Bible teaches us, if I am not mistaken.'

It was the feast of Saint Andrew, and some of the village girls were drinking watered cider after dancing on the green. The sun shone brightly on the trestle tables that were set out there, and all the folk of Tithing Harrow gathered to partake of the sweet honey cakes and the elderflower wine that was traditional to the occasion.

'It was an accident,' Laura told her crossly. 'Anyone can have an accident. He was cleaning his pistol.'

'He was cleaning it in his mouth, then,' scoffed Tilly. 'I heard he blew half his head off.'

'Then you heard a lie,' said Laura coldly, and it was as though a cloud moved before the sun and the cheerful hubbub of the crowd died suddenly away. All that remained were Laura and Tilly's mocking face at her side. Laura's cup slipped from her fingers and broke on the cobbles at her feet.

'Mark Henderson doesn't think it is a lie,' continued Tilly, her lip curled in a sneer, 'and neither does Dr Henderson, his father, who attended on your poor dead daddy.'

Laura felt her eyes fill with tears. A hot wave of rage and humiliation prickled across her scalp, and she clenched her fists into tight balls.

'That's a lie!' she exclaimed again, forcing out the trembling words.

'Say it again and maybe you'll believe it,' scoffed Tilly, 'but I don't think anyone else here's ever going to swallow it.'

'Like your daddy swallowed his gun,' laughed little Josie Critchlow.

'He never!' spat Emily.

In the creeping horror of the exchange, Laura had forgotten that her sister was beside her. But now Emily flung herself at Josie, and suddenly the two of them were shrieking and rolling in the gutter, punching, biting, pulling hair.

'Hey! What's all this?' said big Jack, the butcher's boy, reaching down to pull the two combatants apart and holding each at arm's length like a couple of snarling wild dogs. 'It don't do to disrespect the saint. Today's a day of peace, so it is. Let your differences be set aside.'

'They will,' said Tilly with a proud lift of her chin, pulling Josie to herself and smoothing down her muddied frock, 'but it doesn't alter the fact of the matter.'

'Which is…?' said Mick, giving red-faced Emily a gentle shove in Laura's direction.

'Which is there's no place in Darkharrow for suicides,' Tilly snorted haughtily, hands on hips. 'But Hell reserves a place for their self-murdering father. And the fires of Hell surely reached up for him last year.'

It was only when she was hurrying her sister away that Laura noticed the blood that flecked Emily's lip.

'Hey, stop now. You're bleeding,' she said, stooping to Emily's level, reaching for a rag from her pocket. 'Did that little bitch split your lip, then?'

'No, she didn't!' snarled Emily, twitching her head away. 'I gave as good as I took, did I not?'

'Here, hold still,' Emily intoned while dabbing with the rag. 'Are you wheezy again?'

'A little.'

'Deep breaths, then. Deep, slow breaths.'

Laura pulled away and regarded her little sister with concern. The red flush was fading from her cheeks and there was a familiar darkness beneath her eyes.

'I shall tell Mama. We must fetch the doctor to you again.'

As Laura had dreaded, Dr Henderson took Mama aside later that evening and told her that he feared Emily was consumptive, that the blood on Laura's kerchief came not from her lips but from her lungs. There was a long pause. Laura sat at Emily's bedside and squeezed her hand. On the other side of the bedroom door Laura heard her mother stifle a sob.

'She will not make old bones, I fear,' added the doctor. 'I say this because you must inure yourself to the knowledge… and because you are my friend.'

'And nothing can be done?' tried Mama in a small voice. 'Are there no medicines that can be acquired?'

'There *are* no medicines,' came Jonah's harsh voice. 'You know this, Margaret. You know it. We are in God's hands, and he will measure her days.'

'Indeed,' agreed the doctor solemnly.

'Must I go to Darkharrow?' asked Emily in a whisper.

Laura squeezed her hand some more and forced a smile.

'What will be, will be,' she said simply. 'Ours is to live each day that comes and dwell not on tomorrow.'

The estate recovered some of its former prosperity in Jonah's firm grip, although there was no capital and precious little hope of investing in improvements until a few good harvests had been gathered in. Now that Father's body was no more there was no longer any legal impediment to Mama's remarriage. The law said that although a consort may enter a widow's body, he might not enter her wealth so long as her husband's body was preserved. So long as he had lain on his stone bier in Darkharrow there remained the theoretical possibility that he might awake to a new life and resume his place at his wife's side. Even the dogs in Tithing Harrow knew that this could never happen so long as Father lay there with half his head shot off, but the law made no such distinction. The fire at Darkharrow had ruined many a dream of resurrection, but it brought to pass Jonah's dream of assuming ownership of Groomfield. Upon his marriage to Margaret DeLacey her possessions became his in equal measure and her daughters came under the mantle of his authority. The wedding took place in the spring, when the May was in the hedgerows and the tracksides were primrose-spangled with the promise of new life. The new life that lay ahead for Laura lay heavy on her brow, however, since the intervening months had brought about no greater understanding between Jonah and the girls, no growth in mutual affection. His smiles and his gentle words were reserved for their mother. In her absence he was remote, suspicious, as though he sensed their resentment, and yet, instead of trying to win their trust he treated them with a conceited disdain.

'I cannot rejoice for them,' Laura told Emily quietly as they sat at the high table and watched their new parental couple take their first dance. The hall was alive with life and colour, decked with flowers, the complexions of their friends and family heightened by wine and good cheer. 'He is barely civil to us now. How will he use us when Groomfield is his own?'

'Mama will love us still,' Emily assured her from over the top of a beaker of mead. 'And Jonah will be away with the farm people or his friends most days. And one day we shall be married.'

'But who to?' asked Laura, wondering whether her sickly sister would live long enough to be wed. 'Do you think Jonah cares to see us happy in our betrothals? I think gold is his guiding star and that is all.'

'The chief star in the heavens for many a sweeter man than he, I warrant,' said Emily with a grin.

'You've an old head on young shoulders,' laughed Laura.

Edward Broadfoot, Laura's friend since early childhood, knew things. He was that kind of boy. He didn't know how to play football or cricket with the other boys, and there was a certain awkwardness about his movements, as though the brain that directed his limbs was ill at ease in their deployment. He knew the secrets of the dead, however, and for this reason the other lads of his age regarded him with superstitious awe. His uncle, Prior Noah Broadfoot, was deputy to Abbot Canning, the Keeper of Darkharrow, the man to whom the care of the dead was entrusted, the man whose prayers and ancient rites accompanied their committal to that place and would continue until the day of their awakening or of his own admission to their company. Edward was Noah's apprentice. He spent his days in learning the arcane rituals, the complex procedures by which the dead should be anointed with myrrh and with rare spices, their flesh rubbed with sweet oils, their bodies caressed by cool airs. Such were the paths that might lead to resurrection.

'That Noah, he makes me shiver when I see him,' Laura told Edward one day, four years later, when they were walking in the field below Mustow's broken mill.

Edward was a tall but slight young man, yet to acquire the permanent stoop of those living denizens of Darkharrow. He turned a face to her that was alive with wry amusement.

'Why old Noah? Surely not!'

'He does, I swear!' admitted Laura, her brow furrowed. 'I wonder does he ever smile?'

'Now you're one to point fingers at folks about smiling,' laughed Emily, pushing Laura playfully in the small of her back and then darting away as Laura swung round, hand raised to seize her.

'He keeps sober company,' said Edward through a grin.

'And so do you,' Laura told him, flicking wind-whipped hair from her eyes. 'And you're not... glum and grim...' she paused, eyes momentarily unfocused as she sought inwardly for words, '... and full of bitterness.'

'Not yet,' answered Edward, pressing his hat hard to his head as another fitful gust flattened the long grasses around them. His smile faded. 'Nor yet awhile, I think.' He took off his hat and held it tight to his breast as he turned to look eastward to where the looming bulk of Darkharrow could be seen beyond a screen of trees. 'I think there are those who are made by Darkharrow and those who are made *despite* it.'

'And are you one of those, Edward Broadfoot?' asked Laura seriously, plucking at his sleeve.

He shrugged. 'I think. I hope. Time will tell, perhaps.'

'Time tells all!' cried Emily, skipping past with flowers in her hair and laughter in her eyes. 'And I shall tell that you are lovers.'

'And who'd believe you?' scoffed Edward, the humour draining from his own features now. 'None, I think, for what a creature I am.'

Laura regarded him, and it was true he was a lanky, gangling lad with a shock of dark hair and eyes that seemed too large, too intense for his pale features. His was not a figure to excite a maiden's desire, and so conscious of this, conscious of his awkwardness, she cast her eyes down.

'And you being,' he began, 'and you being...' But whatever was in his mind would not find utterance, and a blush rose to his cheeks.

'Late is what you're being,' supplied Emily as they passed the kissing gate into Tithing Harrow's Westway and came within sight of the church clock. 'Old Noah will have your hide, so he will.'

'Hmm,' said Edward, glancing upward. 'So you might think, although I beg you to cast out the thought that I may tremble at his name.'

And with a tilt of his hat he was gone, with a peculiar gait that bore witness to some internal struggle between the desire to avoid tardiness and the urge to show no evidence thereof.

'Strange boy,' concluded Emily, taking Laura's arm and squeezing it. 'Strange, strange boy.'

'And do you wonder at it,' asked Laura, 'dwelling in that place?'

Chapter Two

Cottersley Park was home to Becky Marchmayne, one of Laura's particular friends. Whereas Groomfield was much reduced in its prosperity and the walls were greying for want of a lick of whitewash, Cottersley Park looked out in proud, high-gabled, three-storeyed pomp over broad acres of profitable agricultural perfection. There was a croquet lawn and a ha-ha in front of it to keep the plump and healthy cattle from straying too close whilst afternoon tea was in progress. Sir Peter Marchmayne, Becky's father, was Justice of the Peace and a Member of Parliament, like his father and his father before him. His swelling belly and his ruddy good-natured features spoke of a man at peace with his own small world – a simple man, untroubled by rumours of disquiet in the wider nation beyond.

It was a walk of no more than forty minutes or so for those who no longer had a carriage, but Laura could cut this to half an hour when she had something of import to share with her friend. Emily often came, too, but Emily walked slowly now that consumption was wasting her lungs, and she often paused for breath, although she passed this off as an opportunity to inspect wildflowers or the half-hidden burrows of small creatures. On one such occasion, in the summer of Laura's sixteenth year, they walked the familiar way past the ruins of old Meg's cottage and beyond the gate, where a view of the wide marshes eastward opened and a hen harrier was often to be seen wheeling high in the sky over the stark black trees on Benchwood Knoll.

Arriving as dark clouds gathered beyond Cottersley Park, the sisters were greeted by Becky at the door with a mischievous glint in her eye, embracing Laura with fulsome enthusiasm and taking Emily in her arms as though she were a delicate piece of china.

'Millie and Eleanor are here,' she told them. 'I left them sitting up in the old attic.'

'The old attic your butler came across?' asked Emily, shrugging off the old coat she wore, even on warm days. 'The one that was hidden behind a wall?'

'Uh, huh. That's the one,' Becky confirmed with a grin. 'It's supposed to be haunted.'

'I never heard such stuff and nonsense,' clucked Martha, the Marchmayne's elderly housekeeper, casting her eyes upward as she took Emily's coat. 'Ghosts indeed! How can folks' spirits be abroad if their bodies is lain' in Darkharrow?'

'Not every corpse lies in Darkharrow,' said Becky, a little sharply as she led them towards the stairs.

'Now ain't that the truth,' muttered Martha, shuffling away towards the kitchens. 'Place's too good for the likes of me an' mine.'

They found Millie and Eleanor waiting outside the attic, peering through into gloom pierced only by a few shafts of daylight that crept beneath the tiles. The wall that had concealed the place for centuries had been partly stripped back, leaving an unswept mess of crumbled lath and plaster. A large and irregular hole gave access to the space.

'What makes you think it's haunted?' asked Laura, conscious of her heart racing as Becky stepped through into the darkness.

'Why wouldn't it be?' asked round-faced Millie Godwin, her eyes agleam with enthusiasm. 'I daresay there's an old retainer walled up in there or a son who shamed the family, no more than a skeleton by now.'

Laura felt Emily's grip tighten on her arm as they followed and stood blinking in the gloom.

'No skeletons,' announced Becky regretfully. 'Pryor's already searched the place; just a big old box full of tiles and a few tools.'

'No hidden gold, then? No walled-up bodies?' enquired Eleanor in disappointed tones. 'And Pryor might have had it dusted. Mama will chide me if I ruin my frock.'

'Well, I think it's exciting,' said Emily, releasing her grip on Laura's arm and moving away towards the bare brick wall at the far end of the attic, sunlight painting a shifting pattern of lines on her frock as she moved. 'Who knows what happened here... and why would they just seal it up like that?'

'I can tell you exactly why,' said a voice behind them.

They turned to find themselves face to face with an elderly woman of distinguished appearance, wearing no more than a nightshirt and with a kerchief trailing from one hand. This was Elsie Courtney. Most of the better families had at least one revenant to call their own, and Elsie was the Marchmaynes'. She had passed within the walls of Darkharrow a century or so ago and reawakened to her second life when Laura was very small. She vaguely remembered the bells pealing to announce the glad tidings, because Mrs Marchmayne was with Mother at the time and had been required to hurry off to greet her newly revived relative. Revenants were at risk of being socially isolated, having awoken to a second life at a time when everyone they knew or loved might themselves be long dead. For this reason, custom dictated they should be welcomed fulsomely into the bosom of the community with prayers, feasting, thanksgiving and gifts. Many revenants quickly integrated within a new social milieu, but some did not. Elsie was one of these. Affecting a marked disdain for her new status, she spent most of her days in the room that had been set aside for her, only rarely venturing out for meals or for a solitary progress around the grounds if the weather was unusually fine.

'Oh, Elsie! You did surprise me. Must you creep around so?' asked Becky with a laugh.

'I do not creep, and I'll bid you curb your insolence!' snapped the old woman, furrowing her pale brow.

'You must excuse me,' conceded Becky with a sly glance of suppressed amusement for her friends. 'But pray tell us why this attic was walled up. You lived in this very house, did you not?'

'I did, and I was no more than your age when your great, great, uncle had this wall put in.'

'But why?' asked Emily. 'Had he a secret to hide? Is there a chest of gold beneath the floorboards?'

'Or a skeleton?' suggested Millie hopefully.

'Nonsense,' scoffed Elsie. 'It was simply that the proportions of this room were found wanting. His wife considered it too long a space to be seemly and insisted that he wall it off. There was meant to be a door by which it might be accessed, but the builders did not comprehend their brief and it was done whilst the owners were away. Then the plague carried them both off, the house stood empty for a time, and it was all forgotten about. There. Is that a dull enough story for you?' she asked, the faintest hint of a smile tugging at the corners of her mouth.

Cottersley Park, with its various wings and labyrinthine corridors, backstairs and passages, offered unparalleled opportunities for games of hide and seek. It was during the afternoon of the same day that Laura came across Elsie once more. On this occasion Laura emerged breathlessly into the long room that overlooked the front lawns, to find the revenant sitting in a corner and staring with apparent interest into the fireplace. It was a warm day in a summer that had so far offered little but rain and wind. Nevertheless, revenants were notoriously prone to feeling the chill, and a small fire was flickering in the hearth.

'Oh, such a hurry!' observed Elsie as Laura stumbled to a halt, smoothing down her hair and glancing furtively about her in case there should be some other present who might lighten the burden of unease that had suddenly settled upon her. Laura always felt a sense of vague disquiet amongst those who had known death, even when their company was leavened with that of those of her own kind. Now she felt an awkward catch in her throat as she mumbled apologies for her haste.

'What are you all flustered about?' demanded Elsie, ignoring Laura's act of contrition. 'Do I trouble you, girl?'

Laura shook her head, muttering an unconvincing denial.

'Well, there's plenty others I trouble,' said Elsie after a pause in which she seemed to consider the notion. 'Here, help me up.'

This peremptory instruction was accompanied by a tilt of the chin and the extension of her withered old hand towards Laura.

Laura bit her lip, approached, took the hand and pulled. At once, as she and Elsie moved in unison, there was a flutter in her chest and a curious sensation akin to a tingling in her fingertips. Elsie felt it, too. Even as she straightened herself, her pale features were enlivened by a small flush in each cheek and by a momentary expression of wonderment that was quickly overtaken by suspicion.

'What's that?' she asked as Laura quickly withdrew her hand.

'Nothing!' Laura snapped back, finding that she was rubbing the hand abstractedly on her smock. The tingling was gone now, but the recollection of the papery coolness of Elsie's skin remained. It was an uncomfortable memory. She knew, with some foreboding, that it would not fade quickly.

Elsie continued to scrutinise her, those rheumy old eyes searching her own, and now the gnarled hand was on her upper arm, causing her flesh to recoil. The big clock on the mantel ticked; the ornate brass pendulum swung beneath it, but the second of time that it announced seemed to hang motionless in the air between them. Laura's mouth was suddenly dry, and a strange tension locked her body into immobility.

'What do you want?' she gasped.

'What do *I* want?' asked Elsie dryly. 'There is something odd about you...'

She nodded and was about to say more when the door burst open and Becky rushed in, with Millie and Emily in close pursuit.

'Oh, hello, Elsie,' said Becky politely, once the joy of finding her friend had faded from her face, and then, rekindled once more, 'Come on, Laura. Papa's just rode in, and he's brought my new pony.'

Laura found herself released, gathered up in an excited progress along stairs and corridors to the stable yard, albeit with Elsie's parting words ringing in her ears.

'We must talk again.'

'Do I seem "odd" to you?' she asked Emily as they made their way homeward at the end of that day.

'You haven't been listening to a word I've said,' said Emily, turning upon her. 'Have you?'

The tone was accusative but brought with it more exasperation than genuine irritation. Emily was used to Laura's absences and those frequent moments when her eyes seemed to look beyond her immediate environment.

'I confess I have not,' admitted Laura, stopping suddenly beneath a spreading horse chestnut tree that overhung the path at that point. A breath of wind stirred the branches above them and a few heavy drops of rain began to patter amongst the leaves. 'Was there something about a horse?'

'I was just saying,' began Emily with an exaggerated sigh, 'that I wondered when you might have a pony of your own. You *are* very nearly sixteen.'

'And do you think my age matters but a jot to Jonah?' scoffed Laura. 'Do you see him loosening his purse strings sufficiently to indulge me so? Even if it were a broken-down old nag fit only for the knackers? I wish I had your sunny outlook on the world... I wish I had some sun,' she added, glancing about as the rain began to fall in earnest. 'And where is your shawl, Emily DeLacey?'

'Oh dear,' said Emily, biting her lip ruefully. 'I fear I may have left it at Cottersley.'

'And us a good two miles from home,' scolded Laura. 'Here, you had best take mine. Mama will take on so if you catch a chill.'

'We could stay here a while,' said Emily, sniffing while wrapping the shawl around her. 'It may pass in a moment, I think.'

'What an optimist you are,' said Laura, gesturing at the leaden skies even as distant thunder rumbled in the east. 'And even you know better than to shelter beneath a tree in a thunderstorm. Come, if we run, we may make it to Jem Brierley's cottage before it sets in hard.'

'Yes, you are,' announced Emily, shawl over her head as they ran towards the distant rooftops, wind and rain stinging their faces.

'Yes, I am what?' cried Laura over her shoulder.

'Odd!' came back the gasping response.

'What?!' Laura spluttered while spinning around, her hair already rain heavy. Emily ran into her so hard that they almost fell in a heap.

'But I still love you!' laughed Emily as she steadied herself in Laura's arms and a squall lashed the puddles in the track around them.

'Do not trouble yourself, Mama,' said Emily as they sat at dinner later that day. 'I am fine – and with barely a wheeze to show for it. Besides, Laura lent me her shawl.'

'Well, the thought of you out in this weather…' chided Mama, removing her hand at last from Emily's forehead. 'You should have been more careful.'

'I swear the sky was blue as your eye when we set out from Cottersley,' said Laura, looking up from the slice of pie she had been contemplating.

'Damn this weather,' observed Jonah, pushing his plate aside. 'And damn this pie, too. Is this really all we have?'

'Mary used Paget's recipe,' said Mama apologetically. 'But she lacks Paget's skill. If you had not dismissed her so…'

'She was a thief, damn her name!' growled Jonah, his dark eyes flashing sudden fire, his napkin cast down abruptly next to his plate.

'She gave her brother a brace of fowl,' said Mama in a low voice, 'because they are starving in that household. Have you seen their children? Thin as sticks they are.'

Laura cast her eyes downward and wished that she were elsewhere. It was unusual to hear her Mama venture

27

such a retort when Jonah was out of sorts. And he was out of sorts tonight, his humour soured by thin gravy and a pastry that offered rather more than token resistance to the knife.

'My fowl! My kitchen!' spat Jonah, thumping the table in a way that prompted a small, stifled cry from Laura. 'And theft, is theft, is theft! I could have had her strung up, had I mind to summon the constable. There's a cancer of theft in these parts, and it's eating the heart out us.'

Jonah went on, at some length and with some passion, to describe recent episodes of thieving and dishonesty in the vicinity, some of which were familiar to Laura's ear. The remedy for such things, it appeared, was hanging, hanging and more hanging, unless a simple thrashing would suffice.

'Yes, I would hang the fear of God into them,' finished Jonah, pushing back his chair and wiping away a few flecks of spittle from around his mouth with the back of his hand, 'if they take things that are mine.'

Laura, who had sat very still during this tirade, as if taking shelter from another thunderstorm, glanced up to see whether her mother's face bore any signs of distress or resentment at being reminded that the things that once were hers were now Jonah's. There was no hint, unless she concealed her inner mind with uncommon skill.

'Calm yourself,' she told him, rising and placing her arm around his shoulders to soothe him. 'I shall enquire in Lavenshall tomorrow, when I go. It may be that we can find somebody even better than Paget. It's not that there aren't plenty of folk in search of employment. There must be a decent cook amongst them.'

'There surely can't be a worse,' grunted Jonah with a wry smile at his own returning humour. 'Here, bring me the ham and some bread. A man must fill his belly one way or another.'

'If we had a pony...' said Emily as Laura brushed her hair at bedtime that night. 'If we had only a small pony, we should have been back at Groomfield long before the rain began.'

'I fear we shall never have a pony,' said Laura. 'Jonah will not allow it.'

'Indeed, it seems he has set his mind against it,' said Emily gloomily.

'Shush now,' hissed Laura as Mary came in with the warming pan for Emily's bed, it being so clammy after the rain.

'And you being sixteen now,' continued Emily after she had gone, in aggrieved tones. 'You could be married.'

'Married!' laughed Laura, tapping Emily's head with the brush. 'I never even had a sweetheart, and you talk of marriage?'

'What about Edward, then? Shan't you marry him?'

'Hah! I wonder sometimes if your wits aren't all astray!' admonished Laura, setting down the brush and crossing to her own bed. 'You know that Edward is betrothed to Mother Church.'

And it was true. Edward had long ago taken the first steps that would lead him on the path towards ordainment in the Camoldolite Order, the priests of which foreswore marriage. The care of the dead was their calling. They were forbidden the delights of the living flesh, forbidden the agonies and the ecstasies of romantic love, at least in theory, at least so far as the world would condone.

If these considerations weighed heavily on the brow of Edward Broadfoot, he gave no sign of it as he and Laura sat together the following day on the old bench that overlooked Tithing Harrow. The rain had passed away during the night and a watery sunlight issued fitfully from between scudding clouds. The bench was still damp, and so the two of them sat upon Edward's folded coat.

'They do say the harvest will be spoiled again if it carries on like this for another fortnight or so,' observed Laura's companion, chewing abstractedly on a stalk of grass.

'Not that Darkharrow will be spoiled by rain,' said Laura.

'You'd be surprised,' countered Edward, turning to her. 'There're parts of the north run that leak like a sieve. Old Noah's forever trying to persuade the abbot to take the roof in hand.'

'Why doesn't he, then? The abbot, I mean,' asked Laura, reaching for the book of mathematics that was their ostensible reason for being there. They were on their way to Mrs Armitage's school but there was to be a test that day, and so Edward, whose understanding of these things was greater, had offered to share his knowledge of geometry.

Edward shrugged and bent forward, elbows on knees, the bones of his long, narrow back standing out against his patched shirt as he contemplated the dark mass of Darkharrow at the far side of the town.

'Abbot Canning is an odd fish,' he said. 'A very learned man, no doubt, and very eloquent when the spirit moves him. Yes, his speech is a fine thing indeed, but I fear he is a stranger to resolution. He should apply to Canterbury for funding. My uncle has told him as many times as he dares, but unless the dead are actually awash down there…' he petered off, turning to offer Laura a wry smile. 'He's happy enough for old Noah and me and the others to dash about with pails and swab the halls and corridors like a parcel of scullery maids.'

Laura smiled, amused by the notion of the serious scholarly youth at her side wielding mop and pail.

'Oh dear!' she chuckled. 'The dignity of Mother Church is endangered, I find!'

'And so is mine,' laughed Edward, lifting an arm to reveal a large tear in the fabric of his shirt. 'Does this apparel speak of dignity, do you think? Am I arrayed as a bishop yet?'

'You should come back to Groomfield with me,' she clucked, poking at his armpit. 'Our Mary could mend that in a trice, and even I in a moment or two. When will you ever learn to wield a needle, Edward Broadfoot?'

'I fear such pleasures will be denied me,' said Edward ironically, his soft brown eyes filled with sudden humour. 'But yet I wield a knowledge of geometry and trigonometry in which I find consolation.'

'Then you must share it with me,' said Laura with mock severity, 'or your shirt must surely remain as open to the elements as the roof of Darkharrow.'

The book was opened. Her instruction began but her heart was not in it, and the complex figures swam before her eyes even as Edward's earnest tones entreated her ears. She found herself regarding him slyly, sidelong. He had become a moderately handsome youth, she decided, although there was a wiry gauntness about him very different to the hard muscularity of some of the other boys of his age. She toyed listlessly with the notion of being kissed by him, of kissing him, in the way she had envisaged such things with others of his sex this last few years. Although there had never been an actual kiss, not really; only a giggling brush of lips at the horse fair last May with Will Mayers, when he and she were intoxicated with dance and a little illicit wine. But Will was a shallow, vacuous creature and Edward was, by comparison, an intellectual giant. They said he might have gone up to Cambridge had his means allowed it. But they would not. His parents were long gone to their grave, and he owed his living to his parsimonious uncle, and to Mother Church, of course. Mother Church... a jealous parent.

Laura found herself studying Edward's neat hands, finished off meticulously with those close-clipped, tidy nails – so unlike the grimy claws his uncle plied about the uncomplaining dead, ingrained with ancient and nameless unguents and oils. She shuddered at this thought and offered Edward a small, encouraging nod when he showed signs of hesitation. She fancied that Edward had considered kissing her, too; had caught a shy considering glance once or twice when he had thought her attention was elsewhere. She was conscious of taking a special care in her movements, in the fall of her hair, in the set of her chin when she was with him. Perhaps this was what it was like to be a woman, she mused, but she was not a woman yet, not quite, and as a woman of her particular station she could have no truck with the likes of Edward.

'Where is Father gone?' she asked her mother later that day. She used this hateful form of words only for Mama's hearing, because she insisted on it and because she knew only bitterness and recrimination would ensue if she did otherwise. Jonah's black mare, Ebony, was gone from the stable, and Tom, the stable boy, had confirmed his departure. That was all she could learn from him, Tom being simple and with a fearful stammer besides.

'He is gone out west on business,' said Mama, looking up from a pile of letters, the late evening sunlight glinting on her spectacles.

This told Laura little, given that most places were west of the Eastings.

'And how long will he be gone, d'you suppose?'

'Your father's plans are his own,' Mama told her, her mouth pursed shrewishly, 'and if he'd cared to share them with us, I dare say he would have done.'

As ever, Laura sought criticism of Jonah in her mother's tone but found none. She found only acceptance. It seemed that after the travails of her brief independence, Mama had craved security above all things and that security was bought at the cost of submission. This submission entailed a shadowing of Jonah's moods and attitudes as one ship changes tack to remain close astern of another. Jonah's approach to his adopted daughters ranged from impatience to barely concealed hostility, so it was hardly to be remarked that they saw little in their mother of the open-hearted affection that once was their endowment. But when Jonah was away, day-by-day, they saw the Mama that once had been seep gradually back into her being.

Consciousness that this was the subtext of Laura's question prompted Mama to regard her daughter disapprovingly. She waved one of the letters.

'This coming out affair of yours... do you have any notion of what it's costing?'

Laura shook her head, crossing to the window to look out over the rose garden that had been so battered by the previous night's rain.

'More than we can well afford,' continued Mama censoriously. 'What with half the tenancies lying idle and last year's harvest being so pitiably poor, here we are trying to launch you into adult life in a befitting manner, and all your sister can do is harangue your father for a pony. A pony, for Lord's sake!' she clucked disapprovingly. 'And this when it's all we can do to keep up the gig. How then should I get me to Lavenshall? Would the two of you have me walk with the peasantry? Would you see me beg a ride on an ox cart?'

'No, Mama,' answered Laura meekly, and then, with gathering excitement, 'of course not. And how many guests shall I have? And when shall I have a new frock?'

Her eyes gleamed and she clapped her hands at this thought. The expression of frigid discontent on Mama's face softened into something approaching good humour. She knew full well that beneath this veneer of disapproval lay an enthusiasm that approached her own.

'We shall see,' she said. 'I suppose we must trouble the drapers this week if this family is to make some show of dignity.'

Laura had celebrated her sixteenth birthday in November, but her official coming out ball was to be shared with Becky Marchmayne, whose birthday was in the following July. In this way Laura's family could take on some of the lustre of the Marchmayne name. Sir Peter Marchmayne was an old friend of Laura's late-departed father and felt a certain obligation to his widow. There were some who said that because of his good fortune at the card table his own estate had swelled even as Father's had dwindled and that this brought with it a certain burden of guilt. Nevertheless, Mama was a proud woman, and despite Jonah's oft-expressed preference for frugality she insisted that she match the Marchmayne's expenditure, pound for pound. On this issue, at least, she was prepared to stand toe to toe with Jonah and tenaciously hold her ground. On this issue, at least, Mama and daughters could find unity in a common cause.

For those who had visited London, or even Cambridge, the assembly rooms at Lavenshall were no great spectacle. Although the ballroom was commodious enough, the ceiling was half-timbered in the antique manner, while even the one at Cordingham, twenty miles or so away, was elegantly plastered and corniced in the French style. But if this, as some said, gave the place a disagreeably rustic appearance, Laura was entirely oblivious to it. Besides, the timber structure was of a pleasing regularity, and chandeliers of impressive size and complexity would surely cast a splendid light upon the gathering after nightfall. After having settled some matters with Mr Hewison, the superintendent of the place, Laura and Mama made their way along the crowded street to Mrs McIntyre's establishment, which everyone said was the finest drapers east of Peterborough. Emily had had to stay at home that day, partly because she was a little wheezy after breakfast and partly because the gig could sensibly accommodate only three. Mama would not countenance driving herself in such circumstances and on this, a market day. Therefore, David had the gig in the stable yard of the Fountain Inn and would doubtless be thoroughly drunk if their errands detained them longer than an hour or two.

'There are so many beggars, Mama!' declared Laura as they made their way through the throng. 'Must they pluck at my sleeve so as I pass?'

'They are uncommon bold here this year,' said Mama, urging Laura away from a group who stood near the great market cross at the head of High Street. 'I wonder that the constables are so lax in their duties. It is little short of a scandal that we should be importuned so as we go about our business.'

'But should we not give them alms?' asked Laura as a thin woman with wild hair blessed her and sought bread for the hollow-eyed child at her side.

'It is not for us to distribute alms in the street,' said Mama, hurrying them through a gap between two passing wagons towards where the drapers stood at the corner of Vintners Row and Elm Street.

'Mr Courtney oversees the poor house, and it is his duty to distribute the alms I gave him only last week. Not that we can well afford it, I might add. But I suppose it is our Christian duty.'

Three burly constables, red-faced, truncheons dangling meaningfully at their wrists, strode purposefully past, and the various beggars and vagrants melted away before them like spring snows in a sudden thaw, only to reappear from alleyways and passageways when they were safely distant.

'It is not the place it once was,' said Mama with a shudder as the door opened to the sweet, clear sound of a little bell and they found themselves in a paradise of rich colours, of lace and lawn, damask and calico, every kind of fabric that Laura had heard of – and many more besides. A chandelier very like the ones in the assembly halls sent specks of wildly dancing light across all the rich surfaces as it moved very gently with the passage of the inflowing air.

'Oh, how I wish Emily were here!' exclaimed Laura, eyes gleaming. 'How she would love it!'

'She will be here soon enough,' assured Mama with a smile of her own. 'I shall bring her next week and we shall open your father's purse for a second time.'

Laura thought to mention that the purse was rightfully her own, the rents and the incomes that filled it her own and that Jonah was no more than a parvenu, an estate manager made good, but she knew full well that the law stood foursquare with Jonah and that natural justice was a will-o'-the-wisp.

'I do wish they wouldn't press their dirty noses to my windows,' said Mrs McIntyre, rubbing her hands together having shooed off a couple of the raggedly girls who stood outside. 'It smears them so, and Meg only washed them two days since. Now,' she regarded them brightly. 'Mrs DeLacey, is it? I thought so. And how are things at Groomfield? I trust that this is Laura; what a pretty girl! All the talk hereabouts is of the ball next month. You would not credit how many other young ladies I have entertained this last ten days and how much finery we have bestowed upon them...'

Mrs McIntyre kept up a steady stream of cheerful prattle, seeming hardly to pause for breath, hardly to stand in need of a single reply as she ushered them towards the rear of the shop, where various elegantly dressed ladies stood about to receive them. Here was one, whose name Laura immediately forgot, who had only recently returned from Paris and had moved in the highest circles there; here another, whose name was Mrs Evans, Laura recalled, and she had a fascinating book of detailed sketches which described the latest styles in London.

It was already dusk when they emerged, laden with parcels and packets and with a boy to summon David from the Fountain Inn with the gig. David was very drunk by then, but the cob knew her business and the way home was familiar enough to her. Even had David turned them into a ditch it seemed unlikely it would seriously endanger their good humour. Laura found her hands toying with the ribbons that secured the parcels, already rehearsing the quick movements that would reveal their splendid contents to her admiring sister.

'I shall look so fine, Mama,' she squealed, squeezing Mama's arm as the gig bore them homeward.

'Surely you shall,' said Mama, 'and we must lay all out in the parlour tomorrow. I wish I had thought to buy another thimble, but I suppose Mary will find us one from somewhere.'

'And what do you suppose Becky will wear?' asked Laura, voicing a concern that had troubled her these last few weeks. She knew that the Marchmaynes' means extended much further than her parents', and there was talk of lace brought all the way from Bruges in distant Flanders.

'Never you trouble yourself on that score,' reassured Mama with a careless laugh that Laura had not heard since Jonah's first arrival at their door. 'All the pearls in India could not make poor Becky's face nor figure match your own, and I fancy I know where all the young men's eyes will be turned.'

Chapter Three

When they returned to Groomfield it was to find Jonah seated at the kitchen table with a mug of ale. Emily was with him, her small face a picture of unease.

'You are returned, I find,' said Jonah, nodding at the parcels in Laura's arms. 'And I can see how you practise in my absence.'

'And you are returned, too,' said Mama, crossing to him and kissing his brow. 'Where have you been this past week? Was it over Northampton way?'

'A man's affairs are his own to know,' grunted Jonah, wiping his mouth with the back of his hand.

'Have you no greeting for me, daughter? Unless that scowl is all I merit.'

'Hello, Father,' said Laura, in a manner that none could reproach, setting down the parcels next to the door and advancing to make her dip before him.

'Hmmm,' said Jonah, placing his hand around his wife's waist and pulling her to him in a manner that suggested the enjoyment of ownership rather than actual affection. 'You had best show me how I have spent my money, had you not? I trust you have used no extravagance.'

How Jonah might define extravagance was anyone's guess, and the joyous anticipation of sharing her acquisitions with Emily was suddenly quite gone. She stooped to pick up her parcels and began to untie them slowly with trembling hands.

Jonah made no comment. He only regarded the threads and the fabrics with cool disdain, indicating with a raised finger the order in which they should be opened. At length he sniffed.

'I suppose you will look well enough,' he conceded, 'if by your combined efforts these items may be assembled into anything approaching the drawing we have here. And if you can deport yourself in a manner that does not disgrace my name, I might add.' This last observation was accompanied by a sniff and a censorious glance. 'And tell me, how much did I spend on this?'

Mama told him, explaining that many of the items were cheaper than they might be had elsewhere, that Mrs McIntyre had arranged a special price. She ran her fingers through his lank black hair, regarding him beseechingly.

'And I am to go next week,' said Emily in a small voice, in tones that suggested more a question than a statement of fact, for Jonah's return had changed everything.

'Is that so?' asked Jonah icily, craning his neck round to see her. 'And am I to be accorded any voice in this household at all?'

'Husband...' began Mama, before his raised hand stilled her protest.

'I concede that convention requires us to parade our daughter before the world in some befitting state, but Emily is known to be an invalid – is an invalid – and I do not doubt that the occasion would further imperil her health. The foul air, the nervous energy to be expended, the excessive stimulation...'

'The additional expense,' supplied Laura bitterly under her breath.

'So, I am not to go?' cried Emily, tears starting in her eyes.

'Daughter, you are not,' said Jonah firmly as Emily rushed into Laura's arms. 'I have advanced my reasoning, and so let that be an end to it.'

'I am not your daughter,' spat Emily, rounding suddenly upon him. The room was suddenly filled with a silence that froze the air in Laura's lungs. A dog barked in the yard. Tom's muffled voice cursed distantly. Jonah narrowed his eyes, cracked his knuckles and rose from his seat, pushing Mama carelessly aside. Mama's face was a picture of horror and confusion as Jonah grasped Emily's hair, pulling roughly upwards so that she was almost lifted from the ground, gasping, whimpering, her feet shuffling for purchase.

'I should thrash you, daughter,' he snarled. 'For if you are not my daughter, then you are certainly a thief at my table and a tenant in arrears. But you are an invalid, are you not, and it ill behoves me to chastise an invalid so.'

He released his grip on her hair so suddenly that Emily collapsed to the ground in a heap, even as Jonah seized Laura by the upper arm in a vice-like grip.

'But your precious sister is not an invalid – she is the very picture of health, and she should certainly be able to sustain your punishment very well indeed.'

Laura gasped, cried out in sudden terror, felt the strength pass out of her and a hot trickle of shame on her thigh as Jonah pushed and pulled her to her chamber with one hand, drawing out his belt with the other.

'Does it hurt very much?' whispered Emily later, when Laura lay face down on her tear-wet pillow.

'I can bear it,' murmured Laura, opening her eyes to see Emily's hand stretched out to bridge the gap between their beds. Wincing, she reached out to grasp the small, warm hand and squeezed.

'I should not have said what I said,' continued Emily. 'I am very sorry for it.'

'Do not be sorry,' Laura told her. 'You only spoke the words that were in my mind, too.'

'No, I should not. It was weak of me…'

'You were disappointed. None shall blame you.'

'I hate him.'

'Hate is an ugly word, sweet Emily.'

'It is the best I have for him.'

'Enough, let me sleep now,' said Laura, closing her eyes and feeling the sting of the welts on her back where Mary had applied soothing lotion to them.

'But Mama...'

'Enough.'

Laura closed her eyes tightly at the recollection of Mama's closed expression, the distance in her gaze as Jonah had dragged her from the room. It was as if a curtain had descended between them once more. Emily's hand released her own. She heard her sister sigh, turn away and begin to succumb to sleep. But Laura did not sleep. The fierce needles that seemed to pierce the flesh of her back would not allow it; instead, they stoked a flame of hatred in her heart that she would nurture now, one that would not be extinguished so long as Jonah breathed.

There were nearly two hundred people at the ball. All the best people of the Eastings were gathered there, all the young ladies who hoped to win themselves a husband, all the young men who wished to secure themselves a wife. But if a proportion of those present were motivated chiefly by the desire for romantic love, marriage and the consequent propagation of the species, the greater part were gathered there simply to eat, to drink, to dance and to enjoy the company of their peers. A band, brought all the way from Norwich, played late into the night, and the tables that had been set up at the south end of the hall groaned beneath the weight of all the foodstuffs that the wealth of the Marchmaynes could provide. On this issue Sir Peter Marchmayne waved aside Mama's protestations and declined to permit her to match him guinea for guinea. The Marchmayne purse, once opened, poured forth a veritable cornucopia of exotic fruit rushed from the wharves of Ipswich and King's Lynn, of stuffed swans and boars' heads, of dressed sturgeon and small fowl in aspic, all presented on glittering silver. Above their heads a thousand candles lit this splendid spectacle, and the acrid smoke of tobacco was leavened with the rich scents of beeswax and rare spices.

'Oh, Mama, I doubt that I was ever so happy!' cried Laura between dances, when she returned to their table for a sip of champagne and a spoonful of syllabub. 'I have had eight dances already and the clock has only just struck nine. What do you say to that?'

'I say you had best not let it turn your head,' said Mama with a wry smile but with a glow of genuine delight in her eye, such as Laura had not seen for many a year. 'Here, let me adjust your dress... just so.'

Turned outward to the throng, Laura could feel the slight tugging as Mama pulled at the upper edge until it concealed the topmost of the ugly wheals that still disfigured her back a full two weeks after her beating.

'There,' said Mama, turning her gently to face her once more, smoothing into place a stray wisp of blonde hair. Then she held her daughter at arm's length, regarding her approvingly. 'There are none here to match you, I declare.'

'Hear, hear,' said Laura's Aunt Catherine, sitting next to Mama. 'You are a vision of perfection, a flower in full bloom.'

Aunt Catherine fancied herself an educated woman and filled her house with books, although no one had ever seen her reading any of them. She too was a widow, having seen her late husband into Darkharrow after a losing battle with cancer.

'And what of Becky Marchmayne?' asked Laura, glancing over towards where Becky stood at the centre of a group of admiring youths. 'Is she not fine, too? Her dress is also perfection, is it not?'

Becky's dress, of brocaded purple silk, incorporated every feature that was held to represent high fashion in London and Paris. It was embellished wherever embellishment could sensibly be placed, and in more places besides, with small sewn pearls, with ribbons and with Flemish lace. A necklace of her mother's pearls glinted at her throat and a diamond tiara perched atop her piled black hair.

'Pah!' scoffed Aunt Catherine's friend Camilla, an elderly spinster with a fine purple nose that testified fulsomely to her affection for sherry. 'She does not compare to you, my dear. Your dress shows a becoming restraint, I find. Such a lovely blue. And it is vain to gild the lily, is it not?'

Laura blushed, almost sure of detecting a compliment in this rebuff, just as Jonah returned to their table, flagon in hand, catching the latter part of their conversation.

'Young Becky, eh?' he drawled as he turned his heavy head that way, stooping to speak in a stage whisper that caused other heads to turn on neighbouring tables. 'I never saw so eloquent a statement of account.'

Camilla covered her mouth to stifle a laugh, but Mama, conscious that others might have heard this indiscretion, shot him a glance of reproach that in any other context might have earned her a slap.

'Do not trouble yourself, wife,' he said, clinking his flagon against her champagne glass. 'I am not yet in my cups.'

'Who is that gentleman with Sir Peter?' asked Aunt Catherine, keen to move things on. 'I swear he is a stranger here.'

'That is Sir Joseph Finch,' said Jonah. 'He is a famous physician from London, I am told, a natural philosopher, too. He lodges with Sir Peter just now, and he has a great interest in wild fowl and in creeping things, it would seem.' He made a gesture with his free hand to suggest the movement of 'creeping things' and then another, close to his head to indicate his belief that Sir Joseph's wits might be astray.

'I see, and are we to be introduced, do you suppose?' continued Aunt Catherine. 'He sounds a man of culture and of learning.'

'He is indeed,' said the Reverend Beale from the adjoining table. 'I could not help but overhear. Sir Joseph addressed the Royal Society only last month on the issue of the mating habits of toads, as they are affected by the proximity of the moon. He has travelled widely abroad. He is on cordial terms with the most eminent of learned men.'

'Indeed,' sniffed Jonah, whose appreciation of learning fell somewhat short of the clergyman's.

'And he has taken Comberwood for what remains of this dismal summer,' continued Beale, undeterred by Jonah's frown. 'He is here for the bittern, I am told, and for other things the fens can offer that London cannot match.'

'Well, I don't doubt these parts offer many attractions for the man of science,' said Aunt Catherine, albeit without giving the appearance of being convinced of this herself. 'Was there not a mermaid trawled up off Loundean at Michaelmas last? I swear there was. The town was all agog with it.'

'I do not think Sir Joseph comes in search of mermaids,' said the Reverend a little stiffly. 'I think the objects of his desire are a little more concrete than that.'

When Laura returned from her twelfth dance, and this with a youth who had shown her particular attention, it was to find Sir Joseph at their table. He was a smallish man of forty years or so, with a round head and a bright eye. His quick, decisive movements recalled those of his namesake.

'I was just saying,' said Mama, after introductions had been made, 'that Sir Joseph has chosen a most inclement season to travel in the Eastings. We have barely known such rain. Not since last year, anyway.'

'Do not trouble yourself on that account,' said Sir Joseph. 'Comberwood's roof seems sound enough, and besides I have a passion for herpetology.'

'I rejoice to hear it; such a rare distinction in these parts,' said Aunt Catherine.

'What is herpetology, Aunt?' asked Laura, reaching for her syllabub.

'Pray do not interrupt Sir Joseph,' said Aunt Catherine after the briefest of pauses.

'Why, herpetology is the study of reptiles, if I may anticipate your aunt's reply,' explained Sir Joseph with a polite nod of acknowledgment in her direction. 'And whereas we might shudder to see another day of rain, our friend Bufo bufo, that is the common toad, looks out on it with infinite satisfaction. For one man's meat is another man's poison, as I believe it is said.'

'You would enjoy speaking to Edward,' Laura told him later, after the table had been regaled with tales of Sir Joseph's travels abroad. 'He is never happier than when he is with a book, I swear, and never happier than speaking of it.'

46

'He sounds a worthy young man,' said Sir Joseph. 'And the love of learning is a rare bloom in the bosom of youth, I find. And where shall I discover him?'

Edward was one of those young men they called "wallflowers", ones who, through timidity or perhaps a simple disinclination to seek the company of the fairer sex, stood in the shadows on the fringes of the company, propping themselves against the walls. For some, this approach was enforced upon them by a consciousness that their features lacked charm and that their fortune offered no compensation for this shortcoming. In Edward's case his calling marked him out as no more than a dispassionate observer of these social rituals. Dressed in the plain dark clothes that befitted his station, he conversed with a young man, a revenant, who was only recently returned from Darkharrow and who had until recently been entrusted to his care, in fact.

Revenants were often wary of moving in wider society, having in many cases been reborn into one quite unlike the one they had known, but there were a number present tonight. Included in their number were Simon Collins and Paul Catchpole, who occupied a table close to the bar, making use of this proximity with rare persistence and determination, as though they sought to drink themselves to death a second time. For Simon and Paul had known each other during their first lives, and although their acquaintance had been marked by no affection at that time, their rebirth into the succeeding century had thrust them together in a kind of involuntary amity. Emboldened by drink, Paul had even tried to win himself a dance from a pretty girl, although Simon had pulled him back. Everyone knew that revenants were forbidden to marry, and so to idly importune girls of marriageable age would only earn them the censure of the company.

47

'You seem to be enjoying yourself,' said Jonah, seizing Laura's wrist as she returned from her thirteenth dance. 'I had wondered whether the absence of your sister would take the edge off your pleasure, but I see that is not so.'

Laura twisted her wrist to withdraw it and narrowed her eyes as she replied.

'I practise to dissemble, Father. And yes, I most fervently wish that Emily were here tonight – she would have enjoyed it so. I pray that she may yet have other opportunities and that your conscience shall not be troubled that you denied her this one.'

'You need not become anxious on that account,' said Jonah with an infuriating leer. 'For my conscience is a hardy beast.'

Laura hurried away to her table, there to dash off half a glass of champagne with a trembling hand, but the damage was done. Intoxicated with the occasion, she had indeed allowed Emily to slip from her thoughts – and Jonah had detected it. His words had found their mark, and the light and the colour were suddenly dulled all around her. She wished she were home.

'I trust you are not bespoken, and that I may engage you for this next dance, when the band have refreshed themselves.'

This, from a tall young man who had appeared suddenly at her elbow. She swung round, taking in a shock of blonde hair, a strong chin and eyes that presently glinted with a knowing anticipation. There was a suavity, a confidence about him, reflected in the cool amusement of those full curving lips, the smooth elegance of the half-bow with which he greeted her.

'Excuse me, allow me most humbly to present myself: John Lovelock at your service.'

There was nothing humble about John Lovelock, as was already disclosed to her through the frankness of his gaze as they danced, as was confirmed by her aunt's entreaties when she returned to their place.

'Perhaps later, my dear. Undoubtedly, we shall speak again,' was his parting remark, accompanied by what Laura would come to recognise as a lascivious wink.

'I beg you be very wary of that young man,' said Aunt Catherine to the accompaniment of an approving nod from her mother. 'He has a silver tongue but an evil reputation, a reputation that has tainted those of girls plainer than you. Why, only last spring Charlotte Hardisty was sent away to London. His motivations are not connected with marriage and the potential conjunction of fortunes. If he engages you in pretty talk, you may be sure that it is not your broad acres he craves.'

'Indeed, for you are uncommonly fair of face and your bosom has developed very satisfactorily,' observed Camilla, in a manner that caused Laura to blush fiercely from those previously mentioned regions to the roots of her hair.

'Oh, Camilla!' snorted Mama. 'Such sentiments are hardly to be...'

'Nonsense, Margaret,' interjected Camilla, waving aside the objections. 'I only say that those in possession of uncommon wealth had better take uncommon care to guard it.'

'And what should Laura guard?' asked Edward, approaching with Sir Joseph and catching the latter part of this exchange.

'I was merely pointing out...' began Camilla.

'Never mind what you were pointing out,' said Mama from the corner of her mouth, and then, to Sir Joseph and his companion, 'are neither of you to dance tonight? I have not observed you take the floor, Sir Joseph. Is the art uncongenial to you?'

'Nothing could be more congenial,' said Sir Joseph with a bow as Edward stood sheepishly at his side, towering over him by half a head, 'but I am a stranger in these parts, and I would not presume to inflict myself on any of the splendid young ladies in which this region rejoices. And indeed, as you can see, I have taken the liberty of introducing myself to your young friend here. It seems we share a common interest in ornithology.'

'That's birds,' said Aunt Catherine *sotto voce* behind her hand to Camilla.

'And Edward has told me that your lands reach far down the estuary into the salt marshes, a region that must be regarded as a veritable avian treasure trove. I wonder if I may importune you to be permitted to wander freely on your property. I am told that the black bittern is frequently to be found in these parts, and it is my heart's desire to see one.'

'Why of course you may,' said Mama delightedly, once it had become apparent that Sir Joseph desired neither money nor services. 'It would be an honour to assist a gentleman of your distinction. And Laura shall be your guide. She knows that area as well as any I could mention, has wandered across it since early childhood and made the fens her playground.'

This was something of an exaggeration, the product of champagne and a momentary excess of enthusiasm, but it was true that Laura and Emily had found in the endless fens a liberty denied them at home and could navigate the trackless vastness with practised ease.

'Delighted,' said Laura with a dip. 'I fancy I know where the black bittern abides.'

'Well perhaps you shall guide me to him some day,' said Sir Joseph with a benevolent smile. 'Just as soon as I am established in Comberwood.'

'Such a small, damp establishment,' said Aunt Catherine. 'I fear for your health. There are no more than a dozen or so rooms, I recall, and only a very few of those fit for reception.'

'My needs are simple,' said Sir Joseph, 'and my servant will set it all to rights even before my effects come down from London. You need not trouble yourself on my behalf.'

Sir Joseph proved to be the most agreeable of neighbours, once he was settled at Comberwood. Although this property lay on the fringes of Marchmayne land, its lawns adjoined Groomfield on the north side, and so the property was barely ten minutes' walk away when Laura went to call upon him. This she did frequently when the weather was fine and occasionally when it was not, encumbered by a large umbrella and borne down by the heavy oilskins he insisted she wear.

'For you see there are many creatures that venture forth most boldly when we shelter timidly under our roofs,' he told her. 'These are the ones I most earnestly seek.'

On some occasions, when she was well, Emily came with them, although they rarely went far from the house when this was so, in case she should be caught in a sudden shower or if she should be seized by one of the prolonged coughing fits that had troubled her of late.

These were happy days, for Emily was entranced by their new neighbour and Sir Joseph was, in truth, a most diverting companion, with a fund of amusing stories which often referred most indiscreetly to members of the royal court. In addition, he was a man of astonishing learning, for whom no creature was too small to be of interest, a man whose pockets bulged with collecting cases and dissecting instruments. Elias Mould, his manservant, was required to follow them in their progress through the fens, burdened heavily with bottles, catch-nets, reference books and sketchpads in addition to the provisions that might be required for luncheon or for tea. A large, loose-limbed man with a lantern jaw and a permanent head cold, Mould was a man of few words and these uttered with an air of world weariness that bordered on the suicidal.

Edward was often a member of their small party, too, when his duties would allow it. Quickly appreciating his skills with a pencil, Sir Joseph set him to work sketching the various species of sedge that were to be found there, the small flowers native to the salt marshes and the milk parsley in which the swallowtail butterflies found delight.

'You have such a sure eye,' said Sir Joseph one day, looking over his shoulder approvingly. 'And a neat hand, too. I am a tolerable draughtsman myself, but I could never approach you for skill.'

'Emily can draw well, when it suits her,' said Laura, from her place on the riverbank where she trailed her hand idly in the cool stream below. 'You should see the figures she has drawn in her schoolbooks. Mrs Armitage quite admires them, I declare.'

'Nonsense, sister,' laughed Emily. 'My skills are nothing compared with those of Edward here. See how he applies tone to each tiny petal. I am amazed by his patience.'

'Would you care to make a portrait of Emily?' asked Laura on an impulse. 'She is in such good looks today, I swear.'

It was a glorious afternoon towards the end of August, after three days of persistent rain. They sat in a small clearing at the fringe of the sedge, looking out past small, stunted trees and bushes towards the endless salt marshes and the sea beyond. The sedge rustled and swayed around them as a small breeze stirred the air.

'I would be delighted to, if I felt at all sure that my skills would be equal to the task,' laughed Edward, 'and that Sir Joseph would welcome such a drawing amongst these flower heads and leaf sketches.'

'Please, do go ahead,' beseeched Sir Joseph from the patch of mud he was exploring a little further on, 'but perhaps you would use the back of the book. It would certainly not do to place Emily's portrait amongst those of moths and coleoptera.'

'Then you must sit very still, Emily,' instructed Edward, shifting his position, 'and I must sharpen my pencil once more. Elias, do you have the small knife there?'

Mould, who had been putting away the things from their luncheon, sniffed and reached into one of the many pockets with which his overcoat was equipped. It was easily the warmest day of the year, and yet he was dressed as though for the exploration of the Arctic.

'Cold-blooded, you see,' he had said, when Emily queried this, 'like the bloody Bufo bufo,' he concluded with a wry grin and a sidelong glance to see that his master was not within earshot.

'I hardly know where to begin,' said Edward, considering Emily's small, pale face through narrowed eyes, 'though I fancy the eyes would be as good a place as any.'

Laura shifted the old coat that lay under her and shuffled alongside Edward so that she could observe the progress of his work, the small confident movements of his quick fingers, the flicker of his eyes from the subject to his page.

There was a strange, forced jollity about the occasion, laughter as Edward admonished Emily for her failure to hold still or as a particularly bold butterfly alighted on her shoulder. And yet there was a palpable poignancy, too, as Edward laboured to preserve on paper a record of a countenance that all knew would not be long for this world.

'I think you flatter her,' said Laura when he pronounced the work complete. 'But I fancy you have the likeness.'

'Is my chin really as small as that,' asked Emily, smoothing back her hair and leaning forward to look over the top of Edward's sketchbook.

'It will look better turned thus,' said Edward, passing her the book. 'There, you are immortal now. I have you captured in this book for all time.'

A silence came amongst them and then a single drop of rain fell on the page, emerging from a sky overhead in which no clouds were presently to be discerned, although a bank of them was approaching westward across the sea. Far away, the white sails of a passing ship stood clear against the brooding mass. Emily wiped away the drop with her sleeve as more began to fall around them.

'I fancy we should retire,' decided Sir Joseph, withdrawing one booted foot from the mud with a sucking sound. He patted his pockets. 'I have enough here to occupy me at the dissecting table well into the night, I should think. Edward, would you care to join me? What a fine portrait,' he added, pulling on his coat. 'You have the essence of her, just so. But now I must urge you to return my sketchbook to the bag. Mould, will you stir yourself? We must not have Emily soaked, if this shower should be the vanguard of some greater cloudburst.'

The summer days marched on, day after damp and rainy day, until all agreed that the harvest was sure to be ruined for another year, with the meagre crops beaten flat by the squalls and the restless footprints of the surging gales. Three ships were lost at sea within the space of a single week, and the price of wheat broke new records in Lavenshall and beyond.

'Damn those lazy scoundrels!' roared Jonah, slamming the parlour door to amplify the expression of his discontent after having received a deputation of estate workers one day. 'Do they imagine I can conjure silver from thin air? How shall we sustain a living if they will not pay their rents?'

'And their rents are little enough already,' said Mama, looking up from her sewing. 'Do they claim to lack the means to pay, just now? How do they seek to justify that claim?'

'They say they lack the means to feed their families, what with the prices so damnably high,' exclaimed Jonah with a sigh, shrugging off his coat and tugging impatiently at his neckcloth.

'I never knew such times,' said Mama with a frown. 'And half the cottages lack for tenants.'

'And tied tenants, too,' growled Jonah, 'bound to our land by legal contract. If I find them, I shall have them thrashed.'

'And do you think that thrashing will correct them, Father?' asked Laura, who was playing cards with Emily at the table beneath the long window whilst rain pattered on the glass.

'Perhaps not,' grunted Jonah, 'but it would give me satisfaction to make the attempt.'

He crossed to the window, abruptly picked up the pack of cards between them and dashed it to the floor. Laura pushed back her chair and regarded Jonah evenly. Emily cried out and shrank back in her chair, fearful of some new outburst.

'And this is all you can contribute to this household?' he said, ignoring Emily, his cold grey eyes engaging Laura's in an unblinking stare. 'Idleness and insolence?'

'What would you have me contribute?' asked Laura, holding his gaze. 'Would you set me to work in the fields?'

'I would have you make a decent match now that you are come of age,' he snarled. 'Perhaps then we may mend our fortunes. Perhaps then we shall have you under the roof of another, where your acid tongue may earn you the censure of a husband less mild than your father. It would be as well that romance took its course before I make a match for you myself.'

'But Jonah, she is only sixteen,' offered Mama, making a cautious and wholly unexpected intervention on her daughter's behalf. 'There is no rush, I think.'

'Old enough in law,' said Jonah, flicking one last card in Laura's face and causing her, at last, to blink. 'Mark my word, daughter. Unless you can demonstrate any other capacities of use to us, your match must be our making.'

Chapter Four

Laura found herself with several suitors in the months after her coming of age, some of them casual in nature, some pressing their claims with a greater degree of persistence. Amongst these was Hugh Redgrave, once a companion of hers at school, a boy four years her senior who had come down from Cambridge for the summer. Hugh's father was Sir Walter, chief magistrate of the county, a man whose wealth outstripped even that of the Marchmaynes and whose riches depended on trade with the West Indies as much as on the uncertain bounty of his lands. For this reason, because he was accustomed to transacting business amongst a broad spectrum of society, he had thought it proper that his son, rather than being tutored at home, should receive education alongside those less fortunate than himself. So, whilst Hugh was necessarily excluded from the company of those unable to pay a penny a day for their education, he was at least to rub shoulders with the offspring of the lesser and the middling gentry in a manner that might be thought mutually beneficial.

Laura had never risen to a full appreciation of her association with this plan, never felt any evident benefit. Nevertheless, she had had the opportunity to see Hugh grow to manhood, although he grew to a height barely greater than hers and with a weak chin and small, cruel eyes besides. But whereas he lacked the physical presence of most of his peers, he was fully conscious of his superior social stature – and this brought him endless delight. The depth of his pockets, the liberality of his expenditure, bought him many friends but few admirers. Laura detested him, which made it even more galling that he insisted on waiting for her and then walking home with her whenever Edward was not present in school. These occasions were increasingly frequent, since Edward was soon to sit the exams that would initiate his admission to the priesthood. Accordingly, he spent many an hour under the watchful eye of his uncle, studying ancient books of lore and learning the mysteries of the care of the dead.

'I often think of our dance at the ball,' Hugh told her as they walked together one evening.

Laura would gladly have hitched up her skirts and run away from him or dashed into one of the cottages at the side of the road had she thought that she might have achieved anything by it. She looked over her shoulder. Two of her friends were further along the street but too distant to offer a realistic chance of diluting his company.

'You do?' she said cautiously. 'I danced with at least a dozen partners on that occasion. I cannot say I recall, although you must believe I mean no unkindness by it.'

'Of course,' said Hugh, 'although I flatter myself that our brief partnership must have outshone all others for elegance and style. My dancing master professes himself amazed by my prowess, and he was trained in Vienna, no less.'

'You have a dancing master?' asked Laura, seeking to encourage Hugh to expound upon his own virtues and perhaps so to distract him from expounding upon hers, with all the awkwardness that might lie along such a road.

'Indeed,' said Hugh, making a few steps about her as though leading her in some waltz of his own imagining, fixing her all the while with a gaze of smug amusement. 'And I have other tutors besides, for fencing, oratory and law. Mrs Armitage, you see, offers only a very basic education for a man, and better folk must look elsewhere for their improvement.'

'Surely they seek in vain for improvement in humility,' said Laura with a hollow laugh.

'I speak in generalities,' said Hugh. 'For I would not have had it otherwise and I could not have wished for a more congenial classmate than yourself when we shared that school room.'

'I was but a small child then. I assist with the younger ones myself, nowadays,' Laura told him. 'Except where mathematics is concerned, as Mrs Armitage is satisfied with my learning.'

'Your parents are a particularly respectable couple,' said Hugh, with a vague nod that excused his failure to acknowledge or respond to her statement. 'How it must gall them to look out upon Groomfield's stony acres and see no prospect of improvement. And their tenants can hardly be retained, by all accounts. You must accept my assurances that I mean no disrespect by saying that I pity them their plight. It must be hard to face the obligations of polite society with barely the means to discharge them.'

'Your kind thoughts oblige me, but your pity is not a commodity I crave,' countered Laura, conscious of a furious blush turning indignantly upon him.

On several occasions in the last few weeks, she had found it necessary to endure his company on this route, and on each occasion the conversation had been no more than mildly irksome to her. Now she felt that matters were moving to a very unwelcome conclusion and there was no sensible way of avoiding it, short of running away, screaming or stabbing him in the eye with her hat pin. A swift glance along the street in each direction offered no hope of immediate succour.

'I'm sorry, I have offended you,' said Hugh, taking off his own hat and wringing it in his hands. 'That is the last thing I would have wanted, for yours is the approval I seek above all others. I tremble at your beauty and your grace. I allow myself to picture a world in which we are united.'

'Then you should not,' she told him shortly. 'For such a world must remain forever a fantasy, I assure you.'

'And yet you are my heart's desire,' stressed Hugh plaintively, 'and experience has led me to expect that what my heart desires I shall presently acquire. I urge you to consider this: it is my most fervent wish that you should gladly accept my advances, for, as you will have gathered, I would have you be my wife someday.'

Glancing around to see that they were unobserved, he took Laura by the elbow and drew her away from the road into a lane between two cottages.

'Will you marry me, Laura?' he asked, eyes shining, taking her hand in both of his and squeezing it emphatically.

Laura regretted the momentary confusion that had impaired her resistance to these advances.

'I most certainly will not,' she replied, recovering herself. 'Why, I am barely sixteen.'

'And I not yet twenty-one,' countered Hugh. 'But I know my own mind full well, and I flatter myself that your parents would rejoice in it. I doubt there is a more desirable bachelor than I in these parts. And besides, it need not be this year or even next. A commitment in my favour would give me full satisfaction.'

'I see. And is this to be the full extent of your courtship?' asked Laura, snatching her hand away from his. 'Are there to be no boating excursions, no walks hand in hand along the river, no evenings spent in earnest conversation to establish that our hearts approach conjunction?'

'We can have all of those things, if you wish,' conceded Hugh, 'but I am a practical man. I wish only to place my cards on the table before you. I would that you were happy to accept my offer, but I foresee that your joy might need instead to grow by gradual increments to its full stature. I admit that initially you might be obliged by weight of circumstances to accept that which is best for you and for those that are dear to you.'

'What?!' exclaimed Laura. She was shocked. 'Do you propose to marry me against my will? Are you insane?'

'I only say that a dutiful daughter must submit to the will of her father,' explained Hugh, some of the pleading draining from his voice to be replaced by a harder note. There was a sudden hardness to his features, too, and a set to his chin that spoke of a fixed determination to prevail.

'Never in life will I submit to such a thing,' she declared with a shake of her head, 'and you have taken leave of your senses, if you envisage it.'

'There are thirty thousand pounds a year that say you will,' said Hugh, taking her by the forearm in a grip that was less than gentle. 'Thirty thousand reasons that will speak in your father's ear with a voice I trust he will find tolerably persuasive.'

'You think that because you have money you can buy anything you want, even me?' she asked aghast.

'As I have mentioned, my experience thus far in life has not taught me otherwise,' answered Hugh, advancing upon her now in a way that caused her heart to flutter. She stepped back and found her back pressed against the wall of an outhouse whilst his face approached her own, a dangerous redness suffusing his cheeks.

'I can restore your family's fortunes,' he said, 'and my own parents would doubtless rejoice to see me unite Groomfield with their own lands. Surely it cries out for investment, but investment it should have. So many good people, not least my humble self, would find joy in our union. Do you presume to stand in the way of such universal felicity for a selfish and momentary disinclination that time will surely remedy?'

'I do so presume,' replied Laura, shaking her head adamantly, 'and I repeat that you cannot buy my… acquiescence in this, this… arrangement.'

'Hah!' scoffed Hugh, who was now fully transformed into a creature of wilful passion and whose eyes glinted with a more dangerous light. 'We shall see about that. For if I cannot buy your acquiescence, I'll wager I can buy your lovely flesh, if all pretentious terms are stripped away, all polite conventions exposed for what they are. You must submit. Though it cost me all my fortune I swear I shall possess you.'

'No.' Laura could only turn her head aside as Hugh's body pressed against hers and his lips approached her own.

'And I fancy I shall take a little on credit now.'

Laura found herself stunned, paralysed as his lips found hers, her mind reeling in shock and despair. It was too late to shout or scream as Hugh enfolded her in his strong arms, as his tongue quested between her lips. A blackness descended upon Laura and with it came rage, bitter indignation that kindled a sudden, unexpected explosion of fury within her. It was like an electric shock of the kind that Sir Joseph had demonstrated to her in his laboratory at Comberwood, a momentary spark of power that tingled in her flesh.

Hugh leapt back, spitting blood that already bespattered his shirt.

'You bit me, you foul bitch!' he cried, his face suddenly pale with fury.

'I did not,' she cried, shaking her head in confusion. 'I don't know… what…'

'Damn you!' he shrieked in outrage. There was his bloodied handkerchief in his palm, two white teeth upon it. 'See what you have done!'

'No!' Laura shouted, continuing to shake her head slowly, edging sideward until she stood in the road once more. She could not take her eyes from Hugh's, and those eyes were filled with shock and suspicion now as he dabbed at his wounded mouth. 'No!' she said once more. 'It was not I!'

And then she turned and ran.

'I never heard of such a thing,' gasped Emily in amazement when Laura breathlessly poured out to her a garbled and halting account of her ill-fated meeting with Hugh.

She sat upright in bed, swinging out her stick-thin legs from underneath the covers and holding Laura in a fond embrace whilst her sister sobbed upon her shoulder.

'Shush, dear sister,' whispered Emily. 'Would you wish our mother to hear?'

Laura bit her lip and looked up as Emily gently stroked away the hair that had fallen over her eyes.

'Now then,' Emily said, as she regarded her sister earnestly, 'tell me again from the beginning, but slowly this time and with everything in its proper order. I fully comprehend that something terrible has happened to you, sister, something to do with Hugh. You are not injured, I trust? Not…?' A shadow of fear passed over her face.

'No, he has not violated me, if that is what you mean. And the injury is all on his side, I fear.'

'He is injured in the mouth, then, I collect. How so? Did you bite his tongue, then? Did you strike him?'

'Indeed, no. I have no savour of his blood in my own mouth,' replied Laura, raising her hands to show her smooth, unmarked knuckles. 'And am I a pugilist? Do these hands look to you like fists that cost a man two teeth?'

'Then how?' wondered Emily.

The sisters gazed perplexed at each other for a long moment.

'I know not how,' answered Laura, at length. 'I swear I do not. I am all at sea.'

'I fancy you may have cured him of his infatuation, at least,' said Emily. 'He may stay away from you so long as he has a tooth in his head and wishes to retain them there. If any good may come of this, it might be that.'

Laura sighed and wiped away the tears from the corners of her eyes.

'Perhaps,' she conceded. 'Although I fear I may have made an enemy of him. Do you suppose I should tell Mama?'

'Then Jonah would know soon after,' replied Emily with a frown. 'And do you think he would rejoice to hear that you have assaulted the most eligible bachelor in the county? I fear he would offer you no congratulation.'

But if Hugh Redgrave had cause to reconsider his intentions regarding Laura, the same could not be said of John Lovelock, whose interest she had awakened on the occasion of her ball. There was an easy charm and affability about Lovelock that made it impossible for her to dislike him, despite the urgings of her elders. Their warnings still occupied a place in the more distant recesses of her mind, but if anything, an awareness of his reputation armoured her against him, made her more confident in her dealings with him. His house lay a little way along the Ditchborough Road. Since the road to Cottersley intersected it at Vernon Cross he was often to be found there waiting for her when she went to visit Becky Marchmayne, and he would walk with her to the gatehouse, amusing her with his endless fund of inconsequential chatter. Becky's need for friendship was regular enough in nature, so it was not hard for him to predict when she would be passing. Sometimes, when she found him to be absent, she would rest a while by the wayside, to see if he would come.

One unusually fine day in the last week of August Laura encountered him there with his fine black gelding, Juniper, leading a saddled mare by the nose.

'She is called Sorrell,' he said, 'and I was taking her to my young cousin Jane, to see if she wished to ride her this afternoon. I find she is indisposed, however. Would you care to ride her instead?'

'I would be delighted,' said Laura, approaching to stroke the mare's soft nose. 'Our own cob Jilly is a fractious mount and will bear only Tom with any good humour.

'Where shall we ride?' she asked, when John had helped her into the saddle and she had felt his firm hand on her thigh, which brought a fine flush to her cheeks.

'There are some woods out yonder,' he said with a knowing smile, indicating the way northwards, 'with some charming little paths and a fine spreading meadow by a mere. I often take my luncheon there.'

They rode out, and soon Becky's fretful wait for her was all forgotten and the sun moved westward in a cloudless sky. The woods were full of flowers and late-summer butterflies, while the mere, when they reached it, was clear and still and cool.

John tethered their horses a little way from the edge, and they sat in dappled shade, sharing sweet watered wine from his flask.

'You will not mind if I swim?' he asked. 'It is such a perfect day and I find I am almost overcome by the heat just now.'

'I shall not mind,' laughed Laura, 'as long as you do not expect me to join you, and as long as you do not propose to swim as nature made you.'

'I do not,' said John, stripping off his coat, neckcloth and stockings and then kicking his shoes aside. 'Shirt and breeches it shall be.'

Laura settled back in the long grasses and watched with languorous amusement as her companion splashed into the shallows, hooting with the chill of it. Soon he was swimming with strong, confident strokes, diving beneath the waters and then emerging like some great fish in a gasping explosion of spray.

Toying idly with a dandelion, plucking the seeds one by one, blowing them into the still air with a gentle breath, Laura noted that John was a beautiful young man, notwithstanding all his faults, if those tales were to be believed.

'Do you think we have been observed?' she asked when he lay beside her once more, white shirt clinging wetly to his tanned skin, propped up on one elbow the better to regard her.

'I think not,' he said. 'Though I wonder you should mention it.'

'You know why I should mention it,' said Laura, poking a finger at his chest. 'My Mama would be scandalised if she knew with whom I rode and where I presently recline.'

'Then I wonder that you are here at all,' teased John with a soft smile and a look of dreamy directness that began to kindle a strange fire in her loins. 'For I recall no coercion on my part. Tell me, sweet Laura, have you ever been kissed?'

'I might have been,' said Laura, dismissing from her mind the inauspicious circumstances of the last. 'Why should you ask?'

'Because you are the most bewitching creature I ever met,' he said, reaching for her hand. 'And I am completely under your spell.'

'Such stuff,' she laughed, squeezing his hand. 'You seek to steal a kiss from me, do you?'

'I cannot steal what is freely given,' said John, shifting a little closer to her.

'But I have heard that a kiss is but the first step on a dangerous road,' whispered Laura in a low voice, stroking his hand idly with a finger.

'A road with many diversions,' replied her companion, flicking damp black hair away from his face. 'And besides, there are occasions when it is better to live in the moment than to exist, a prisoner of past and future. Moments of such bliss are few enough in life, treasures to be gathered when we can.'

'And am I one such treasure?' asked Laura, regarding him coyly, sidelong.

'The brightest jewel of all,' he answered earnestly, moving smoothly towards her. They kissed, and it was as unlike Hugh's kiss as anything she could have imagined. His lips were soft, his breath fragrant and soon she found herself opening to him like the swift blossoming of some exotic flower. Her heart was aflutter, his hand was on her, and she found herself carried along on a warm tide of passion. She might have surrendered herself to him entirely, trembling on the brink of that sweet oblivion, when there was a faint snap of dry grass stems behind them.

At once, John sprang to his feet, straightening his clothes, turning to face the intruder. A man dressed in soiled and torn clothing stood above them on a grassy bank, his face lost in the shadows of a deep hood. He bore a hunter's bow with an arrow nocked ready on the string.

'What do you mean by this, sir?' demanded John indignantly, brushing grass from his sleeve. 'How dare you accost us so on my own land. Do you know who I am?'

Without further speech the man raised his bow and sent his arrow unerringly through John's throat. With a sharp cry, John toppled and lay twitching at Laura's feet, blood pumping spasmodically from the wound. She gasped and drew her clothing about her, too terrified to speak.

'I know who you were,' answered the man dryly to John's corpse while stooping to tug the arrow free.

'And who are you?' asked Laura in a trembling voice. 'Do you mean to slay me, too?'

'My name is Vengeance,' said the man with fierce satisfaction, casting back his hood. 'Though you may know me better as Richard Hardisty.'

'Charlotte's brother?' asked Laura, pulling her skirts down over her legs.

'The same. And this here wretched creature put a child in her belly, just like he did to half a dozen others before her. And she died in the getting out of it. Well, he'll get no more bastards now.' He nodded grimly, stirring the corpse with his foot. 'You may be sure that I mean you no harm. In time you may even come to thank me for sparing you from my poor Charlotte's fate. And now she is at rest, perhaps. For myself, I too shall be at rest now that this here swine has breathed his last and may not work his charm on other foolish maidens like the one I see before me. For you remain a maiden, I collect, although things may have been otherwise had I arrived a little later.'

He settled to his haunches to wipe his bloody arrowhead on John's shirt.

'Let them hang me now, if they can find me. For you will tell the constable, I suppose. If you dare, that is. For it may test your powers of explanation to describe the nature of your purpose here.' He then laughed. 'Although it's plain enough to see. He had a subtle tongue, had he not? You would need one subtler still to preserve your reputation.'

'What should I do?' asked Laura, fighting back the tears that threatened to trickle from her eyes.

'I followed you from the road back there,' grunted John's slayer. 'I suggest you let loose the horses and get you home as quick as you can, making sure that none see you hereabouts.'

'And what of you?' asked Laura, recovering her spirit somewhat. 'The noose shall claim you for this murder in the end, you know.'

'If it is God's will,' he shrugged. 'For, I shall fly with the Raven.'

'The Raven?'

'Aye, for the Raven will have his day before this world is much older, and I shall be at his side.'

'Oh, Emily, I have been such a fool,' cried Laura later that day. Jonah was somewhere about the estate and Mama out as a guest of Aunt Catherine, so she was required to make no immediate explanation for her tear-streaked face or the rip in the hem of her skirt. Already she had sent Tom out in the gig to convey a scribbled a note to Becky offering apologies for her failure to attend upon her.

'I said that you were too ill to be left,' sobbed Laura. 'How one lie leads to another. Surely my sins will find me out.'

'Nonsense, sister,' said Emily, who was out of bed for once and had been reading a book of poetry that now lay abandoned on her windowsill. 'For sure you have been very foolish, but simply to be present at a murder leaves you with no taint of that crime. Besides, and although you will not wish to hear it just now, there will be many who will rejoice to hear of John Lovelock's passing. They will say that fate has stalked him since first his sweet tongue seduced a virgin.'

'He was such a beautiful young man,' sighed Laura, screwing up her eyes in a vain attempt to dispel the image of his face that occupied the forefront of her mind.

'But fatal to innocence and virtue. You know that to be true.'

'I know,' Laura admitted as she sat down heavily on the edge of Emily's bed. 'So now what shall be done?'

'Who knows?' shrugged Emily. 'I suppose the horses will return to Madeley Hall and the alert will be sounded. I suppose he will be found at last, and the constables will be summoned. They will blame brigands. There were said to be brigands off to the north, although I never heard of them this close to Tithing Harrow. Then they will bury him. I wonder if he will go into Darkharrow? I suppose his family can afford it.'

The thought of John's cold, still form on a slab in those dark halls provoked Laura into a new bout of weeping.

'And what did Richard Hardisty mean by "the Raven"?' wondered Emily out loud, picking up her book at last and crossing to embrace her sister.

'Oh, Emily,' sighed Laura. 'I don't know what I should do without you.'

The prominent knobbles in Emily's thin back were hard under her hand.

'I shall always be with you,' replied Emily sadly, looking up to Laura under her curtain of blonde hair. 'You know that.'

Laura found coherent speech denied her. She could only press her lips tightly together and nod bleakly.

Dr Henderson had become a frequent visitor to Groomfield as August drew to its damp conclusion. On one occasion he brought Sir Joseph with him, for the two had become fast friends. Dr Henderson claimed that he valued a second opinion in these matters, but in truth Sir Joseph was a far more distinguished medic than himself, and so Dr Henderson stood by mildly whilst Sir Joseph went about his business, tapping Emily's back, listening to her heart and her poor, wasted lungs through his splendid silver stethoscope.

'I fear these damp climes will soon be fatal to her,' Laura heard him tell Mama, her ear pressed to the parlour door. 'The condition progresses with lamentable rapidity.'

'Well, what can be done?' asked Mama plaintively. 'Are there medicines we must acquire?'

'None that offers any hope of her salvation,' answered Sir Joseph sadly. 'The only course is to remove her from this environment, to take her to climes more amenable to her health. I know a physician in the southern part of Italy who may be prepared to take her into his care. He has an excellent reputation.'

'Italy? But how shall we afford it?'

'I do not presume to discuss your circumstances,' said Sir Joseph a little stiffly. 'I only say that any prospect of prolonging her life depends upon such a contingency.'

'I am to go to stay in Italy,' said Emily, eyes gleaming, the next morning when Laura came up to see her after breakfast.

'I know, and I am heartily glad of it,' said Laura with a smile, taking her hand. 'Sir Joseph recommended that course to our mother.'

She did not mention the atmosphere of gloom that had prevailed in the breakfast room just now, with Jonah cutting savagely at his cutlet and presenting a countenance of settled discontent to the world. Mama's own face held an expression of cool determination, her chin raised in defiance. There was not a moment of eye contact, not a word of conversation to dispel the chill in the air between them. The puffiness around her eyes and the pallor of her complexion spoke of a battle hard fought that night, a victory hard won.

'And we are to mortgage land out Melbury way to pay for it,' said Emily more cautiously. 'Mama told me and that I mustn't worry about it.'

'Indeed, you must not,' said Laura, a glance between them sufficient to agree that this statement was intended to armour her against Jonah, should he seek to question the expense, for it was certain that his present ill-humour was financially induced.

'And I have a note from Becky,' said Laura, brandishing the paper. 'She says that she would have me stay a few nights when you are better.'

'I am better now,' said Emily, raising herself to her elbows. 'Already the warm sun of Naples is on my brow.

I can feel it. You must go, sister,' she grinned. 'And besides, it will perhaps drive, shall we say, "recent events" from your mind.'

It was hard to conceive of any circumstances that could have driven the previous day's events from Laura's mind. Her walk to Cottersley Park was a melancholy one that morning, her gait akin to that of some creeping somnambulist as she reflected bleakly on John Lovelock's death and of her own folly that had, perhaps, contributed to it. The sharp gasp that John had made as death claimed him came again and again to her ears. At length she clasped her hands over them and rubbed fiercely until her hair stood awry and her flesh aglow. Not that this helped; nor did it drive his pale face, his twitching corpse, from the focus of her inner eye. John's eyes, had held a fascinating inner light but now they were blank and expressionless, that once beguiling spark extinguished. Nevertheless, they looked into her own until she held these tight shut, knuckled them and shook her head from side to side. Only as she passed the woods did she hasten her pace, hardly daring to glance that way, fearing that the body should have already been discovered, that constables would be questioning all who passed along the road.

There was, as yet no indication that the world at large was aware that anything untoward had occurred, however. The crossroads where she had been accustomed to await him was deserted, and a crow regarded her bleakly from the old wooden signpost there. 'Tithing Harr' said the finger of wood that pointed at her as she approached, for the signpost had long been broken. Two carriages and a farm cart went past her, one of the former bearing with it the post for her village, but although she trembled at each approaching hoof beat there came no contingent of constables to investigate poor John's disappearance.

'Damn you, crow,' she called out as she passed, for it was sure that the creature's black brethren would be pecking at John's sightless eyes just now, and it was all she could do to stop herself from turning aside to Madeley. Surely it was her duty to go there and to tell them where his body might be found. Her conscience argued but argued in vain. Pace by pace she grew closer to Cottersley, leaving the crossroads far behind her, its voice growing ever fainter with every step.

Why had she been so foolish? As the next mile crept beneath her, she strove to drive out the persistent image of John's dead face that loomed before her inner eye by a renewed programme of earnest self-censure. Already this campaign had kept her wakeful half the night, but the self-same questions still nagged at her. Why had she not heeded the advice of those wiser than herself? A rather large cohort, to be sure. Why had she knowingly placed her person and her reputation in such mortal danger? And to what end? This question at least was readily answered. She knew exactly what end, and that surrender to the mortal sin of lust was no mere male distinction. For what else should she call it, the hot consuming passion that had clouded all her higher senses and stilled her ears to the urgings of good sense and moderation? Her mouth was bitter with the taste of folly, haunted by the taste of his mouth in a way that two whole jugs of water last night could not wash out.

'I am a fool,' she said out loud to a small dog that yapped at her from a roadside timber yard, 'and my body shall not be my master again. I swear it.'

The dog tilted its head on one side, seeming to accept her assurance, even as the gatehouse of Cottersley Park came in sight around the bend.

'Now,' she said out loud once more, glancing around to see that the road was empty. 'I must gather my wits and present a smooth façade of normality. I shall glide serenely through these next few days, and soon, as I pile day upon day, hour upon hour, my yesterday will be buried deep, too deep to trouble me. Yes, so it will unfold.'

'Good day, Chapman,' she said jauntily to the gatekeeper as she passed through with a bright smile and what she conceived to be a casual step.

'Mornin', Miss DeLacey,' said he, leaning on the gate and lifting his cap. 'I trust you have not turned your ankle?'

'I swear you are a dull companion,' said Becky to her later. 'Why are you so out of sorts today? We have had so few fair days this month.'

'And a picnic in the woods would be perfection itself,' said Millie ruefully. 'Why do you set your face against it so?'

'Old Kimble at the timber yard told me that it would rain later this afternoon, that clouds were gathering in the west. He felt it in his water,' replied Laura, conscious of the burden of accumulating untruth.

'Pah, what stuff!' snorted Becky. 'Since when did Kimble's bladder predict the motion of the skies? Since when did Kimble know anything but larch and lime? I will have Partridge make something up for us. Besides, we shall take umbrellas.'

'I have heard there may be brigands in those woods,' tried Laura, her eyes darting from Millie to Becky in an attempt to keep a note of desperation from manifesting itself in her voice.

'Then we shall take Jim Mason with us, and he shall have his gun,' decided Becky, naming Cottersley Park's fearsome gamekeeper, a man held in awe by the poachers of the locality. 'I should like to see a brigand tangle with Jim. He would put them in the ground swiftly enough, I should think. What say you?'

'Indeed,' conceded Laura with a sigh, giving up the fight, 'but those woods up towards Lintenham have the better claim on us, I should think. And there is a fine view of Lavenshall from there.'

'A better claim than which?' asked Millie, eyebrow raised.

'A better claim than all the others, of course,' answered Laura, conscious of the treacherous flush in her cheeks.

'And where is the bracelet I gave you for your birthday?' asked Becky, seizing Laura's forearm. 'Have you wearied of it already?'

'Indeed not,' gasped Laura, a dread sensation striking coldly to her heart, for she had been wearing it yesterday and now it was gone. Nor could she recall setting it aside last night, although last night, in truth, had been an unfathomable whirl of events and emotions. Could it have slipped from her wrist as she lay with John Lovelock? Would those who found his corpse find her bracelet next to him? She felt hot tears start in her eyes, and a rush of blood to her head that almost made her swoon.

'What is it, Laura?' cried Millie. 'You look as though you have seen a ghost.'

'Oh, my heart!' sobbed Laura, waving her hands about her face to fan herself. 'I love that bracelet so and I fear I may have dropped it by the wayside as I walked.'

'My dear Laura,' cooed Becky, deeply touched, brushing away the single tear that had escaped from her friend's eye. 'You must not grieve for it so. Perhaps you shall find it upon your return. Should I send some of the servants to look for it? I shall certainly buy you another, if it is lost.'

Later that day, at dinner, a servant came into the dining room and spoke quietly into Sir Peter's ear. Sir Peter's large, round face had been a fine brick red, induced by roast pork and claret, but now this colour faded to an unhealthy mottled pink, as what was evidently grim news was imparted to him.

'What is it, Papa?' asked Becky, setting down her fork.

The pleasant hubbub of conversation around the long table died away.

'Something bad has happened, I can tell,' said Jessica, Becky's younger sister. 'Papa always looks like that when bad things happen.'

'Hush, dear,' said Lady Marchmayne, setting down her napkin and getting to her feet. 'Would you tell me privately, Sir Peter?'

'No, no,' said Sir Peter, waving aside this notion. 'Terrible news, indeed! Young John Lovelock is found murdered in Madeley woods. Knifed in the throat, they say.'

There were general expressions of dismay around the table, in which Laura felt obliged to participate, resisting the perverse impulse to state that the instrument of his death had been, in fact, an arrow.

'Why, Laura warned us that there might be brigands about only this morning,' said Millie, turning upon her. 'How prescient you were. I shudder to think that we might have ventured there.'

Laura, having done her best to stretch her countenance into some reasonable semblance of shock, was able to conceal her distress in the gloom and alarm that settled more generally upon the company. John's faults and predilections were widely known, but his family were close neighbours and the Marchmaynes shared their grief. Besides, it was disquieting to know that there were murderers at large in the vicinity. All the doors were securely double-locked when the family retired, and a roster of servants set to keep watch.

'I swear we have not had a murder in these regions for five years or more,' said Becky as she conducted Laura to her room, lamp in hand. 'But you must sleep tight. None shall trouble my father's house that value their necks, and I daresay the constables will apprehend the culprit tomorrow. I hear that half the county is alerted.'

But Laura did not sleep tight. Hardly did she sleep at all for what seemed hours, and then, just as the soft tendrils of sleep were about to extinguish her consciousness, she heard her door open. Laura's eyes sprang open, and she turned to face the door, peering into the gloom. Her lamp was long put out, but enough vague light crept in between the curtains to disclose to her a figure in a white nightgown, standing at the foot of her bed.

'Do not be alarmed, my dear,' said old Elsie's low voice, although this was a tolerably vain injunction.

'What is it?' stuttered Laura, her tone conveying mingled anxiety and irritation. 'It is the middle of the night. You scared me.'

'I didn't intend it so,' replied Elsie. 'It's just that I have been thinking of you.'

'You have?' asked Laura, when Elsie offered no immediate addition to this information.

'Indeed,' said Elsie after a long pause in which Laura felt her settle herself upon the foot of her bed, 'and there are things that I wish to say to you.'

'And breakfast would not do?' enquired Laura with a strange sense of foreboding.

'No, it would not, for I would not wish to say these things to you when Becky, Millie or the others are about.'

'Oh,' said Laura sitting up in bed, beginning to see Elsie more clearly now that her eyes were becoming accustomed to the dark.

'Do I scare you, Laura?' asked Elsie, a palpable note of sadness in her voice.

'A little,' admitted Laura.

'Because I have known death? Is that what it is? I fear that is our common lot – of revenants, I mean,' she clarified, before Laura could bring any thoughts of her own to utterance.

'No matter how well integrated we are within our community, we are never quite accepted, I find, and we generally have more in common with our own kind than with those we live amongst. The shadow of Darkharrow or of other such places is always on our faces. A very few of us can see that shadow, mark it out, even in bright daylight and know what we see. We know our own kind when we meet them, regardless of rank or circumstance.'

'What do you mean?' asked Laura perplexed. 'Why are you telling me this at all?'

'I am telling you this because I think there is something remarkable about you,' answered Elsie after a long pause. 'When my flesh encountered yours a little while ago, I felt a sensation I have felt only once before – and that was in a dark dream many, many years ago, a dream that brought me stumbling towards the light at long last. You felt it, too, I fancy. I saw it in your eyes. But that is not all. I have not told you anything yet, not really, and what I am about to disclose to you I have thought long and hard about sharing. At last, I resolved that you had best hear this information, and then you may do with it what you will. I shall have discharged my duty to myself... and perhaps to you, my dear.'

'What information?' Laura asked, now thoroughly alarmed, her mouth quite dry.

'The man who asks to be called your father is not infrequently a visitor to this house,' began Elsie, leaning forward towards her and pronouncing the words with exaggerated care, 'and he is a revenant.'

Chapter Five

Thus, Laura passed another sleepless night, albeit for very different reasons, and rose to meet a cheerless new day replete with low cloud and a thin rain from the east. Mid-morning, when Laura had viewed with appropriate declarations of approval the new bonnet that Becky's mother had bought for her, they retired to the white drawing room, where tea and cakes had been laid out. Millie had acquired a new novel that was said to have scandalised half of London, and they spent a pleasant hour or two looking for the parts that might be thought scandalous, reading these passages out with much delight. Laura's participation in this was more measured, however, as her mind turned continually to recent events.

'I declare you are in strangely low spirits this afternoon,' Becky told her. 'I do not usually know you to be coy when such matters arise.'

'Oh, Becky,' giggled Millie, her cheeks flushed pink with delight. 'I wish you would choose your words more carefully.'

'Well, when such issues raise their head…' said Becky, sharing in the mirth.

'I hardly think we may consider that an improvement,' laughed Millie, tapping Becky's shoulder with the book. 'But observe, we have caused Laura to smile, if that brief twitch merits the description.'

'And indeed, I believe it is your turn to read,' said Becky, pressing the book into her unwilling hand. 'I don't doubt you can find us a diverting passage.'

There was much more of this entertainment to be wrung from "The Maiden Undisclosed", and Laura did her poor best to contribute to the jollity. She was heartily glad, however, when Lady Marchmayne offered her a ride home in their carriage at the end of the day.

'I tremble to think what news you might bring me next,' said Emily, when Laura told her of old Elsie's remarkable disclosure. 'I curse my weakness that I am not able to spend more time abroad in your company, the better to protect you from the world. How dull things were for us when we went everywhere together.'

'And how comfortable!' exclaimed Laura with an ironic laugh. 'How I regret their passing. I lie in my bed and screw my eyes closed shut and wish only that dull normality may prevail as once it did. But I fear that the genie may not readily be confined to his lamp once more.'

'You astonish me. You encountered a genie, you had three wishes, and that was what you chose?' observed Emily with a wry smile. 'Dull normality?'

'Indeed not. You take me for a fool, of course,' laughed Laura bitterly. 'My metaphor was not well-chosen, I concede.' She lit a lamp of her own, now that dusk was settling around Groomfield, and drew up a chair next to Emily's bed. 'Oh, dear Emily, what does it all mean? Why do all these dreadful things come crowding in?'

'I don't suppose Elsie is dreadful,' said Emily, her brow furrowed, 'and her nature does much to explain her strangeness. And Jonah is no more dreadful for being a revenant. I suppose his status confers no special wickedness on him that cannot be attributed simply to the content of his character.'

'But what should we do?' asked Laura, standing up and pacing restlessly around the room. 'We have been given this knowledge, but what use should we make of it?'

'Perhaps we may make no use of it at all,' answered Emily, sitting up in bed and swinging her pale legs out over the side, 'because to disclose such knowledge to others would destroy Mama as surely as it would destroy Jonah. Her marriage would be dissolved, her reputation ruined beyond hope of redemption.'

'I wish she had not told me,' admitted Laura, stooping to poke a little life into the small fire in the grate that warmed Emily's room, even on the brightest of days. 'For the knowledge is a burden to me now.'

'And one that I gladly share,'replied her sister. 'But I fear it must lie unused within us.'

Emily's condition continued to worsen with the dampness of the climate, and so Laura spent much of the next week at home – and much of this time at her sister's bedside. Emily was afflicted with a high fever, and the doctor had to be summoned one night. He prescribed various medicines, and on this occasion, they seemed to have a beneficial effect. The patient began to recover her strength and her wits. At times, when the fever led her mind astray, she lay pale, perspiring, eyes wide but unfocused, muttering inconsequential nonsense that could barely be understood. Laura's name featured large in her ramblings, and Laura lived in dread that she might utter some indiscretion that would bring suspicion upon her. So, for many reasons, Laura was a devoted nurse, content to remain with her sister, to soothe the clammy heat of her brow with a cool cloth, to squeeze her hand and speak softly to her when she called out suddenly in her disordered dreams. In truth Laura had little appetite for the society of her peers during this time, and so she welcomed the seclusion that her sister's illness occasioned from her. All the talk of the village was of the murder in Madeley Woods, and Laura felt sure that her attendance at the scene of the crime must somehow be written indelibly in her features. Even the servants at Groomfield were heard to discuss the murder, and a party of constables were said to be patrolling the fens that lay beyond Madeley in the hope of apprehending the culprit.

'What if they catch him?' Laura murmured to Emily when her fever had subsided, and she was lucid once more. Such considerations had dominated her thoughts in recent days, and she was relieved, at last, to be able to share them with her sister.

'What if they do?' asked Emily huskily.

'Well, they may mistreat him as they question him, and who knows what he will then reveal.'

'Laura, my sweet sister, you are quite innocent of all charges that could possibly be levelled at you. Why do you torment yourself so?' asked Emily with a faint smile. 'It was not you that put an arrow through poor John Lovelock's throat.'

'I know, but I was there,' sighed Laura. 'And I fear shame... disgrace.'

'It will pass,' assured Emily. 'Surely it will all pass. All is in the Lord's hands, and you must have the grace to accept it.'

'But it is so hard,' sighed Laura.

'Life goes on,' said Emily in a small voice, 'like a great river, and you must submit yourself to its flow. Although like a strong swimmer you may pass hither or thither across its breadth, no good thing comes from resistance to that current.'

'Indeed,' said Laura. 'Wise words – the words of the Reverend Beale's last sermon, if I recall.'

'Some of his best,' agreed Emily with a smile.

At length, as Emily recovered something of her former vitality, Laura was persuaded to resume the life that she had recoiled from since the day of John's murder. Becky Marchmayne, who had keenly felt the deprivation of her company (or so she claimed in a note from Cottersley), urged her to come and stay for a few nights. She made it abundantly clear that she understood that this should only come to pass if the doctor vouchsafed for Emily's recovery and if Laura could be spared from her bedside.

'You must go, Laura dear. I insist,' Emily told her after Laura had read her the letter and the various earnest enquiries of concern for the patient's health that it contained, 'for I am quite recovered now. Besides, I am heartily fatigued with the sight of you looming over my bed by day and night. A few days with my books and with Mama to tend to me will do me the power of good, I swear.'

The mischievous glint in Emily's eye assured Laura that she should take no offence.

'Well, if you are sure,' conceded Laura, biting her lip.

'I have never been surer of anything,' replied Emily. 'Besides, Mama and I have Italy to prepare for. I am to go in October, if all remains well, and I should like to know a little Italian by then.'

The thought of remaining in the house with Jonah, whilst Mama and Emily removed themselves to warmer climes, was not one on which Laura cared to dwell, although she rejoiced that Emily was to have that opportunity. Nevertheless, the familiar circumstances of Cottersley Park and the society of her friends did much to distract her from this prospect and from recollection of those troubling events that were beginning to seem a little more remote.

She was almost restored to her former habitual cheerfulness by the third day of her stay. After luncheon she settled down with Becky, Millie and Jessica to work on the play they were meant to be performing to celebrate Sir Peter's birthday.

'I fancy I should enter at this point, with a lamb under my arm,' declared Millie, tapping the text. 'It seems to me the shepherd is under-represented in this act.'

'What, and interrupt the magistrate's speech?' asked Becky disapprovingly, who was cast as the magistrate in question. 'Have you no notion of legal procedure? The court officials would surely have prevented it.'

'Well, I would simply point out that the play is entitled "The Watchful Shepherd" and I should have asked to play another role had I known the shepherd featured so slightly,' grumbled Millie.

'Then you should attend more closely to that title, Millie,' Becky admonished, making a small amendment to the script with a stub of pencil, 'for the shepherd in question is not defined as a "talkative" or an "assertive" one. If you had not wished merely to be watchful you should have chosen another character.'

'And besides, you can never remember your lines,' said Jessica scornfully. 'Whereas no one can fault your watchfulness.'

'And what shall I take from that?' asked Millie in outraged tones.

'She only means that your mere presence lends dignity to the stage,' sighed Laura wearily. 'I saw Miss Cadogan's Boadicea at the Norwich Hippodrome last autumn. She had no more than three lines in the second act, and I swear all eyes were fixed upon her throughout. For sure, the best actresses can hold an audience's attention even whilst entirely mute.'

'I see,' said Millie somewhat mollified. 'I suppose that might be so.'

'That's exactly what I meant,' said Jessica gratefully, conscious of having over-reached herself just now, and then, 'I say, is that Groomfield's gig approaching on the drive?'

'Why yes?' confirmed Millie, crossing to the window even as Laura joined her. 'I believe it is.'

Suddenly Laura's heart was like a stone within her chest. She was at the front door even as the butler drew it open, to find Tom standing there with a face ghastly pale, wringing his cap in his hands.

'I had best go straight away,' said Laura, fighting back tears. 'You will excuse me, I trust, Lady Marchmayne.'

For Tom had stammered out the news that Emily lay gravely ill, that she might breathe her last at any moment.

'Of course,' said Lady Marchmayne, her round face suddenly grave. 'Shall I summon a servant to go with you?'

'Not at all,' replied Laura, drawing on her coat with all the haste she could muster, kissing her wide-eyed friends and snatching up her bag. 'Please don't trouble yourself. Tom will suffice and I shall be home within the hour, I think.'

Laura's mind reeled with anguish as the gig turned out onto the rain-wet road and the cob carried them homeward with all the haste that could be coaxed from her. There was little point in conducting a thorough interrogation of Tom, for he was distressed almost to the point of incoherence, but she gathered that Emily's condition had taken a turn for the worse during the night and that the doctor had been summoned. The Reverend Beale had been summoned, too, and it was this that caused Laura's throat to constrict, her heart to pound painfully within her breast as the hedgerows hurried past. They were going too fast. The gig slipped into a ditch on a muddy corner, turning out Tom upon his face and leaving Laura sprawling across the seat.

'No, no, no!' she cried, hauling herself upright and snatching for the reins. 'Lord preserve us! There is not time for this!'

It was whilst they were attempting to ease the wheel from the ditch, heaving with all their might, that a group of young men emerged from the trees above the road. They wore scarves about their faces and carried stout staves in their hands.

'Good day, lads,' said Laura warily, looking up from her work, stepping back to regard the newcomers who had formed a loose arc around them. She was conscious that she must fight down the rising tide of panic that threatened to extinguish her mastery of mind and body, to face this new crisis with a bold front.

'Never mind "good day", Miss,' said one of them, extending an open hand towards her. 'You had best empty your purse for us or it will be the worse for you.'

'Is that you, Jeb Ferney?' asked Laura, ignoring this injunction, addressing a boy whose shock of red hair proclaimed his identity with more certainty than his scarf could conceal.

'No, it ain't me,' said the boy with a blush and a shake of the head.

'I told you that were the Groomfield cob,' said another lad in aggrieved tones. 'Now we'll catch it.' This was Jacob Cutler, by the sound of his voice, whose parents were once tenants of Groomfield but had now absconded to places unknown.

'Not if we kill 'em first,' said another boy with bravado belied by his quavering voice.

'Oh yes, and who's about to start the killing?' said Laura, stepping forward and pulling the scarf down his face. 'Seth Cartwright, I thought as much! Do you really propose to murder me, when my mother dandled you in her arms that time you were sick with the whooping cough and your own mama was in despair. Really? Is that where you have come to?' She glanced around the group, who were now sheepishly pulling down their own scarves and regarding her fearfully. 'You should be ashamed of yourselves,' she told them. 'You do know you could swing for this kind of thing?'

'At least hangin's quick,' retorted red-haired Jeb. 'I ain't eaten for three days now, and starvin's an ugly long way to go.'

Laura settled her lips in a taut line and looked back at the gig.

'Well, you'd best lend a shoulder with this, then. A sixpence should recompense you for your efforts, should it not?'

It was too late. Laura had known in her heart it would be too late, and her mother rushed out to meet her in the hall, cradling Laura's head on her shoulder as they wept together, swaying to and fro. Jonah stood awkwardly aside; his sallow features arranged to represent respectful sadness if not outright grief.

'I must go to her,' said Laura when at last she could form coherent speech.

'Indeed, but you may not presently touch her,' warned Mama.

'She is in the grip of the rigor,' grunted Jonah. 'It is unlucky. And the undertaker will be here presently, as

89

soon as the doctor has signed her papers. But you may say farewell.'

Laura stood at the end of Emily's bed and regarded her poor dead sister with a sadness that permeated every atom of her being, a bitter sadness that ached within her soul. She was so small, so pale, lost in the whiteness of her pillow, her hair brushed neatly about her.

'Emily,' she began, clutching for support at the rail of the brass bedstead, but she could make no other words, and besides Dr Henderson was still there, writing in his notebook, glancing at his watch.

'She knows, dear child,' he said, placing a hand on her shoulder as he turned to leave. 'She knows what you would say.'

'You must speak to your father,' said Mama urgently the next day. 'For he would have Emily consigned to the earth and I cannot prevail upon him.'

Laura had been looking out into the garden with no particular attention, a note to Becky lying unfinished on the table before her. Now she turned to her mother, who seemed as though a mantle of ten years had been draped upon her and from whom the last vestiges of youth and vitality had been visibly drained. Her cheeks were hollow and her eyes sunken, but a wan determination was written therein.

'But surely she must go into Darkharrow!' cried Laura, rising from her seat.

'Indeed, she must,' replied Mama bleakly. 'Perhaps you can persuade him of that need, for all my entreaties have fallen on deaf ears.'

Jonah was in his study, surrounded by papers, sleeves rolled up, his coat thrown over the back of a chair. He swivelled in his seat, removed his spectacles and glared at her as she entered.

'And would it injure you to knock, daughter, before you destroy a man's train of thought?'

'This is my family's house, Jonah,' said Laura coldly, 'and I do not need to knock.'

Jonah regarded her speculatively for a moment, whilst the implications of this sank in, and then he crossed to close the door softly behind her.

'I see,' he said. 'And to what do I owe this... approach? For you may be sure I resent the manner of it extremely.'

'I do not care what you resent, Jonah, and you may be sure that I care little for your approval,' answered Laura boldly, her arms folded. 'I do care that my sister should be committed to Darkharrow to lie with our ancestors, as is her right. I will not have her mouldering in the earth. I am here to see that you attend to this matter, for I can see that my mother's desires carry no weight with you. I am here to insist upon it.'

'And you conceive that you have the power to command such a thing?' scoffed Jonah. 'You are overcome with grief, daughter, and your wits are all astray or you would not presume to speak to me in this manner. For surely, they would earn for you a beating were I not sensible of your distress, were I not minded to make fair allowance as a dutiful father should.'

'You are not my father,' spat Laura, her eyes flashing defiance, 'and I shall never call you that again in this house. I know exactly what you are.'

'You do?' pondered Jonah carefully after a long pause in which the clock ticked heavily on the mantel. He regarded her steadily, returned to his seat and picked up his pocket watch, toying abstractedly with its chain. 'And what would that be, then, dear child?'

'A status that invalidates your presence here and that would, of necessity, annul your false marriage to my mother and strike out all the legal rights that accrued to you as consequence of that falsehood. For you are a revenant, are you not?'

Laura allowed herself a small, tight smile of satisfaction as the blood drained slowly from Jonah's face. His eyes narrowed and his fingers were suddenly stilled upon the chain. Part of her had feared that old Elsie had been mistaken, but the strange, hunted look that she glimpsed momentarily in Jonah's eyes was all the confirmation she required. She nodded.

'So, it is true,' she said, 'for if it was not, you would surely have given me the lie by now.'

'A grave accusation, indeed,' retorted Jonah in a low voice, leaning back in his chair, regarding her through tightened eyes.

'And one that you may easily refute by showing me the sole of your foot,' said Laura. By law, and by ancient tradition, the dead were tattooed there with the mark of the cross upon their entry into Darkharrow or into other such places. It was the indelible mark of the revenant.

'How did you come by such a notion?' asked Jonah, ignoring her request after a moment in which Laura feared he might snatch off his boot and stocking.

'You do not deny it?' replied Laura.

'I asked you where you came by such a notion,' growled Jonah, a dangerous edge to his voice.

'And I declined to answer you,' said Laura, 'just as you declined to show me the sole of your foot. I suppose we must call it an impasse.' He did not respond to this, only regarded her in the manner a fox might regard hens behind wire, so she pressed on. 'And does my mother know?' She asked in the knowledge that it was entirely possible that their marital relations were conducted in darkness or that Jonah insisted on retaining his stockings.

'You find this amusing?' he countered, detecting the faint glimmer of this thought in her eyes. He shook his head. 'No, she knows not. Do you know your mother for a dissembler?'

'And what if I were to disclose this to her?' suggested Laura warily, judging her distance from the door in case he should suddenly fly at her.

'Not for a moment do I think that you would,' answered Jonah in a low voice, recovering some of his composure, 'because it would break her heart, as you well know, and I do not think that you would countenance such a thing. For this changes nothing, except necessarily in the relations between us, and then only in private. What have you to say to that?' he offered grimly, allowing his posture to relax.

'I have nothing to say to it,' replied Laura, 'except to reiterate what I said to you when first I stepped in here. Emily must go into Darkharrow. I assume the funds set aside for Italy would make some contribution to her committal to that place. No possible contingency is too grave to dissuade me from exposing your crime if you do not bring this about. I beg you must believe me on this point, for I shall bring ruin upon us all, if I must, and if you do not oblige me in this concern.'

She was conscious of the tremor in her voice, but she held her chin high, her gaze true and steady, her fists clenched at her side. There could be no mistaking her sincerity.

Jonah cleared his throat, leant forward and reached for papers from his desk. She knew that she had won.

'You would not so cheerfully urge that course if you knew the state of our accounts,' said Jonah. 'Peruse this, if you will,' he said as he extended a paper to her, which she vaguely recognised as some account of income and expenses. She gave it only a peremptory glance before pushing it back to him.

'I am no clerk,' she said, 'but I know that if Emily had been your own true offspring, you would have given the shirt from your back to win her the chance of her second life. Her first was brief enough, Lord knows.'

'When I first came here the estate stood on the brink of ruin,' Jonah told her. 'Mortgaged to the hilt with the threat of insolvency hung over us like Damocles' sword. Why, half the tradesmen for miles around would extend us no more credit. You and your sister were still quite small, and your mother, still eaten up with grief for your late father, was driven to distraction.' He tapped his chest. 'I was the salvation of this estate. It was I who consolidated the loans and arranged for better terms. It was I who improved the drainage in the south reach, I who brought in new livestock and improved our yields five-fold. We would approach the prospect of some moderate prosperity were it not for this accursed weather and these last two dismal harvests. You would have me prejudice these hard-won gains merely so that your sister can be housed in Darkharrow? What makes you think that you will ever see her living face again? You might be long dead and forgotten, if she ever wakes to see another dawn. And she might not. We all know the Lord raises a tiny proportion of those who pass through those portals. You are content to gamble our chance of prosperity on such uncertain odds? What are we to gain?'

'I am,' said Laura. 'Add up your columns and do what is necessary, for I will not have you deny to Emily what you once had for yourself.'

Emily was committed at last to the care of the Camoldolites and passed into the day-less gloom of Darkharrow, where Edward was amongst those who must attend upon her, though he would never speak of it. Emily's funeral took place in the abbey church alongside the great necropolis, and when it was done and her casket had been carried away by six black-clad brothers, Laura allowed herself a moment of quiet triumph. She dared not make eye contact with Jonah, who sat on the other side of her mother on the hard oak pew whilst the procession came past, swinging censers and chanting the orison. She felt sure that he was lamenting the diminution of his wealth even as her mother and she lamented for Emily. And with the satisfaction of her own immediate desires came the sudden fear of what the future might hold for her. She had barely looked beyond this day, so caught up had she been with Mama in the arrangements for the committal and for the wake that must follow. Jonah was known to be a vengeful man, and nothing could be more certain than his resentment of her intervention. But what form might his vengeance take? Laura felt a chill in her bones that owed nothing to the cool stone of the abbey as she made her way out blinking into the light of a September day.

Chapter Six

But if Jonah plotted to wreak vengeance upon her there was no sign of it in the weeks to come, and life resumed its normal round as though there had been no secret understanding between them. Laura called him 'Father,' at least in her mother's presence, and showed him every outward mark of the respect that was due to a parent.

'I'm not sure what it was you said to him,' Mama told her one day, shortly after the funeral. 'And I do not wish to know. But whatever it was softened his heart most effectively, and I thank you for it.'

In truth it seemed unlikely that Jonah's heart was susceptible to softening, unless first removed from his person, but fortunately his attention was wholly absorbed by the settling of the estate's affairs as the present tax year approached its end. Tithing Harrow was so named because it had been, since time immemorial, a local centre for the collection of the tithes or taxes that were due to King and Church. There were four tithing days, one for each quarter of the year, and each taxpayer, whether humble or noble, was allocated to one of these quarters, according to the date of their birth. On the appointed day they were obliged to attend the tithing fair in the county of their birth and settle their debts to the state. Naturally, this was a complex and time-consuming undertaking. The Lord Lieutenant was required to stand guard with the county constabulary whilst the King's Receivers did their work. This took place in the great tithing hall that stood opposite and across the square from Darkharrow. Here the Lord Lieutenant held court twice a month, and here were kept the county records that detailed the wealth of each subject and the extent of their resultant tax commitments. It was for this reason that the complex of buildings of which it formed part was sturdily constructed. It was a squat, unlovely building with a single entrance on the second floor, reached by a timber staircase that might quickly be removed in time of need. There were no windows on the ground floor at all. Three times in centuries past, when the exactions of the state had surpassed the endurance of the populace, the people had risen and attempted to burn down the hated hall of records. On each occasion they had failed, precipitating a gruesome campaign of hangings and floggings by the vengeful state. There were some who suspected a similar crisis was approaching. Amongst them was Jonah.

'They will not tell me, damn their eyes,' he complained as he threaded his way through the crowded streets towards the marquees set up in the square, where he was due to make his payment. 'I know there is something going on, but as soon as I begin to probe a little, they close up tight as tight can be.'

He was talking about the estate workers, who had become unusually surly in recent weeks, many of them responding to his entreaties with dumb insolence, if not outright defiance.

'And look at this,' he blustered, snatching up a printed handbill that showed an ill-drawn records office with curling flames issuing from it and the word 'LIBERTY' in bold uppercase letters underneath. 'If this is not sedition, I don't know what is! Here!' he barked as he thrust it at a sweating constable who had an armful of similar items. 'Do your duty, sir. The gutters are awash with these rags.'

'I suppose they will find the culprit and break his press,' said Sir Peter Marchmayne mildly, walking at his side. Several of his burlier servants and employees carried the burden of his tax dues behind him and made it unlikely that either he or Jonah should be robbed.

'They should break his body, too,' snarled Jonah, glancing at another bill nailed to a door that showed what was evidently meant to represent Darkharrow, this too with curling smoke and flames. "One Life for All" was the caption. 'Here, take that one, too, you blind bastard!' he shouted after the receding constable's back.

Jonah was bound to be out of sorts, given that he was shortly to be divested of a large proportion of his income. His ill-humour was intensified by the knowledge that the wealthiest and best-connected contrived to pare down their own commitment through ingenious accounting or downright dishonesty. In this, at least, the present age stood squarely in line with tradition. Cottersley Park, with lands ten times the extent of Groomfield, paid barely twice as much, due to a complex arrangement of special concessions and exemptions set in place over generations. In addition, he was conscious of a palpable tension in the air as though some great tempest was about to break across the land.

Laura felt it as well, walking behind with her mother, several of Groomfield's staff and the Marchmayne girls. Becky's cheerful chatter suggested that she, at least, remained insensible of the gathering storm.

'Oh dear,' remarked Jessica, rather more aware of their immediate surroundings. 'I do wish your father would not kick the beggars so.'

'Well, if they will importune him as he goes about his business,' said Becky, intervening to protect the reputation of her friend's family, 'they must expect to be admonished.'

'They are uncommonly bold just now,' said Mama with a shudder. 'Mrs Gillard had one snatch at her bag yesterday, and this under the eyes of a constable. They are intolerably lax in their duties, I find. Here is a shilling,' she said to Laura and her friends. 'Will you go amongst the stalls and amuse yourselves awhile? David shall come with you. I am to go to Cranage's to get me some ribbon,' she added, mentioning Tithing Harrow's haberdashers, 'and I shall meet you under the sign at the King's Head.'

'I never saw the tithing fair so busy,' noted Laura as they made their way through the throng towards the stalls that were set up around the edge of the town square. 'Surely there are more folk here than are due for this quarter.'

Away at the north end of the square, in the lee of the abbey church, wooden staging had been set up for the miracle plays traditionally provided for the entertainment and instruction of the masses on these occasions. Brightly coloured costumes and ingenious stage props were typically to be seen, but in this instance, there was only a red-faced man, haranguing the crowd, a book held in one hand, his other punching the air to emphasise the sincerity of his words. The crowd jostled to move closer as the girls moved around its perimeter, weaving amongst those who sought merely to pass through or to shop amongst the stalls. It seemed clear to Laura that something momentous might be about to occur, and she felt a shudder of disquiet.

'Here, let me get me a toffee-apple,' said Becky, oblivious, as ever, to anything beyond the urgings of her stomach or of her inner mind. 'Will you attend a moment?'

'Hear him!' bellowed the stall owner over her shoulder, nevertheless opening his palm to receive her penny.

Sentiments of this kind were being expressed by others in the square, and there was a murmur of approval that rippled through the throng. Most of them were humble people, Laura saw, as she began to attend for the first time to the nature of the speaker's discourse. It was clear that this was no mere religious exhortation, and all the time more people were joining the press. They were spinners, weavers and the labourers from the land, cotters, carpenters, workers from the tannery and the timber yard. Every trade was represented, every age and stature. There were apprentice boys from the foundry on the edge of town and gnarled old men leaning on their sticks. Yet, amongst this diversity, they had this one thing in common – a leanness that bordered on starvation, for many of these folk trod that perilous margin every day. A hollowness was in their cheeks and a rising anger in their eyes.

'Listen,' instructed Laura, tugging on Becky's sleeve as she made to move away. 'I want to hear what he is saying.'

'I don't much care for this,' muttered David, who had been sent to accompany them. 'I think we had best get us to the King's Head to await your mother, like she said.'

'Not yet, David,' said Laura impatiently. 'Do have forbearance just a while.'

'What is he saying?' hissed Jessica, listening for the first time. 'Does he preach sedition?'

'He ain't no preacher,' grunted David. 'That's a rabble rouser, if ever I saw one. Thomas Sheridan, if I ain't mistook.'

'Hush!' Laura shushed, rounding on him and pressing her finger to her lips.

'… and take the bread from the mouth of babes,' the man was saying, or rather shouting, with a loud, clear voice that carried to every corner of the square, 'that the Church, with all its fat prelates, might be enriched… and the corpses in Darkharrow eat up the gold that we have earned with the sweat of our brows? Is this right, I ask you?'

'No!' roared the crowd, with many a raised fist shaken.

'And our sons and daughters must moulder in the earth, whilst the rich can dream of a second life as they lie at our expense in this cursed place.' A sweeping gesture of his arm encompassed the looming mass of Darkharrow behind him. 'Anointed with all the oils of Araby brought halfway across the globe at our expense. I ask you, is this right?'

'No!' roared the crowd again.

'Well, that is surely sedition, and he will swing for it if they catch him,' muttered David. 'Come on, now. This may take an ugly turn, I think.'

For it was certain that once Thomas Sheridan had finished posing questions, he might move on to proposing remedies, and raising a petition seemed unlikely to feature amongst them. David was not the only one present to foresee that recourse to force of arms by the common people might soon be recommended. Amongst those who shared his anxiety on this point was the Lord Lieutenant, who now sent a party of constables to arrest the miscreant. He had left it far too late.

'Now you see the true face of the state,' roared Sheridan as a party of grim-faced constables began to make their way through the crowd towards him. 'Now they will take me to the gallows for speaking God's truth. For speaking with your voices,' he added. 'Will you have your voices stilled?'

There was a great shout of protest. First the constables were booed and spat at, then pushed and jostled. Soon they were marooned, quite helplessly, in a hostile sea of faces made bold by their numbers and intoxicated by Sheridan's exhortations. The agents of the law were cursed and abused until one of them unwisely drew his sword and blood was spilt. There was a scream and more agonised cries. A huge roar of pent-up rage rose from the crowd and suddenly all was chaos.

'Oh, my sweet God! Come quickly,' cried David, snatching at Laura's sleeve, but now there were troopers urging their mounts through the press, beating about them with sturdy sticks, and as the crowd surged this way and that, Laura found it all but impossible to keep her feet, forced hard against a mass of angry bodies, David's anguished face drifting from her like a ship in a storm. The sound was like nothing she had ever heard. Where were her friends? Nowhere to be seen. Close by, a struggling trooper was dragged from his mount. Cursing, he subsided beneath a heaving mass of people. Sticks rose and fell, his shrill screams of sudden terror drowned out by animal sounds of fury Laura had never heard issue from human throats.

'Where are the rich?' went up a cry. 'Kill the rich!'

More people were flooding into the square, and Laura, heart pounding, was acutely conscious of her neat shoes, her sky-blue Sunday dress, the straw bonnet on her head. How clearly these marked her out against the dull browns and greens of peasant garb. The eyes of her social inferiors were suddenly hostile as she pushed against their unyielding shoulders, holding back her tears to maintain some semblance of dignity, making her way towards the edge of the square. Spittle flecked her dress and clung in her hair when she reached the soaring wall of Darkharrow, and twice, with a yelp, she had slapped aside a hand that quested at her clothing. One such hand snatched away her bonnet now, to a raucous cry of triumph, but the sudden overturning of a stall offered other distractions. Whilst all attention was turned to thieving, she darted away into a side street, no wider than a hand cart, and ran along it for a few paces, pausing for a moment to catch her breath and to regain her composure as best she could muster. She was smoothing down her skirts and wondering how she might find her way in safety to the King's Head when a door opened in the wall next to her and she found herself face to face with Edward.

'Edward,' she gasped.

'Laura,' he replied. 'I am surprised to see you.'

'And I, you.'

Two large youths bearing cudgels appeared at the end of the lane, breathing hard. Their gaze fell upon Laura.

'It would be a kindness if you would admit me,' she added.

'Certainly.'

And then they stood in a dark passage, lit only by the lamp that Edward bore and by a few faint gleams from around the outline of the door. Heavy footsteps sounded outside, dull voices and then only the distant sounds of the turmoil in the square.

'What are you doing here?' asked Edward, picking a cobweb from her hair.

'I was running to escape the mob,' she said, 'and I could ask you the same question.'

'We can see nothing at the front with the great doors shut. The Abbot heard a commotion outside and, thinking that some miscreants might be setting faggots against them, sent me to go out by the side door there and observe from the other side. You see,' he moved the lamp up and down to illuminate the shabby workman's clothes he wore, 'I have set aside my robes so that I may not be discovered. Oh dear...' He frowned. 'And you must certainly not be discovered here. I shudder to think how many taboos would be broken then, even if it were not actually a crime. I should surely be punished for admitting you.'

'What, simply for preserving me from the wrath of the mob?' asked Laura, contributing a frown of her own. 'I call that very illiberal of them.'

'Call it what you will. You well know that the living may not enter Darkharrow unless they are of my order,' he said. 'Here, you had best take this lamp and await my return. I shall summon a constable to take charge of you, if a living one can be found. If all is well by then I shall let you out and we each may go about our business as though this had never happened.'

Then he was gone, and Laura was left blinking in the passage, wondering how much oil was in the lamp and whether her friends and family were safe. After a while, finding it draughty by the door, she moved a little way along the passage to where an inkier patch of darkness hinted at the presence of a side chamber. Stepping inside, the flickering lamplight illuminated a space that contained six wall niches, three on either side. Each niche was occupied by a corpse, their eyes closed shut, sunken cheeks cast in shadow by the yellow light. Laura's immediate impulse was to recoil in revulsion, but after a moment she calmed herself and took another step. The motivation for this second step was not clearly evident to her then, or ever, even after long reflection, and most girls of her age would surely have retired trembling to the passage within a moment. Beneath each niche there was a stone plaque with an inscription recording the occupant's name, their age and the date of their admittance. Two of them were women and four were men, ranging in age from eighty-one to fifteen. On one side of her were Dorothy Chapman, Reginald Fairchild and Timothy Thorpe. On the other lay David Beer, Mary Hickwold and George Hemingway. Each of them had died within the fifth and sixth decades of the previous century, more than a hundred years since. The dead were draped in plain white sheets, pulled up to their breasts to leave their wizened arms and faces exposed. Part of Laura marvelled that she was able to gaze with such equanimity upon those lifeless countenances, but the greater part of her was affected by a strange fascination. If she had not been so affected, had not found herself in such a state of mind akin to a trance, it is doubtful that she would have placed her hand upon George Hemingway's cold brow. There was immediately a tremor along her arm and a sensation similar to that she had felt when she had touched old Elsie at Cottersley Park.

'How curious,' she wondered out loud, reaching up to try the same with Mary Hickwold.

There was no such sensation on this occasion, only cool, dead flesh like the hams that were hung in Groomfield's cellar. The same was true of David Beer and of Timothy Thorpe on the other side of the chamber. But with Dorothy Chapman and Reginald Fairchild she likewise received the sensation of a small, sharp tremor within her. Fascinated now, all fear set aside, Laura replaced her hand on Dorothy's brow and kept it there, closing her eyes the better to explore the sensation. Eyes closed, she felt as though with some alternative inner vision she could see within Dorothy's body, past the skull and down through the desiccated tissues of her mouth and throat. Down, down her mind's eye swam, through paper-dry lungs to that shrunken, long-stilled heart. How cold it was, how hard and with a granular coating of frost crystals that glinted in some inner light. With David Beer it was quite different. There was no ice, no light of any description. She was conscious only of hardness, of immobility, of a heart that might as well have been carved from granite.

'What are you doing?' came a loud, abrasive voice behind her.

Her own heart leapt within her, and she swung round to find herself face to face with Noah Broadfoot, prior of this place and Edward's uncle. Two of Edward's robed comrades stood next to him, faces aghast. 'I say, what are you doing here?' he repeated in outraged tones, approaching with his own lamp to shine it in her face. 'Is that you, Laura DeLacey? It is! What do you mean by this sacrilege? The dead are not to be trifled with for your amusement, and you well know that the living may not enter here. How dare you! Is my nephew's hand to be detected in this? I ask you again, what are you doing here?'

'Why nothing,' said Laura, attempting to recover her wits, to shrug off the trance-like state that had she had entered. 'I meant no harm; I do assure you.'

'And yet you disturb the dead,'

'Some may be not disturbed, I think,' she gestured about her mildly, 'for these hearts are of ice and those of stone.'

The Hall of Records was burned down that day, and if the militia had not been summoned from Lowestoft, Darkharrow might have joined it in the flames, for the common people had grown to hate it. Indeed, there were some who said that such malcontents might have set the last fire to afflict it, full five years since. Their social superiors shivered behind the stout doors of their houses and looked nervously into the eyes of their servants as the peasants unleashed their fury on the land.

Three of the king's best regiments were sent down from London to restore order. After a few skirmishes, in which the common mob succumbed bloodily to grapeshot and musketry, a surly quiet was restored to the Eastings. It could hardly be described as peace, since the woods and the fens crawled with bandits and fugitives from the vengeance of the law. A consignment of spice destined for Darkharrow was ambushed on the road, despite the presence of a file of troopers assigned to protect it, and the precious cargo set on fire. The pungent smoke could be seen roiling across the fields from miles away.

'Damn their impudence,' bellowed Jonah, turning from the window several weeks after what was already becoming known as the 'Eastings Revolt.' He had been standing there for some while, watching the smoke drifting past the tall elms at the end of the fields that marked the western limit of the estate. 'If his Royal Majesty doesn't presently take a grip in these parts, we may be sure the contagion will spread elsewhere. I warrant there's scoundrels just like that damned Thomas Sheridan in every county of the realm, pouring their poison into the ears of the wicked and the ignorant. There're rogues hung up in the gibbets from here to Lavenshall – and still they come. But we shall have gallows enough, I swear, if we must string up half the county.' He emphasised this point with a fierce rap of his stick on the floor.

For Jonah had walked with a stick these last few weeks. With a party of armed gentry, he had ridden out one night to drive off a mob that was burning down the barns at High Mallow, a few miles away. In the ensuing violence and confusion, he had been wounded by a pistol ball.

Laura well recalled his return to Groomfield later that night, supported on either side by his friends. She could have wished the ball had been a cannon ball and taken off his head, but instead the projectile had merely grazed the heel of his foot, passing through his boot.

'Left foot or right foot?' she had asked as her anxious mother came hurrying through the parlour with bandages and scissors.

'Left,' she said over her shoulder, confirming Laura's suspicions.

'And why should that matter?' asked Mary, with a frown, bringing through a bloodied stocking in a bowl.

'No reason,' said Laura with a grim nod. 'I was simply curious. I'll warrant the ball has carried away the flesh of his heel.'

'It has that,' agreed Mary with a puzzled tilt of her head. 'Although you've no way of knowing it. I do wonder at you sometimes, Missy.'

Laura pursed her lips into a tight line and glared at her hands before her on the table at which she sat. She fancied she knew exactly the circumstances in which Jonah had sustained his wound. He must have thought it worth the pain to shoot away the only evidence that marked him as a revenant, and the skirmish would have offered the perfect opportunity, in the din of battle with steel clashing and musket balls flying.

There was a sly triumph in his eyes as well as pain when Laura had seen him later and he had spared her a secret glance that declared his victory.

'Your father is fortunate,' Dr Henderson had told her, wiping his hands. 'It could have been much worse. There may be scarring but no worse than that, I should think. I doubt he will be crippled by it.'

'Oh yes, my father is fortunate indeed,' said Laura under her breath as the doctor buttoned his coat.

'And how do you fare?' asked Dr Henderson, when he had closed his bag. 'I have heard troubling accounts of your doings in Darkharrow. There is to be an investigation, I hear. I suppose the church might have overlooked the intrusion had you not interfered with the dead. I imagine the greater part of humanity might have quailed at being stranded in darkness there, might have confined themselves to the immediate environs of the point of entry. It seems strange that you would venture further within, well beyond the bounds of what we might describe as normal behaviour.'

'I cannot explain it,' offered Laura, 'but if you seek to make the case for some mental disturbance or incapacity, I should tell you that I resent it extremely. Nor did I "interfere" with the dead, as you term it. I merely placed my hand upon their foreheads. That is all. In no way did I injure them.'

'And you do not concede that your behaviour might be considered... the issue of a mind that is in some way... disturbed?' asked Dr Henderson with a frown.

'Certainly, I concede that some ill-informed persons might form that opinion,' said Laura, 'and might continue to do so unless those who know better strive to enlighten them.'

'Indeed,' said the doctor with a slow, considering nod. 'Well, I shall bid you all goodnight.'

Whilst Laura's activity in Darkharrow was a source of controversy in that place and beyond, they were also a source of great confusion and perplexity to their perpetrator. Those moments in the darkness of the tomb were never far from the surface of her mind, and there were times when she shared the good doctor's evident doubts about her sanity. Poor Edward had been severely admonished for admitting her, even though he had almost certainly spared her from insult and injury by so doing. He had undergone a hostile interview with the abbot and a still more awkward one with Noah, who was smarting from the censure he himself had endured on his nephew's behalf.

'Do not trouble yourself on that score,' Edward told her a week later. 'I do not criticise you for your actions, although I do not pretend to understand your motivation.'

'I am no closer to understanding it myself,' admitted Laura, 'and this after seven days in which I have thought of little else.'

She explained the sensations she had experienced and the strange visions she had seen. Even speaking of it made her own heart beat faster and brought a flush to her skin.

'I have never heard of such a thing,' said Edward, stroking his chin. 'Have you mentioned this to anyone other than me?'

Laura shook her head. 'I have not. I begin to think that I am mad, although naturally I would not wish to induce others to form that opinion. I believe Jonah would like nothing better than to have me locked away.'

'You are not mad, Laura,' said Edward adamantly. 'I believe what you have told me, although your experience lies well beyond my own. Perhaps you should confide in Sir Joseph when he returns from his travels. He is a man of rare wisdom and knowledge.'

'Perhaps I should,' conceded Laura.

Chapter Seven

Jonathon Lamb, the Archbishop of Canterbury, was a mild and saintly man, but like many saintly men he was beset by devils within. Like Saint Antony in the desert, he was tormented by fleshly temptations of the most distressing kind. Only through night-long prayer vigils and the mortification of his flesh was he able to keep these devils at bay. Only through fasting, meditation and solitary retreats was he able to cast out from his mind tempting visions of unnatural sins of the flesh. The rigorous nature of his prayer regime, his other-worldly focus on the spiritual, won for him a reputation for holiness, which he did nothing to discourage or oppose. Naturally, such preoccupations interfered with the execution of his daily duties and made it essential that he should delegate many of these to his deputy.

William Turnbull, the Bishop of London, was the man who shouldered most of this burden – and shouldered it gladly. The bishop was an ambitious and able man with a ruthless determination to advance his cause that had seen many more scrupulous than he pushed aside or trampled underfoot. At the age of forty-two he was the fourth most powerful figure within the Church of Britannia. He was an intelligent man, with a sharp eye for weakness in those around him and a forensic knowledge of scripture that enabled him to enlist it in support of any cause. His guiding passion was to do God's will, or so he claimed; there were those who said it was remarkable that God's will so often coincided with his own, that William Turnbull's will, and God's, were scarcely to be distinguished, in fact. Nevertheless, God took no obvious steps to distance himself from his dutiful servant, and so the bishop's management of the archdiocese's financial affairs enabled him to enrich himself to an extraordinary degree. The archbishop, bound up with his own internal preoccupations, seemed oblivious to his subordinate's machinations, and Turnbull, keen to perpetuate this situation, was careful to ensure that the altar boys in Saint Paul's were of a most distracting comeliness.

When, on Turnbull's earnest recommendation, the archbishop made a pilgrimage to Rome it appeared that at last the ambitious bishop might have over-reached himself. In the absence of his distinguished protector, his enemies proposed that a man as active and as able as Turnbull might be wasted within the administrative structure of the archdiocese, that he might be employed more generally to address the problems with which the realm was beset.

'This is an outrage!' Turnbull told Lord Clarey, the King's High Treasurer and one of the most exalted nobles in the land, when first this commission was presented to him. The noble lord, an old friend of Turnbull's, was also in possession of one of the most penetrating minds in the realm and was aware of Turnbull's ambitions within the Church.

'I see,' said Clarey with a disapproving cluck of the tongue. 'You wish me to convey to His Majesty that you feel he has perpetrated an outrage upon you.'

'I wish nothing of the sort, as you well know, Clarey,' said the bishop, a flush rising to his cheeks. He removed his spectacles and set down the paper that contained the lines that had so inflamed him. 'Allow me a moment to order my thoughts, if you will.'

Turnbull turned to the window, which offered a view of London rooftops stretching out towards the majestic grey bulk of Saint Paul's. He bit his lip, took a deep breath and turned once more to Lord Clarey, who sat with his legs outstretched before him, an expression of languorous amusement set in his fine, ascetic features.

'There must be others better suited to the execution of this task,' said Turnbull in measured tones, taking up the paper from the desk once more but brandishing it in a trembling hand that betrayed his agitation. 'I am a servant of Mother Church. My talents lie in the administration and the ordering of affairs within the Church. The commission outlined here would seem to require a man of action, a man with a mind that can competently encompass a broad range of activities and with the energy and experience to take decisive action. Whereas I am a simple man of God.'

'Hah!' snorted the noble Lord. 'My dear Turnbull, I wonder those words don't lodge in your throat.'

'I must say I resent...' started Turnbull, his brows knitting.

'Dismiss such resentment from your mind, I urge you,' warned Clarey, leaning forward in his chair suddenly, so that his posture was abruptly transformed from languid detachment to one of earnest regret. 'You are in no position to refuse, and besides, His Majesty has detected in you a set of attributes that befit you to deal most effectively with this crisis. You should be flattered. Would you wish to call his judgement into question on this issue?'

'Whose judgement, in truth?' asked Turnbull suspiciously. 'Which of my enemies has attached the august royal cipher to his own?'

'You are overly cynical, I find,' said Clarey, shaking his head slowly. 'We have known each other a long time, have we not? And I think we understand each other's minds.'

'This is a poisoned chalice,' said Turnbull bitterly.

'Not one that I have prepared, you may be assured,' replied Clarey in emollient tones. 'Besides, success in this enterprise could burnish your reputation still further, and of course you would be well rewarded.'

'Hah!' scoffed Turnbull, and then, after a few moments to reflect that there seemed little possibility of escape from this unwelcome commitment, 'How well rewarded?'

'I take that as assent, then,' said Clarey with a wry smile. 'The rather extensive revenues of several defunct abbeys in the north are to be yours, I believe, although I have heard it said that virtue is its own reward.'

'Not one that you would yourself deem sufficient, I suppose,' scoffed the bishop. 'And once established there amid all this… chaos, am I to "pour out on the earth the seven bowls of the wrath of God", as we hear in Revelations?'

'There will be many who hope that your interpretation of your role savours more of the New Testament than the Old,' said Clarey. 'But the commission is extraordinarily wide-ranging. His Majesty has entrusted you with all executive powers appropriate to these duties and the resources to execute them with all necessary resolution.'

'I see,' said the bishop with a sigh. 'And when am I to begin?'

'I believe you already have,' replied Clarey, rising from his seat.

And therefore, William Turnbull found himself at the head of a commission of enquiry with executive powers to investigate and to extirpate sedition with all necessary severity, to restore order to those regions in which the proper authority of Church and Crown was under threat. In short, he was dispatched to the Eastings to stamp out the smouldering revolt there, before such a cancer of treason could spread elsewhere throughout the realm. Bishop Turnbull was most displeased by this commission but quite unable to refuse it. Accordingly, he determined to act with unprecedented speed and resolution, in order to impress his royal master and hasten his own return to London. The bishop had barely set foot out of London in the last twenty years or so and had only the sketchiest notion of what might await him in the Eastings. It was said that conditions of the utmost barbarity prevailed there, that folk still dwelled in mud huts, that incestuous relations were the norm. Looking bleakly out of his carriage window as it bore him ever eastwards away from London and civilisation, he mused bleakly upon the circumstances that had brought him there.

'You have an ill look, I find,' said Turnbull, turning his attention eventually to his assistant and chief of staff, Canon Abel Ward.

'I fear that the hake we ate in that last inn has disagreed with me,' said Ward, whose thin face wore a colourless, waxen appearance. 'And the motion of the carriage seems likely to dislodge him.'

'Well,' said Turnbull with a fastidious sniff, 'if your belching and flatulence is any guide, he knows not which exit to prefer.'

'And I had thought that Norwich stood at the end of the earth,' said Turnbull a little later, whilst the carriage stood idle behind him, and Ward rid himself noisily of the hake behind a bush. 'I see that I was wrong.'

He stretched the stiff muscles of his back and arms, glaring out despondently across a landscape empty of any sign of human habitation, a landscape of heath and sedge with nothing to divert the eye other than a few stunted trees bowed by the prevailing easterlies.

'Why, not at all,' said young Canon David Warburton brightly, another of his staff and a man forever keen to parade his learning. 'Why, there is Yarmouth beyond that and then the North Sea until the shores of Holland or Germany are reached and...' He stopped, quelled by Turnbull's knitted eyebrows, the pursing of his lips. 'But I see I weary you, my Lord,' he finished awkwardly.

'I spoke figuratively,' Turnbull snapped. 'When I need you to instruct me on geography, I shall certainly let you know.'

'Do you get the feeling that we are secretly observed?' asked Canon Paul Dawson, approaching from the second carriage and then turning to the bushes. 'Oh dear. Ward is unwell, I collect.'

'I think it very likely, on both counts,' agreed Turnbull, pulling his coat around him as a cold squall flattened the grasses and the sedges. 'This wasteland is alive with brigands and assorted savages, by all accounts. If it were not for these fellows...'

Turnbull indicated the troop of cavalry that accompanied the carriages and wagons of his retinue, strung out along the puddled and rutted road for half a mile or so.

'I suppose they know their business,' said Dawson, glancing about anxiously.

Much of the escort were dismounted now, talking amongst themselves and attending to their horses, but a few stood mounted here and there, out in front or on their flanks, regarding the endless flatlands for any sign of threat.

'I suppose they do,' agreed Turnbull, 'but I fancy we shall need more than this to root out the sedition that infests these lands.'

'They say we are to have the Scarlet Band,' remarked Warburton, recovering his composure at last.

'Then they are correct,' agreed the bishop, turning to him. 'And I daresay Danny Blanchflower and his boys will strike fear into the hearts of the king's enemies here.'

'He strikes fear enough into mine,' muttered Dawson. 'Terrible man.'

'But he has his uses,' grunted Turnbull. 'I suppose you will concede it. If the people will not love the king, then at least they will fear him, and their compliance, their sullen acquiescence, is all that I require. Pacification is what His Majesty requires of me, and pacification is what he shall have, if I must string up every wretch east of Norwich to achieve it.'

'Then Danny Boy is the man for you,' said Dawson with a shudder. 'And God help the Eastings!'

'I'm told that Bishop Turnbull and his commission are established in Lavenshall,' said Laura as she walked with Edward one mild October morning. 'David was saying that the whole town is in turmoil. What is he like, this bishop? You have some understanding of the church, I find.'

'And yet not of its more exalted circles,' admitted Edward, pausing to adjust the strap of his sword belt. 'I have a fair notion of its workings in the Eastings, but the fellows in London have been sadly remiss in informing me as to affairs in the capital. I only know that Turnbull is judged to be an efficient and ambitious man. He seeks to make his reputation by distinguishing himself here, it is said. To have pacified an important region such as this would doubtless burnish his credentials. And he is already set up in the Lord Lieutenant's house. Sir Joseph is acquainted with him, has met him on several occasions in London, although I don't think they are friends, exactly.'

'Here, let me help you with that,' offered Laura, clucking as Edward struggled with his task. 'I swear that sword is a greater danger to you than to any potential miscreant.'

Edward blushed, looking away across the common towards where the outlying houses of Tithing Harrow could be discerned beyond the tannery.

'And yet when I am ordained, I shall be forbidden to bear arms,' he said. 'How then shall I protect you when we walk out together? There are still any number of thieves and vagabonds out there.'

He made a vague gesture that encompassed the woods and fields to their south and west.

'Do I detect a hint of regret in your voice?' quizzed Laura, squeezing his forearm. 'Regret that you are to be swallowed up by Darkharrow and spend your days in the service of the dead.'

'Not at all,' answered Edward with an ironic curl of his lip. 'Who could regret such a cornucopia of good fortune?'

'Oh, Edward,' said Laura with a laugh. 'How I shall miss you.'

'You make it sound as though I am to emigrate to some foreign parts. I shall emerge blinking, from time to time, to rub shoulders with the living. I shall not be entirely a stranger to you.'

'And yet Sir Joseph will regret your absence,' said Laura as they approached the ruined drover's pen that marked the centre of the common. 'I conceive he has a high regard for your mind and your capacity for learning. I swear he has come to rely on you.'

'Dear Laura,' said Edward, turning suddenly to her. 'One might almost imagine that you sought to dissuade me from the path that fate has marked out for me?'

'Not at all,' replied Laura, making a space for herself to sit down on the crumbled wall. 'I'm surprised that you should nourish such a thought.'

For a while they sat silently next to each other, content to watch the clouds pass majestically across the pale-blue autumn sky.

'And this... Raven, the one that the bishop is sworn to hunt down. Do you think he will discover him?' asked Laura at length. 'If he hides himself away in the marshes, he will be a most elusive bird, I think. He is a heretic, I am told, although in truth fine distinctions of doctrine are lost on me. Jonah curses his name constantly which, I confess, rather makes me warm towards the object of his ire. He says the man must surely swing when they catch him. I fancy he knows little besides the name, however, and has no more than some general notion of his role in these disturbances.'

'I know little more than Jonah,' said Edward with a shrug. 'I have heard that his real name is Matthew Corvin and that he is a fugitive from the law. The nature of his heresy is no fine distinction from the established doctrine of the church, however. Even you shall readily comprehend it. He dares to preach that the sleep halls should be closed, and their incumbents buried in the earth. He preaches against my order, and he is at war with Mother Church.'

'A bold proposal indeed,' declared Laura, eyes suddenly wide. 'How you must resent it!'

'I do. Of course, I do,' admitted Edward after a moment of reflection, 'and yet I concede that there is some substance to his complaints.'

'On what basis?' Laura asked, regarding him levelly now as a small figure approached across the common.

'He argues that there are too many of the dead for the living to sustain,' answered Edward, 'and that with each passing year their ranks increase. The poor and middling folk resent the taxes that they pay for the upkeep of their betters in Darkharrow and such places. Those burdens may one day become intolerable, I suppose, when enough of us have passed within those portals. Perhaps one day there will not be enough of the living to support the dead.'

'Perhaps that day is already at hand,' agreed Laura. 'Half the Eastings stand at the door of starvation and still the taxman extends his hand. Perhaps there may be more riots such as those we saw at Lavenshall three weeks since. Do you think there will be a more general uprising?'

Edward's views on this issue were to remain undisclosed, at least for the present, as a boy several years younger than Edward but wearing the familiar robes of his order arrived before them.

''Abbot desires to speak to you,' he said baldly, addressing Edward but with eyes that darted at Laura in a way that spoke of fear and suspicion.

'For what purpose?' asked Edward, sliding down from the wall and rubbing his hands. It was plain that something was amiss, and some of the colour was already draining from his face. It was not every day that Edward was summoned by the Abbot of Darkharrow.

'I'm not to say,' said the boy solemnly, but now he looked directly at Edward as though having made a conscious decision not to acknowledge the presence of his companion.

'I see. Then I had better come,' said Edward somewhat awkwardly. 'Perhaps I shall see you tomorrow,' he said to

Laura, before adjusting his sword once more. He glanced around, concerned that Laura might be unprotected now.

'Go, Edward, I shall be fine,' she told him. 'For there is Mick the miller's wagon across the way. I shall walk alongside with him to the village. I don't suppose any brigand will trifle with Mick.'

If Laura had been given cause to wonder what issue had arisen that had required her friend to be so abruptly summoned, she had no immediate opportunity to question him about it. Edward was absent from his usual haunts and nowhere to be found for the next few days. Laura assumed that whatever business had required his urgent attention continued to detain him. However, the mystery began to unravel when she returned home one afternoon to find half a dozen cavalrymen in the stable yard. Here they were drinking the beer that had been brought out to them and exchanging ribald remarks about Jen, the scullery maid, as she handed out the flagons. The bright red sashes worn by these men and the red feathers in their broad brimmed hats marked them out as troopers from the Scarlet Band, a regiment with an evil reputation. Laura knew that this unit had been assigned to the Eastings as part of the king's campaign to stamp out sedition in these parts and that they had distinguished themselves in the recent wars with France. Some said that they had found fame more through the bloody swath they had cut through the common citizens of that nation rather than through any special prowess on the battlefield. Laura's impression was of slouching, loose-limbed bravado as she walked past them to the rear door, conscious of their eyes upon her, even as she cast her own downwards. There was something sinister, something unwholesome about them that caused her heart to beat faster and the saliva to drain from her mouth. It was all she could do to maintain a pace that would pass inspection for unhurried.

'And why would they have a cart with an iron cage upon it?' she asked herself as she surmounted the three steps and made her way past two leering troopers, who doffed their hats for her and made a low whistle.

In the hall she found her mother, and immediately she knew for certain that something was terribly wrong. Mama's face was ashen-white and there was a hunted look in her eyes. She raised a finger to her lips, to stifle Laura's first urgent enquiry.

'Hush, dear!' she cautioned. 'Captain Renshaw of the Scarlet Band is here to convey you to Lavenshall. You are to be interviewed by Bishop Turnbull himself.'

'What?!' Laura gasped, her hand flying to her mouth and a cold prickle of horror traversing her scalp. She thought she must surely faint, but her mother's arm steadied her.

'Shhh!' she said. 'You must allow me to do the talking unless you are directly addressed. I have sent for your father, but he is over towards Morden and I know not when he will return.'

Further discussion was curtailed by the opening of the parlour door. A huge soldier stood framed in it, swathed in black leather, slashed in the Spanish style and with a broad scarlet sash from shoulder to hip.

'This her?' he grunted with a nod to Mama.

'Indeed,' she said, making a visible effort to compose herself and sparing Laura a glance of mute appeal, 'and she is glad to answer the bishop's enquiries, for I'm sure this must be a mistake.'

Laura followed her mother through into the parlour, where a moustachioed man in a splendid but mud-spattered uniform stood looking out through the window. His knee-length boots had besmirched the Turkish rug in a way that Mama would bitterly resent in ordinary times. But these were not ordinary times.

'And this would be Miss DeLacey, would it not?' he said, turning to the room and favouring them with a frosty smile. He was a slender man with cold blue eyes and an ugly scar that rippled lividly across his nose and cheek, utterly extinguishing any charm his features may once have held.

'Captain Renshaw, at your service,' he said, acknowledging Laura's curtsey with the faintest of nods, 'and I have been sent to convey you to the bishop.'

'But no doubt there is some simple error,' said Mama to Laura, 'and you must not be alarmed. Doubtless all will soon be resolved. May I enquire as to the nature of His Lordship's business with my daughter?'

'You may not,' answered the captain curtly, with a glance at his larger companion, who had followed them into the room. 'It is not our duty to disclose such information, even should we be privy to it.'

'Could we not await my husband's return?' asked Mama, whose voice betrayed a tremble, whose grip on Laura's arm was tighter than was necessary. 'I have sent for him, and he may return at any time.'

'I have no business with your husband,' said the captain coldly. 'I trust you mean to make no difficulty.'

Laura gasped as she remembered the cage-laden cart in the stable yard. Her mother's grip tightened still further.

'Not at all,' Mama assured him. 'May I at least convey her to Lavenshall myself in our gig, under your escort, of course? It would never do for her to be seen...' She broke off, swallowed hard, unable to complete a sentence that mentioned so hideous a prospect.

'That would be highly irregular,' said the captain, casually opening the cigar box that stood on the table next to the fireplace. 'I should have to give it due consideration – these look as though they might be capital cigars.'

'Please, take them all,' said Mama hurriedly. 'It would be my pleasure.'

'But I suppose I might permit it,' continued the captain suavely, rolling a fat cigar between his fingertips. 'The end result would be the same.'

It proved impossible for Laura to have any conversation of consequence with her mother during the journey to Lavenshall. One of the smaller troopers sat with them in the gig and made it quite plain that he was assigned to report on any exchange between them. Mama sat as though carved from stone, looking neither to the left nor the right as the gig conveyed them through the village, with its clinking, clattering escort of cavalrymen. It had begun to rain, but even so there were moments when the cavalcade was accompanied by whooping boys who ran alongside or when they were stared at by half-seen faces from the doors of shops and cottages. Laura knew that their reputation would be amongst her mother's preoccupations, but it was clear that she feared for her daughter's wellbeing, too, and consciousness of this notion struck terror into Laura's heart. For once in her life, as they approached the outskirts of Lavenshall, she found herself wishing that Jonah was there.

Turnbull had spent a dismal night. His lodgings in the Lord Lieutenant's apartments left much to be desired and his bed was disagreeably hard. In addition, the fierce itching in his legs and around his rib cage made it seem likely that he was far from being its only occupant. Accordingly, those who necessity brought within his presence during the day found it to be a chastening experience.

'Get them to send my own bed down, will you?' he grunted to Ward, 'when next you send a dispatch to London. And what about those intelligence reports from Mason? Do we have those yet?'

'We do not, I fear,' admitted Ward, looking up from his own desk at one side of the large office they shared.

'Damn their indolence!' fumed Turnbull, dashing his pen to the desktop where he had been unenthusiastically perusing a pile of petitions. 'How am I supposed to go about my business when I am half-blind? Do they imagine I am gifted with second sight?'

'I believe that the better people are already interviewed,' ventured Ward, 'but that work remains to be done with the middling and the lesser gentry. We have hardly been here a fortnight, after all.'

'You don't have to tell me how long we've been here!' snapped Turnbull. 'I am aware of every minute of it. Lousy, pestilential sewer of a place. And what do you want?'

This last, terse enquiry was directed at young Canon Dangerfield, whose entry into the room had been preceded by a faint and timid knock. Turnbull had quickly identified Dangerfield as a weakling and accordingly took every available opportunity to bully a little spine into him. Not that this policy seemed to be having any beneficial effect.

'The girl...' he stammered, eyes wide, gesturing vaguely at the door.

'What girl?' snarled Turnbull.

'The girl who caused such a stir over at Darkharrow,' supplied Ward smoothly, once it became apparent that Dangerfield was incapable of further speech. 'You asked to see her.' He consulted the notes in front of him. 'Yes. Here it is. Miss Laura DeLacey, I believe.'

'Yes, yes, yes,' said Turnbull stroking his chin. 'Now I recall. Pass me the notes.'

'You should indeed recall,' Ward told him in the manner of someone confident of his indispensability to his master. 'The circumstances were quite remarkable, were they not?'

'They were,' agreed Turnbull in ordinary tones, and then addressing Dangerfield testily, 'Well? What are you waiting for? Send her in!'

With a yelp, Dangerfield withdrew, and after a moment Laura advanced cautiously into the room.

'Your Lordship,' she said, making a passable curtsey, the pallor of her cheeks, the tremor in her hands making her anxiety plain to all.

For a moment Turnbull only considered her, leaning back in his swivel chair and swinging it slowly from side to side. She was reminded of stories she had heard of cobras in India, hypnotising their prey. She was struck, when he spoke, by the deep richness of his voice and the metropolitan elegance of his accent, strange to her locality. This was the voice of learning and of the court. Sir Joseph's voice had many of these qualities but lacked the hard edge of menace that distinguished the bishop's now.

'You are Laura DeLacey?' he stated, looking down at the page before him and then directly at her with a gaze that suggested smouldering resentment. 'Of Groomfield, in Tithing Harrow.'

'I am,' she said. 'And how may I assist you, my Lord?'

It was all she could do to form these words and bring them to utterance. Surely her presence at the scene of John Lovelock's death must have been discovered.

'You may begin by telling us everything you know,' said the bishop, tapping his finger on the desk. 'And I would remind you that the Lord's eyes are upon you and that your punishment will be severe if you attempt to conceal anything that we later discover through our own enquiries or that you later disclose under further investigation.'

What Turnbull meant by 'further investigation' could only be surmised, but grim tales were circulating about the mistreatment of those detained in the cells beneath this building. Laura felt a sudden flush grow in her cheeks that rose, spreading to the roots of her hair.

'I was there,' she blurted. 'I was there when John Lovelock was murdered. I saw who did it.'

Turnbull said nothing, although one eyebrow twitched upward. He swivelled in his chair and exchanged a quizzical glance with Ward.

Turnbull's injunction had been his standard opening statement, one designed to scare the hapless subjects of his investigations into frank disclosures of their guilt. Usually, these disclosures were entirely in line with his expectations, but occasionally they brought forth information that was entirely unforeseen. This was one of those occasions.

'I see,' he said levelly. 'Do go on. Do supply more details in support of this... statement, in order that we can cross-check with our own information.'

From the corner of his eye Turnbull could see Ward leafing through some of the many sheets that recorded recent murders and disturbances in the vicinity.

Laura supplied the date and the circumstances of the crime, her voice breaking, tears overflowing at last from her eyes, knuckled fiercely aside as she fought to maintain some semblance of dignity. Turnbull regarded her with steely severity throughout. Ward scribbled notes, the soft scratching of his pen occupying the intervals whenever her account momentarily faltered. At last, her story was complete, and she stood silent, dabbing at her tear-wet cheeks.

'It is well that you have made this confession at last,' Turnbull told her. 'I'm sure you are aware that it is a grave offence to withhold from the authorities information that may assist in the detection of a crime. You may also be aware that under the present extraordinary circumstances such conduct is typically punished with severity. Are you indeed aware of that?'

'I am,' sobbed Laura, suddenly in despair, 'and I am very sorry for it. What will my poor parents think of me?'

A snort of disdain was Turnbull's only response.

'And there are other matters that have come to our attention,' he said after a while, to allow Laura more time to consider the seriousness of her circumstances. 'It appears that you have molested the holy departed in Darkharrow, that you were discovered there having intruded within the consecrated halls – quite at variance with law and tradition.' He consulted his notes. 'You were found with your hand upon the forehead of one of the deceased. How do you answer this charge, for charge it is. You may be aware that to disturb the dead is a serious offence in canon law.'

'I meant no harm by it,' wept Laura. 'You must believe me. I was allowed to take refuge in one of the outer passages of Darkharrow when my life stood in peril from the riot there on tithing day. I ventured a little way inside, that is all.'

Haltingly, her account punctuated by bouts of sobbing, she explained how she had been drawn to the dark opening of the chamber and found the dead lying within.

'You will not be surprised if I question your motivation for such a course,' said Turnbull, narrowing his eyes. 'I would have supposed that a typical girl of your age would have felt constrained by a certain natural caution in such circumstances. In fact, I do not think it too broad a generalisation to say that any ordinary girl would have remained as close to the outer door as circumstances would allow.'

'Perhaps, then, I am not an ordinary girl,' sniffed Laura.

'Perhaps not,' agreed Turnbull. 'That is the conclusion that we have been approaching. A conclusion made more certain by subsequent events.' He rose from his chair and stepped around his desk to approach her, looming over her like a dark cliff thrown into silhouette by the window behind him. Laura cast her eyes down, unable to behold his face.

'I had word from the abbot at Darkharrow yesterday,' he continued. 'He had some extraordinary things to tell me. Oh yes, most extraordinary. He described to me your exact form of words when apprehended in that place. "Hearts of stone", you mentioned, and "hearts of ice", it appears, identifying three of each within that chamber. It is by no means extraordinary that the dead should arise to a second life. It happens every year, a central tenet of our faith and of our shared experience, is it not? But what is extraordinary, what is wholly unprecedented, is that three of the departed should arise simultaneously from their slumbers. The abbot assures me that the three whose hearts you described as "ice" have embarked upon the process that will lead inevitably to their reanimation. Am I making myself clear, Laura DeLacey? It seems that you have awakened the dead.'

Laura gasped. Her hand flew to her mouth as her mind reeled, cast momentarily into a state of confusion quite inconsistent with rational thought.

'No!' she cried. 'Dear Lord, it cannot be!'

'You may well appeal to the Lord,' said Turnbull gravely, stepping back a little. 'For you have dared to appropriate to yourself the Lord's prerogative. For it is only God who may choose those who are to be summoned to a second life, and to presumptuously anticipate his desires in this most sacred of matters is to offend most gravely against our common faith. It is an abomination, in fact, for such powers offend against nature.'

'No!' Laura shook her head. 'It was an accident, I swear it. I did not intend…'

'Your intentions will be investigated in due course,' said Turnbull, turning from her now, pacing to the window with his hands behind his back and looking out over the courtyard where workmen were erecting a new scaffold. 'As will all aspects of this matter. I must inform you that the circumstances make it likely that you will be accused of a crime of the utmost severity.'

He turned back to her and wagged a bejewelled finger. 'For we have two words for those seemingly in possession of unnatural powers. One of those words is "saint". Do you know what the other word is, Laura? For I do not think you are a saint. Hmm? Do you know?'

'What?!' Laura felt dread claw at her heart. 'No! I am not a….'

'Witch,' supplied Turnbull with a grim smile. 'Is that what you deny? You deny that you are a witch? For that is what our investigations must reveal. And I do assure you, our investigation will be of the most rigorous kind.'

Chapter Eight

Laura was led away, along passages and down staircases that became ever darker and more forbidding, until she was within the prison that formed the basement of the Lord Lieutenant's house. Ordinarily, the cells here might be occupied by no more than a dozen or so malefactors awaiting trial or punishment, but now the place was crowded many times beyond its official capacity. Two grim-faced gaolers led her past rows of open-fronted cells where wretches pressed themselves against the bars, calling out lewdly, leering at her, reaching out to pluck at her dress until the gaolers' cudgels knocked them away. The stench was appalling, and the gaolers' lamps shone jerkily on eyes and faces made desperate by fear and hunger. It was like a vision of hell. Laura fixed her eyes on the heels of the man in front of her as she was led to a quieter place where the cells were smaller and furnished with stout wooden doors. With a great clinking of keys, the taller of the two gaolers opened a door and thrust her within, not without first having placed a questing hand upon her rump, causing her to reel upon him angrily.

Hot words rose into her mouth, but she held them back, glaring at him, surprised to find that outrage had the power to drive out terror and despair, at least for a moment.

'Ain't you a pretty missy,' laughed the gaoler, 'and you'd better be real nice to me, if you want things to go your way. It ain't unheard of for folks in here to get piss in their water and spit in their vittles. And that's if they get any vittles at all. Think on that, I should, my sweet dearie.'

He swung the door shut with a monstrous clang and his key ground in the lock. Then the sound of his laughter and of footsteps faded away. She was alone in darkness relieved only by what little light filtered down through a tiny slit of a window high above. The cell, which was hardly longer than she was tall, was furnished only with a pile of filthy sacking and a bucket. She slumped against the wall and subsided slowly to the cold flags of the floor. Then the hot tide of tears that had been building within her breast burst from her at last and she wept uncontrollably, her whole body wracked by great despairing sobs, for surely, she was ruined now, damned beyond hope of redemption.

'And so, you will have her burnt?' asked Ward, when Laura had been led away.

'If she is proved a witch,' confirmed Turnbull, taking a decanter of cognac from a wall cupboard and pouring himself a measure. 'When the investigation has been completed, the trial conducted, and the proper legal formalities have been observed.' He shrugged. 'But yes. She must certainly die. You saw the report.'

'Indeed,' agreed Ward, observing with mild but by now chronic disappointment when the decanter was replaced without having first been offered to him. 'The abbot was most emphatic. He knows his business, I am told, and it appears that the young girl you propose to kill seems genuinely able to reanimate at least a proportion of the dead. She is clearly a remarkable person. May I enquire as to your motivation?'

'Do you seek to question my decision?' asked Turnbull acidly, swishing the remaining cognac in his glass.

Ward did not immediately answer, which was as close he dared venture towards open subordination.

'Consider, if you will,' grunted Turnbull, showing no immediate resentment of Ward's insolence, 'how events might unfold if this girl proved genuinely capable of raising even a small proportion of the dead.'

'You have given this some thought...'

'I have,' he interjected. 'And I have been told that there are more than thirty thousand of the blessed dead confined within Darkharrow. Imagine, if you will, the consequences if even a quarter of that number should emerge once more to take their place in society.'

'I suppose the vicinity would be hard pressed to accommodate them,' conceded Ward. 'And the social consequences might be profound, particularly if the same scenario were to be enacted in all the sleep halls across the length and breadth of this land. But why should we assume that she would be permitted or invited to encompass such a feat?'

'That potential alone should be sufficient to identify her as a threat to the peace of the realm.' Turnbull resumed his seat, swinging it once more from side to side and pursing his lips. 'I invite you to exercise your imagination once more, Ward, and I fear that we must stray into the realm of high politics for a moment. Consider what might transpire if word of this girl's remarkable talent were to spread more widely abroad, were to become known even in the most elevated circles of the court.'

'Uh, huh,' nodded Ward, possibilities beginning to suggest themselves to his questing mind.

'And what might happen if some of the more distinguished amongst the deceased were to be awakened?'

'Good Lord,' said Ward softly, nodding slowly.

In the cool darkness of the crypt beneath St Dominic's Abbey lay the bodies of the kings and queens of Britannia.

In five hundred years none had been awakened, but who was to say how many of their hearts were of ice and not of stone? King Henry, in the fifteen years of his reign, had proved himself to be a drunkard and a fool. His mother, Queen Charlotte, had died under circumstances that some deemed to be suspicious, since, at more than seventy years old, she had nonetheless shown no obvious signs of ill health. There were dark rumours that poison might have been administered, that the prince had grown impatient of his succession to the throne. The "old queen", as she was affectionately known, had inspired the devotion of the nation in a way to which her son could only aspire. There were many who looked back upon her long reign as a golden age. What if she proved susceptible to reawakening? There were factions at court that might unite behind their renascent queen. The lawyers would surely rejoice. The king's legitimacy would certainly be called into question, since a monarch's title was officially Steward of the Realm, so long as the body of his predecessor remained intact and at least theoretically capable of reanimation. There might be popular discord, perhaps even civil war. It was not necessary for either of the clerics to discuss this out loud. A mere meeting of eyes was sufficient to signal their understanding. It could not be countenanced. Above all, Mother Church stood for stability and the maintenance of social order.

'Then I suppose she must die,' shrugged Ward. 'Pity, pretty little thing...'

'Quite, but evidently a freak of nature – and one that may not be permitted to survive.'

'And I suppose you will notify London of this matter?'

'Of course. That is our duty. But we shall exercise our duty in a tolerably understated manner, in order that it might not attract undue attention. Let it be a footnote in your account of events, buried amongst the trivial and tedious details of the other trials conducted under our jurisdiction.'

'It shall be so,' agreed Ward, taking up his pen.

'Do you confess that you are a witch?' asked King's Investigator, Canon Richard Tong.

'I do not,' said Laura in a small voice.

It was the day after her appearance before the bishop, and Laura had spent a largely sleepless night reflecting upon her likely fate. Now that fate seemed at hand, for the King's Investigators were known for the rigour of their methods – and the infliction of pain featured prominently amongst them. Richard Tong was a man of unremarkable appearance, with lank black hair and the manner of a career civil servant rather than a medieval torturer. He also had a streaming head-cold and had paused from time to time during her interrogation to blow his nose into a large white handkerchief.

'I see,' said Tong sadly. 'That is most unfortunate, for the facts suggest otherwise, do they not? And it is my job to reconcile appearance with…' he made a vague gesture with his hand, searching for a word '…actuality.' He offered her a thin smile, pleased with himself for this recall, 'and you may be aware that I have extraordinary powers to extract a confession from you.'

You will not, were the words Laura wanted to say, but she found that she was unable. The spark of defiance that had prompted them died on her lips. She swallowed hard and regarded her captor fearfully.

Laura sat on a hard chair in a large, ill-lit chamber that stank of human filth and of something less tangible besides – sheer naked terror. A single lamp hung from the ceiling above her. There was another chair where Tong had initially sat, but now he paced around her, advancing and retiring into the circle of light as he spoke. There were others there, too, some standing in the shadows behind her and some against the wall by the door through which she had entered. These did not speak; they only observed.

Laura had already given a full account of her actions in Darkharrow and described in detail the sensations she had felt when her hand was placed upon the brows of the dead. A clerk, somewhere behind her, had noted down the facts of this encounter.

'You would agree, I take it, that the things you have described lie outside the experience of ordinary humanity?'

Laura could only nod.

'And you have already admitted that you can offer no rational explanation for it. It is my belief, Miss DeLacey, that there is a perfectly rational explanation for this and that the unusual powers that you disclose arise from your communion with Satan.'

'No,' Laura blustered, squeezing her eyes tight shut, so that they brimmed with tears, and shaking her head.

'But perhaps a single example of such unnatural power is insufficient to condemn you,' Tong suggested as he approached closer, bending towards her so that his sallow features were fully illuminated, nostrils and eyes red-rimmed. 'Perhaps an additional example would serve to strengthen the case.'

He made a signal to one of his unseen assistants and she heard the door creak open. Hugh Redgrave advanced into the circle of light. Laura gasped.

'Perhaps you would care to recapitulate the facts you disclosed to me earlier,' suggested Tong to Redgrave, who nodded and licked his lips. There was a malevolent glint in his eyes.

'You are known to each other, I believe,' said Tong, 'and so no formal introductions are required.'

He gestured with his handkerchief and then pressed this pensively to the lower part of his face. 'Remind us of what you told me earlier, Mr Redgrave,' he said. 'It was most illuminating.'

Laura's heart sank as Hugh gave an account of the occasion when he had tried to steal a kiss from her and had paid for the attempt with two of his teeth.

'She is certainly a witch,' he finished, 'for how else could she split my lip and injure me so? Do I look as though I would succumb to such a blow from so slight a maid? Besides, she drew me on towards her with uncanny wiles in the preceding weeks and days, ensnaring me most skilfully before capriciously smiting me. I can offer no other explanation for it. I would not normally risk censure by associating myself in such a manner with a person so far beneath my station.'

'Naturally,' agreed Tong, waving the handkerchief absently. 'Your concerns are quite understandable.' He then turned to Laura, whose spirits had sunk still further during Hugh's description of their encounter. 'And how do you explain this outrage upon the person of Mr Redgrave, if we are to discount a physical assault by yourself? I take it you deny that you struck him by ordinary means?'

'I know not how to explain it,' murmured Laura.

'And that is your only response?'

'It is,' she said, feeling strangely numbed.

'Hmmm,' Tong nodded slowly, before turning to Hugh. 'Thank you, Mr Redgrave, that will be all.'

After he had gone Tong pulled up the other chair, its legs grating on the rough flags of the floor, and he sat astride it facing her, resting his forearms on its back.

'You are evidently in possession of uncanny powers,' said Tong levelly, 'and that makes you a witch.'

'No,' moaned Laura, shaking her head slowly from side to side, a single tear escaping from one closed eye and trickling down her cheek.

'As a witch you will burn,' said Tong matter-of-factly, 'although if you confess it, we may see you hang instead. Do you wish to burn, Miss DeLacey? I have seen people burn. It is not pleasant. I imagine it is still more unpleasant for the victim,' he chuckled grimly, smiling nastily at his own wit. 'Imagine the flames licking at your flesh, your lovely fair skin blackening and shrivelling from your tormented flesh. Most unpleasant, no doubt. It would be better for you if you confessed, don't you think? Hmmm?' He rested his own chin on one arm and with his right hand lifted hers.

'Look at me, Laura,' he said gently. 'For I shall call you Laura, as we shall shortly be on the most intimate of terms if you do not soon recognise the hopelessness of your situation.'

Laura opened her eyes and stared into his hard and of the palest blue, with not the faintest glint of genuine humanity within them. A tremor of renewed terror passed through her as the implications of his words became apparent to her.

'You are going to die, Laura. Accept it. We shall refer your case to the highest tribunal of all. You will stand before the Lord, and there you may make account of yourself and be judged. The manner of your passing there is the sole choice that remains to you. Hanging is a swift death, they say, no more than a moment of pain as though you had pressed a thorn to your finger. Your confession will secure you that release. Should you choose not to confess we will be obliged to draw that confession from you contrary to your will. In due course we shall break that will and the body that sustains it.'

He removed the hand that had supported her chin and leaned back. He made a gesture that encompassed the shadows, where Laura could make out the dark shapes of Tong's colleagues.

'There are others here whose business is the infliction of pain, and they are exceedingly expert in it, as many a miscreant could testify, were they alive to do so, were they in possession of a tongue with which to declare it. Invariably the starting point is to strip the subject naked, for in order to bare the reluctant soul we must first expose the flesh of the body in its entirety. Is that what you want, Laura? Or would you prefer to submit yourself willingly to the fate that the Lord has marked out for you?'

'I want to see my mother,' replied Laura in a small voice.

'In ordinary circumstances that might be possible,' said Tong after a snort of disdainful amusement. 'You might even be permitted to speak to a lawyer. But these are not ordinary circumstances and the tribunal I serve has unlimited powers; powers that serve to suspend established legal procedure. I regret to say that you will not see daylight again until the day you depart from this vale of tears, this unfortunate earth that we inhabit. You will appear before the bishop's tribunal in due course and then you will confess your sins as we have discussed. That is how it will be, Laura.'

She pressed her lips hard together to prevent their trembling, gripped the seat of her chair as though she feared that she would be thrown from it. A great sob rose in her breast, and she fought to suppress it, fought to maintain some semblance of dignity and self-mastery.

'It is late,' said Tong, consulting his pocket watch, 'and you are tired. I shall give you this coming night to reflect upon your situation. You will have one more chance voluntarily to confess your sins tomorrow morning and then, if you have not repented of your obstinacy, duty requires that I should submit you to the tender cares of my colleagues here. Consider well, sweet Laura. As I have said, the only choice that remains to you is the manner of your death.'

Once more in her cell Laura gave herself up to the despair that assailed her, that had threatened to overwhelm her in Tong's presence. She wept until her eyes would shed no more tears, her nose was red raw, and her throat ached from sobbing. Her mother's name and that of Emily, after frequent invocation, became no more than a murmur on her swollen lips. Their names were like a prayer, the comfort of those syllables, the dim vision of their faces in her inner mind a beacon in the darkness of her anguish.

'I am not a witch,' she told herself, repeatedly. 'I am not.'

But as the long night crept past her minute by slow untold minute, that muttered assertion began to seem a hollow thing indeed. What if she were a witch? What if the devil moved secretly within her and was yet to make his purpose clear? What if she was unwittingly the vessel of some evil that was yet to disclose itself? She could not now deny that there was something strange about her. The sensations she had experienced in Darkharrow, the unexplained wound she had inflicted on Hugh Redgrave, these things marked her out as something more than ordinary. She knew it and she knew that of necessity she would confess it when dawn came.

At last, she slept, curled foetal in the corner of her cold, dark cell, and dreamt. She dreamt of her mother pacing the yard of the Lord Lieutenant's house and demanding to see her daughter –demanding in vain. She dreamt of Emily lying somewhere in darkness in the cool embrace of Darkharrow. She dreamt of placing her hand upon that white brow and of reaching down through her tissues to where her small heart lay stilled. But was her heart of ice or stone? In vain she strove to clear her inner vision and to peer through the shifting veils of darkness that concealed that precious organ. Her fingertips moved over a surface that was rough and hard and brutally cold, but when she opened her eyes, it was only the edge of a flagstone beneath her hand and dawn's first light was softening the gloom around her.

Laura was not to be permitted the formal procedures of a trial. Instead, in common with any number of unfortunate wretches apprehended by the bishop's forces, she was to have her case heard in what was termed a "judicial hearing". This took place in Market Lavenshall's ancient courthouse, but the bench was occupied only by the bishop, the Lord Lieutenant and a pair of elderly legal advisors, one of whom was asleep and seemed likely to remain so. In addition, Tong was there as prosecuting counsel, to present the evidence that had been marshalled against her. The public galleries were empty except for Jonah and for Mama, the latter of whom seemed aged and diminished by events, dabbing at her eyes with her handkerchief throughout. Laura felt a strange sense of detachment from her surroundings, partly because of fatigue and partly from her resignation to the fate that was shortly to claim her. She felt numbed. She could scarcely focus her eyes and the courtroom swam blurrily around her. Once, in a moment of clarity, her eyes met those of her mother and found only grief and despair. The formalities of the hearing droned in the voices of the officials before her, their white wigs dark against the oak panelling, their red robes patches of brilliance. She was conscious of the ache in her bones, of the thin buzzing in her ears, of a warder's hand holding her arm to steady her as she swayed.

'You have heard the evidence against you,' said the bishop at last, his great, clear voice ringing around the sunlit space. 'How do you plead?'

Laura's eyes opened wide, and she looked straight ahead, past motes of dust that danced in a sudden sunbeam, to the bishop's grim features, to his hard grey eyes. It was easy. She knew she was already condemned, that the hours of her life were measured and that nothing of value could be achieved by resistance. In her heart she nourished the hope that the Lord would judge her more kindly and that she would soon look upon Emily's face once more.

'Guilty,' she heard herself say.

'No!'

There was a sudden commotion as her mother leapt to her feet, pulled down once more by Jonah's firm hands and by the court officials around her.

'She is no witch!'

'Silence!' roared Turnbull, turning his ferocious gaze upon her, his face suffused suddenly red. 'Lest you be charged with contempt. Is that what you want, woman?'

Laura found herself suddenly looking upon Jonah, and there was an expression in his features that briefly jolted her mind from the lethargy that had afflicted it. Was that concern she saw there? Certainly, it fell far short of the mingled love and grief that she had seen in her mother's eyes, but there was something wholly unexpected there, an emotion that she was quite unable to identify. Slow consideration of this occupied her thoughts as the proceedings continued around her.

'… hereby sentence you to be hanged by the neck until dead,' intoned the bishop, pronouncing her sentence, the black cap seated squarely on his head.

And thus, her fate was sealed, along with the fates of a score or so bandits, preachers of sedition and assorted malefactors whose hearings were held that day. The gallows would be busy on the morrow. The prison was loud with the protests of the condemned, the groans and cries of those for whom the torment of their flesh had brought forth their inevitable confessions. Laura, whose flesh remained unmarked, walked calmly back to her cell, her mind insulated from her grim surroundings by the trance-like state of acceptance that had settled upon her. She was barely conscious now of the lewd remarks and catcalls as she passed the open-fronted holding cells, hardly aware of the gaoler's hot breath on her ear as he whispered, 'Tonight, my sweet. Tonight, or never.'

She might, had she been in her ordinary mind, have been alarmed to hear such a form of words and been given cause to fear their significance. But Laura settled herself amongst filthy straw in the corner of her cell and occupied herself with thoughts of happier times and of the next world that the scriptures had promised her. She sang some hymns in a small, quiet voice and said some prayers, the familiar words having a comforting effect, and soon she fell asleep.

She was awakened by the sound of a key grating in a lock and of the cell door creaking open. The two gaolers were there, unshaven faces lit unevenly by the yellow light of a lamp. One of these men, the one who had whispered in her ear, was large, ugly and with a permanent stoop he owed to years of moving through these low passages. He was called Jeb, she gathered. The other, whose name was perhaps Dan, was much younger and of a slighter build. He seemed inferior in status and of a less assertive character. She had barely heard him speak.

'On your feet, little missy,' said Jeb, taking her by the upper arm and dragging her roughly upright. 'You're coming with us.'

'Where?' she asked, her mind a whirl of confusion, blinking in the sudden light and stroking hair from her eyes.

'Never you mind,' said Jeb, pushing her before him out of the cell and into the passage beyond. She was conscious of his firm grip on her flesh as he impelled her forward along passages and corridors that were unfamiliar to her, until they emerged through a sturdy iron gate into an area that might be presumed to be the gaoler's quarters. There were windows overlooking the street, a simple kitchen and a room that had the appearance of an office. At last Jeb threw open a door into a room that was already lit with lamps. The room contained a bed, replete with a stained mattress with a few rough blankets thrown upon it. Laura's mind reeled, rising suddenly from quiescence in which it had languished as the implications of these circumstances cut sharply though her consciousness.

'Let me go!' she cried shrilly, trying ineffectively to shake Jeb's grip loose, finding her voice at last.

Her captor thrust her upon the bed and grinned lasciviously at her as he drew down his britches.

'You're for the drop tomorrow, sweetheart,' he said. 'But it'd be a crime to let you die a virgin, if virgin you be.'

Suddenly he was upon her, pushing her back, his foul breath in her face and his rough hand groping beneath her skirts, forcing her writhing thighs apart.

'No!' she panted, wriggling away from him until the wall arrested her progress. 'You shall not!'

The weight of him was huge upon her, her skirts pushed up, his hairy flesh against hers and she knew within an instant she would feel the alien heat and hardness of him within her. At that moment, in some unfrequented recess of her mind, something awakened. Something beyond conscious control caused her to press her hand to the taught sinews of his neck. Instantly, as it had in Darkharrow, her mind swam down through the tissues of throat and lungs. On this occasion those tissues were living, moving flesh filled with pumping blood. There was the heart, huge and livid red, held in its matrix of blood vessels and sinews, throbbing and jerking in its rhythmic contractions. Laura reached out for that heart, held it in the insubstantial grasp of the hand that accompanied her mind's eye and squeezed hard.

At once, Jeb's head sprang back from her, his eyes suddenly wide. He rolled aside, clutching his chest, fighting for breath as his heart spasmed within him and a searing pain transfixed his chest.

' Ahh!' he gasped, eyes bulging. 'Stop it!Ahh!'

Laura rolled to pursue him, hand pressed still to his neck, her inner grasp continuing to squeeze the heart as its owner writhed next to her, his legs kicking spastically.

'Jeb! Jeb! What is it?' squealed Dan, his face suddenly pale with alarm.

And then Jeb's heart was still, except for a residual twitch or two. IIis body slumped lifeless, and his tongue lolled from his mouth. Laura let go, raised herself on her hands and stared hard at Dan. A strange power coursed through her veins now and her mind was incandescent with a fierce triumph. Her eyes met those of Dan, who backed away towards the door.

'Stop right there,' she commanded. 'I stilled his heart. I killed your stupid friend and I'll kill you likewise if you do not do exactly as I demand of you.'

Dan whimpered, stood stock still, eyes wide. Suddenly, her mind was fully awake, crystal clear. She slid from the bed and seized Dan's hand, holding it firmly after his first instinctive attempt to snatch it away. Now it was easy. Her mind's hand darted to Dan's trembling heart, brushed it lightly, causing Dan to jerk spasmodically and cry out with alarm.

'D'you feel that?' she asked, pressing her face close to his, so that she could look into his terrified eyes. 'That's a witch's finger on your heart, that is. If I choose to close my witch's hand around it you will surely die, as sure as your foul friend there. Do you understand?' She jabbed again, causing another jerky movement and a gasp that became a whimper. He nodded, breathing hard. 'Please, miss,' he begged, a dark stain appearing on the front of his britches.

'Get me from this place,' she snarled. 'Conduct me to the street.'

Moments later she emerged in a narrow passage at the rear of the Lord Lieutenant's house. The small door through which she passed swung shut, but not before a final exchange of words with her erstwhile captor.

'I can see into your heart,' she had hissed, as he fumbled for the key that would open the external door to the gaolers' quarters. 'And I shall be watching you. If you raise the alarm before dawn I shall certainly still that organ as I did your friend's. Do we understand each other?'

'Yes,' gasped Dan as the door opened to admit a breath of pure fresh air into the fetid gloom.

'Then you may yet live,' were her final words as she slipped away into the night.

The streets were quite empty, except for a cat or two, and Laura guessed that it was the small hours of the morning. She could not be more exact, as she dared not make her way to the market square for sight of the clock on St. Peter's. There was another clock in the lower town on St. Antony's, but that one had told ten past eight since time immemorial. The moon shone intermittently between scudding clouds, but Laura knew her environs well and there was enough light for her to thread her way through deserted back streets towards the edge of the town. Once, she saw a pair of patrolling constables pass across the mouth of one of the wider thoroughfares, but she shrank back into the deeper shadows of a gateway and soon they were gone. The town was eerily silent except for the occasional barking of a dog that alone remarked upon her passage. There were soldiers in a wooden shed that had been set up to monitor traffic entering by the Tithing Harrow Road and they had a small brazier alight beside them, playing cards by its light. Laura could hear their low conversation, their occasional laughter as she approached. It was easy enough for her to cut through the field that lay behind it and come out onto the road that led homeward well beyond their sight. It was at this point, with the rooftops of Lavenshall silhouetted against the starry sky behind her, that Laura succumbed at last to the emotions that she had held in check this last hour. She did not subside to the road verge in an exhausted heap, as her body demanded, and she fought hard to keep another tide of tears at bay. Knuckling her eyes fiercely, taking deep breaths, she stood still for a time, except for a sway of the hips, an arching of the back and a spreading of the arms to stretch muscles that ached from continual tension. Her mind continued to race, however, even as her body took pause. The fierce exhilaration of her triumph over her captors was already beginning to drain from her, leaving her in a state of renewed anxiety. It was remarkable that the calm acceptance with which she had faced her impending death only a few hours previously had been quite dispelled, supplanted by a new determination to survive. Jeb's intended outrage upon her person had rekindled a spirit that was almost extinguished and awoken in her a power the magnitude of which she was only beginning to explore. She held her hands up before her, so that silver moonlight limned her fingers.

'Here I hold life or death. Perhaps I am a witch, indeed,' she told an owl that flew past on hushed white wings. 'But what now shall I do?'

It was clear that she could not return to Groomfield, or to any of her familiar haunts, for it was certain that the bishop's men would come looking for her as soon as it was light and as soon as Dan, the surviving gaoler, had summoned the courage to raise the alarm. She felt certain that he would do her bidding. The glint of mortal terror in his eyes had assured her so, and the recollection of this afforded her a grim satisfaction.

'They will surely burn me if they catch me now,' she said with a small, taut smile. 'But let them catch me first.'

Chapter Nine

'Beggin' your pardon, sir, but we have a visitor,' announced Mould, coming with a lamp into Sir Joseph's bedchamber.

'Hmmm?'

His master rolled over in bed, reaching for his spectacles and pocket watch.

'It's four of the clock, sir, just past,' said Mould forestalling Sir Joseph while crossing to place the lamp on the table that stood by the window.

'What the devil?' barked Sir Joseph, sitting bolt upright now and swinging his legs out of bed.

'Ain't no devil, sir,' said Mould with a twitch at the corner of his lips, which in other mortals might have flourished to become a smile. 'Ain't no angel neither. 'Tis Miss DeLacey.'

'What?!'

'I am escaped,' Laura told Sir Joseph when he walked into his study and found her sitting by what remained of last night's fire, 'and I am entirely at your mercy.'

The coat that Mould had placed around her shoulders was still in place, and wild, loose strands of her unkempt hair were strewn golden on its collar. She looked up and her eyes were wide with the calm trust of a small child.

'I have cheated the gallows for now. What next should I do, if I would confound them at last?'

Sir Joseph sat opposite her and stirred the glowing embers of the fire with a poker, before settling back in his chair and regarding her over steepled fingers. For a while he said nothing. Distantly he could hear Mould preparing a cup of tea for her. Then he sighed, pursed his lips and spoke.

'You are a fugitive from the law, I collect, and it is a grave crime that I commit if I do not soon turn you over to the authorities. You are aware of this.'

'I am, Sir Joseph. And yet I am here.'

'None can deny it. Then you had better give a full account of your travails,' he said.

She did so, required by her host to describe even the slightest and most circumstantial details of the events that had led to her arrest and to her subsequent escape from gaol. She felt as though she were a subject of his forensic dissection, cut and peeled apart layer by slow layer until all aspects of her lay exposed to his keen eye. Naturally, Sir Joseph was particularly interested in those encounters of hers that lay outside of everyday human experience. On several occasions he asked her to reiterate her sensations when what she had begun to know as her mind's hand reached down through the flesh of the quick and the dead. At last, he seemed satisfied. He regarded her steadily as the growing light of day found its way past curtains to paint a narrow line across his Persian rug.

'I believe you,' he said, 'for I do not take you for a deceitful creature. Nor do I believe you to be a witch, for that title is but an artful confection designed by the Church to oppress those in possession of powers that surpass their understanding. A tolerably large category, I might add; if their small minds may not encompass it then surely it must be the devil's work. And then it must be destroyed, of course, lest it assail the citadel of their certainty. The Church is surely the ball and chain that humanity must laboriously drag with it as it creeps towards the light.'

'I am not a witch?' she asked, cautiously.

'No, indeed; on the contrary, it seems that you are a very remarkable person, one whose abilities should excite wonder and gratitude. As you know, I am a student of nature and I do not doubt that these abilities arise from some fortunate conjunction of entirely natural phenomena and not by the whim of this notional "Devil" that they use to oppress us.'

'Your words would seem to condemn you as a heretic,' said Laura doubtfully, setting down her empty cup. 'Not that I would share in that condemnation.'

'I execrate that baleful conformity of thought and belief that the state practices to impose upon us,' said Sir Joseph with feeling. 'For the pursuit of knowledge is the highest purpose of all, and I am the devoted servant of that enquiry. Knowledge and belief are uneasy bedfellows, however, for knowledge is susceptible to growth but belief remains content within itself, a jealous dwarf beside a waking giant. So yes, defined by those terms, I am indeed a heretic. I count myself fortunate that there are many others, like myself, who value learning and enquiry. A new spirit is abroad in this land and further afield besides, across the whole of Europe. We represent the future. The bishop and all the vast established forces for which he is no more than a brutal battering ram represent the past. Sclerotic, myopic and resentful of change they may be, strong they may be, but a shaft of light is deadly to them in the end.'

Sir Joseph moved his hand into the broadening shaft of light between them and made of it a fist. Then he placed it on her own, squeezed gently and regarded her seriously.

'And you are one such beam of mysterious luminance, one that the bishop feared because he did not understand it and because he feared the consequences of its use. That is why he determined to destroy you. Do you see? And that is why I shall do everything in my power to preserve you.'

'Thank you, Sir Joseph,' said Laura, a sensation of warm relief stealing over her. 'You do oblige me beyond my powers to describe. But shall I never return home? Shall I never see my mother again? I cannot tell her distress…'

'You may not,' said Sir Joseph gravely, shaking his head, 'at least not in the immediate future. For you have embarked upon a journey that obliges you to rise above the simple circumstances that were the making of you. The past shall be a foreign country to you now. You have outgrown it. A larger future awaits you; I suspect.'

'Or the gallows,' said Laura in a small voice. 'But I fear you gild me with a grandeur that I scarcely merit. I am but a fugitive from the law.'

'You are more than that, Laura,' assured her host, rising from his chair and crossing to draw the curtains aside so that the room was suddenly bright with the clear light of an October day. 'I see in you what the bishop saw,' he turned to her, 'and I do not fear it.'

'You do not?'

'I do not,' affirmed Sir Joseph, 'but we must conduct you to a place of safety. I have some acquaintance with Bishop Turnbull. We have met at various functions, and he seemed to me to be a determined and able man. Surely, he will spare no effort to recapture you, and I expect his forces will be scouring this vicinity from end to end within the hour. I do not doubt that the gaoler you so terrified will have raised the alarm by now. I imagine they will go first to Groomfield, but then their search will expand from there and soon they will come knocking on my door.'

'But where shall I go? Should I journey to Lowestoft, do you suppose, or even Ipswich?' asked Laura, getting to her feet. 'And I am so fatigued, I swear.'

'Indeed not,' said Sir Joseph, regarding her torn and stained dress disapprovingly. 'We must certainly give you some brief time to wash and find you some clothes more appropriate to your status as a fugitive. But then I shall conduct you to a friend of mine.'

'A friend?' murmured Laura as her host summoned Mould, calling for warm water, for jug and bowl so that she might wash.

'A good friend,' said Sir Joseph, turning back to her. 'You may have heard of him. His name is Matthew Corvin.'

'The Raven!' Laura gasped, her eyes springing open.

Whilst Laura washed the filth of days from herself and brushed the tangles from her hair, Mould made her breakfast and Sir Joseph inspected the contents of various chests that the owners of the house had stored in their attic, returning with the drab patched garments that some servant had once worn.

'Later, we must do something with your hair,' he said as she tried on shoes, 'but for now this must suffice. You may tie back those locks within your cap, at least.'

'Trouble,' said Mould urgently, setting aside the usual formalities and putting his head around the door.

Sir Joseph crossed to the window from where he could see a party of horsemen approaching along the drive. They were undoubtedly a contingent of the Scarlet Company. He cursed, turned to Mould and frowned for a moment as several possibilities occurred to him. Then he beckoned to Laura.

'You must come with me, my dear. Hurry, I beg you! Mould, conduct their officer to my laboratory, if they insist on entry. Tell them I am at work.'

Sir Joseph led Laura along corridors to the rear of the house, to a large, well-lit room that once had been used for dining by the previous occupants. A long table occupied much of the space. A partially dissected cadaver lay on the table, placed on an oilcloth that draped almost to the floor. From throat to belly the corpse was cut open, ribs pulled back to reveal the chest cavity within. Buckets and bowls of all sizes stood around, filled with dark blood and what might be internal organs. Laura gasped as the stench assailed her, and she clasped her hand to her nose, felt bile rise in her throat.

'Yes, I must fling open a few windows in due course,' said Sir Joseph apologetically. 'I was working here until late last night with my friend Mr Phillips, who has a particular interest in the pancreas. The pancreas, you see, is a fascinating organ. I was investigating its blood supply, which differs markedly from that of...' he broke off, caught sight of the pallor in Laura's face and remembered their circumstances. 'But now you must surely secrete yourself beneath that table.'

Once Laura was hidden there, doing her utmost to keep herself from retching, Sir Joseph pulled on his bloodied apron. He thrust his hands into the corpse's exposed abdomen, withdrawing these gorily and picking up a scalpel even as Mould admitted two cavalrymen into the room. Their reaction to these circumstances was akin to that of Laura's, causing Sir Joseph a wry smile, inadequately suppressed. He set down his scalpel and approached the senior of his two visitors, who wore the insignia of a sergeant, with open hand extended.

'Sergeant Bateman, is it not?' he enquired cheerily, and then, when the sergeant twitched his own hand away, he affected to notice the gore that besmirched it for the first time. 'Oh dear. Of course. Do forgive me. I believe you were with Captain Reeve when last he called upon me. To what do I owe this pleasure?'

'I have been sent to ask you if you have seen Laura DeLacey, of Groomfield house,' said the Sergeant, eyes darting from the partially dismembered corpse to Sir Joseph. His companion stealthily withdrew and closed the door behind him, leaving his superior alone. The sergeant, keenly aware of this, also took a step backward. 'She is a fugitive from justice,' he managed to add.

'Is she indeed?' said Sir Joseph, advancing upon him, rubbing his hands together and then stroking his chin thoughtfully, leaving a livid smear. 'Well, I cannot claim to have seen her. Are you interested in anatomy at all, Sergeant? I have a most delightful spleen here, if you'd care to see it. It has a morbid growth upon it of a most unusual kind.'

'I would not,' said the soldier emphatically. 'Meaning no offence, sir, but I have orders to search the premises of all those who are known associates of Miss DeLacey – and you are on my list. Doubtless it will be a formality in this case, but you will understand that I must do my duty.'

'Of course,' said Sir Joseph. 'I quite understand. Do ask Mould if you require any assistance.'

There was a long interval during which Laura was required to remain crouched quietly beneath the table. Sir Joseph did not speak but busied himself around the room, humming to himself as though quite untroubled by events. In the narrow space between the hem of the oil cloth Laura could see only his feet and a few of the bloody vessels that stood about on the floor. The stench that had first affronted her nostrils seemed at length to lose some of its foul pungency, but the horror of her circumstances remained to clutch coldly at her heart. At times, she could hear the distant sounds of the soldiers' conversation and their heavy boots as they moved about the house. Unsurprisingly, none of them sought to investigate Sir Joseph's laboratory in detail, and the brevity of their presence suggested that their search of the premises was cursory enough in nature. At last, Sergeant Bateman opened the door a little and spoke from the corridor outside.

'Well, that will be all then, sir. I thank you for your patience. I trust you will send notification if you chance upon her.'

'I most certainly will,' said Sir Joseph with a nod. 'And it would be kindness if you would you ask my good friend Captain Reeve if he would send me another cadaver, when convenient.' He gestured behind him. 'This one is a little ripe, I find.'

It was as they were preparing to leave the house that Edward arrived.

'Laura?' he stuttered; eyes wide. 'Is that you?'

'Edward,' she cried. 'I thought I should never see you again.'

There was an awkward moment in which the urge to run into his arms almost overwhelmed her, but after no more than a faint twitch she remained where she stood; instead, they grasped hands before them.

'And I, you. How are you escaped? You are become a servant, I see.'

'Explanations will have to wait,' said Sir Joseph, pulling on his coat. 'We need to convey Laura here to Corvin. We have already entertained a party of the bishop's men this morning, and I don't doubt the vicinity will fairly be crawling with them.'

It appeared that Edward had an engagement to assist Sir Joseph in his work that morning, making detailed drawings of the structures identified within the cadaver's pancreas the previous night. It also appeared that there was much more to their relationship – that both he and Sir Joseph were confederates of the notorious rebel and heretic, Matthew Corvin, known to friend and foe alike as the "Raven". There was much to be discussed, many questions to be answered as the three of them made their way across the field that lay behind Sir Joseph's house and through an arm of Pinchbeck Wood to the fringes of the fens. Mould remained behind to undertake the unenviable task of cleaning up and disposing of the cadaver. He would join them later. It was a grey day, with a thin wind-blown rain from the south-east, and they met no others as they walked. Laura, intimately familiar with these regions, recognised many an occasional distant landmark – the steeple of St Swithins-at-Holme, the abandoned windmill at Cowlin Reach – but soon they were passing through an area that was unknown to her and came upon a decayed wooden jetty by an arm of some creek, waters almost obscured by the low stunted trees that hung over it. Edward pushed through the sedge a little way, parting the reeds to reveal one of the small boats that the local people called "lighters".

'Be wary here,' Sir Joseph warned Laura as she approached the boat. 'These timbers have mischief in their rotten hearts, and they are slippery besides.'

Soon she was established in the stern of the boat whilst Edward and Sir Joseph conducted them through the shallow waters and the endless sedge. At times the channel was wide enough for them to row. On other occasions, when the murky waters were barely wider than the boat itself, barely more than a glinting thread that reached ahead amongst the rushes, it was necessary to use the long pole that occupied the full length of their vessel. Then, Laura would be required to move to one side whilst Edward thrust this into the mud to drive them forward, withdrawing it dripping, stepping past her to place it down once more. It was slow progress, and the many twists and turns of their passage, with scarcely a landmark more prominent than a stunted bush, made it certain that they could never be pursued. Laura began to feel the cold grip of anxiety withdraw from her mind.

'Listen,' she implored, tugging at Sir Joseph's sleeve, 'for that is certainly the voice of the black bittern you once sought.'

He turned to smile at her.

'It is not, although I concede it is very similar. The voice you heard springs from a human throat and signals that we are detected, for we are almost arrived.'

Raising his hands to his mouth, Sir Joseph made a sound very like that they had heard, and this was repeated from ahead. The waters widened until their vessel emerged into a broader reach of water with a low eminence at its far side and a stretch of clear shore before it. Here there was a jetty, and beyond it a cluster of low timber-framed dwellings walled with wattle and daub, roofed with rushes. From some of them smoke rose, curling to be dissipated by the brisk south-easterly that rippled the waters of the mere.

'Behold,' said Sir Joseph with ironic grandeur, stretching his arms wide. 'The Kingdom of the Raven. You should be aware that I am known to the people here as plain John Cordwell, although Corvin knows my true identity well enough. Accordingly, I would be glad if you would not refer to me by my proper name.'

Edward guided the boat to the jetty where a few other such vessels were tethered, and he handed Laura ashore to where a swelling group of men were gathered to meet them, emerging from various huts or advancing along the shore. Some of them bore arms. Although there was the occasional bright neckerchief or weskit to be discerned, most wore the drab clothes of the peasantry or the small folk of the towns. Sir Joseph exchanged familiar pleasantries with a few of them as he secured their boat to a stanchion, but soon the murmur of the crowd fell silent as a tall man stepped from amongst them. Surely this was the Raven, concluded Laura, smoothing down her skirt. He was perhaps forty years old, with greying hair and the rough skin of one who had seen more than his share of sun and weather. It was the skin of a mariner. He had the prominent nose of his namesake and dark, deep-set eyes that immediately fixed themselves upon Laura as he strode forward to the jetty.

'Greetings, friends,' he said, returning his gaze to Sir Joseph. 'This is an unexpected pleasure, Cordwell. I had not thought to see you this side of the full moon. And I see that you have brought us a guest,' he said, nodding at Laura in a manner that denoted no great leap of pleasure in the heart.

'Those events are intimately connected, as you shall presently perceive,' countered Sir Joseph, shaking Corvin's hand vigorously. 'I trust you still have coffee in your little realm. It would an act of mercy if you would have some prepared.' He gestured at Laura. 'My daily routine has been somewhat altered by circumstance, as you see, and there was no time to break our fast.'

'It shall be yours,' said the tall newcomer, regarding Laura in a considering way that made her cast her eyes downward apprehensively, 'but pray, will you not introduce me to your companion?'

'Certainly,' said Sir Joseph. 'Permit me to introduce Miss Laura DeLacey of Groomfield House.'

Laura made her dip, conscious that all eyes were suddenly upon her, a blush rising to her cheeks.

'And Laura, allow me to introduce my friend, Matthew Corvin of...' Sir Joseph gestured with his hand '...this place,' he finished lamely, with a self-deprecating grin.

'Indeed, my material circumstances may strike you as unprepossessing,' said Corvin with a humorous glance at Sir Joseph, 'and to dwell on a mud flat amongst frogs and voles was not my fondest imagining as a child. However, my kingdom lies not here but in the minds of men, Miss DeLacey. And that kingdom extends the full breadth of Britannia. Is that not so, my friend?'

'It is,' nodded Sir Joseph, 'and a kingdom the bounds of which expand with every passing day. But we must talk, for I have brought you a most promising new subject.'

The crowd of men drew back respectfully, many with bowed heads, as Corvin led them away from the shore and towards the highest point of this reach of land, where the largest of the single-storey dwellings faced east across the sea of reeds towards the distant ocean. Inside, the floor was of packed earth and the walls unplastered, lit by unglazed windows with shutters thrown wide. Here, in the main room, stood a simple pine table and a few chairs. Various cooking vessels and some hams hung by hooks from the rafter above them. There was no stone chimneybreast, only an open fire in a hearth of cobbles. Most of the smoke from this crept up through a square opening in the roof above, but enough remained to sting Laura's eyes as she drew up a chair. Edward, whose presence she had barely been conscious of since their arrival, drew up one next to her. Matthew Corvin, having exchanged various remarks with some of his men, soon arrived at the head of the table. He settled himself into the carver chair that was evidently his only mark of rank, placing his large hands on the table before him, turning to regard Laura quizzically.

'Well,' he said, 'do tell me why you have conveyed Miss DeLacey across the briny wasteland to my court. I yearn to be enlightened.'

'And you shall be,' said Sir Joseph, 'for Bishop Turnbull believes her to be a witch, and had she not taken it upon herself to withdraw from his custody she would be a-swing on the gallows by now.'

'I see,' Corvin replied, raising an eyebrow. 'I take it you escaped from the gaol in Lavenshall, then. No small accomplishment. And are you indeed a witch? Have you indeed welcomed Satan to your body and your heart?'

'I should point out that Mr Corvin shares my own views of such ignoble superstitions,' said Sir Joseph said to Laura while gratefully receiving a steaming cup of coffee from the boy who had suddenly appeared at his elbow.

'I am not, and I have not,' said Laura quietly, 'unless one can be a witch unawares.'

'I think it unlikely,' laughed Corvin, accepting a cup of coffee for himself and sipping it cautiously, wiping his mouth with the back of his hand, 'but then I have never had the privilege of meeting one. I have seen a few burnt here and there in my travels, but I never came across one whose skin was proof against flames or whose powers were sufficient to spare them from the pyre.'

'But witch or no, Laura is in possession of remarkable powers,' continued Sir Joseph. 'Do tell Mr Corvin what you were able to accomplish, my dear.'

Laura stared anxiously at Sir Joseph for a moment before returning her gaze to Corvin. She swallowed hard, folded her hands before her on the table and looked fixedly at them as she spoke.

'It appears that I can raise some of the dead.'

Corvin regarded her in silence, his face betraying no obvious emotion, although Laura fancied, she observed a slight stiffening of his posture.

'And your other little skill...' prompted Sir Joseph gently.

'And it appears that I can still the hearts of the living, if I choose,' admitted Laura reluctantly.

'Thereby rendering *them* dead,' added Sir Joseph cheerfully. 'I told you she was remarkable.'

Laura was required to give a full account of her activities, of her experiences in Darkharrow, of her encounter with Hugh Redgrave and of the manner of her escape. Corvin listened attentively, occasionally asking her to reiterate part of her story or to provide more detail where she had hurried on. At last, he was satisfied and the sun was already low in the western sky.

'Remarkable indeed,' he said, subjecting Laura to a particularly penetrating and considering stare. She found herself blushing, and when raising her own gaze momentarily she found herself looking into his dark, unblinking eyes.

'Would you excuse Mr Cordwell and me, my dear?' asked Corvin at length, settling back in his chair. 'There is much that we must discuss. If you and Mr Broadfoot make your way a short distance along the shore towards the jetty you will find our communal kitchen. I'm sure they will furnish you with a little something to eat.'

'I find that you are suddenly a person of consequence,' said Edward as they walked towards the kitchen.

'If you mean to imply that my previous status was *inconsequential,* I take that very ill,' Laura told him, with a wry smile and a glance that told him no genuine offence had been given. She was feeling more cheerful and optimistic than she had felt for days, and there was a lightness in her step as she picked her way along the broken duckboards that been laid upon the mud.

'Witch or no, your tongue remains a lethal blade,' laughed Edward, 'but seriously, this turn of events has left me quite amazed. I thought never to see you again.'

'And I, you,' said Laura as they stooped beneath the low lintel of the kitchen.

Here, in a large and smoky space lit by a great fire, a cook behind a long counter was ladling out some lumpy brown fluid to a waiting line of men. They joined the end of this queue, conscious of many curious eyes upon them, and presently they found themselves each with a bowl of thin stew.

'I suppose this is nutritious,' said Edward doubtfully as they settled at a low bench close to the door.

'It had better be,' said Laura, making a face. 'For surely it has no other virtue.'

'Corvin's army can never amount to much,' said Edward, gesturing around. 'Not here, at least. For although the fens offer some security, they offer no sustenance beyond frogs and fish. An occasional ship from Holland finds its way along the creeks with a cargo of wheat and such provisions but brings with it also the risk of discovery. We may never feel entirely secure here.'

'You say "we",' Laura noted, regarding him quizzically while setting down her spoon. 'Since when did you become a disciple of the Raven?'

'It was Sir Joseph who introduced me to Corvin,' said Edward with a sigh. 'He found in me a willing student and an open mind. In Darkharrow I learned only ritual and the dead words of uncounted generations. There was poetry in them and a satisfaction that derived from the wholeness of our existence there, but it was not enough. It could never have been sufficient for me. Sir Joseph is a remarkable man. He opened my eyes to the new learning. He opened my mind to the light, to the existence of possibilities that are not to be found in monkish books or intoned by candlelight in shadowed galleries whilst the world sleeps. I am awakened, Laura,' he announced, reaching across the table to grasp her hand, his eyes shining with passion, 'and my mind shall not slumber again so long as I live. I shall not go into Darkharrow, not now.'

'Then what will you do?' she asked, squeezing in return. 'For you cannot remain in this place forever, I suppose.'

'I shall follow Sir Joseph and I shall follow Corvin wherever he leads me,' said Edward, his mouth set grimly, 'Even though it leads me to the gallows I shall follow him, for Corvin is an idea as much as a man, an idea of change that shall release the dead hand of the past from this land and set the people free.'

'You speak with passion, a passion I have never heard in you before,' said Laura, genuinely moved.

'I feel it,' said Edward, gesturing around at the others in that place, 'and so do these fellows. It is a joy to be a small part of something bigger than myself, something that grows stronger with every passing day. Perhaps one day you shall feel it, too.'

Laura's heart swelled with a sudden affection for her companion.

'Perhaps, I shall,' she said, 'but what do you suppose they have in mind for me? I gather Sir Joseph regards me as something of a prize specimen in his collection, a curious creature to be observed and recorded. I should not wonder if I were to be labelled and pinned to a card.'

'You are not to think of yourself in those terms,' scolded Edward. 'There could not be a finer, more honourable man than he, and not for a moment do I conceive that he would...'

'Ah, so, this our witch then,' said a young man who sat down suddenly beside them. 'I thought I should find some wart-pocked crone.'

'She is no witch, Thomas, as well you know,' said Edward with a cluck of disapproval. 'Laura, permit me to introduce you to Thomas Corvin, son of Matthew, raucous hatchling of the Raven. He has a liberal, unfettered tongue and no obvious social graces, as you see.'

'So I gather,' said Laura, regarding the newcomer coldly. 'And I regret that I can offer you no warts.'

Thomas showed no sign of quailing before her disapproval or that of Edward's. Instead, he turned to survey Laura with what she had been brought up to identify as an impudent stare.

'No apology is necessary,' he said, with an airy wave of the hand, 'for disappointment was the least of my sensations. On the contrary, it is a rare delight to see so fair a face amongst these unsightly rogues and villains.'

Thomas Corvin was a tall, muscular lad in his eighteenth or nineteenth year – so Laura judged. He had a shock of unkempt dark hair and a wide mouth well suited to the expression of wry amusement. It split now into a broad grin and his soft brown eyes glinted with a keen intelligence. They were unlike Edward's eyes in every way. They held Laura's gaze steadily and directly, professing an interest only occasionally to be glimpsed in her companion's. She blushed and then cast her eyes down at last as Edward began a conversation with Thomas about a party of newcomers that had arrived from the south. It appeared that there had been rioting in Ipswich, too.

'The word spreads,' said Thomas Corvin with satisfaction. 'My father's name is on the nation's lips.'

'Perhaps, but does he also dwell in their hearts?' asked Edward. 'That is where victory will spring from at last.'

'We shall see, in good time,' replied Thomas, returning his gaze to Laura. 'But what brings you to this place? The manner of your dress is humble enough, but it seems unlikely you are of humble stock.'

Laura and Edward exchanged glances.

'It is a lengthy tale,' answered Laura, 'but it appears that I am thought a witch.'

'I have heard,' said Thomas, rubbing his chin thoughtfully. 'And are you a witch?'

'I am not,' said Laura, regarding him seriously.

'I thought you were not,' said Thomas with a grin. 'Then I'm sure you and I will get on.'

Chapter Ten

Later, when it was growing dark, and lamps were being lit amongst the low dwellings of Corvin's small kingdom, Laura and Edward were summoned once more to his house. They found him with Sir Joseph but with others besides, a gathering of his trusted counsellors and lieutenants. It appeared that her story had been told to them, and so they regarded Laura with frank curiosity as she settled herself in the chair that was set out for her.

'I know her,' muttered one of these men to his neighbour, and immediately Laura knew him, too. There stood Richard Hardisty, who last had looked upon her with the corpse of John Lockwood and her skirts about her thighs. She felt the hot blood rise to her cheeks and averted her gaze hastily as Matthew Corvin greeted her.

'It appears that a person of some significance has come amongst us,' he said, 'but the nature of that significance remains to be determined. Naturally, we extend the hand of friendship to you, as we do to all who flee the spiteful state, but that refuge brings with it obligations. All of us here are sworn to the overthrow of that state, and all of us are committed to serve that cause in any way we can. We serve, Laura, according to our strength and according to the nature of our talents.'

'And it seems that your talents are unique,' observed Sir Joseph.

Laura glanced around her at Corvin's companions. Apart from herself he was the only one seated, but despite this he seemed to dominate the room. Half of his face was cast in shadow by the single table lamp with which the room was lit. It appeared that circumstances had placed her entirely at his mercy, and yet she did not feel afraid. A calm authority exuded from Corvin's person, reflected in the respectful silence and attitudes of those around him. Her audience with Bishop Turnbull came suddenly to her mind. There she had known terror, seen death glint malevolently in his eyes, but now there was no fear. The circumstances were quite different, but there was more than that; the person who sat before Corvin was not the same person who had sat before the bishop and before Tong, his inquisitor. She had changed. The consciousness that she held death in her fingertips had never been far from her mind since she had trodden the road from Lavenshall. That consciousness brought with it an inner resilience that she had not known before. It was as though the child had been supplanted by the woman, and the woman was only beginning to understand her strength.

'Indeed. It will be our business to see how those talents might be employed,' said Corvin, leaning back in his chair and narrowing his eyes. 'The bishop feared you, or rather he feared your potential, and he determined to snuff out your life's spark before it could grow into a flame. Perhaps we shall nourish that spark and kindle a flame that will burn the mighty in their halls. Perhaps we shall set a fire that will cleanse the land from end to end.'

Laura found that she rather resented the notion of being employed as a tool or a weapon in any cause, but she held her tongue for now.

'And you imagine she is so significant?' asked Thomas Corvin at her shoulder. 'I am amazed. I had not thought.'

'Imagination is what defines us,' responded his father. 'And what sets us apart from our foes. We can imagine a better world. They cannot. They seek only to perpetuate the present that sustains them and oppresses the wretched masses that they tread beneath their feet.'

'And when this fire that you conceive has left a blackened waste – for that is my experience of fire – what do you seek to build amongst the ruins?' asked Laura. 'For if I am to contribute to your cause I would know the nobility of those aspirations.'

A discontented murmur amongst Corvin's companions suggested to her that she might have uttered some impertinence, but Corvin raised a hand and the rumbling subsided.

'A reasonable request,' he said. 'And I could, of course, place in your hand any number of pamphlets and handbills that proclaim our manifesto. But I shall describe its outline for you. Doubtless you are aware that we are declared heretics, that we are known as Monozoeists, that we maintain that one earthly life for each mortal man must be sufficient.'

Laura nodded. She had heard this said. Everyone knew that the Raven wished to burn down Darkharrow and bury the sleeping dead to moulder in the earth. Everyone knew that he desired to close the sleep halls throughout the land. The green and hollow hills which housed the dead in all their myriads should empty out their denizens and stand at last deserted. Thus, he preached, and the princes of the Church thundered back in resentful fury. Her own feelings on the issue were conditioned by concern for Emily, whose own body lay within the belly of Darkharrow. Whatever weight she might concede to his arguments would always be counterbalanced by that knowledge.

'The living are oppressed by the weight of the dead, and we can sustain them no more,' continued Corvin. 'With every passing year the burden grows. The vast legion of the Camoldolites that tend the departed, the numberless ranks of church officials that regulate the process, the scouring of the earth for the spices with which the dead are anointed – these are a burden that can no longer be sustained.'

'Not to mention our opposition to the fundamental iniquity that only the wealthy may dream of walking the earth a second time,' added Sir Joseph.

'Undeniably,' nodded Corvin gravely. 'But you have asked what I would put in place once these things have been set to rights. The power of the Church must be curbed and likewise the power of the monarch. In the old queen's day parliament stood respected and her ministers were elected from its ranks. Now the king declines to summon parliament at all and his ministers are entirely his own creatures, answerable only to his whim. Queen Charlotte, God bless her, would never have behaved in such a manner. She was drawing up plans to enact laws that might have accomplished the bulk of what we desire, and she might have done so had not death overtaken her.'

There was a low muttering at this notion, and a few bowed their heads.

'A tolerably suspicious death, I might add,' said Corvin, glancing around, 'and there are many who accuse the king of hastening the end of her days.'

'And do you?' asked Laura simply. 'Do you think it was the king that murdered his own mother?'

'I say only that the circumstances were remarkably propitious for him, that Her Majesty's sudden death occurred at a time when his own place in the succession stood in doubt,' Corvin frowned.

'He should answer before a court, if clear evidence can be produced,' added Sir Joseph.

'And we shall all travel to that court in a crystal carriage pulled by unicorns,' said Thomas with a grin, provoking several other humorous observations.

'But for now, our voices go unheard,' said Corvin, when the laughter had died away. 'There are no legal means by which the people may express their grievances. We have no alternative but recourse to force of arms, to summon the people from the bench or the plough, to march on London and force the king's hand. We shall humble the over-mighty Church and open the king's eyes to the suffering of his nation. We shall cast down his arrogant counsellors and oblige him to summon a parliament that shall represent the views of all his subjects, great and small.'

'Noble ends,' observed Laura, 'noble indeed. But do you suppose that you may achieve them?'

'There are some ideas that surpass us all, notions that are greater than the mere continuation of the existence of the individual,' said Corvin. 'And my body is committed to the service of those ideas, even though that service might encompass its destruction. It is the same for us all. We have sworn it. We have laid down our lives on the altar of this great undertaking. If we cannot achieve our ends, we do not wish to live to see the consequences of that failure. We shall bring about the downfall of the king and the church, or we shall die in the attempt.'

A chorus of approval accompanied this declaration, and Laura found herself swept up in the passion of the moment. There was a messianic glint in Corvin's eye, and his knuckles were suddenly white as he gripped the arms of his chair. It was easy to see why he inspired such devotion in his disciples.

'I believe you,' she said.

It was raining hard when Laura awoke. She could hear its rustle in the thatch of the roof above her and the occasional soft drip that made its way through. The vague

171

light of dawn crept through closed shutters, and by this she could discern the sleeping form of the girl whose accommodation she shared. The girl had been a servant in one of the great houses north of Ipswich and she had fled to Corvin when her brother had been hung for sedition. She was a plain creature but kindly, and her soft snoring made it certain that Laura would sleep no more that morning. Outside, she could hear occasional voices as those whose duties obliged them to rise with the dawn went about their business. Laura settled back on the sacking that served her as a bolster and drew her rough blanket about her, reflecting on the changes that had come about in her material circumstances during the last few weeks. As ever, the faces of her mother and of Emily formed within her inner vision, and after a while Emily's pale features crystallised to form an image that was almost tangible in its clarity. She squeezed her eyes tight shut, stifled a sob that caught at her breast and gazed with her mind's eye upon her poor dead sister's face with a poignant fervency. She was in a state between sleep and full wakefulness now, a state in which her mind trod the uncertain border between reason and fancy. She gasped, however, as Emily's eyes flew open and fixed her with a meaningful stare. Laura's own eyes followed suit and she glared unseeingly into the dark thatch above as the meaning of her vision became apparent to her. Then, after a moment, she slipped from the lumpy straw mattress that had been her resting place and groped for her shoes.

She found Matthew Corvin already awake and eating boiled eggs for his breakfast. Still chewing, he waved aside the objections of a bodyguard who had sought to deny her entry and set down the paper that he had been perusing.

'Miss DeLacey,' he said. 'Good morning. I had meant to speak with you again a little later, but I see that you have anticipated me.'

'Please excuse my intrusion,' said Laura, sitting on the chair that Corvin drew out for her, 'but I awoke just now, and I saw…' her voice faltered as she wondered at the wisdom of describing the crystal clarity of the vision that had motivated her visit, 'and I had an idea,' she finished.

'An idea?' asked Corvin mildly, dabbing at the corner of his mouth with a napkin. 'Do go on.'

'What if I could raise Queen Charlotte from the dead?' she asked. 'How then would your cause be advanced?'

Corvin appeared momentarily paralysed. He regarded her with eyes whose gaze was directed inwardly, and his lips moved silently.

'Do you think you could?' he asked at last.

'I could try,' she said. 'If I could be conveyed to her resting place and could place my hand upon her brow, I could tell whether her heart is of ice or of stone. It may be of stone, of course…'

'But it might be of ice,' concluded Corvin, jumping up and throwing down his napkin, 'and that ice might be melted.'

He crossed to the window and looked out across the wasteland of sedge and water beyond for a long moment, whilst Laura sat and regarded his powerful shoulders. At last, he turned upon her and his eyes fairly gleamed with passion.

'How the mighty would tremble in their halls if you could encompass this,' said Corvin. 'Queen Charlotte would surely curb her son's excesses in a moment.'

'If she were permitted to live,' said Sir Joseph, coming into the room. 'For there might be some who would wish to restore her former bodily status before news of her revival was widely known.' He nodded to Laura. 'A most extraordinary proposal, however. A most captivating notion.'

'Captivating indeed,' agreed Corvin with an emphatic nod. 'And one we must explore with urgency. My mind seethes with the possibilities...'

'And mine,' interjected Sir Joseph, regarding Laura with a new respect.

'That would be the moment for a general uprising,' observed Sir Joseph, when various matters had been discussed. 'A swelling declaration of support in every town and city across the land. If then we called our supporters to the streets...'

'Most certainly,' nodded Corvin. 'If a resuscitated queen were to survive, her survival must be generally known and the extent of her support full known to every waverer in the court and administration. We must march in defence of queen and constitution.'

'But first the queen must be revived,' reminded Laura in an apologetic tone that derived from her reluctance to quash the enthusiasm of her companions.

'Yes,' agreed Corvin, after a reflective moment in which the fire faded from his eyes, 'of course.'

'And she may not be susceptible to reawakening,' continued Laura in the same tone. 'Her heart may be of stone.'

'It may,' conceded Corvin, 'but I am a believer in fate, Laura, a believer that immutable destiny guides each of our courses, a plan of unimaginable complexity set in place by our creator. On occasion, in dreams and visions, we are privileged to see a glimpse of that plan and know our places in past, present and future. Surely, you have drawn aside the veils of obscurity that darken mankind's labours and disclosed to us a momentary flash of that great design. It was meant to be, Laura.' His eyes shone once more. 'Surely it was meant to be. I believe it with all my heart.' He grasped her forearm in a fervent grip. 'You were meant to awaken the queen.'

'And we must do everything in our power to provide you with the opportunity,' said Sir Joseph, likewise caught up in the fervour of the moment.

'Then I shall surely play my part in the attempt,' said Laura, but there was a hesitance in her voice, a reticence that Sir Joseph immediately detected. He cocked his head on one side, narrowed his eyes quizzically.

'But I detect a reservation,' he said. 'Unless I am mistaken.'

'I too,' agreed Corvin, resuming his seat before her, resting his weight on his elbows as he leaned forward across the table, steepling his fingers beneath his hawkish nose. 'Pray, what troubles you? I trust it is not fear of the enterprise itself. I do not detect in you a coward.'

'Not at all,' replied Laura, shaking her head vehemently. 'I know I shall live forever a fugitive unless your plans come to fruition, and that is no life at all.'

'Then what?' pressed Corvin, brow furrowed.

For a long moment Laura hesitated whilst she turned in her mind the words that she must use, setting them together in various combinations and with a variety of intonations appropriate to her intention. For to insist on a bargain with the famous Matthew Corvin was no small matter for a girl of her years, or indeed for any woman at all.

'Then you must first help me to go to my sister in Darkharrow,' she said at last.

For what seemed an even longer time no one spoke at all. Beyond the walls of Corvin's house, Laura could hear the shouts of fishermen, the bark of a distant dog. Her host's face appeared to darken, his eyes to fix hers with a steely glare.

'You seek to awaken your sister?' said Sir Joseph, when it seemed that the silence should endure forever.

'I do. I know that my touch may awaken no answering spark in her heart, but I am determined that I must try. That is my first duty, and I beg that you will help me to accomplish it.' There was a pleading note in her voice now and she leaned across the table towards Corvin, placing her hand on his forearm. 'I do not doubt that I can persuade Edward to accompany me, and he knows Darkharrow as well as anyone alive. If you could only provide us with a few good men to convey us there in safety, then I should be your servant in the matter you propose. I swear it.'

Corvin stared into her tear-rimmed eyes, his arm like a rock beneath her fingers, but at length his face and his flesh softened.

'It shall be so,' he said, 'though I hesitate to place you in unnecessary danger. Conveying you to London will be dangerous enough, God knows.'

'Then I shall go tomorrow,' she said, a warm rush of relief suffusing her breast.

By nightfall of the following day Laura found herself once more in the vicinity of Tithing Harrow. Edward, whose familiarity with Darkharrow was essential to her purpose, had accompanied her. Corvin had also sent his son, Thomas, and two of his companions in case they had need of protection. It felt strange to walk as a fugitive amongst the familiar lanes and byways on the fringes of the village, head bowed whenever they encountered a passer-by. Her servant garb was muddied from their passage through the fens and her hair dyed a dull brown by the girl whose quarters she had shared. The disguise would not long have deceived one who knew her, had they had the chance to look full into her face, but Laura kept her eyes cast down as she walked and fumbled with the beads of a rosary, as though in silent prayer. Certainly, none spoke to her as she made her way along the shallow creek that ran behind Darkharrow, past the timber yard and the market gardens. Thomas Corvin walked at her side, his two friends a little way behind, and Edward strode out in front, tipping his hat to those he passed, exchanging familiar greetings with an old man at his allotment gate.

'He knows what he is doing, I trust,' muttered Thomas as they slowed their pace.

'He does,' said Laura, glancing up at her companion, whose taut muscularity could barely be concealed by the voluminous coat he wore. Underneath it, she knew, nestled a loaded pistol and a wicked long knife, honed to a murderous edge. These things did not contribute to any sense of security in her. 'And he must certainly hail those he knows here, or his behaviour will be judged accordingly. He has no quarrel with the law.'

'Not yet,' laughed Thomas softly as they moved on towards the towering bulk of Darkharrow beyond the weavers' houses and the stockyards, empty now as darkness settled over the looming mass. Here, the east wing stood still in ruins as it had since the great fire, though the yard around it was stacked with the various building materials that were slowly being assembled for the purpose of rebuilding it. The perimeter wall was tumbled halfway across a lane here, and the fence that secured the holy precinct was a rickety one. It was easy enough for Edward to prise open a gap between the rough stone and the moulded timbers to let them through into the yard. Scudding clouds drew shifting veils across the rising moon, but Edward was sure-footed as he conducted them amongst piles of stone and tiles to the smoke-blackened flanks of the necropolis. Above them broken fingers of stone reached unevenly for the darkening sky, and they trod with care amongst huge black slabs of crumbled masonry. At last, passing through a tall gothic arch and the shell of what once had been a refectory, they came to a small door that gave access to the yard. The place was in deep shadows now, and in the breathless silence Edward could be heard running his hand across the aged planks in search of the lock.

'Do you want a light?' asked Robert, one of Thomas's companions, in a low voice, groping for his tinderbox.

'No, I shall manage,' murmured Edward. 'Here, I have it.'

There came the sound of metallic grating and a sharp click, horribly loud, as Edward's passkey did its work and the door creaked open.

Laura stepped after him but there was a momentary hesitation amongst the others as superstitious dread caught at their hearts. It was no small matter to intrude amongst the sleeping dead, and although each of them had sworn their unswerving commitment to the destruction of this place and all those like it, venturing in darkness amongst the ranks of the departed was not to be undertaken with a quiet mind.

'I think now is the time for a light,' conceded Edward, once the door had been shut once more and they stood in complete darkness, their own breathing loud in the narrow passage. 'None shall see it, I think. No one comes this way by night, and besides, all will be at supper.'

Soon the small lamp they had brought with them was lit, and by its dim glow they made their way through a maze of passages and courtyards open to the sky.

'I wouldn't care to have to find my way back through here without 'im,' remarked George softly, the fifth in their party, indicating Edward's back ahead of them, cast into sharp silhouette by the yellow glow of the lamp. 'It's like the bloody labyrinth.'

'Hush,' hissed Thomas, turning upon them angrily. They had emerged into another courtyard. He waved his arm meaningfully at a light in a window above the cloister on the far side.

Laura's own anxiety was not occasioned by the proximity of the dead; rather, it derived from the uncertainty of what she would find when she came to look upon Emily's face once more. Would her cheeks be hollowed and sunken, the lank strands of her hair dark around a parchment-pale brow? And when Laura placed her hand there, reached down to find her heart, would she find there the unyielding chill of stone or the delicate frost of ice? Her own heart beat faster; her tongue moved restlessly in the dry cavern of her mouth as they entered upon a region where the dead lay in stone-cut niches on either side of the passage and the dark maws of chambers opened on either side.

'Here,' said Edward at last, when it seemed that they must have traversed the whole breadth of Darkharrow at least a dozen times. 'She is within.'

A narrow opening in the wall gave access to a chamber that housed some of the more recent dead. Laura followed Edward through with the lamp whilst the others stood guard in the passage, content rather to stand in the chill blackness than gaze upon the withered countenances of the departed.

'At least… she was,' said Edward a moment later, his lamp revealing an empty niche.

'No!' gasped Laura. 'It cannot be!'

Her heart froze within her, and her throat was suddenly tight, as though unseen hands sought to strangle her. She shrank back against the wall, shaking her head. 'No!' she gasped in barely controlled anguish.

'Are you sure this is the place?' asked Thomas, venturing into the space.

'Why yes,' said Edward, shining his lamp on the stone plaque beneath the bier. 'Here is her name, you will observe, "Emily DeLacey", and the date of her admission.'

'Uh huh,' Thomas nodded. 'Then where is she now?'

'I don't know,' conceded Edward with a shrug. 'This is most irregular. I have never known…'

'They must have taken her,' wept Laura, finding her voice once more, if only a hoarse whisper. 'The bishop's men – to punish me.'

'They would not dare,' scoffed Edward, placing a comforting arm around her shoulder. 'Hush now. I never heard of such a thing.'

'Are we to stand here all night debating it?' asked Thomas. 'I trust you will agree our purpose is defeated.'

'Indeed, we must be away. Come, Laura. We can accomplish nothing here now.'

The long journey back to Corvin's stronghold had been without incident. For Laura, her stumbling progress through the benighted reed beds and the sedge had seemed almost a dream. Her mind was quite overwhelmed with shock and disappointment as she grieved afresh for her vanished sister. She was quite oblivious to the muttered speculation, the hoarse exhortations of her comrades as they urged her onward towards the hiding place of the boat that had conveyed them across the waters. Edward sought to assure her that her status as a fugitive from justice could not possibly relate to the absence of her sister's body, that his colleagues must have removed it temporarily to the chambers where the dead were cared for periodically, especially when the subject had only recently been admitted. His earnest entreaties and soothing words were in vain. Nothing could convince Laura that Emily's removal was not a consequence of the bishop's spite and that her hopes of reviving her sister were not yet utterly dashed. Perhaps she was already consigned to the dismal earth in some unmarked grave, her flesh assailed by worms.

'I will find out, I do assure you,' promised Edward, grim-faced, as they stepped out once more on the wharf in Corvin's stronghold. 'I shall return directly, as soon as I have spoken with Sir Joseph and with Corvin.'

Thomas Corvin, far from being disappointed, seemed to have regarded the episode as a great adventure. Already, as soon as news of their return had spread, a crowd of his friends gathered, eager to hear of their invasion of Darkharrow. Laura felt numb. She could contribute nothing to the tale. Soon she detached herself from the crowd and slipped away to her quarters, there to lie on her bed and stare sightlessly into the thatch above.

'It will not do, I tell you,' said the bishop, running his hands through his meagre hair. 'If the Lord Lieutenant cannot keep an orderly house he must hardly be surprised if I recommend that he should be dismissed from his post.'

'This prisoner,' said the soldier, 'this girl – I take it she was important to you, then?'

The soldier, a colonel, dressed in the dishevelled flamboyance that distinguished him from officers of the regular army, was the famous Colonel Danny Blanchflower of the Scarlet Band. His feet, much to the bishop's disgust, were on Turnbull's desk. The rest of him lounged in one of the comfortable chairs with which his host's office was now supplied and regarded his surroundings with an easy-going indulgence quite at odds with his reputation. Blanchflower was known to be a dangerous and irascible man, a psychopath, some said, whose enthusiasm for violent mayhem was matched only by his devotion to his master, the king. There was a dash, a charm, an open-handed generosity about him, too, at least where his men were concerned, and the three hundred cavalrymen he commanded served him with unswerving devotion. But he was a dangerous man, a very dangerous man, and Turnbull was entirely aware of this situation. For this reason, the bishop only spared the occasional peevish glance for the soldier's muddy boots and the irregular slew of papers they pinned to his desktop.

'She was a witch,' said Turnbull evenly. '*Is* a witch, but you may be sure I would resent it equally were any prisoner of His Majesty to escape from our custody.'

'It's a wonder she didn't take opportunity to turn you to a toad,' observed Blanchflower with a wry grin, looking up from where he was cleaning under his grimy fingernails with the point of an exceptionally sharp stiletto. 'Or infest you with a plague of warts,' he added with a meaningful glance.

Turnbull, whose forehead was disfigured by a number of sizeable moles, shifted uneasily in his seat, declining the opportunity to mention the distinction. He was all too conscious that Abel Ward, seated at his desk behind him, had his gaze cast into his lap and that the whole of his being was focused on betraying no impression of amusement.

'I want her caught,' said Turnbull after a lengthy clearing of his throat in which he attempted to order his thoughts. 'A principle is at stake here, and you may be sure that I should call upon your extreme diligence in this matter regardless of the identity of the fugitive. Rumour of this escape risks giving hope to our enemies.'

'Not much hope, I should have thought,' said Blanchflower, tapping the paper in his lap that Ward had passed to him some moments previously. 'Since rather more than a thousand of His Majesty's enemies have made their way to your gallows and perhaps as many have perished by our steel. I hardly think the rebel councils are raising a glass to their success.'

'You don't know what the rebel councils are doing,' countered Turnbull bluntly. 'Your business is simply to maintain order in this region, and I might add that the indiscriminate torching of villages, the abuse of the common people where blame does not attach to them – these things do not advance our cause.'

'Omelettes, eggs,' said Blanchflower with a shrug. 'One requires the breaking of the other, does it not? Where now are the armed bands roaming the open country? Where are the rioters in the streets of the towns? Omelettes and eggs, I say.'

'When His Majesty sent me here it was not with culinary intent,' replied Turnbull acidly. 'And when the next tithing comes to pass it would be agreeable if there were sufficient taxpayers remaining to settle your wages. All those with blue blood in them have long since decamped to London, and I have a list of complaints from the gentry the length of my arm.' He extended a hand in

Ward's direction, who, after a moment's hesitation, placed a sheaf of papers there.

'There are accusations of extra-judicial killing, of common brutality, theft and rape,' said Turnbull, having perused the top sheet, 'some of them in which you stand personally accused.'

'I am the arm of the law,' said Blanchflower, a dangerous glint in his eye. 'Naturally some resent it, make scurrilous accusations that reflect more their own attitude to authority. Perhaps they merit further investigation. Give me their names and I shall visit them. Then we shall see if they press their complaints.'

For a moment the two men held each other's gaze, but then Turnbull placed the papers on his desk.

'In good time,' he said. 'For now, I urge you to remind yourself that we are all subject to His Majesty's law and that our personal circumstances may change over time.'

A snort of amusement signalled Blanchflower's appreciation of this subtlety.

'Oh yes, indeed,' he said, withdrawing his feet from Turnbull's desk, standing up and stretching himself languorously. 'Even the mightiest can fall, can they not? But a good length of steel stands between me and ruination,' he said, slapping his hand on the basket hilt of his sword. 'And what of yourself?'

'The Lord preserves the virtuous,' answered Turnbull, rising to his feet now and being disagreeably reminded that he was a good head shorter than the soldier.

'Is that right?' laughed Blanchflower. 'Virtue, eh? Well, it's to be hoped he makes a tolerably vague interpretation of that quality, or I can think of some that'll be roasting in Hell for a good long time.'

Turnbull, rarely at a loss for a cutting riposte, could think of no immediate response to this and stood, lips moving wordlessly, whilst the colonel crossed to the window and regarded the gallows with evident satisfaction.

'About this girl...,' he said at length.

Chapter Eleven

The girl in question stood with Thomas Corvin on a sand flat and watched as a distant vessel negotiated the tortuous passage from the open sea to his father's camp. There was a brisk north- easterly to whip Laura's hair around her face, and beyond the wind-ruffled sedge close-reefed topsails glinted white in the pale midday sun.

'They'll have to put out a boat and warp her in before long,' Thomas observed. 'The pilot is pulling out to meet her away to leeward, see?'

'Where does the ship hail from?' asked Laura, glancing sidelong at her companion.

'She's the Marigold, out of Southend,' said Thomas, turning to her, 'and she's bringing supplies from Holland. Perhaps news, too. Perhaps visitors for my father.'

'Have you been to Holland?' asked Laura, brushing hair from her eye.

'Uh, huh,' answered Thomas. 'Of course, many times. And to France and to Spain, too.'

'I've never been anywhere,' said Laura ruefully. 'Not even to London.'

'I fancy that may be about to change,' said Thomas. 'At least where London is concerned.'

'You know, then?'

'Of course, my father tells me much. He relies on me.'

'He does?' A certain wry amusement tugged at the corners of Laura's mouth, and she turned away to conceal it.

'You sound surprised.'

'I do?'

'You do,' he replied, his face burdened with a frown.

'Then I am sorry for it,' said Laura, smiling brightly to dispel and feelings of hurt while tugging at his arm. 'Tell me about Holland.'

Thomas did so and about other places besides, whilst the ship drew closer, sails furled, yards struck down on deck now, towed by one of its boats, oars rising and falling rhythmically whilst a bosun's harsh voice carried across the waters to them.

'My father will triumph in the end,' he said at last, looking out dark-eyed towards the dim horizon.

'I desire it most fervently,' said Laura, 'but how can you know?' She glanced around her at the endless wind-scoured marshes under cloud-roiled skies.

'Do not be deceived by the appearance of obscurity,' said Thomas seriously, 'or by the manner of our living here. My father's finger is on the pulse of the realm, and he has agents and followers in every corner of it.'

'Like Sir Joseph?'

'Like Sir Joseph,' agreed Thomas. 'Although I think he would remind us to refer to him as John Cordwell whilst we are here.' He glanced around to see that no one else was within earshot whilst Laura blushed at her indiscretion. 'There are many like him,' he continued, 'although few with his peculiar usefulness and versatility. His reputation for eccentricity, his well-known passion for birds and creeping things enables him to travel widely without fear of suspicion.'

'He is a good man,' observed Laura.

'He is indeed,' agreed Thomas, 'but in every city there are good men like him, ready to respond to my father's summons, ready to call the people to the streets and rise up against their oppressors. Then we shall see what we shall see.'

Thomas's mouth was set in a grim line now, and Laura was reminded strongly of his father. He flexed the muscles of arm and back, placing his hand on the hilt of his sword. Unlike Edward's sword this seemed to hang naturally at his side, to be organically a part of him as much as the hand that caressed it.

'There will be an end to skulking on mud flats and a time to test steel on steel,' he said. 'You mark my words.'

'Our investigations occasionally unearth information of unexpected value,' said Richard Tong, handing a report to Abel Ward. 'And I wouldn't trouble you with it at this hour were I not entirely sensible of its significance. I trust His Lordship is indisposed, then.'

'He is,' replied Ward, having glanced at his pocket watch a moment since and found, in line with his general expectations, that it told three of the morning. 'Pray, do come in.'

Ward opened the door to admit Tong to his quarters in the south range of the Lord Lieutenant's house and drew his gown more closely around him, moving within to where his servant had hurriedly set a small lamp on a table.

Tong drew back a chair and sat, regarding Ward with a certain grim satisfaction, as the canon fumbled for his spectacles and began to read, holding the papers up to the uncertain yellow glow of the lamp, the same unflattering light disclosing the hairs in his nostrils and a spread of uneven stubble.

'I am astonished,' he said at last, setting down the papers. 'So Corvin is close at hand.'

'Within fifty miles or so of where we sit,' said Tong. 'He has returned from the low countries, no longer an exile but a fugitive still. There have been rumours to that effect for some time, but nothing concrete that might be relied on.'

'And this unfortunate wretch that you have questioned,' said Ward. 'If he were intimately acquainted with Corvin's hiding place, might he be prevailed upon to guide us to him?'

'Regrettably not,' said Tong with a sigh. 'He yielded this information late in the investigation, when his body was already past the point of sustaining life, even had medical intervention been undertaken.'

'You tortured him to death?' said Ward with a shudder. He loathed the methods employed by Tong and his confederates. Even in the full light of day the cold, grey eyes of the man before him betrayed not a flicker of humanity. And yet he had a wife and four children. How could the man reconcile his daily round of state-sanctioned devilry with any semblance of normal family life?

'Of course,' agreed Tong with a grave nod that fell somewhere short of regret. 'He was a craftsman who repaired a boat used by the rebels and overheard some of their private conversation as they awaited him. He knew only that Corvin was hiding somewhere in the fens east of Tithing Harrow.'

'And you trust this information?' asked Ward, handing back the papers. 'I believe information acquired under these… circumstances… is not always to be trusted.'

'Uncorroborated accounts are no basis on which to form settled policy,' agreed Tong, as though quoting from an official document, 'but may inspire further investigation. It would accord with what little we know of Corvin's recent movements – he has been required to leave Holland; you know.'

'I heard,' said Ward. 'The recent treaty…'

'Truly required both parties to desist from giving succour to each other's domestic opponents. It was assumed that he had fled to Scandinavia or even further afield.'

'But to take up residence in these desolate wastelands on the fringes of the realm, do you really think it credible?'

'It would offer certain advantages,' answered Tong carefully. 'I have been turning the matter over in my mind on the way here. He could readily be supplied by sea, I suppose, and his spies could come and go on foot without exciting suspicion.'

'And I imagine he would be the very devil to winkle out by land,' said Tong, 'if forces were to be sent to search for him. These endless fens make a formidable fortress.'

'And yet he must be supplied,' said Ward thoughtfully. 'And those who supply him must certainly know his whereabouts. We should notify London immediately, I suppose,' he added.

'I expect that the bishop would wish to adopt that course,' nodded Tong.

'Then we must certainly inform him directly.'

'I imagine he will be encouraged,' said Tong. 'I have heard that he is in low spirits.'

Turnbull's spirits were indeed depressed. In one respect this stemmed from a persistent head cold that left him with gritty, red-rimmed eyes and a streaming nose. On another account he was oppressed by a sense that his mission showed no signs of drawing to a speedy conclusion and that the murderous zeal of Colonel Blanchflower, and his band of cold-eyed ruffians seemed likely only to stand in the way of this objective. In addition, a communication from London assured him that Archbishop Lamb was settling his affairs in Rome in readiness for his return to Britannia. Bishop Anthony Craddock, who might be expected to squeeze every possible advantage from Turnbull's absence, had sent this letter to him. Craddock's intolerable satisfaction at this development positively radiated from every line of the document so that Turnbull was unable to read it through without uttering a series of most unchristian sentiments.

At breakfast, as he was contemplating a disagreeably runny boiled egg, he found himself unexpectedly face to face with Abel Ward, admitted by a wide-eyed and apprehensive servant. There was a pink, exuberant glow in Ward's features that caused the peevish enquiry that rose from Turnbull's throat to wither on his tongue. Only raised eyebrows and a look of wary discontent remained to signal his resentment.

'I have news,' announced Ward with satisfaction, placing a sheaf of papers neatly in front of his superior.

'I thought you must have,' grunted Turnbull. 'Otherwise, I should simply have assumed that you had lost your mind. Could this not have waited until we meet in the office in...,' Turnbull squinted at the clock on his mantel, '... twenty-five minutes. Am I to enjoy no privacy at all? Do you know what time it is?'

'Yes, yes, of course,' clucked Ward, tapping the papers. 'But I perceive you have forgotten that you are to spend the morning with the Deputy Lord Lieutenant and will not have leisure to discuss matters with me until much later in the day. And this is important.'

'It had better be,' warned Turnbull, reaching for his glasses.

Some moments later he set them down once more, a congealing egg driven from his mind by the keenest sense of emergent possibilities, all resentment set aside, at least for now.

'And Tong vouches for this information?' he said.

'He does,' replied Ward. 'And he placed such store in it that he thought it necessary to awaken me in the small hours.'

'He believes that there is not a minute to be lost?'

Ward turned the implications of this query in his mind for a moment before answering.

'He believed that the information should be placed at your disposal with all possible dispatch,' he said at last, 'and that you would inform London in due course.'

'As is our duty,' said Turnbull, wiping his mouth with a napkin, 'in due course.'

'Indeed.'

'Were Corvin to be apprehended in these regions it would deal a mighty blow to His Majesty's foes, would it not?' mused Turnbull, gazing sightlessly beyond Ward, who took the opportunity to draw back a chair and sit opposite the bishop.

'I imagine that it might,' agreed Ward, thinking that it would also add mightily to Turnbull's reputation and that this entrancing prospect hung glittering in his master's mind.

'But Corvin's residence is of uncertain duration,' said Turnbull. 'This may merely be a pied-à-terre, a staging post for some more permanent lodging, in this realm or further afield.'

'Of course,' agreed Ward, eyeing a piece of buttered toast acquisitively and wondering idly whether Turnbull's state of distraction might render him insensible of his eating it.

'And any action that must be taken must be taken with urgency and resolution,' continued Turnbull, eyes glinting now.

'Exactly so. Should I compose a message for London?' asked Ward, getting to his feet.

'No!' Turnbull's hand was on his forearm, pressing him back. 'I think not. Not yet. I imagine it would take a considerable time for the various departments to evolve an appropriate response, whereas we are here, on the spot, well-placed to deal immediately with the issue.'

'I see,' said Ward, creasing his smooth brow with a wondering frown. 'But I believe Tong intends that his intelligence should be transmitted directly to London.'

'Tong's duty ends upon his passing his document into my hands,' said Turnbull heavily. 'The intelligence it contains is now my responsibility and I shall act upon it as I see fit. Such is my duty as His Majesty's representative here.'

'And it may simply be a chimera, of course,' said Ward in soothing tones, observing with alarm the colour that had risen in Turnbull's cheeks. 'You may well judge it incumbent on you to seek confirmation from other sources before troubling His Majesty's intelligencers with what may try their patience unnecessarily, information that may prove to be insubstantial.'

'My thoughts exactly,' said Turnbull, eyes narrowed. 'We must build a portfolio. What contacts do we have in Holland, do you suppose?'

Corvin's mud-girt kingdom was a place in a state of almost continual flux. There were always agents coming and going on their missions across the fens, boats arriving at the wharf with fish caught locally or with provisions from further afield, refugees guided through the wastes by those followers of Corvin authorised to admit them. There were a few score permanent residents, however, amongst them a band of men who dubbed themselves the

'Ravenguard' and wore a black sash as the mark of their role. It was hardly large or experienced enough to be dignified with the title of a "regiment", but its members took their duties seriously and drilled in ranks on the firmer reaches of mud flat within the environs of the camp. There was swordplay, too, with a splendid variety of obsolete or inadequate blades in evidence, wielded with more enthusiasm than finesse. Occasionally, when powder could be spared, a dozen or so muskets were brought out and the younger volunteers instructed in their use, whoops and cheers accompanying the thunderous discharges, clouds of acrid black smoke drifting away across the waters. A few of the Ravenguard were grizzled veterans of a dozen or so European conflicts, but most were strangers to the art of war and seemed unlikely to prosper in any imminent encounter with the enemy. As a swordsman of some repute, Thomas Corvin's days were devoted to the improvement of this unpromising military material.

Laura often went to watch him training his young comrades in the days after Edward had returned to his place in Darkharrow. A few of the younger girls would go out with her and make small talk and pass comments about the personal or physical virtues of the various swordsmen, seating themselves comfortably enough on a length of oilskin brought out from the camp. Class distinctions mattered little in this context, and although Laura's mother might have frowned to see her chattering so comfortably amongst those marked down irredeemably as her social inferiors, it seemed natural enough in her present situation. Besides, there were no idle hands, no useless mouths in the camp and all were required to make their contribution, regardless of their status. Laura spent much of her days in plying her needle to mend clothes or in working in the rudimentary laundry that had been set up behind the kitchen.

Jen, the girl with whom she shared lodgings, was her constant companion, a simple, cheerful soul with an engaging gap-toothed smile and quick, nimble fingers. Plain, rather thickset and with no discernible waist, she was nonetheless popular with the young men. Her open, affectionate nature and her willingness to please more than compensated for any shortcomings to be found in face and figure, although her liaisons were never enduring ones. Laura's person might ordinarily have excited the interest or admiration of her male peers, but word of her deeds and reputation had spread widely, and although she was treated with every mark of respect none of the boys could look at her without betraying at least some subtle indication of superstitious dread. It was said that she could stop a man's heart by placing her hand on his flesh, and there were none too eager to put this to the test. When once she tripped on her petticoat and went sprawling, it was only Thomas amongst them who offered his hand to help her to her feet. For this mark of acceptance Laura was grateful, and besides there was a fire in his eyes, an urgency about him that set him apart from the other young men and set her own heart a-flutter when his flesh touched hers.

'I reckon Thomas Corvin's a-lying in your head,' Jen suggested one day, glancing up from the bucket of potatoes they were peeling. 'All naked he is, with his dark curls next to yours,' she laughed. 'Tell me if I'm wrong. Your eyes are all glazed over, and you haven't twitched a muscle this minute since.'

'Fie! What stuff!' laughed Laura, pushing playfully at Jen's round shoulder. 'Since when could you know the content of my mind?'

'That flush in your cheek tells me all I need to know,' said Jen, gesturing with her peeler. 'And besides, he's sweet on you, too. Everyone knows it.'

'I'm sure you exaggerate,' countered Laura demurely, although not without a satisfaction that she was hard pressed to conceal.

'But then I suppose that there Edward fellow is your sweetheart,' continued Jen, wiping her brow with the back of a grubby hand and leaving a dirty smear. 'I suppose you're all set up for him.'

'Then your suppositions are quite wrong,' Laura told her, finding it strange to be obliged to define her feelings thus. 'We have been friends since early childhood, that is all. He was destined for a career with the Camoldolites. You have heard of Darkharrow, no doubt?'

'Of course,' nodded Jen. 'Who hasn't?'

'Well, he's to take holy orders there soon.'

'Is he, now?' wondered Jen, the tone in her voice suggesting a degree of scepticism, although the necessity of selecting another potato to peel stifled further comment.

If Laura had hoped that this would be sufficient to curtail discussion of the inclinations of her heart, she was to be disappointed. Jen's mind was rarely capacious enough to hold more than one thought at a time, and it was quite clear that Thomas Corvin occupied its forefront now.

'He does cut a fine figure, though,' she said.

The substance of this declaration made it immediately apparent that she was referring to Thomas and not Edward.

'I suppose he does,' conceded Laura, completing, with some satisfaction, a peeling that entirely encompassed the potato she was working on and holding it up for Jen to admire.

'And he works that sword like a livin' thing,' said Jen with a vague nod of acknowledgement but a misty distance in her eye that spoke of her own attachment.

'And you dare to accuse me of carnal imaginings featuring young Thomas,' grinned Laura. 'You should look at yourself.'

'I don't have no business with mirrors, as you know,' said Jen wryly, 'but as to imaginings – well, there's more prospect of yours taking shape than mine, I'll wager.'

Lying abed later that night, with the dark thatch above her, it was hard not revisiting that earlier conversation and dwelling languorously upon the possibilities that had been awakened in her mind. The place that she now occupied in the world, and the circumstances that had brought her here, seemed almost a dream to her, and so the limitless imaginative scope of the dreamer brought within the compass of her mind's eye a time in which she and Thomas might be lovers. Days passed and grew into weeks. The sedge-girt horizons of this small place were the bounds of a world in which her life's expectations and experiences were set aside. Her mother and her extended family had no contribution to make to it, except to exist darkly on the fringes of her thoughts. All the familiar faces that she had known were withdrawn and a new reality confronted her. At the heart of this reality stood Thomas Corvin.

'How long do you suppose we shall remain here?' she asked him one late November evening when they were in the porch of his father's house and darkness settled around   them.

'I know that I shall remain until my guard duty is

complete,' replied Thomas, his mouth curling into a wry smile. 'I cannot speak for you.'

'You know that wasn't what I meant,' laughed Laura, nudging him playfully.

'As to how long you must remain in this place of safety and evade the clutches of those who would burn you as a witch, then I fear I cannot say. But do you chafe at your confinement? Would you rather wander abroad and take your chances with the king's men?'

'You know I wouldn't,' answered Laura, pulling her shawl around her shoulders. 'I ask only if your father has decided when I might venture forth to London and try my hand at waking the old queen. I trust that will be proof enough of my courage.'

She sat upon one of the long benches that stood on either side of the door and that were used by those awaiting audience with the Raven, but now she edged along to warm her hands from the glowing brazier at the edge of the porch. Thomas, whose duty of vigilance forbade him to sit down, regarded her thoughtfully.

'Pray, do not for a moment entertain the notion that I doubt your courage,' he said. 'You may be sure that I have the highest regard for...'

The object of Thomas's regard was to remain unclear for the moment as two of the Raven's councillors emerged from audience with him. They were still deep in conversation and, after a nod to Thomas, they disappeared, still talking, into the darkness between the various rudimentary shacks and huts that lined the only street of the little settlement.

It was almost completely dark now and firelight glinted in Thomas's eyes as he regarded her.

'You were saying...' prompted Laura, who had hoped that some further declaration of his admiration might be forthcoming, perhaps one couched in more endearing terms. There was suddenly a warmth in her brow, a tingling in her fingertips. Standing up, she crossed to her companion's side and squeezed his arm.

Apparently aware of the content of her mind, Thomas drew himself to his full height and turned to gaze out into the darkness. He did not draw his arm away, but Laura was conscious of a slight stiffening of the smooth muscle which she held.

'It is no small ambition, to cast the world into a better shape,' he said. 'And to dedicate one's flesh and blood, one's living soul to that noble cause. To focus the whole of one's being upon bringing one's dreams to fruition admits of no... distraction. And yet... and yet...'

Thomas turned back to her, and for a moment his lips moved wordlessly as though the notion that had formed in his mind could not be brought to utterance. His eyes, though, were wide and suddenly rimmed with moisture that spoke of some high emotion with great difficulty contained.

'Of course,' agreed Laura hurriedly in tones that, she hoped, betrayed no resentment at being thought a distraction. 'Your dedication is to be admired.'

'You oblige me,' said Thomas with a slow nod, finding his voice at last. 'I set a high value on your opinion. It would be agreeable to think that one day the nation will stand at peace and that justice will prevail throughout the land.' He patted his sword hilt. 'And this blade shall know retirement on a wall above some mantelpiece. Perhaps then, but then, perhaps...'

He moved towards her, and he seemed afflicted by an uncertainty she was quite unused to in him. Leaning in, her face uplifted to his, it seemed for a long moment that he might kiss her.

'Indeed,' she said wistfully, even as the door opened behind them and the Raven himself stood in the threshold, cast into silhouette by the warm yellow light behind him.

'Miss DeLacey,' he said after taking a moment to assess the situation, after a moment in which Laura and Thomas drew apart. 'May I trouble you for a moment of your time?'

She followed him within, and soon she was seated opposite him across what she was already beginning to think of as his "council" table. Plates were laid out there with the remains of a rudimentary meal, cheese rinds and a few crusts. There were two empty ale flagons, but the Raven's remained half-full – he was famously abstemious.

'I would offer you refreshment,' he said, a regretful glance encompassing the table before them.

'No matter, I have already eaten,' she said. 'Pray, how may I assist you?'

'You may certainly assist me by making no amorous advances upon my son,' said Corvin with a wry smile, causing Laura to blush furiously. 'For I see that he is quite smitten by you and will be unmanned by cow-eyed devotion to Eros, if offered the slightest encouragement.' He leaned back in his chair and regarded her levelly, eyes narrowed in a considering manner that caused her heart a momentary flutter. 'It would be as well if our plans moved forward with all reasonable despatch, and I am glad to say that I have made provision for your accommodation in London. Thomas will remain here, but you will travel there in the capacity of maidservant to Sir Edward Fishburn, a merchant of my acquaintance, there to await a propitious moment for you to make your contribution to our plan.'

'I am glad of it,' said Laura firmly, feeling no small sense of disappointment, however. 'It was a kindness of you to admit me to your company, and you must believe me when I say I am impatient to serve you in any way I can.'

'If you are able to serve us as you propose it will be to strike a mighty blow for our cause,' said Corvin in level tones.

Their eyes met and Laura lowered her gaze as modesty dictated, but not before having noted a certain reticence in the set of his features.

'He entertains no real hope that I will succeed,' she told herself. 'But he will do what he can to support me, because even a slender chance is better than none.'

She wondered whether Matthew Corvin had the capacity to serve as the figurehead for the frustrated hopes of the nation – as so many here claimed. To pronounce his name, to hear it whispered on the lips of the oppressed, was to conjure up a fleeting vision of a world that might yet be, that existed in the collective imagination of the downtrodden, beyond the reach of the vengeful state and all its agencies. To embody those accumulated hopes and aspirations, to exist as the physical vessel for so many dreams, seemed to Laura to be a ponderous burden to bear, perhaps more than any one man could shoulder. Yet shoulder them he did, although there was a weariness about Corvin tonight, written in the pallor of his brow and the slackness in the skin about his jaw.

'We shall see what we shall see,' he said at length, as though having read her mind. 'You will depart on the Marigold when next she returns from Holland, and a vessel from Rotterdam will convey you thence to London. Would you wish to take your friend Jen with you?'

'If she wills it,' said Laura.

'Then you should ask her.'

Chapter Twelve

It was with Jen at her side that Laura stood on the jetty a few days later, awaiting the docking of the Marigold. It was a cold afternoon, the first day of December, with frost rimming the ancient timbers and a low carpet of swirling fog drifting around them on the icy breath of winter. They saw the limp topsails of the vessel above the grey gloom long before her bulk could be discerned, the pale canvas occasionally half-filling in some fitful gust that stirred the slowly rolling fog banks and rustled across the sedge. They could hear the splash of distant oars as the boats warped her in, the curse of a bosun, the creak of a cable stretched taut.

'And will you have everything you need, when you sail tomorrow?' asked Thomas, who stood with a few of his companions watching the ship come in.

'I will have everything that my supposed status requires,' answered Laura with a shiver, pulling her shawl around her.

'As shall I,' said Jen with a wry smile and a sidelong glance at Laura, 'should you be interested.'

'My enquiry was of you both,' said Thomas in injured tones that nevertheless proclaimed that her barb had been well placed.

'I'm sure,' said Laura, squeezing Jen's arm to show her understanding of this and then, turning to Thomas, 'What troubles you? I swear you…'

'Hush!' Thomas waved her enquiry aside, his face suddenly grave. 'Listen.'

'What?'

There were various muttered conversations amongst the other bystanders gathered on the jetty, but these subsided into silence as Thomas's injunction took effect. The sounds of muffled voices carried to them through the fog bank, but there was a curious reticence in them as though untypical restraint was being imposed on the crew. There were no cheerful cries or exchange of ribaldry, and the dispersed splash of oars suggested the approach of more than a single boat. The ghostly forms of four launches emerged from the veils of fog almost simultaneously. At the same moment, awful realisation dawned amongst those waiting.

'We're under attack!' cried Thomas, even as the first shot rang out, oddly dulled by the fog, an angry flash of orange from the leading vessel. 'Raise the alarm!'

Suddenly, all was chaos, a flurry of half-seen, half-heard events in a tumbled succession too rapid for comprehension. Jen, more alert than Laura, was stooping, tugging at her arm. More shots rang out. There was an anguished cry and a body dropped at Laura's feet even as she ran. A bell clanged out behind them. Sword drawn now; Thomas turned to her as she glanced over her shoulder. There were more shots. He gasped and lurched forward, clutching at his head, vanishing with a splash into the chill waters, even as the first boat touched, and a stream of roaring soldiers clambered onto the jetty, brandishing swords and pistols. Laura was aware of colliding with another stumbling body, tripping over an outstretched arm, her own heart leaping in her breast. In retrospect, her brain's groping attempts to impose order on a sequence of fleeting impressions crystallised in her mind's eye a few vivid images that could not readily be dispelled – a boy, no more than ten years old, sinking to his knees, stupidly to regard the sword point that had suddenly emerged from his chest. His eyes met hers as she passed, eyes from which life leached even as the red blood flowered on his shirt. An elderly woman, crust of bread in hand, emerged from a doorway and then a musket ball caught her full in the face, an explosion of blood and white bone. A small dog, squealing, running amongst lurching feet with a line of flapping laundry caught about its collar.

Now she was amongst the sedge at the mud flat's edge, gasping for breath, her own whimpering harsh in her throat as she pushed the brittle stems aside, desperate to place the frosted brown curtain of reeds between her and the storm of death at the settlement's edge. She tripped over the root of a stunted bush, fell headlong and groped for purchase in the crusted mud.

'Enough,' hissed Jen at her side. 'Lay still now.'

Together, oblivious to the chill seeping through their clothes, they stared back through the shifting sedge to where the settlement that had been their home died in flame and swirling black smoke. Their mad rush had carried them a few hundred yards, but beyond rooftops they could hear the crackle of musketry and the clash of steel. There were cries of pain, abruptly cut short, and one wretch's agonised screams, again and again, until Laura shut her eyes and prayed that sweet, swift death would claim him.

High tide had brought with it this sudden wave of destruction, but the late hour of that tide, the shortness of the winter day, brought salvation with it, too. Even now daylight was fading and the crackling flames that consumed the Raven's house cast into sharp silhouette a pair of figures that detached themselves from deeper shadows, splashing through shallow water and approaching their hiding place. Groups of men with flickering torches were hunting down fugitives amongst the low buildings and at the edge of the fen, but these two eluded them, sometimes crouching still when danger threatened, sometimes hurrying onward. One figure supported another, clearly injured.

'Why, 'tis Thomas,' gasped Jen. 'And young Michael Coldicott, if I ain't mistook.'

'Is that you, Jen, Miss Laura?' asked Michael as he settled down next to them and Thomas slumped at his side, muttering incoherently.

'Thomas!' cried Laura, hushed instantly by Jen and Michael. 'You are injured!'

'I am not yet dead,' he muttered indistinctly, through pain-clenched teeth. 'Not quite yet.'

It was almost completely dark now, but sufficient light remained to disclose that blood from an open wound trickled from his forehead into one eye. He blinked distractedly and wiped this aside with a damp and gory sleeve. There was another wound in his side, wet with an ominous dark ooze.

'We must bind it,' said Laura urgently. 'Or he will surely bleed to death.' She began tearing strips from her petticoat as her companions pushed stems aside to make a space for Thomas to be laid out to receive what rudimentary treatment they could offer.

'My father,' stuttered Thomas. 'Is he escaped, too?'

Michael, a thin young man with an immoderately large nose, exchanged a grim glance with Laura. A shrug of his narrow shoulders was sufficient to express his view that death or captivity was their leader's likely fate.

'Quiet! You are our only concern just now,' Jen scolded Thomas, pulling his shirt aside to reveal the wound, pursing her lips, accepting a strip of pale fabric from Laura. 'Here, Michael, hold him up whilst we bind him. That's it, just so.'

It was now too dark to see clearly, and there was much fumbling as they struggled to wrap and tie their makeshift bandage.

'Do you suppose that will hold?' asked Laura doubtfully, wiping her hands on her skirt.

'It will have to,' said Jen, standing to peer back towards the burning settlement as a few curls of pungent smoke found their way to their nostrils, "cos we must be away.'

'Stay here,' sighed Thomas vaguely, who trod the uncertain verge of consciousness.

'No way,' disagreed Michael with a shake of his head. 'We needs must be far away from here by dawn. The place is going to be crawling with the military.'

For a while it was easy enough to judge the direction of their travel, simply by ensuring that the fiery orange glow remained at their backs, but in time even that vague light faded from view, and they trudged on blindly, groping amongst the reed stalks. A few stars emerged in the firmament but there was no moon and there could be no certainty that they were proceeding in anything approaching a straight line. Besides, Thomas was wearying, and it became necessary for one of them to support him on either side in a halting, laborious progress that left them gasping for breath. At times the ground was firm enough underfoot, but at other times a glutinous black mud clung to their feet, making it an arduous task even to drag them free. It was clear that exhaustion lay close at hand when they stumbled upon a fragile reed-built shelter of the kind that huntsmen use when shooting fowl. The wattled reed walls offered some protection from the cold breeze that had sprung up, but now that they lay still the bitter chill of December gnawed at their bones. Like sheep in the fold, they nestled together, encasing

Thomas in the small warmth of their bodies. Sometimes he was sufficiently wakeful to mutter that they should leave him, look to their own salvation, sometimes to assert improbably that the dawn would find him quite recovered. Mostly he slept, and the others also lapsed into a fitful slumber whenever exhaustion overwhelmed the urgings of discomfort.

'We must have been betrayed,' whispered Michael at a time when he and Laura were both wakeful. 'They must have found out the Marigold was ours an' took her over, so they must. Some bastard sold us out, Hell rot his soul!'

Michael Coldicott was a weaver's son. When soldiers found a seditious leaflet in his cottage, they arrested the father and smashed his loom. When the elder Coldicott went to the gallows his son found his way to the Raven. A thin, undersized youth, there was nevertheless a wiry hardiness to him, a resilience that had carried him through many a scrape.

'We escaped, did we not?' pondered Laura across Thomas's shoulder. 'Perhaps many others also made good their escape. The fog shrouded their coming, but it also concealed our getting from that place.'

'Do you suppose... the Raven?' The dread possibility that Matthew Corvin was dead or captive was too awful for Michael to bring to utterance. They lapsed into silence, oppressed by the thought of this contingency, silence broken only by Thomas's laboured breathing and by the rustle of the brittle rushes beneath him as he shifted his weight.

'I was a coward back there,' announced Michael at last, in solemn tones. 'My spirit broke. My conscience prompts me to declare it and I cannot contain it a moment longer, try though I might.'

'How so?' asked Laura as Michael suppressed a sob. 'You surely saved our friend Thomas here.'

'By chance, I did,' admitted Michael with a sigh. 'When first the alarm was raised the others drew their swords and rushed to make a fight of it.' He laughed bitterly. 'Much good it did them. My first thought, my only thought, was the saving of my skin, and so I plunged headlong off the jetty even as the soldiers were coming ashore. There I found Thomas, of course, unnoticed in the confusion, half-drowned in the shallows.'

'Then, you picked him up and brought him away,' said Laura encouragingly. 'That was courageous in you. I suppose you could have left him there and looked to your own salvation.'

'I suppose,' conceded Michael. 'I suppose I could. Anyways, I kept his head above water and dragged him under the timbers of the jetty until the fight had moved away. Then I brought him away, when it seemed they were all taken up with looting and burning.'

'And you have saved his life,' Laura told him. 'So perhaps your initial want of bravery was no bad thing. Perhaps, had you raised your sword against them, you would be dead now and so would Thomas.'

'You could say so,' agreed Michael reluctantly. 'And I thank you for applying such sweet salve to my poor, wounded conscience.'

'Let it be at rest,' said Laura kindly, although in truth Michael's conscience was the least of their concerns. It seemed likely enough that the next hours would be fatal for Thomas unless they could convey him to a place of safety and secure medical attention for him.

At last, a growing glimmer in the east brought with it vague perception of the reed beds and a shallow mere before them, with a hint of higher ground to the west. Stretching aching limbs, they raised Thomas to a pitch of consciousness that promised some mobility and set off through the sedge, following the little muddy track that the huntsmen might use to make their way to their hide. Soon, the extent of Thomas's injuries became clearly apparent – a graze to the skull through which bone gleamed pale amongst congealed blood and a wound to his left side from which fresh blood continued to issue despite their best efforts at binding him.

'I'm seeing two wounds, front and back, yes?' said Jen, as she tore cleaner strips from her own garments.

'Uh huh,' agreed Michael. 'And he's bleeding from 'em fit to empty hisself out. Hurry up with that.'

'I will,' said Jen, passing a length of petticoat round his abdomen. 'But that's a good thing, see? There ain't no musket ball in there, now, is there? No one needs to go digging around in there to fetch it out.'

'Jen's right,' concurred Laura, nodding as she struggled to tie the ends. 'But we needs must find someone with the skills to stitch him up before long. Oh, how I wish Sir Joseph were here. He would stitch him up in a trice, I swear.'

Within an hour or so it could be said that the new day had fully dawned and this with a cold wind and a little driven snow, more particles of ice than true flakes, that stung their faces as they walked. By midday a distant smudge of smoke appeared beyond the rustling sedge and beneath the smoking chimney the scattered buildings of a farmstead. In the main yard a man of middle years and stature paused in his wood chopping, wiped his brow and regarded them suspiciously as they approached. He did not set down his axe, holding this loosely at his side in a casual but meaningful manner. A dog barked alarm, racing out from a barn to confront them, waved aside by its master, whose eyes darted rapidly from Thomas to Laura, who now walked in front. She spread her arms wide in a beseeching gesture, turning to indicate her companions.

'Pray assist us kind, sir,' she implored, regarding the dog warily. 'As you see, our friend is gravely wounded and in dire need of shelter.'

The man bit his lip, glanced over his shoulder and seemed to weigh the situation. It was obvious enough that Thomas's injuries derived rather from violence than through accident, and the penalties for aiding fugitives from the law were well known to all. Within the last week the bishop's men had visited the place, carrying away four chickens and a keg of cider without payment or permission, leaving behind a stern warning that any suspicious visitors should be reported to the local constable.

'Please, sir,' said Laura once more, gesturing at the pale-faced invalid, at Jen and Michael who supported him on either side. 'I fear he will soon breathe his last, else.'

The farmer made up his mind, tipped his hat back on his head and jerked his thumb at the farmhouse behind him.

'Best get him inside, then,' he grunted.

'Brigstock! Have you taken leave of your senses?' demanded the woman that must be his wife, dropping a half-plucked fowl from her lap as they carried Thomas through into their kitchen.

'I won't turn my face from folks in need,' said the farmer. 'And nor shall you. Here, bring him through to the back. There's a bed there you can lay him in. Martha, boil water, if you will, and bring us some blankets from the chest.'

The woman regarded him aghast for a moment, hands on hips, but she quailed before his stony glare and hurried to the well to draw water, muttering gloomily under her breath.

'Get us both hanged, he will, foolish old mule,' Laura heard as she cast down the bucket.

'Have you any skill with a wound, sir?' enquired Jen of the man they would soon learn was called Ewan Brigstock, as they stripped Thomas's damp and filthy clothes from him, setting him down moaning in the clean white sheets.

'None more than the average, but I know well enough that you must clean them, lest corruption set in,' said Brigstock, plucking at the crude knots that secured Thomas's bandages. 'And there's a rare, good doctor, down in the village, Dr Foley by name. Retired now he is, but once he earned a good living in Norwich, and London before that, so they say. You should certainly seek him out.' He looked up from his work, bawling, 'are you ever going to set that kettle to boil, woman?'

'Curb your lip, husband, I'm going as fast as ever I can,' came the reply from the kitchen as she set the kettle in place over the fire.

Sent to fetch scissors, Laura regarded the roaring fire and the comfortable armchairs on either side with longing, the delicious warmth already tingling in her fingertips. And yet a glance at the pallor in Thomas's sleeping face was enough to dispel any thought of lingering there a while to drive the chill from her bones.

'We will fetch the doctor at once, if he is there to be fetched and willing to come,' she said. 'If you would just give me directions…'

Jen remained with Thomas to assist in the cleaning of his wounds and to reassure him should he awaken. With Michael at her side, Laura set off along the farm track to the road and thence to the broader route that wound its way around the fringes of the fen to Meldon; perhaps a hundred houses clustered around a Saxon church, with a smithy and an inn facing each other across the village green. It was mid-afternoon by now and quite impossible to avoid the attention of passers-by as they made their way to the doctor's house, a large white dwelling that stood at the corner of the green. None challenged them but they received a curious glance or two, and one small boy stopped to watch them pass, tugging at his mother's skirts. With no more than a curt nod to an elderly man, who in turn tipped his hat to them, they pressed on past the green. But here they must also pass by the inn. On the forecourt, with their horses tethered to the rail, a group of three of the Scarlet Band stood swigging ale. There was no alternative but to pass them by, once the curve of the road had brought them into view and the doctor's house lay beyond them.

'A bold face and a confident gait,' murmured Laura to Michael as they approached.

'Good day to you, pretty missy,' said the tallest of the three soldiers, sweeping off his feathered hat and making a low bow. 'And what might your sweet name be?'

Laura made a vague murmur of acknowledgment as they passed but did not slow her pace, which she hoped might indicate righteous urgency rather than barely contained panic.

'I see you have lost none of your skill with the ladies, Corporal Bailey,' laughed a second soldier.

They were part of a larger patrol that had been passing through earlier that day, but the corporal's horse had shed a shoe and they had been left to wait whilst the smith fitted another. The sound of his hammering could be heard from across the green.

'Hey, young missy,' shouted the corporal after Laura's back, red-faced now, smarting from the derision of his comrades. 'Have you no gentility or manners in these parts?'

Laura exchanged a despairing glance with Michael and debated whether she should press on regardless; the doctor's house was within a score of yards or so. But it was no use. She needs must address this threat. She turned; Michael carried on.

'And you, there. Both of you stand still this moment,' called the corporal in icily commanding tones now. He set down his flagon on a wall and approached them, brushing a fold of his tunic aside meaningfully to reveal the pistol in his belt. His comrades came up at his side.

'I'll have you tell me your business,' he said, narrowing his eyes as he considered her, sparing a brief glance for her companion. 'For there's something in your manner that ain't quite right and etiquette's got no bearin' on't. Tell me your name, missy, and his too and that may be a fair beginning.'

'My name is... Anna, Anna Blashford, and this is Peter... Finch,' she said, groping for lies, feeling the flush rising in her cheeks, 'my cousin. And we are sent to see the doctor, for my mother's sake. She is ill, has been ill this last week with the...'

'Never mind your mother,' said the corporal, 'for we have no business with her. Whereas you, my dear, are the object of my keenest interest. I am a curious man, you see,' he said, plucking at her clothing, causing her to wince, 'and I see shoes and garments so bespattered with mud I wonder at where you've been a-travelling. Likewise, filth all splashed in your hair and on your sweet cheeks,' he said, running pudgy fingers through her lank locks.

'I'd say you were strangers in these parts,' he added, his hot breath on her ear now, 'for I'm an observant man and I observed just now that three people passed you on the street and not one of them seemed to know your face. How's that so, Miss Anna? Not from round here, are we? I might ask where you do abide.'

'We have a house on the lane yonder,' said Laura conscious of anxiety welling up within her, of tears gathering in her eyes, 'and I took a tumble as I went out to feed the pigs last night. Mama's been so ill, I found no moment to change my clothes.'

'Corporal'd like to take a tumble on you,' said one of the troopers with a lewd wink at his companion.

'It's true,' said Michael, in querulous tones. 'We must see the doctor urgently, I say. There isn't a moment to lose.' He had pulled himself up to his full albeit inconsiderable height and looked the corporal full in the face to simulate confidence. Nevertheless, Laura saw the gallows in his eyes.

'I'll be the judge of that,' snapped the corporal, shoving him in the chest, 'and you'd do well to speak when you're spoke to and leave it at that, for she's of gentle birth, unless I'm very much mistook, and you are not.'

He returned his attention to Laura, who could not meet his eye now and stood biting her lip as a tide of despair rose within her breast.

'But what's a gentlewoman doin' dressed just so, I ask myself, and why does she need to dissemble? From these parts, are you? I reckon not. I reckon if I take you into the inn there'd be none there who'd know your face. That so, missy? On the right tracks, am I? I daresay Sergeant

Bradman would like a word wi' you when we catches up with him.'

'More than a word, I'd say,' laughed the third soldier, taking her roughly by the arm.

There seemed little point in further protest. Laura tried to compose her features and resigned herself to an interview with the sergeant of the patrol. He was said to be searching properties in the next village. What he would deduce from her it was impossible to say, but the dread possibility that she might be recognised as the fugitive witch clutched at her bowels as the corporal, mounted once more, led them away along the lane that ran north along the fringes of the fen. Michael, head hung low now, trudged wordlessly at her side, despondency written in the set of his narrow shoulders. Laura nourished some faint hope that Thomas might remain undiscovered. For the sake of the kind folk who had taken him in she prayed that this might be so. And had that been the twitch of a curtain in the window of the doctor's house as she passed by? She saw in this an indication, some slight hope, that her passing was not entirely unremarked, that somehow word of her detention might reach those with the power to help her. She had said no more to her captors, regarding them with stony-faced indifference as they bound her wrists and secured her by a long cord to the saddle rigging of one of the horses. Michael had received the same treatment, suffering a brutal kick to the groin when he resisted the binding.

'Not so fine now, missy, eh?' laughed the corporal, yanking on the cord to make her stumble forward.

'And yet I could have killed you a moment since,' thought Laura, recovering her balance. The notion had certainly come into her mind as the soldier's rough skin brushed against hers. But the moment had passed before the necessary focus could be established or the resolution to use it. Besides, she wondered whether killing the corporal would have spared her from destruction. His two comrades were close at hand with weapons drawn, and her witch's power had no answer to pistol balls, she supposed. Nevertheless, the consciousness that she had the capacity to still a man's heart, should she choose to, raised her spirit somewhat above the very deepest abyss of despair as they made their way along the lane. She was giving some thought to the story that she must concoct for her impending interview with the sergeant when five riders emerged suddenly from a side lane. They were dressed in dark clothes with voluminous cloaks that billowed in the wind. Long muskets hung from their saddles. Deep hoods cast their faces into shadow, and they wore scarves that concealed noses and mouths.

'What do we have here, then?' asked their leader, sparing her a glance and then addressing the corporal. 'More trade for the hangman?'

The corporal, who showed no alarm at their arrival, chuckled and jerked a thumb back at Laura.

'That's yet to be seen,' he said. 'More than likely, though, when the sarge looks at 'em. Waste 'o prime rump, mind you.'

Laura might have resented this last assertion had her mind not been reeling under the assault of sudden recognition. She knew that voice.

'Jonah!' she gasped as Michael swivelled to regard her.

'Hmmm?' he murmured.

Her involuntary outburst passed unnoticed as the men before them exchanged cheerful greetings and began a conversation that confirmed their prior acquaintance. It appeared that the five riders were members of a vigilante group operating in the area. They carried with them the authority of the military to assist them in hunting down brigands. Clearly, they were well known to the soldiers, and they spoke in humorous terms of a lively chase a few weeks ago in which the corporal had been unhorsed by the branch of a tree.

Laura's grim conviction that this was indeed Jonah grew increasingly firm with every word he uttered, and finally, when he threw back his hood, all remaining doubt was dispelled.

'We'll take the girl off your hands,' he said with a glance in her direction that carried with it a spark of intense satisfaction.

'I don't think you will,' growled the corporal, his hand moving towards his pistol.

'Well then, you must think again,' said Jonah, drawing his own pistol from within his cloak and discharging it full in the man's chest.

The man's horse reared as its rider toppled, shock still written in his anguished features, falling to earth in a crumpled heap. Then the creature lurched away, dragging Michael with it through a rough hedge and into an adjacent field. It was all over in moments. Before the remaining soldiers could draw their weapons they too were pistoled and had dropped heavily to the ground. Spooked horses reared, whinnied and rolled their eyes until Jonah's companions seized their reins. Jonah cut the cord that secured Laura with a swipe of his sabre and pulled her to him.

'Daughter,' he said with fierce exultation in his voice, 'I had feared never to see you again in this world. How I rejoice in this unlooked-for meeting!'

His voice was heavy with irony. There was no great gentleness in his hands as he pulled away the bindings from her wrists.

'You may be sure I do not share your joy,' she said suspiciously. 'Though you have surely spared me from the gallows.'

'What about this one?' asked one of Jonah's companions, standing over a groaning soldier who had risen to his knees. His sword point was at the man's throat.

'Do you imagine we are in need of prisoners or witnesses?' asked Jonah, without turning his face from Laura's. 'Finish him.'

The man shrugged and thrust his sword into the soldier's throat. With a gasp and a gurgle his victim slumped face down onto the muddy track.

Another dark-cloaked rider emerged through the broken hedge, holding the reins of the horse that had bolted.

'What of their other prisoner?' asked Jonah, regarding the broken cord that trailed behind the jittery mount.

'Gone,' answered the rider with a shrug. 'Should we pursue him?'

Jonah cursed, rising in his saddle to survey the scrubby, broken land beyond the hedge. There were many places that a man might hide.

'No,' he said regretfully. 'There is no time. We should be away before we have the Scarlet Band on our heels. They are a vengeful company, I have heard.'

Chapter Thirteen

By nightfall they had put ten miles of rough Eastings lanes between themselves and the scene of the soldiers' murder. Laura, astride a captured cavalry mare in a manner of which her mother would certainly have disapproved, was subject to a range of conflicting emotions. On the one hand she was relieved to have been removed from the danger of an interrogation that might reveal her identity, but on the other she was anxious for her friends. Perhaps Michael, who had surely made good his escape, would by now have summoned the doctor to treat Thomas. Perhaps that kind farmer would allow him to remain there until his wounds healed sufficiently for him to move on. There were too many uncertainties, not least of which was the motivation of the man who rode at the head of their small column, the man who had once demanded that she call him "Father". What was Jonah doing? Since her liberation he had barely spoken to her, even in the two brief halts they had taken for the horses to drink. She had hardly expected any great show of emotion, given the difficult nature of their relationship, but this apparent indifference left her baffled. She had enquired after her mother and been rebuffed. After a moment to regard her stonily, Jonah had turned his back to her and exchanged a few inconsequential remarks about their location with his comrades. And who were these men that were his companions? Laura had never seen any of them before. One of them was a tall, pale-faced figure with high cheekbones, deep-set eyes and an expression of brooding menace. Laura barely ever heard him speak and then in a low rumble that was barely audible. His name, she deduced from remarks addressed to him, was Mortlake. Another, whose name was evidently Boyle, had a rasping cough and a countenance hideously disfigured by smallpox.

As dusk settled over the flatlands, fog gathered once more across broad drains and leats, the artificial waterways by which the land was preserved from the encroachment of the sea. They approached the outskirts of a larger village, obliging Laura to dismount, releasing her horse into a roadside copse.

'It would not do for you to come riding into town on a cavalry mount carrying the brand of His Majesty's armed forces on its rump,' said Jonah. 'I fancy that might excite suspicion. There is an inn just yonder. You will continue that far on foot.'

The inn was a sizeable one, the Black Lion, standing at the junction where the byway they had travelled met the main Ipswich road. Jonah had decided that they should stay there overnight, arranging for the stabling of the horses, sending two of his comrades down into the village to acquire a fifth mount that Laura might ride on the morrow. Dining upstairs, in the largest of the three rooms they had secured, Laura had the opportunity to learn a little more about her company and in turn to be questioned about her own movements. She formed the opinion that they must be foreign despite the English-sounding names of most of them, since their speech was heavily accented in a manner strange to her ear.

Mr Blood, he who had dispatched the last of Laura's erstwhile captors, carved the joint and then proceeded to eat his meal with an urgency and appetite that did much to explain the generosity of his paunch. Nonetheless, he was clearly an active, lively fellow with a litheness of movement that belied his bulk. Mr Maigret, by contrast, ate only a crust of bread rubbed in olive oil and drank water with a little vinegar. Thinner even than Mortlake, there was a translucent quality to his skin, this stretched taut over cheekbones and knuckles in a manner that drew attention to the faint network of blue veins beneath. None of Jonah's companions had much conversation, and it was an oddly cheerless meal despite the circumstances of her liberation. Laura came to wonder if they were in awe of her, that their reticence stemmed in part from a respect for her quite at variance with their leader's example. There was muted discussion of the route they might take when the new day dawned, but Jonah, when he acknowledged her existence at all, regarded her with a glance that betrayed only the satisfaction of possession. No stranger would have guessed that their relationship – in law – was of parent and child. The others, however, would not meet her eye at all, and when circumstances dictated that they must address her it was with a remarkable deference that puzzled her extremely. After dinner, Blood set himself to cleaning his pistols, and Mortlake, who was evidently very pious, took to reading a well-worn book of religious tracts, this bound with cracked and fraying leather. The other two sat by the fire and spoke with Jonah in low voices that were largely inaudible to her, occasionally looking over to where she sat by the window. Here, she immersed herself in anxious thoughts of Thomas, Michael and Jen, with the occasional interlude in favour of Edward and Sir Joseph. Looking through the gap between the curtains, she could see that a little snow had begun to fall in the road outside, a road quite empty all evening except once for the patrolling watchman and his mate, burly in their thick coats, stamping their feet in the warm glow from the inn's downstairs window, wreathed in the silver of their own breath.

At last, when the distant church clock chimed eleven, Jonah's companions withdrew to their own rooms, and she was left alone with him. She had at once dreaded and welcomed that moment. It was clear that there could be no unconstrained conversation between them so long as they were accompanied, and there was much that needed to be resolved.

'Sit here with me, by the fire,' he said, leaning forward to pat the chair opposite him when the last of Mr Boyle's productive cough faded away along the corridor outside.

'Well?' she asked cautiously, when she was established there, and the heat of the fire was on her cheek.

'Well indeed, daughter,' said Jonah with a nod and a wry smile.

'And am I to consider myself your prisoner?' she asked when he appeared satisfied with this wholly inadequate riposte.

'A very curious notion,' laughed Jonah, reaching for his pipe and tobacco. 'And one quite at odds with my duties as a parent. I had expected no great show of gratitude for sparing you from the attentions of the Scarlet Band, but clearly your immoderate hatred of me sets aside such normal human considerations. You will reflect, I suppose, that my actions today have placed me in the same relationship with the law as yourself. For now, I am a fugitive, too, or will be, should word of my deeds reach the ears of those in lawful authority. As they may well do. Your friend was witness to those events, after all. I suppose he has a tongue in his head that might be made to wag. There are many who would cry "shame" upon you, no doubt. I do not place myself in their ranks. I know your limitations.'

Laura bit her lip and felt a blush suffuse her cheeks. It was hard to contest the truth of his remarks, and the awkward desire to concede an apology rose in her breast.

'And what of my mother?' she asked instead. 'I will not call her your wife, for we both know your status gives the lie to that false union.'

'She is well,' he said. 'Or was when last I saw her, two weeks since. Naturally, she was distraught beyond my powers to describe when you were condemned. And she has been shunned by society, of course.'

Laura nodded and bit her lip. She could well imagine the distressing social consequences of being identified as the mother of a witch.

'And now you must give account of your own doings,' ordered Jonah, pulling at his pipe and throwing away the expended match with an exaggerated flick of his wrist.

The distant clock had struck the half-hour before Laura had completed her story and supplied the many additional details that Jonah demanded. She told the story in its entirety, except in one respect; she omitted from her account the part that Sir Joseph had played in her escape, saying instead that Edward had conveyed her to the Raven's camp. At last, a great weariness crept over her and a feeling of resignation to whatever fate awaited her.

'You found your way to the Raven,' said Jonah at last, when the fire was diminished in the grate and the blackened, shrunken logs glimmered red, reflected in his eyes.

'I did,' she said. 'And he was kind to me and now I am his follower, a rebel of the kind you daily excoriate, committed to the overthrow of the king and all his works.'

'More than that,' said Jonah. 'For I know full well that Corvin would overthrow the Church and empty all the sleep halls, condemning the sacred dead to be consumed in the earth by worm and beetle.'

'As is the fate of the common man, the greater part of humanity,' said Laura, her eyes flashing defiance. 'And had justice prevailed in days gone by you would not sit before me now. You would long be mouldered to the white bone.'

Jonah regarded her thoughtfully for a few moments before replying, puffing contentedly on his pipe.

'I would,' he conceded. 'And perhaps if I were dust you would be on your way to the scaffold once more to take your place amongst the faggots and await the flames that would consume you. But to speak of such notional contingencies is idle, is it not? We are where we are, and we must enact the roles that fate has marked out for us.'

'And what role has fate marked out for you, Jonah?' demanded Laura, with a look of disgust that encompassed the whole of the room.

'I shall tell you,' he said evenly. 'And I shall tell you your own, but first I must disclose to you a little about myself.'

'You are a revenant,' said Laura. 'That much I know.'

'But that is just the beginning,' said Jonah. 'And you must attend closely.'

Setting down his pipe carefully on the hearth, he drew a small book from the bag at his side, opened it at a page marked with a slip of paper and passed it to her.

'What do you see?' he asked.

It was a very old book. Laura's eye settled upon a yellowed page with a copperplate illustration of a king, sword and sceptre in hand, enthroned amongst a crowd of courtiers. Beneath his feet was a stylised map of Britain. Above his head God and His angels were enthroned amongst the seven circles of Heaven. "King Stephen, Rex

Britannicus" read a curling scroll across the top of the page, marred by an ancient stain.

'King Stephen,' said Laura with a frown. 'He that is called the "Wytch King", who reigned three hundred years ago or more.'

'And he that is my father,' said Jonah with a taut smile.

'You sent for me,' said Edward, shown by Mould into Sir Joseph's study.

'I did,' replied Sir Joseph, rising from his desk and reaching for his spectacles. 'I have just received some very grave news from a friend of mine in Rotterdam.'

Sir Joseph had only returned from London the previous afternoon, and much of the furniture in the house remained draped in large dustsheets. His study had been made habitable, however, and a fire blazed in the grate. He indicated a leather upholstered armchair next to this and handed Edward a letter as he settled himself down.

'Tea, if you would be so kind, Mould, and do we have any of those small cakes?'

Mould shook his great head regretfully, combining this with the slightest of bows as he withdrew from the room.

'Pity,' noted Sir Joseph with a sniff. 'Mrs Armstrong, my housekeeper in London, has a talent for these things.'

'This is in Dutch,' said Edward, having peered at the letter for a moment. 'A tongue with which I am shockingly unfamiliar.'

'Oh, yes. Of course, how presumptuous of me,' said Sir Joseph, accepting it from Edward's outstretched hand. 'Then you must accept my assurance that it is from Professor Pieter Van Buuren, whose brother-in-law is the harbour master at Rotterdam. There is a coded section herein, within a paragraph ostensibly devoted to an account of migrating geese in the Rhine estuary. He writes to tell me that His Majesty's intelligencers have been at work in the city and that he believes Corvin's operations there to have been penetrated. Certainly, large sums of money have changed hands in those regions of officialdom known to set a monetary value on their honesty, and only last week the master of the Marigold was fished out of the Scheldt.'

'Dead?' enquired Edward, without much hope of any other outcome.

'Indeed,' said Sir Joseph sadly. 'With a throat cut, and an empty purse. Doubtless it was intended that he should be thought to have fallen victim to some dockside footpad. He was in the melancholy habit of frequenting the less salubrious whorehouses. And Dorffman, his second in command, well, I do not care for him at all.'

'I see,' said Edward carefully, 'and the Marigold was due to visit only yesterday, if memory serves. I remember Thomas Corvin declaring that the first of December was a day that would be fixed in all their memories as the last day of plenty before the festival of St Felix, and that in mid-February.'

'It was?' Sir Joseph's eyebrows twitched upwards. 'Then that makes matters more urgent still. I had not realised.' He folded the letter and placed it carefully in the pocket of his tailcoat. 'And I rather fear that we may be too late to give warning. This letter reached me only two hours since, having followed me up from London.' He patted his pocket.

'But we must certainly try,' said Edward, springing up. 'Good Lord! What if they are betrayed?'

'Quite,' said Sir Joseph. 'I had thought to bid you warn them when next you journey there, but this changes everything. We must get word to them at once.'

'Unless it is already too late,' breathed Edward. The two of them exchanged grim glances.

'Your tea,' announced Mould, coming into the room. The tone in his voice and the absence of any preliminary knock suggested that he had been listening from outside. Certainly, there was no raised eyebrow, no darkening of his countenance when the tray was waved dismissively aside, and coats called for instead.

'Very good, sir,' he said with a nod. 'And will sir be requiring his pistols?'

'Very possibly, Mould,' replied Sir Joseph, taking a spyglass from his desk drawer. 'And I'd be glad if you could look out my fowling piece, too.'

'My relations with my uncle could hardly be worse,' said Edward an hour later as they made their way through the fringes of the fens towards where their boat was hidden, 'and I have not been able to discover where Emily's body has been removed to. It appears that I am marked with suspicion. Certain regions of Darkharrow are denied to me and the other brothers will not say anything of consequence when approached. My connection with Laura is well known and the taint of witchcraft is upon me. I have never felt more miserable.'

'Then certainly you must come to dwell with me now,' said Sir Joseph, ducking to pass beneath the low branch of a stunted hazel, 'and accompany me in my travels, if you would oblige me in that.'

'Why thank you! I should be delighted,' exclaimed Edward with feeling, 'for I feel my usefulness in these parts is ended and it would be a privilege to serve you, a privilege, I say.'

'It is not another servant I require,' said Sir Joseph with a glance over his shoulder to where Mould laboured beneath the various bags and baskets that comprised his master's scientific equipment. 'Although perhaps Mould may beg to differ with me on that score. No, indeed; rather, it is an assistant, an apprentice, if you will, and you have already proved yourself very promising in that regard.'

'Quiet!' came a hiss from Mould at their rear, and all three of them paused to crouch amongst the reeds. A gesture of his large hand indicated the area to the north, where a flock of birds rose raucously above a stand of tall elms. Minutes passed and a lone huntsman with two dogs emerged, heading away from them towards the distant settlement of Harleston.

The boat was where they expected to find it and the hiding place showed no signs of disturbance or discovery. Soon Mould and Edward were taking it in turns to propel the vessel cautiously eastward as the pale winter sun reached its apogee and its light danced on the slow ripples of the waterways.

'And do you miss her very much?' asked Sir Joseph as Mould took his turn and the dripping pole passed between them.

Edward glanced uncertainly at the servant before replying. To be asked to make frank disclosure of the content of his heart was an unfamiliar experience for him. The upper classes, of which Sir Joseph was certainly a representative, tended to regard servants as deaf and mute unless directly addressed. Edward had known all manner of delicate issues to be discussed in their presence, with no consideration given to their unexpressed opinions, their potential amusement or revulsion. Mould's habitually blank expression offered no indication of having heard this enquiry, to which Edward presently replied, 'I presume you refer to Laura.'

'Of course, who else?' said Sir Joseph, collapsing his spyglass, having surveyed the largely featureless horizon for some minutes. 'I have perceived a certain intimacy there and an undeclared affection, at least on your part.'

'Undeclared?' asked Edward, swallowing hard.

'Undeniably, for I suppose you consider your station inferior to hers, whatever the inclinations of your heart.'

'Why should I not suppose it?' asked Edward. 'I was destined for the Camoldolites, who have no truck with marriage, as you know. And were I subject to such feelings, why would I ever venture such a vain disclosure? What could it achieve?'

'Vain indeed, but not a consideration that has invariably deterred star-crossed lovers, not since Cupid placed his first dart.'

'Well, since you ask, yes, I have missed her,' conceded Edward a little peevishly, having beaten down a rising resentment at his companion's presumption.

'Have you? Have you so?' laughed Sir Joseph with an indulgent nod. 'Well, I thought as much. You are no great dissembler, you know, and to see you together requires no great student of human nature to detect that connection.'

'And do you see its reciprocation?' asked Edward, compelled by some inner urge quite at variance with the demands of dignity or self-respect.

'I do not,' admitted Sir Joseph, 'at least not in the same quality or with the same fervour. There is affection, of course, unmistakeably so...'

'But nothing in the romantic line – is that what you're saying?'

'Dear Edward, I don't suppose you need me to interpret the whims of Miss DeLacey's heart,' said Sir Joseph with a smile, 'and the tone of your question admits of no great uncertainty.'

'And now I feel a fool,' said Edward glumly, looking out over the reed beds bleakly.

'Then you should not,' assured his companion. 'For circumstances change, do they not? And I have preserved you from Darkharrow, at least.'

'You have,' agreed Edward, 'and for that...' He raised a hand suddenly and sniffed the air. 'Do you smell smoke?'

'I do,' said Sir Joseph grimly, 'and we are yet some way distant from camp.'

'Look, away there on the left, sir,' interrupted Mould, leaning hard on the pole to bring their small vessel to a halt. 'Beneath that there willow.'

Half-hidden amongst the low brush and the reed stems was a figure, lying prone, face turned from them.

'Bring us ashore,' said Sir Joseph in a low voice.

'He's alive,' said Edward, moments later as the boat was drawn up on the low bank. 'Is it Dan Biggar? I think it is.'

'I don't recall the name,' said Sir Joseph, gently turning the body to examine it, 'although you may be right. Look, here.'

There was a wound in the man's abdomen from which blood leached as they held him. His lips were already blue and a deathly pallor in his brow. It was clear that what little life remained to him ebbed swiftly.

'Dan, can you hear me?' asked Edward, bending close, having exchanged grim glances with Sir Joseph.

'I hear you,' came the faintest of murmurs.

'What happened, Dan?' asked Sir Joseph, feeling for the man's pulse and finding the faintest of flutters.

'We was betrayed... the Marigold... all gone,' muttered the man.

'What about the Raven? Did he make good his escape?'

'Don't know... all gone... soldiers came... bastards.'

The man drew one last breath and then lay still. Sir Joseph placed a hand on his cold neck and then withdrew it with a frown and a shake of the head. Beyond his shoulder, Edward saw movement on the waterway behind them. He gasped. Sir Joseph whipped round, half-crouching, and gestured to Mould for his gun. A boat like their own but occupied by four soldiers was gliding into view. At the same time, some way further along the muddy shore, several geese emerged from the sedge. Standing to his full height, Sir Joseph raised the gun to his shoulder and fired. There was suddenly a great commotion, a flurry of white wings as the geese flapped away. Across the water the soldiers, all alert now, had their own weapons raised.

'Halloo!' cried Sir Joseph to them, waving his arm cheerfully.

'I trust you've a truer aim than I,' he added loudly as their boat approached. 'Is that Corporal Dennison, I spy amongst you?'

"Tis that, Sir Joseph Finch I were tellin' you about,' said the last named to his crewmates. 'Half-cracked in the head they do say, but the biggest brains in the country and a rare hand with a scalpel, too. Cuts up corpses in his dining room just to see how's they're put together. Spleens and livers all over the place.'

"Tis I,' he called presently when the boat lay close at hand. There was no room on the narrow strand to draw their boat ashore, and Dan Biggar's corpse was concealed from them by Sir Joseph's intervening vessel. 'And what might you be doin' in these parts, sir, the place bein' fair a-crawl with rebels an all?'

'Is it? Is it indeed?' Sir Joseph asked, giving a fair impression of being surprised and perplexed. 'How very bold of them. I should have thought your presence here would have discouraged such miscreants. For myself I am in search of the black bittern – a very rare fowl nowadays. You may have heard his call, which is not unlike that of his close cousin the…'

'That's all very well, sir,' said another of the soldiers. 'But this region is out of bounds just now whilst we search the area for fugitives.'

'Fugitives?' Sir Joseph scratched his head and glanced around at Edward and at Mould.

'Yes, sir,' replied the corporal. 'They had a camp just yonder and we took it yesterday afternoon. Killed scores and took scores more. What with time and tide, though, we reckon as many again made off through these here fens. You ain't seen any on 'em?'

'Not a living soul,' said Sir Joseph, his boot an inch or so from dead Dan Biggar's nose.

'You come here lookin' for birds and so did we,' laughed another soldier, pleased with his wit. 'For 'twas the Raven we winkled out of his hiding place.'

'Good Lord, d'ye hear that?' cried Sir Joseph to his companions, giving a passable impression of enthusiasm. 'I give you joy of it, sirs! You have taken him alive; I collect?'

'Not yet, sir,' said the corporal with a disapproving glance at his comrade. 'He's another elusive fowl, if ever there was one. But I daresay we'll catch up with him in the end. There's a couple of companies on the dry side of these fens and they'll be lookin' out, too.'

'Well, I wish you luck in it, corporal,' said Sir Joseph, tipping his hat back on his head. 'And a clear shot and a steady hand, too. Steadier than mine at any rate. The Raven, eh? I daresay there's a bird that'll fetch a good price at market.'

'A good price indeed,' laughed the corporal, nudging his comrade to pick up his oar. 'Well, I'll wish you good day, sir. But my conscience would be clearer if you made your way back west. I have my orders, see.'

'Of course, we'll be on our way presently, just as soon as I've collected a few of these here rather curious molluscs. They have a most intriguing internal structure, you   see...'

'No doubt they do, sir, but I'd be glad if you'd get moving sooner rather than later.'

'Without delay,' Sir Joseph assured him. 'And good luck in your worthy endeavour.'

He waved his hand once more as the soldier's boat withdrew, accompanied by restrained mirth as the corporal made some inaudible but doubtless comical remark about the gentleman's mental status.

'Do we have a map of these parts?' asked Sir Joseph, sotto voce, as the soldiers disappeared from sight.

'Why, Sir Joseph, it is good to see you!' declared Dr Foley, appearing at the foot of the stairs. 'And such a surprise. I had certainly never expected to encounter you in these barbarous regions. A delightful surprise, I might add. I well remember your lecture at the Marine Society two years since, on elasmobranchii as I recall, a most intriguing topic and one that my colleague Dr Warburton was particularly enamoured of. Do please come through. I shall have tea brought directly. Smeaton,' he said to the undersized and elderly servant that had admitted them, 'do bring tea, if you will. And in the best china, mind.'

All the while the equally elderly Dr Foley had been beckoning his guests along the hall and into his study, a large room with walls lined with bookshelves and with a few chairs around a table strewn with books. He indicated these with one hand whilst regarding, with disapproval, the glowing embers in the grate. 'Oh, and I shall have this built up, too, lest we freeze to death. Such sharp weather we've been having, don't you think, although Lord knows I prefer it to the sodden, dripping weeks before that.'

It was the following day, and examination of the best available map of the Eastings had indicated that the village of Meldon was one of three that stood directly west of where Corvin's ruined camp might be supposed to lie. It was entirely possible that any fugitives from that place might have passed this way, and since Sir Joseph was acquainted with one of its more distinguished residents it seemed a likely enough place to begin their search. The doctor kept them engaged with inconsequential chatter, with enquiries after mutual acquaintances, with recollections of Sir Joseph's lectures, until tea was brought, and the fire stoked to a fine blaze once more. Then, when Smeaton had withdrawn, doubtless to entertain Mould in the kitchen, he closed the door firmly, listened attentively for a moment and turned upon them with a conspiratorial air.

'I trust this is not entirely a social call,' he observed.

Edward and Sir Joseph exchanged glances.

'How so?' asked Sir Joseph. 'I'm not sure I take your meaning.'

'I think you do,' said Dr Foley, sitting down and regarding his guests seriously across the corner of the table. 'We have had the military here for the last few days, stamping about in their great boots, lording it over the villagers like the petty tyrants they are, once safely ensconced in a uniform. And these Scarlet Band ruffians are the worst of them. They've taken quite a few prisoners, so I'm told, poor creatures fleeing from the marshes out east. It's said that Corvin was hiding out there and his refuge was betrayed to the authorities.'

'And how would you know this?' asked Sir Joseph, setting down his cup, 'if it is not an impertinence to enquire.'

For a long moment the doctor appeared to look beyond Sir Joseph, fixing his attention on a stuffed bird in a glass case before resolution settled upon him.

'Very well, I shall declare myself,' he said at last. 'I am too old to fear the consequences of a misplaced trust. I have a fellow in bed upstairs brought here in a sorry state by two such fugitives from those soldiers. There, I've said it. You have me at your mercy.'

'You have?' Sir Joseph and Edward were instantly on their feet. 'You have a patient, I mean?' added Sir Joseph.

'Indeed. And his name is Thomas Corvin, if that name means anything to you.'

'It does,' said Sir Joseph emphatically. 'It most definitely does. And I must see him directly, supposing he is capable of rational thought or speech. How fares he?'

Thomas lay amongst clean white sheets with his wounds neatly bound. It was clear that he was very weak, but he raised a hand as Sir Joseph approached and murmured a faint greeting. Michael and Jen were at his side, their countenances filled with relief as the identity of their visitors became apparent.

'There is no corruption in the wounds,' said Dr Foley with satisfaction. 'And given rest he should do very well.'

'But what of Laura?' asked Edward as soon as preliminary expressions of surprise and delight had been exchanged. 'Is she captured… dead?'

At once the atmosphere was altered. Jen approached to place her hand on Edward's arm.

'She is taken,' she said.

Edward and Sir Joseph listened to a halting, disconnected account of their escape across the fens, of their brief sojourn at the farmer's house and of their encounter with the soldiers in the village.

'Smeaton happened to witness the encounter from a window and informed me directly,' said Dr Foley, 'and after a little while Michael here came running back down the road as though all the hounds of Hell were at his heels, hammering on my door, no less, and giving us a very alarming account of events.'

'And you say the soldiers were accosted by five men in the lane outside the village,' mused Sir Joseph. 'Five men who seemed to know them?'

'Yes, sir,' agreed Michael. 'It seemed like they'd been helpin' 'em hunt down rebels hereabouts. But they wanted, Laura, see. As soon as they saw her, they wanted her, and when the soldiers made their objections, they shot 'em down in cold blood, just like that. I reckon they'd have done me, too, if the horse I was tied to hadn't carried me through a hedge. Then the cord broke, and I legged it, hid in a ditch until they'd gone.'

'But you say they appeared to know Laura?' asked Sir Joseph, his head cocked on one side.

'They did, sir. At least one of 'em, anyways. And she him, too – their leader, I mean. She gasped when she saw him and cried out his name. Only quiet, like. She quickly hushed up. Jonah, it were. At least I think…'

'Jonah?!' cried Edward. 'Tall, dark fellow with an ill look?'

'Aye, that'd be 'im, with a murderous glint in his eye, too. Gi'd me the creeps just to look at 'im.'

'Well, at least she is safe, it appears,' said Sir Joseph.

'Safe!' snorted Edward. 'Perhaps she is spared from death, but you well know her opinion of Jonah.'

'And what of the other riders?' asked Sir Joseph, 'and of their direction of travel? Were you able to observe their departure?'

Michael shook his head regretfully.

'Like I say, sir, I was skulkin' in a ditch, up to my neck in water.'

'Well, at least Thomas is spared,' conceded Sir Joseph, looking over to where the invalid offered him a weak smile, 'and there remains some hope that the Raven will likewise have made good his escape. As that soldier mentioned yesterday, he is a most elusive fowl. And you are content for these to remain here until Thomas is ready to move on?' he asked the doctor, who knitted his brows and nodded.

'I am. Any friend of yours, Sir Joseph, may be sure of a warm welcome here.'

'I thank you,' said Sir Joseph, 'but Laura must be our concern now.'

'The girl,' said the doctor. 'It appears that she is with an acquaintance, at least.'

'Of course,' said Edward. 'And for that we must be grateful in some measure. But she is rather more important than you might conceive. Much depends on finding her.'

Chapter Fourteen

'Your father!' Laura looked up from the page.

'Yes, and my name is not Jonah; rather, it is Leo. And before this present incarnation that you see before you, I breathed my last in the autumn of 1497, as did my friends.'

Laura swallowed hard and looked into Jonah's eyes, finding a fierce jubilation there, as though he rejoiced in her dismay. It was an extraordinary claim to make, and yet there was no doubting such blazing sincerity. She wondered, for a moment, if he were mad, but such considerations were rapidly dismissed. Jonah had given no previous indications of irrationality. On the contrary, his actions had always seemed guided by the most calculating of minds. Hers reeled, nevertheless, under the assault of this circumstance.

'The Wytch King,' she murmured, incapable for now of coherent speech.

'He that is called by that name,' agreed Jonah. 'By his enemies, those who prevailed over us at last. Although in truth he was the Priest King. The Priest King, I say, God's servant and the realm's. History, however, goes as spoils to the victor, does it not? And a hundred lickspittle scribblers have poured their venom on his deeds.'

Jonah rose to his feet now, his eyes strangely glazed as he recounted for her the events of the distant years before his death. She had learned of those events in school, and although in truth she was no keen student of history, the broad pattern of events was familiar to her. To hear those events reinterpreted by one who had lived through them was certainly strange to the ear. There had been wars of religion in those days, of course, long and bitter wars that had sundered families as they had sundered the nation, setting brother against brother, father against son. The warring factions each fought to promote their view of man's relationship with his creator and with the state, and both came to be known by names that had once applied to factions amongst the Jews before Christ's coming. The Sadducees argued for the separation of Church and State, for the admittance of ancient philosophies to guide their interpretation of the faith. The Pharisees, by contrast, held to an austere severity in their understanding of God's word, arguing for a distribution of wealth in accordance with principles of equality and humility advanced by Christ himself. In their view monarchy should be absolute, and the king, God's sole representative in the realm, should answer only to his maker. Stephen had been the first and only Pharisee king. His regime died with him in an orgy of cruelty and bloodletting that scoured the realm from end to end in a manner that only hard-held faith could sustain and left a legacy of bitterness that endured in some parts to that day.

'They say that he could kill a man with a single glance,' said Laura when Jonah's account seemed to have run its course.

'And they say that you can do likewise with the touch of your hand.'

Laura shrugged. 'It appears so. And was it true, of your father, I mean?'

'God's righteous anger blazed through his eyes,' said Jonah, 'and struck down sinners where they stood.'

'Or those who simply differed with his views,' noted Laura, remembering some of what she had read in the history books.

'His judgement was God's judgement,' said Jonah firmly.

'And yet he was defeated in the end,' said Laura. 'How so, when he was the chosen vessel of the Lord?'

'I do not presume to know His great design for us.'

'Unless it suits you to,' retorted Laura with a snort.

'And we are but vessels of his grace, bound by love and fear of Him to do our duty as it is revealed to us,' continued Jonah, his eyes narrowed.

It was strange to hear Jonah speak in this manner. He had never previously shown any special piety or religious enthusiasm, had been observed to sleep through some of Reverend Beale's less diverting sermons and had made infrequent reference to the Creator in his everyday speech, unlike many of their acquaintance. Laura's own religious convictions might be described as conventional for her time. She rarely called upon the Almighty for support or guidance except in times of great distress, and for his part, the Almighty seemed content to communicate only through others. She always felt uncomfortable in the presence of those who seemed to have Him forever in their ear or on their tongues.

'So how did your father meet his end?' asked Laura, keen to move the discussion towards matters of more practical relevance. 'I recall that there was some doubt regarding the fate of his body.'

'There was,' agreed Jonah. 'After the battle of Todmorton, in which our enemies were victorious, my father and his paladins were forced to take refuge in a nearby manor house.'

'They ran away,' scoffed Laura. 'They did not make some glorious last stand with God's name on their lips, I collect.'

'My father was unconscious, gravely wounded,' stated Jonah icily, 'and as dusk approached and smoke obscured the battlefield his comrades bore him away to this house,

240

even as our broken army fled the field, pursued by our foes, leaving a trail of hewn corpses halfway to Bristol. The building was searched and set alight, but they did not find my father, who was taken to the attic. The fire was later extinguished by a violent rainstorm that scoured the battlefield from end to end, but not before my father and his companions had perished through the inhalation of smoke. Later, when the victorious army had passed away to visit destruction upon my father's loyal cities, the bodies were discovered by his faithful followers. Naturally, they were hidden away for fear that his enemies would insult them. Already, my uncle's head adorned a spike on London Bridge.'

'So where did they secrete the bodies?' asked Laura. 'I imagine the new king would have been keen to discover them.'

'Indeed, they were,' agreed Jonah. 'And the risk of corruption in the corpses made the hiding of them more urgent still. Fortunately, the weather was uncommonly cold in the next few days as rain turned to snow and ice. The bodies were conveyed into the west where they were entrusted to the care of Camoldolites loyal to our cause. And there they lay, whilst three hundred more winters came and went and twelve generations of mankind lived out their allotted spans.'

'And were there seven of them, perchance?' asked Laura as Jonah leaned his weight upon the mantel, regarding his brooding reflection in the mirror there.

'There were,' he said.

She was reminded of an ancient legend in which seven sleepers lay deep within a green hill in the heart of Britain. It was said that when Britannia's need was direst, they would rise once more and ride to her salvation. But perhaps the legend was founded in ancient truth. Perhaps there was substance to that myth.

'Seven sleepers?' she said.

'Aye, seven,' he said regarding her sidelong, reaching for his pipe once more. 'In the grip of death. But we all know that grip might be relinquished, do we not? And by whom the hour of their reawakening is determined. Fate marks out a path for each of us on Earth, and your fate has long been apparent to me.'

'And what is that fate, Jonah?' asked Laura, obliging him to declare it, although the answer already resonated in her head.

'To wake the seven sleepers.'

'And you have still received no communication from your husband, Mrs Stephenson?' asked Sir Joseph of Laura's mother.

It was cold in Groomfield and many of the rooms were closed. All the servants had been dismissed except for Mary, and it had been she who showed the two visitors into the green drawing room. Here, at least, it was a little warmer, but Mrs Stephenson, showing no signs of having detected this, sat swathed in coats and shawls like an Arctic explorer. She did not rise to greet Edward or Sir Joseph, nor did she show the lively pleasure in their arrival that they had come to expect from her in days gone by. Emily's death might have been endured had Laura remained to her, but now Laura was declared a witch and even this solace was denied to her. The stream of family, friends and acquaintances who once had found their way to Groomfield's welcoming door had long ceased to flow, and now it was only her sisters who came. Even they, although outwardly supportive, laboured to conceal their resentment at the burden that Margaret, through her daughter, had imposed upon their family.

'Not for three weeks or more,' answered Mrs Stephenson with a sniff, 'as you already know, so I wonder that you should ask. As I have told you, he has engaged himself wholeheartedly with the county militia and his duties take him very far afield.'

This was their third visit to Groomfield since they had heard of Laura's falling into Jonah's hands ten days since. On each occasion they had enquired of Jonah, on each occasion been told that he had yet to return. Edward knew through Laura that her mother could never be induced to criticise Jonah and that this description of his activity omitted mention of his unconstrained satisfaction in stringing up miscreants, his consequent neglect of the grieving wife to whom he owed his rank. They had hoped that Jonah would soon return with Laura to Groomfield or at least, if this was judged too dangerous, send word of her wellbeing. It had been a dispiriting ten days, with word neither of Jonah nor of the Raven. Perhaps Mrs Stephenson was keeping something from them. It seemed time to declare their hand.

'I have heard that he is a mainstay of that worthy band,' said Sir Joseph, 'and we have it on good authority that he engaged in those duties no more than a day's ride from here on the second of this month.'

'Indeed,' said Mrs Stephenson suspiciously. 'That sounds entirely likely. I confess myself perplexed that you should mention it.'

'But you have not seen him, have received no communication from him?' asked Edward.

'I have not,' sniffed their host, her face betraying no small irritation now, 'as I have previously assured you.'

Edward glanced hesitantly at Sir Joseph, who made the slightest of assenting nods.

'I only mention it because we believe that he has Laura in his company,' he continued.

'Laura!' Mrs Stephenson's eyebrows twitched upward; her hand flew to her mouth. 'You have word – pray tell me how she fares. I had given up all hope.'

'We know no more than we have disclosed to you,' said Sir Joseph gravely. 'But it seems most strange that your husband would not have shared this intelligence with you by now.'

'Why so?' objected Mrs Stephenson after a moment's thought. 'My daughter is a fugitive, and even to assist her is a crime of the most heinous kind. He must have his own reasons. I do not doubt he wishes only to spare me from the taint of such a crime.'

'Perhaps,' conceded Sir Joseph as their host wiped away tears. 'Pray do not distress yourself.'

'It is vain in you to urge me so, Sir Joseph. Vain and cruel, too. I wish you had not told me this, for I knew not what to hope for, but I do know that my daughter's preservation in this manner can bring no lasting resolution or satisfaction. Surely the agents of the law will catch her in the end, and she will burn for it. How my heart quails at the thought. And now my poor husband will swing, too. How you distress me with your detestable news. I truly urge you to desist from it.'

'Mrs Stephenson,' said Sir Joseph kindly, sitting beside her now and placing a consoling hand on her arm. 'That, if I may venture the opinion, is a counsel of despair. In the first place, let us not acknowledge the scandalous falsehood that your daughter is a witch. Certainly, she is seemingly in possession of some very remarkable powers, but that should not condemn her and there is not a grain of wickedness in her character, as I'm sure you will allow. I'm sure you are the first to deny that she has any truck with the Devil and his works.'

'Of course, she is no witch,' wept Mrs Stephenson, leaning her head on his shoulder now whilst Edward looked on awkwardly and wrung his hat between his fingers, 'but of what avail are my denials or hers? The law has pronounced her guilty and she walks the earth beyond her appointed hour now whilst vengeful death pursues   her.'

'And yet Laura does not give herself up to black despair,' said Edward. 'She has fought back against those who would destroy her. Perhaps you might take courage from her example. She has joined the Raven, who does not perceive in her a monster that must be destroyed; rather, he sees in her the very spark of hope that the bishop sought to extinguish lest it set a conflagration that will consume all their houses.'

'So now she is a rebel, too,' moaned Mrs Stephenson.

'And doubly condemned for it, no doubt, should she fall into the bishop's custody once more,' admitted Sir Joseph, 'but I have contacts in officialdom and they would have surely notified me by now if Jonah or Laura had fallen into the hands of the authorities. Besides, she has but one neck to hang, one skin to burn, so her situation is not materially the worse for it. Now at least she plays a role in a drama that unfolds as we speak and that may yet result in the overthrow of the king and all his creatures.'

'I suppose treason is no great advance on witchcraft,' conceded Mrs Stephenson bleakly. 'And you are conspirators, too, I collect. You are very frank.'

'We are frank with you because we need to understand your husband's motives,' said Sir Joseph. 'And in all likelihood, he finds himself prey to violently colliding impulses. On the one hand, he is known to be fierce in his condemnation of rebels, but on the other, a rebel with whom he is intimately acquainted has fallen into his hands.'

'And his bonds of attachment to Laura are not perhaps quite as strong as might be expected from a parent, albeit a step-father, if what she has disclosed to me is correct,' added Edward haltingly.

'Do you think he would betray her?' demanded Mrs Stephenson, her brow clouded with suspicion. 'Do you presume to make me choose between husband and daughter?'

There was an awkward silence, in which Edward and Sir Joseph pursed their lips and directed their attention respectively at fireplace and shoes.

'Then I reject that choice,' snapped Mrs Stephenson.

'I very much fear that your rejection might be in vain,' said Sir Joseph in a low voice, 'and I rather suspect that your husband has not been entirely honest with you.'

'Honest? What do you mean?' she asked, regarding them suspiciously.

Edward and Sir Joseph exchanged glances once more before the former continued.

'You will be aware that Laura's relationship with your husband was a difficult one...'

Mrs Stephenson nodded cautiously.

'She once told me that she thought he was... is... a revenant.'

'A revenant?!' Mrs Stephenson's eyes sprang wide. 'That is a scandalous accusation. How dare you?! If the sole purpose of your visit here is to make false accusations against my husband and to afflict my poor mind with further anguish, I must ask you to leave this house at once.'

'I am sorry for it, but I think that dissembling is in his nature,' continued Edward grimly. 'And that you have been deceived. At least hear me out, and then we will retire gladly.'

After a moment in which she regarded them stonily, Mrs Stephenson made the smallest of nods. Edward proceeded to tell her what Laura had told him, of her conversation with old Elsie, of her confronting Jonah with her suspicions.

At last Mrs Stephenson waved a hand vaguely. It seemed that all the strength had gone from her, and she slumped in her seat, handkerchief pressed to her nose. It seemed to Edward that she had been brought to recognise a truth that she had denied to herself for many years and that this recognition might be fatal to her self-respect.

'So, what would you have me do?' she asked in a small voice. 'Am I to make this accusation when next I see him?'

'I cannot advise you in that respect,' said Sir Joseph softly. 'But we do feel that we need to know more about him and of his origins, in order that we might find some clue as to where he might have taken your daughter. Perhaps you might answer some questions?'

Mrs Stephenson seemed afflicted by a great lethargy now. She responded to her visitors' enquiries with no obvious reserve or resentment, although some of her responses called her own wisdom and judgement into question. It appeared that she had resigned herself to whatever fate awaited her, and she made no objection when Sir Joseph asked if he might investigate Jonah's study.

'We might chance across some correspondence that could offer some clue as to his present whereabouts,' he explained, accepting the key from her outstretched hand.

Jonah's study served also as the estate office, so there were many papers relating to the administration of that business. But there was also correspondence from some surprising sources, including some from the abbots of monasteries in the north and west of the country. The content of these letters was inconsequential enough, referring to the transfer of breeding stock and of charitable works.

'Look at this,' said Sir Joseph, holding up one such letter. 'Did Jonah strike you as a man given to a particular piety?'

'He did not,' said Edward, looking up from his examination of one of many aged leather-bound ledgers that occupied a broad shelf on one side of the room.

'You would not think so to read these words, couched in a form that implies a particular fervour.'

'Perhaps he desired to conceal it,' suggested Edward. 'It would not be the only thing he sought to conceal.'

As he went to replace it upon the high shelf the heavy volume slipped in his hand, and in the act of recovery the pages fanned suddenly open, so that a number of folded letters fluttered to the floor.

'It would appear that these fall into that category,' said Sir Joseph, gathering up the letters and sorting through them on Jonah's desk. 'And there are no fewer than eight items from the Abbot of Breasham.' He adjusted his spectacles and held one of them up to the light of the window. 'More dull platitudes, more details of seedstock and rent adjustments. One might almost think them some form of cipher. Are you familiar with ciphers, Edward?'

'I know what they are, that it is all.'

'Well, I have some limited acquaintance with them, enough to recognise one when I see it, although I fear my knowledge is too slight even to attempt to decode this one.'

'Why would Jonah be corresponding in code?' asked Edward, his brow furrowed. 'And why would he seek to conceal these particular letters?'

'Interesting questions, certainly,' agreed Sir Joseph. 'And I have a friend in London who may be able to unlock their   secrets.'

'But should we really take them?' asked Edward doubtfully. 'We have already far exceeded the bounds of acquaintance by searching Jonah's office, even with Mrs Stephenson's permission. Are we to venture into outright criminality?'

'Do you wish to see Laura's living face again?' asked Sir Joseph   grimly.
'Of course.'

'Well, your moral qualms, worthy though they are, are a luxury we may not afford ourselves; I think.' He tapped one of the letters, an expression of perplexity and then growing satisfaction spreading across his face. 'What do you know of Breasham Abbey?'

'Breasham? Why, nothing,' admitted Edward. 'I have never heard of it.'

'It lies adjacent to a great dark hill and carved within the depths of that hill is a sleep hall, managed and administered by the Camoldolites of the abbey.'

'I see. And why should that circumstance be of such particular interest?'

'Because, my dear boy, the hill is so shaped as to resemble a great grey whale. When seen across the wide lake that laps its slopes on one side the resemblance is particularly apparent, and for that reason it is known universally as "Whale Hall".'

'I see.' said Edward, mystification clouding his eyes.

'And a revenant who emerged blinking from that place and wished to assume for himself a fresh identity; what might he call himself, do you suppose?'

Edward's stroked his chin pensively. 'Jonah!' he said.

Laura learned much more about Jonah and his companions during the next few days as they made their way westwards, leaving the Eastings far behind. It appeared that Jonah had breathed his last in his first incarnation at the age of fourteen. The youngest son of the dead king, he had been too young to fight in the decisive battle, and so, unlike his elder brothers, he had survived the downfall of his father's kingdom. He had been smuggled away with his mother and sisters into the west that had been the heartland of his father's support. Here, he had led a fugitive existence for a few months before succumbing to death by his own hand, and his body had been committed to a sleep hall, given over to the care of the Camoldolites. What had happened next, the circumstances of Jonah's reawakening and the motivations that inspired him, thereafter, continued to resonate in Laura's mind long after he had shared them with her.

'It is written here in the Book of Romuald,' Jonah had told her, that first night of their re-acquaintance. He had passed her the same book in which she had seen the picture of King Stephen, opened now on a different page. 'St Romuald's work was suppressed by the church soon after my father's death, when those who had supported him were harried and persecuted mercilessly. Many copies of this book were seized and burned in those days. Even today, to be found in possession of one is to incur the suspicion of the established church and state.'

'St Romuald?' Laura had furrowed her brow. 'I confess the name means nothing to me.'

'Of course, it wouldn't,' snarled Jonah. 'His name was stricken from the historical record and from the common knowledge of mankind. Only in the more remote places did his word survive, in a few monasteries on the far western fringes of the realm. St Romuald was a seer, gifted with divine visions of the distant future, and his book was once a standard adjunct to the scriptures. His word has given solace to twelve generations of those remaining Pharisees in the time since my father's death. They have endured the long sorrows of their existence through the hope of his second coming. Read this page, if you will...'

'I cannot,' she said after a moment to peruse the closely printed page, with its spiky Germanic text. 'It appears to be in Latin and my grasp of...'

'Give it to me,' huffed Jonah impatiently, holding it to the light of the oil lamp on the table between them. 'Then shall the fallen lie inviolate and the stars in weeping heavens move in their constant courses and the tide of generations shall lap the shores of His sleep. And the brows of the oppressed shall hold hard fast the seed of the tree. And that great tree shall flower once more unending in the sun of second birth and the land run red with the rivers of His wrath. For the son that slept shall awake at last and the son shall wake the father and the seed of the seed of his seed shall be the summoning of him.' Jonah lowered the book, and his cold eyes regarded her levelly.

'The seed of the seed of his seed, Laura. That is what you are.' After a moment's reflection he continued to read. 'That seed shall be unknowing. Hard by the marsh-girt timber tombs three hundred years shall summon her, daughter of earth's husband, seed of seed of seeds. Life shall breathe in the touch of her, the archer's fair daughter and the crown of victory she shall be.'

'It was no accident that brought me to Groomfield,' said Jonah. 'I awoke from the long sleep thirty years ago, and since that time I have lived with this prophecy. It was these words that brought me to the Eastings, where I had heard that the dead slept within a great wood-built hall. It was the riddle in these words that eventually led me to Groomfield and to the daughter of "earth's husband", born in the three hundredth year since my father's birth. Your mother's maiden name was Strongbow, "archer's fair daughter". When I first set eyes upon your mother, I felt that deliverance stood at hand and the ancient prophecy within sight of fulfilment. She was born three hundred years after my father's birth. I told myself that it must be she that the prophecy foretold, so I made her my wife. It was meant to be.'

There was a smug self-satisfaction in Jonah's tone that made Laura bite her lip lest she utter some untimely reproach.

'But I was wrong,' continued Jonah. 'Of course, I was. You may be sure that I observed your mother with the closest attention for signs that she might fulfil her destiny in the manner that was foretold. And of course I was to be disappointed, even though I set in place all measures that might hasten the fulfilment of that prophecy. She showed no signs of God-given powers, none, and my years passed by in growing bitterness and despair.'

He smiled grimly, eyes clouded with the recollection of those times, and Laura reflected that there was indeed a sourness about the man that spoke of disappointment long endured.

'But then you went into Darkharrow,' he said, turning suddenly upon her, 'and it was like an epiphany for me. I saw, in a vision of blinding clarity, that I had mistaken the mother for the daughter. The "archer's fair daughter" must mean instead a child born under the sign of Sagittarius, the celestial archer, as you are. The last words in the prophecy foretold "the crown of victory she shall be". I assumed, in my folly, that those words spoke only of the victory she should bring me. I was wrong. Your name, Laura, recalls the sacred leaves of laurel with which victors were crowned in ancient times, which the very emperors themselves wore on their brows.'

'But what of the three hundred years foretold?' objected Laura. 'You mentioned that my mother was born three hundred years after your father's birth.'

'But this year marks three hundred years after his death,' explained Jonah. 'And so Romuald's vision is fulfilled. Thirty years I have waited, and now that waiting is done. Do you not feel the tremor beneath your feet as the earth prepares to give up its dead?'

'I do not,' murmured Laura, whose mind reeled before the onslaught of these words.

'Then you should,' chided Jonah, 'because you have the God-given power to awaken the dead and you shall awaken my father as it is written. That is your destiny, written in the stars and in the revelation of St Romuald. Do you see that now, daughter?'

'I am not your daughter,' said Laura, but from force of habit rather than through conviction.

'Perhaps not,' conceded Jonah, 'but my blood and the blood of my father runs in your veins. Consult the genealogies as I have, and you will find that your ancestor fled into the Eastings after Todmorton and made his home there on the lands that you call Groomfield. He was married to my father's daughter, my youngest sister. You are the seed of the seed of his seed.'

'And you genuinely believe this to be true, this prophecy?' asked Laura, although in truth there could hardly be any doubt.

'I do,' said Jonah. 'As my life and death have confirmed. I chose to die, you see, daughter, in order that I may be awakened as the prophecy described. I chose to die, and my four comrades, the bodyguards appointed by my father, chose to accompany me to the long sleep. We took poison and lay down and entrusted the faithful monks to the care of our mortal remains until the day of our awakening.'

'That was surely a leap of faith,' mused Laura, 'for only a tiny proportion of the dead ever awaken, and to awake at the time appointed by the prophecy? Well, that is strange. I had thought your comrades to be foreign,' she added.

'They are as British as you or I,' said Jonah, 'but they speak with the accent of the fifteenth century and are, perhaps, too old to adapt their speech. For myself, when I emerged from my sleep, I was sufficiently young to acquire contemporary patterns of speech from those around me.'

'You do amaze me, Jonah,' admitted Laura.

'If your amazement signals belief, I applaud it,' said Jonah. 'But you may call me Leo, for that is my given name: Leo, son of Stephen.'

'Stephenson – of course,' said Laura. 'But I shall always call you Jonah. It all makes sense now.'

'It should.'

'But what makes you think that I will do your bidding? What makes you think that I will come with you and wake these seven sleepers? What makes you think that they are even susceptible to waking? You know that there are hearts of ice and hearts of stone. What if their hearts are of stone?'

'I know that you will try,' said Jonah grimly. 'If you would look upon your dear sister's living face again.'

Laura felt the blood drain swiftly from her own face and a curious lightness in her head.

'You have Emily?' she asked.

'I do.'

Chapter Fifteen

'Well, I had not expected any great declaration of gratitude,' sniffed Turnbull, setting down the letter. 'But some appreciation of our success in stamping out that nest of vipers might have been appropriate.'

'But Corvin...' began Lord Clarey, stretching himself languorously before the window and looking out over the square beyond.

'Yes, I know. Corvin made good his escape,' snapped Turnbull. 'Do you imagine I am not aware of this?'

'And there are those in high places in London who are asking themselves why the intelligence committee was not privy to this information regarding his whereabouts that you were able to act upon so precipitously. Naturally, I have done my best to present the facts in a favourable light, but you place your friends in a difficult situation. I have made this rather tedious journey to apprise you of these things in person and to place that letter,' he nodded at the folded document on Turnbull's desk, 'in its proper context.'

'What context?' snarled Turnbull, leaning back in his seat, exchanging an irritable glance with Abel Ward, who sat in his own place, observing with the detached amusement to which his master had become accustomed. Were he not so impressively efficient in his duties, Turnbull might have dismissed him long ago.

'Well,' said Clarey patiently. 'His Majesty's words, as written there...'

'Which are undoubtedly those of the Duke of Lauderdale...'

'Which may indeed emanate from that noble Lord...'

A loud harrumph from Turnbull signalled his opinion of the lord in question.

'… are nevertheless a true reflection of his opinions.'

'Or those opinions that have been impressed upon him, when he can spare time enough to listen between whoring, gambling and drinking,' remarked Turnbull, whose state of irritation caused him momentarily to forget the nature of his present company.

There was a brief silence, punctuated by the creak of Ward shifting his weight awkwardly in his chair whilst Turnbull reflected that he might have over-reached himself. A glance in the direction of Danny Blanchflower, who slouched against the fireplace with a half-smoked cigar in his hand, suggested that he thought so, too. A wry smile tugged at the corners of his mouth.

'Oh dear,' said Clarey in a low voice, eyes narrowed. 'I wonder whether you have been spending too long in the company of rebels, whether merely having spent so much time in their company whilst you condemn them to the gallows has resulted in some melancholy contagion.'

'I meant no disloyalty.'

'It would be hard to interpret such intemperate language in any other way,' observed Clarey. 'And I would urge caution upon you, unless your commitment to His Majesty's service be called into question.'

'My commitment is unwearied and enduring,' said Turnbull in more emollient tones. 'As you well know. As everyone knows. And I humbly acknowledge your correction. As we hear in Proverbs: "Better is open rebuke than hidden love. Faithful are the wounds of a friend; profuse are the kisses of an enemy".'

'Indeed,' said Clarey with a slow nod. 'Although I'll thank you not to trouble me with your trite scriptural platitudes. I am not some trembling acolyte to be overawed by such pretension.' He smiled. 'Unless, as Matthew says in Chapter 23, you "outwardly appear righteous to others, but within are full of hypocrisy and lawlessness".'

'Yes,' said Turnbull, who found himself momentarily lost for speech.

'But I wonder if we might speak privately for a moment,' continued Clarey smoothly, indicating the door to Turnbull's adjoining bedroom.

Once in there, Clarey listened for a moment with his ear to the door and then rounded upon the bishop, his voice hushed.

'Really, Turnbull, have you taken leave of your senses? To act and speak in that manner? I consider myself to be your friend and your loyal advocate at court, but I really wonder whether you have been too long in this benighted wilderness. There is a limit to what friendship can endure. I was duty-bound to be seen to admonish you just then, given the circumstances.'

'Of course,' groaned Turnbull miserably. 'I have not been sleeping well. You don't understand...'

'I understand perfectly well that you have mishandled things badly in some respects,' Clarey interjected. 'As your friend I must tell you this and that my own judgment has been called into account for lending my support to your appointment.'

'So, it was you,' Turnbull accused, raising a finger.

'It was not I who proposed it,' said Clarey adamantly with a shake of his head. 'But naturally, I found it expedient to declare my support once it was clear which way the wind was blowing on that committee, and now, bizarrely enough, I find myself censured for it. Such are the wiles of our enemies.'

'And Lamb is now come back, I collect,' said Turnbull, his mind returning to the archbishop as it had been wont to do, all too frequently, in recent days. 'And I daresay Craddock is already fawning upon him. My reputation is in tatters, then. Is that what you have come to tell me?'

'Not at all,' assured Clarey soothingly, placing an elegant hand upon his shoulder. 'You may be sure that I have advised His Majesty that your swift action badly disrupted Corvin's organisation and abruptly curtailed any plots that he might have been concocting. He can hardly focus on undermining the security of His Majesty's realm when his first concern must be his own survival. And besides, I understand that several captives were taken. Doubtless these will furnish us with valuable information in due course. No, Turnbull, your initiative was by no means a complete disaster and I have resisted all attempts to portray it as such.'

'And I thank you for it,' said Turnbull humbly, feeling a warm sense of relief across his brow.

'But you will recall that your mission here was of local significance only, whereas Corvin's insidious movement aspires to incite the whole nation to revolt. As such, there are agencies whose attentions are wholly dedicated to dealing with him and better placed to do so.'

'But I...'

Clarey raised a hand. 'I know your intentions were of the noblest. You sought only to nip out the bud of Corvin's nascent revolt when the opportunity presented itself,' Clarey smiled wryly, 'and burnish your own credentials in the eyes of the court by so doing. But only complete success would have accomplished those aims – and your success was far from complete. You do understand me?'

'Of course.'

'And your performance is also judged according to the situation here in these regions that first occasioned your appointment and dispatch. How do you suppose that performance is judged?'

'I think you will find that security is restored, that the roads are reasonably safe, that the better sort of people find that their property is safe,' said the bishop warily, 'and that there is no imminent risk of a general insurrection.'

'But at what cost?' asked Clarey. 'The streets of London are clogged with those who have fled from this region in fear of their lives. Your own records indicate that the better part of five hundred convicted malefactors have made their way to the gallows in the past few months, and that is without consideration of those who have met their ends by less official means.'

'There have been some irregularities, it is true,' admitted Turnbull. 'But order has been restored, for the most part, as was my remit.'

'And these... irregularities,' Clarey nodded at the closed door behind them. 'Do they arise from Colonel Blanchflower's activities?'

'They do,' conceded Turnbull. 'By and large. His men are sometimes, shall we say, overzealous.'

'Barbarously savage, if what my sources tell me are true,' snorted Clarey.

'Indeed, but not at my direction, I assure you. And his regiment is not here at my request, as you know. They were sent here at His Majesty's pleasure, I believe.'

'His Majesty's intentions are inevitably interpreted by those creatures around him best placed to hear his views,' said Clarey.

'What are you saying?' asked Turnbull, eyes narrowed. 'Are you saying that someone close to His Majesty foresaw that Blanchflower might overstep the mark and sent him here with the express intention of undermining my campaign of pacification?'

'It is not beyond the bounds of possibility. Do you find that Blanchflower responds positively when offered criticism?'

'I do not.'

'Then I shall speak to him myself.'

Turnbull, whose acquaintance with Colonel Danny Blanchflower was already well-developed, observed with satisfaction as Lord Clarey questioned him about his activities. Blanchflower's reaction was entirely in line with his expectations. Clarey's assertion that the civil power held primacy over the military was greeted with a stifled yawn, his warning that the spilling of innocent blood in the pursuit of the guilty could not long go uncontested seemed to leave Blanchflower unmoved, unless the vigorous working of the cigar between his jaws could be interpreted as a sign of regret. All the time, Turnbull was pleased to see the colour rise in Clarey's cheeks and hear the ascending pitch of his voice. The soldier's arrogance and self-confidence knew no obvious bounds. Finally, when Blanchflower blew a long stream of pungent blue smoke into the noble lord's face, Clarey's patience reached its limit.

'I have tried to impress upon you our profound dissatisfaction with your conduct in this region,' Clarey barked. 'Clearly, I have failed, and I am minded to recommend your unit's deployment elsewhere and your own dismissal from its command immediately upon my return to London. Given that I may, with a single stroke of my pen, consign you to oblivion, you may wish to reflect that all your muscular barbarity is mere pretension and that the pen is indeed mightier than the sword!'

There was an awkward moment of silence in which Blanchflower's chewing abruptly ceased and he narrowed his eyes, regarding the noble lord as a snake might regard its prey.

'Not in this room it isn't,' he grunted, approaching within a hand's breadth of Clarey's face and pressing the steel of his sudden-drawn dagger cold against his chin.

In all her sixteen years Laura had never set foot outside the Eastings, so it was a matter of some interest for her to travel westward and northward into the marches of Wales and then onward to the mountains of Cumbria. Whereas the company she travelled with could hardly have been less congenial, the landscape, with its snow-capped mountains, its cloud-reflecting meres beneath great grey crags and its fast-flowing streams, was a source of constant wonder to her. The endless flatlands she had known from birth, the wind-scoured marshes and the long skies of her homeland began to seem a distant dream to her as day by day she was borne away. They were hard, harsh lands that nurtured an iron-hard people, Jonah assured her. Within their hearts they nourished the spark of an ancient hatred, within their minds they held fast the memory of a time when their people had briefly held sway across the land, when King Stephen, those the unbelievers called the Wytch King, raised his standard above London's White Tower. Here the sleep halls nestled in the hearts of mountains, the abbeys of the Camoldolites hard beneath their shoulders, carved from the living rock, the same substance that once had filled the halls where now the dead lay waiting. They waited for Laura, for the touch of her hand and the warmth of her breath on their brows.

Consciousness of the role Jonah had cast for her was never far from the surface of Laura's mind, as the party made its way along roads that became progressively worse as they left the great cities of the plain behind. In time, she would be called upon to wake the seven sleepers of the ancient legend, but first there were others she must summon from their death-bound slumbers – and she had not the means to resist or to refuse. For how would she ever look upon her sister's face again unless she acceded to her captor's demands? And Jonah was surely her captor. His blood, in some infinitesimal proportion, might flow in her veins, but there remained no affection between them, no growth of sympathy or understanding as the days passed by. She was his prisoner, bound only by the ties of necessity but bound nevertheless and nourishing a growing, if futile, resentment.

'And this is she that the prophecy foretold?' asked the Abbot of Roundknott, master of the first sleep hall that they visited.

This place was high on the Cumbrian fells, in a cleft between two looming grey crags, where the bare trees were bent by the sweep of the prevailing winds and a blanket of deep snow softened the hard bones of the land.

'It is she,' grunted Jonah as Laura stood blinking in the abbot's study.

The abbot was very elderly but with a bright eye and a litheness of movement that belied his years. He approached Laura closely and looked into her face as though scrutinising a chart on a wall. For her part, Laura shrank back, repulsed by the stink of his breath and the hairiness of his ears and nostrils. She felt like some prize animal, poked and prodded admiringly at the county fair, but for now apprehension and a sense of resignation to her fate kept rising irritation at bay.

'And you reckon you can raise the dead, girl?' he sniffed skeptically.

'She can,' said Jonah.

'I wasn't addressing you, sir,' said the abbot, without shifting his gaze from Laura's face.

Laura glanced uncertainly at Jonah, who inclined his head.

'I can,' she said. 'At least, I have been told that I have so done.'

'Yes, yes, I read your letter,' said the abbot as Jonah made to explain the circumstances of those resurrections. 'And you claim to be the son of King Stephen?' He turned his myopic gaze upon Jonah now, wiping his nose on the sleeve of his stained black robe. 'Extraordinary claim, don't you think?'

'We live in extraordinary times,' said Jonah patiently, 'as the prophecies foretold. I am Prince Leo, son of Stephen. I come to summon the Congregations and to wake the ancient dead. Laura is the instrument of that awakening. She is the chosen vessel of the Holy Spirit.'

The Congregations were assemblies of the faithful who were otherwise known as Pharisees and who clung to the beliefs of their forebears, the beliefs that King Stephen had briefly brought to prominence. Since his fall their faith had known three hundred years of persecution and suppression. And yet it was not extinguished. Although its possession brought with it the taint of heresy and the risk of arrest, the Book of St Romuald was secreted in many a cottage thatch or chimney nook in the north and west of Britain.

'She does not look like any kind of chosen vessel,' said another cleric, this one a tall man whose head was permanently bowed through dwelling amongst low passages and doorways.

'And you had expected the light of Heaven to shine from her eyes, fool?' snarled Jonah. 'And glowing angels to whirl insubstantially in the air around her? Is your faith so unsophisticated?' He cast his eyes upward in disgust and then glared at the abbot and his companion, who now regarded each other thoughtfully.

'If your faith requires confirmation then I suggest you put it to the test,' said Jonah in more measured tones. 'How many of the dead awoke here last year?'

'I do not see...' began the abbot.

'Just tell me!' snapped Jonah.

'Two,' replied the abbot after a long moment in which Laura wondered whether they might be invited to leave.

'Two,' said Jonah. 'Just two, out of the thousands who doubtless lie within the belly of that mountain? Not all may be awakened – their hearts are as stone within them – but those that may yet be summoned will surely respond to Laura's touch upon their brows. As I have said, she is the vessel of the Lord. The hour foretold by Romuald approaches. Consult your registers and mark out twenty strong and faithful men from along the dark centuries, that Laura might summon them from their slumbers. Then you shall have your proof.'

The abbot and his companion regarded each other doubtfully.

'What have you to lose?' asked Jonah. 'I ask only that my party be housed in the hostel here until the awakening becomes evident to you. Then you will regret your caution. Then you will bow before us and spread the glad word amongst the Congregations.'

Laura found herself once more in the cold darkness of a sleep hall, once more with the brows of the dead beneath her fingertips. On this occasion she was accompanied by

Jonah, the abbot and a party of his monks, their lamplight setting shadows racing across the gaunt faces of the dead in their stone-cut niches. The party watched in reverential silence as she placed her hand upon the cold, dry skin, focused her mind and looked within to determine the nature of their hearts. Of the twenty that she was called upon to summon, twelve were no more than lifeless, chilled flesh, but eight hearts responded, the ice crystals shifting subtly in a manner that she began to recognise as the first sign of reawakening.

'It is done,' she said at last, looking up from the sallow features of a man with a long blue scar across his brow, feeling a strange bone-weariness that caused her a momentary faintness, a sensation of having poured out something of herself.

'And you say there are eight,' said the abbot.

'Eight indeed,' said Jonah, a fierce glint in his eye. 'As she has told you. And now you must wait.'

It was only a week before the first signs of awakening began to manifest themselves, seven days in which Laura was confined to a cold and draughty room in the hostel that stood next to the monastery. Sometimes her mind turned to escape, revolving within it the notion of going to the stables and taking a horse, slipping away unseen during the night. But such notions were no more than dreams. She knew that there was no real hope of escape. At night, pulling the thin blankets more closely around her, she could see Jonah's dark sleeping form on the opposite side of their room, hear Boyle's soft cough in the corridor outside. Others stood guard, too. It was to be assumed that that they each took their turn in her confinement, but it was Boyle whose presence she was most aware of, and his cough came to have a curiously grating effect on her nerves. When she heard it, she clenched her teeth hard together and then lay awake, waiting in tense misery until its next occurrence. And Laura was truly miserable. It might have been supposed that Jonah would have treated the Lord's chosen vessel with respect if not adulation. And yet his attitude to her remained as cold, as wintry as the frost-bound wilderness beyond the monastery walls. His approach suggested that he was able to separate the role from the person that enacted it, to treat her person as no more significant than the jug that poured the beer at their supper time. Nor would he discuss her mother. It appeared that the life they had once shared was forgotten, pushed away to the dark fringes of his mind.

'Why will you not speak of Mama?' she asked him once. 'Am I to assume that you never loved her at all, that you seduced her only to achieve a measure of financial security and to gain access to myself in due course?'

'What I have done was necessary to my purpose,' he told her. 'And that is all. I acted in accordance with the prophecy, but for many years that prophecy seemed to sleep within me. I became the person my role had cast me in, within the lives of your sister and your mother. The years passed by and there were times when the prophecy seemed no more than a distant memory, no more than the half-remembered legend that lingers in these remote places hereabouts. But then fate took you to Darkharrow, and as you kindled fire in those cold hearts, so the prophecy stirred in my mind once more. You were my awakening, too, child, and I shrugged off the clothes of my deception.'

'And did you ever love her? The garment of deception that you called your wife?'

Jonah had regarded her long and hard and then he had turned away, reaching for his book.

'There is no love in me, child, not like that, unless the fiery passion that guides me, that burns eternally in my breast might be so described.'

'But my mother…'

'Hush now! Will you never be told?' he snarled, stamping from the room.

It was the abbot who came to Jonah at breakfast on the seventh day and whispered in his ear. He looked up from his plate and there was a quiet triumph in the eyes that met hers. The abbot now regarded her with wonder.

'It has begun,' he said. 'And surely she is as you described, as the prophecy foretold.'

'They are awakening?' asked Laura, although she knew in her heart that this was so.

'They are,' nodded the abbot. 'And I beg your forgiveness for having doubted you.'

'Then you have it,' grunted Jonah. 'But now you must redeem yourself by doing as I urge. You must send word to the Congregations – but in secret, mind. A letter to the abbots will suffice, to say that we will come to them and to prepare a list of those they would have awakened. Now,' he clicked his fingers imperiously, 'bring me a map of these regions. Our work is only just begun.'

'My work,' corrected Laura. 'I suppose that is what you mean.'

'The Lord's work,' said Jonah with a grim smile.

'I trust you are well enough to ride?' asked Sir Joseph of Thomas Corvin as he entered Comberwood, shaking snow from his boots.

'You do not see a corpse before you,' laughed Thomas. 'And in truth I am much recovered. That good man, Dr Foley, was much grieved by my departure but expressed himself satisfied with my chances of making it at least this far. Besides, I have news for you that will make you glad.'

It was the third week in December and a few modest Christmas trimmings had appeared in the hall at Comberwood, sufficient to indicate that the occupants spared some regard for the season. This was more from a desire to impress visitors with a sense of normality than through any genuine celebration of the approaching festival in a year when the Eastings was a bleaker place than at any time in living memory. Many of the farms and smallholdings stood empty, the larger settlements half-deserted, the blackened rafters of burnt-out buildings stark against skies pregnant with the driving snows that now held fast the fields and fens.

'You have?' asked Edward, helping Thomas to shrug off his heavy coat.

'Most certainly,' replied Thomas. 'And I shall waste no more time in telling you that I have word from my father.'

'Good news indeed!' exclaimed Sir Joseph, taking Thomas's hand and pumping it vigorously. 'And I trust he is well. He is? How wonderful! He is an elusive bird indeed, our Raven. I knew in my heart that he would have made good his escape. Lord knows he is well-practiced in that art. Where does he dwell now, pray?'

'In London,' said Thomas, a glint of pleasure in his eye. 'In the heart of the enemy's camp, where he plots their destruction beneath their very noses. The city is so engorged with refugees from the provinces he can move freely with no great risk of detection.'

'I rejoice to hear it,' said Sir Joseph as Michael and Jen came through the outer door with Mould, bringing with them a sudden icy draught and a flurry of snow. 'But come, you must warm yourselves by the fire and we shall find you a little something that will drive the chill from your bones. Now tell me, how came your father to slip through their net?'

It appeared that the Raven's escape had been not unlike his son's. With two of his councillors, he had hidden in a secret compartment beneath the floor of his house and then, when darkness fell, made his way through the marshes to where a small boat was hidden expressly for that purpose. In this boat the small party had threaded their way along the sea fringe of the fen until their arrival at the small fishing village of Lodney, where they were able to secure passage on a larger vessel that would take them to London. Naturally the bishop's raid had done much to disrupt Corvin's organisation, but he was unharmed and in time that organisation could be rebuilt.

'And what news is there of Miss Laura?' asked Jen at last. 'If you will pardon my asking.'

Despite their evident delight to see their hosts, she and Michael had both seemed afflicted by an awkward consciousness of their rank, sitting ill-at-ease in Sir Joseph's parlour whilst Mould brought them hot drinks.

'Well, that is the curious thing,' said Sir Joseph. 'We have no word of her, although I think I should have heard were she apprehended by those in authority. We can only assume that she remains in the custody of her father.'

'I cannot imagine she rejoices in that circumstance,' said Thomas frowning. 'I had dearly hoped to see her.'

'I know,' agreed Edward with a disapproving glance. 'I'm sure we all do. And some curious information has come to light regarding Mr Stephenson.'

'He is certainly a revenant,' said Sir Joseph, 'and one whose motives are entirely unclear to me. It is not unheard of for revenants to attempt to conceal their status – there are certain legal encumbrances upon them, of course, but I suspect that he is concealing rather more than that.'

'You are a man of science,' observed Thomas, gratefully accepting a cup of steaming chocolate.

'I flatter myself that scientific principles are generally my guiding lights,' agreed Sir Joseph. 'But on this occasion, where evidence is disagreeably hard to come by, more fundamental instincts come to the fore. My late friend and colleague Dr Gator would have said that he "had a feeling in his water". Well, I have such a sensation myself, although by no means localised to the bladder, and that sensation tells me that Jonah Stephenson, whatever his true name might be, is a person of far greater significance than his supposed status would suggest.'

'And he has Laura,' added Edward.

'Indeed, he does,' nodded Sir Joseph. 'And we all know her significance, her potential.'

'Then surely we must track him down,' said Thomas.

'Do we have no clue as to his present whereabouts? None, sir?' asked Jen, with a deferential glance at Sir Joseph.

'None,' answered Sir Joseph, 'but we do have an idea as to his place of origin in this second incarnation, and I suppose that is as good a place as any to begin.'

There was something about the kindling of life in icy hearts that Laura began to find unsettling. After three weeks of travelling from sleep hall to sleep hall in the western regions of the realm the process became no more than routine. On each occasion she was conducted through dark passages to the bodies of the dead that she must attempt to summon from their slumbers, guided by monks or abbots bearing lamps and with lists of those deemed worthy of a second life. The names were carefully chosen. Jonah had soon realised that the task took a toll of Laura, that to attempt more than a dozen or so reawakenings each day left her in a state of enervation that placed her own health in jeopardy. At Comberwood, in Sir Joseph's makeshift laboratory, she had witnessed a spark of what he termed "electricity" flash between two copper spheres: this in one of his many investigations into the properties of materials. When she placed her hand upon the brow of a corpse and her spirit's hand reached down through dead tissues to the icebound heart within, she felt as though a similar phenomenon occurred. It was as though a spark of life passed out of her to re-animate that heart. There were occasions, when she lay in her cold bed at night in some monastery hostel, when she wondered whether those miraculous sparks of life were inexhaustibly renewed within her. The strange inner fatigue that found her stumbling to her bed each night, pushing away the food that was placed before her, admitted of no innocent interpretation. Each new day found her a little less refreshed by sleep and by rest. She began to fear that her life and vitality were being slowly, inexorably drained from her even as the grateful dead blinked in the first light of their new existence, and this fear gradually solidified into a terrible certainty. The cost of new life for others was the slow leaching of her own. Her captors saw it, too.

'She's had enough. Can't you tell?' she heard Boyle say to Jonah in the adjoining room, one night as she lay half-asleep.

'One more day, at Speeth Abbey tomorrow, and then she can rest a few days,' conceded Jonah.

'You know what ails her, do you not?' asked Mortlake, who rarely spoke and whose voice, when heard at all, reminded Laura of the dull creaking of doors in Darkharrow.

'Aye, I know it,' conceded Jonah with a sigh. 'But it must be done. You know it must. She is the chosen vessel.'

'And a vessel that may soon be emptied out,' said Blood dryly.

The draughty hostels in which they stayed were rarely furnished in a manner that might delight a maiden's heart, and the Camoldolites took a particularly dim view of vanity, so it was some weeks before Laura was able to catch sight of her reflection in a mirror. When she did, in the hall outside an abbot's office, a sensation of cold bewilderment afflicted her. The face that looked back at her was robbed of the clarity of complexion that once had been there. Her skin was dulled, puffy around the eyes, drawn taut over cheekbones and sunken beneath. She placed her hand to her cheek, feeling a disagreeable roughness at her fingertips where once there had been only smooth softness. Jen's dark dye was long ago washed from her hair, but the glint of her golden tresses was dimmed now. She lifted a lank lock with one finger and frowned.

'I am aged,' she murmured, 'and yet I am but sixteen.'

'You will revive,' grunted Jonah with no great conviction, taking her not too gently by the arm, 'but first you must set vanity aside and let Abbot Earnshaw have sight of you.'

Chapter Sixteen

Breasham Abbey was four days' journey from the Eastings, in the Somerset levels, beneath the great isolated hill that gave Whale Hall its name. Once, long ago, when the levels had been an extension of the sea, that hill had been an island, but now the marshes and lakes that surrounded it were not unlike those of the Eastings, likewise locked in the icy grip of winter. The party had celebrated a meagre Christmas in a roadside inn a few days previously, but now, as dusk settled over the ice-rimmed mere, they stood in the abbey stable yard whilst a groom tended to their mounts. Michael and Jen had remained at Comberwood, so it was only Sir Joseph, Edward, Thomas Corvin and Mould who waited upon the abbot of that place, stamping their feet and blowing upon cold hands. Thomas was still heavily bandaged, but his wounds were healing well. Sir Joseph had forbidden him to ride with them, but such injunctions meant nothing to Thomas, and he had accompanied them anyway.

'Besides,' he said, when Edward objected, 'if I remain skulking here at Comberwood I shall be denied the care of one of the finest physicians in the realm. I am quite well enough to ride, I do assure you. The wholesome activity, the vigorous action of the blood, will doubtless work favourably upon the healing process.'

'I wish I shared your conviction,' sniffed Sir Joseph, but there was a glint in the young man's eye that spoke of a fervour that might not be opposed.

Edward glanced at Thomas now as he stretched himself cautiously and yawned. He knew well-enough the passion that inspired his companion's commitment to their quest – knew it with a deep-seated devotion of his own that he seemed to have known all his life. Laura was their common pre-occupation; the guiding light that at once united and divided them. Edward had soon enough come to realise that Thomas loved Laura, that the glint in his eyes when he spoke of her betokened of no other explanation. And with that realisation had come another awakening as he regarded the complex strands of his inner mind and recognised therein a love of his own. Here was no sudden fiery leap of passion akin to that kindled in Thomas's heart but instead a slow accumulation of affection, year by year, which only now coalesced into a form that demanded to be known as love. It was as though Thomas's transparent devotion to her provoked his own in jealous reaction. Such alien sensations worked strangely within his breast, and it was all he could do to speak, to think with any convincing semblance of the rational creature he had once considered himself to be.

'Do you think they will keep us standing here all night?' asked Thomas, catching Edward's pondering eye.

'I know not,' Edward began to say, but at that moment the door creaked open before them and an elderly monk stood framed within it, a warm, yellow glow behind him.

'Visitors,' he observed. 'Unseasonal ones, I should say,' he added, glancing around them at the falling snow. 'But I suppose you know your business, and ours is to offer what hospitality we may. Do step this way.'

Sir Joseph made introductions and it became apparent that their host was the prior of this place, temporarily in charge whilst the abbot was away conducting business in the north. He seemed a cheerful soul, holding forth with a stream of anecdotes and observations, cursing the weather, bemoaning his arthritic back whilst they shrugged off coats and bags in a chamber to the side of the entrance hall.

'Doubtless we shall find you a room or two in the hostel wing,' he said, having issued a few muttered instructions to a monk of less advanced years, 'but for now I imagine you would wish to eat. Perhaps you would care to join me in my chambers. The brothers are about to be summoned to their communal supper, and unless you prefer to sit in silence with them whilst the scriptures are read aloud...'

'I'm sure that would be delightful,' declared Sir Joseph, adding, 'your chambers, I should say. We should be loath to distract the community from their worthy contemplations.'

'Of course, of course,' beamed the prior, whose name, it appeared, was Hardiman. 'I shall ask the vintner to set out a little wine, too. It is not often we receive visitors in this season.'

'And what inspires this visitation?' asked their host, when they were seated at the table in his chambers and food was being placed before them. 'From the look of you I don't suppose you are in want of charity, and it seems unlikely that you would wish to buy or sell anything in this inclement season. I imagine you are in search of the legend, then, like so many others who come this way. Would that be it?'

'The legend?' Sir Joseph raised an eyebrow. 'I'm afraid...'

'The seven sleepers,' offered Hardiman helpfully. 'I take it that you are not, then,' he added, the lively enthusiasm in his face diminishing somewhat as he perceived the blankness of the expressions around him.

'I confess, I was unaware of that legend,' admitted Sir Joseph, brow furrowed. 'But then, now I come to think of it, perhaps I do recall mention of it in some childhood story.'

'Indeed,' said the prior, enthusiasm rekindled, beaming

about him benevolently. 'A childhood story, yes. The green hill in the heart of England wherein lie the seven sleepers who will…'

'… ride out to the nation's salvation in her darkest hour,' supplied Edward, his eyes shining. 'I have heard of it, although I had not heard it connected with any particular place.'

'Well, there are various candidates for that honour,' said Hardiman. 'But Breasham, although strictly some way from the geographical heart of the realm, seems to attract more than its fair share of visitors, at least in the summer months.'

'That is doubtless a fascinating story, but we came in search of something a little more substantial than legends,' said Sir Joseph a little later, cutting himself some cheese. 'There is a person of great interest to us, a revenant, a fellow we think may have emerged from here some years past. He calls himself "Jonah Stephenson". That may not be his true name, of course. We would be most interested to know if he was indeed an incumbent of this place and to be acquainted with any other information relating to him you might care to supply.'

'Hmm, Jonah,' mused Hardiman. 'A pun on the name Whale Hall, I suppose. He would not be the first to adopt that name, I'm afraid. And may I enquire as to the reason for your interest? We do not usually disclose such details to the casual enquirer, you will understand.'

'Of course,' nodded Sir Joseph. 'I perfectly understand that you have a duty of confidentiality to the risen and the dead. However, I beg that you will waive such considerations if I tell you that this person is guilty of a crime, that they have abducted a young woman of our acquaintance.'

'I see,' said the prior, taking a thoughtful sip from his wine, 'and would this be an official enquiry, then? Do you represent the sheriff?'

'The abduction took place in the Eastings, beyond your sheriff's jurisdiction,' said Sir Joseph with a glance at Edward, 'but I wonder that your hall is not even more widely celebrated, if what you say of the legend is true. Pray, what causes those with an interest in such things to connect Breasham with that tale?'

'Ah, well, there are a number of telling clues for those with the wit to discern them,' replied the prior, setting down his napkin and rising to his feet, 'and I have gathered together various sources over the years.'

He crossed to one of the bookshelves with which one side of the room was provided and, after momentary scrutiny, selected a book which he proceeded to blow upon and to open at a page marked with a piece of ribbon.

'There is Cordingly, of course,' he said, reaching for his spectacles from a pocket in his habit. 'One of the earliest but still the best-regarded sources. This is what he wrote in his Britannia.'

He read a lengthy passage in a loud, clear voice, pausing from time to time to regard them quizzically, receiving in return many nods, smiles and expressions of encouragement.

'A fascinating tale,' said Sir Joseph when the prior set down his book, 'and I agree that the geographical references could perhaps be interpreted to refer to this place. But what of the sleepers themselves – your source is frustratingly vague, is he not?'

'He is,' agreed the prior. 'And there we find no general agreement at all. But Mitchell has some interesting suggestions to make,' he noted, crossing to the bookshelf once more, replacing his spectacles on his nose and then turning to them, eyebrow raised. 'I trust I do not try your patience...'

'Not at all!' said Sir Joseph, whilst Thomas cast his eyes upward in private despair. 'Nothing could be more congenial to us. A legend is an object of fascination to the vast bulk of humanity.'

'It is certainly one that has fascinated me,' laughed the prior, drawing out another book, 'and the late Abbot Cole was a particular expert in the field – stimulated my own abiding interest in due course, indeed, God rest his soul.'

It appeared that the late abbot had died some years previously in a fire and that his replacement had proved less congenial to the prior. The prior was somewhat guarded on this point but disclosed enough by way of facial expression and tone of voice to suggest that their relationship was not marked by any amity.

'And where is the abbot today, if I may be so bold as to enquire?' asked Sir Joseph, looking up from the remains of an excellent apple pie.

'Why, he's gone to a meeting at Willenshaw, two days' ride from here,' replied the prior, 'and I don't suppose we shall see him returned before Wednesday.'

The glint in his eye told of a degree of inward satisfaction at this circumstance.

'Your accent would seem to mark you as an immigrant to these parts,' observed Sir Joseph. 'I do not detect that distinctive western burr in your intonation.'

'You are in the right of it,' laughed Hardiman. 'I am indeed a stranger here after twenty years and more. Even after so many summers and winters have passed us by my fellows scarcely clasp me to their collective bosom in perfect acceptance. They are a strange set, these westerners, close, secretive, mired in ancient heresies they can scarce be prevailed upon to admit or discuss.'

'I suppose it is only natural that each region should have its eccentricities,' said Edward.

'I suppose,' conceded the prior with no great conviction. 'In the late queen's time it was briefly decreed that more senior personnel in the order should be rotated throughout the nation to combat regional particularism. Not that it amounted to anything in the end, of course. I don't imagine anything of lasting value was achieved. Fortunately, I have my great-nephew Mark to console me when I feel a foreigner amid an alien nation. He has journeyed out here from my hometown of Guildford to join us as a novice, and he now studies under my tutelage.'

'I am myself a novice in the order,' volunteered Edward, 'although I am presently engaged in a sabbatical before taking my final vows.'

'You are?!' cried the prior delightedly. 'Then you should have said so at once. I shall summon Mark directly. Doubtless you and he will have much to discuss, and I do not doubt he would delight in the diversion from his studies.'

A tall, gangling youth with a shock of dark hair and the soft beginnings of a beard, Mark quickly overcame his shyness and conducted his guest in a tour of the abbey and of the sleep hall that lay adjacent to it, within the belly of the great hill.

'There are four levels,' explained Mark as they progressed by flickering lamplight along one of the lower passages, 'but the infirmary is on the upper level, which I believe is uncommon in these parts, although that placement is quite general further to the east.'

The infirmary was the chamber in which those for whom the grip of death was loosening were cared for during the awakening process. Edward was aware of the general principles involved, although he had never actually been present on such an occasion. Typically, the process took between thirteen and sixteen days from the first stirrings of renewed life to the complete awakening. During this period there was a complex and demanding sequence of religious and practical interventions into which Edward was only partly initiated.

'We have not needed the infirmary yet this year,' said Mark, showing Edward through into the oil room that was a vital institution in any sleep hall, 'and we only had a single awakening last year, a lady who promptly went out and hanged herself again, can you believe. Such ingratitude!'

'I suppose those for whom life is a burden might resent its re-imposition,' suggested Edward, looking around at the various bottles and jars with which the room was crowded. The rituals of the Camoldolites required that the dead should be regularly anointed with such commodities.

'Indeed, but it does seem a mite ungrateful,' continued Mark. 'This is where the fire began, five years ago now, and consumed poor Abbot Cole.'

'How curious,' observed Edward, picking up an empty unguent jar and regarding its label thoughtfully. 'There was also a fire in Darkharrow five years since.'

'Really? Well, it is not uncommon, I suppose, that fires should break out when so many flammable materials are stored together. They say the fire could be seen thirty miles away and half the neighbourhood were engaged in moving bodies to a temporary refuge in case the flames should penetrate the halls and consume the dead where they lay.'

'It was a similar situation at Darkharrow,' observed Edward 'I was only a boy at the time, but I well recall the coming and going as the dead were taken into the cool crypts of churches and other such places. Was the abbot the only victim of the flames?'

'He was. A very learned man whose demise was much regretted. They say he knew more about the legend of the seven than any man alive. My great uncle, who was his disciple in these matters, maintains that he had made a vital discovery, was about to disclose it to him when death overtook him.'

'How unfortunate,' said Edward. 'And how did the fire begin?'

'It appears that the abbot, whose duties required that he should check the oil room every day, knocked over a lamp and the flames quickly spread to a jar of spice that had been left uncovered.'

'And he was on his own at this time?' asked Edward as they re-emerged into the corridor and Mark locked the door behind them.

'He was,' answered Mark. 'I suppose he was quickly overcome by the fumes and by the time the alarm was raised this wing was well ablaze. It caused quite a sensation in the locality, as you may imagine.'

When they returned to the prior's chambers some hours later, it was to find Sir Joseph and his host poring over various books that were strewn across a table. It appeared that they had discovered a common interest in etymology and were studying local place names that betrayed an origin in Roman times. Thomas and Mould, whose interest in these matters was strictly limited and whose ability to dissemble had expired some hours ago, sat by the fire and took refuge in the sweet mead for which the abbey was locally famous.

'Why, Edward!' cried Sir Joseph as the two young men came in. 'I never thought to be entertained here by a man of such broad learning. To be sure the abbeys are known to be repositories of ancient wisdom, but you will be delighted to hear that our host is a noted botanist as well as an antiquarian.'

'Really? You do amaze me,' supplied Edward obligingly. 'And Mark here has acquainted me with the very remarkable arrangement for the accommodation of the dead in this place; on no fewer than four levels, would you believe, which places it in the first rank of such establishments in the west. Is that not the case, Mark?'

'Yes, it most certainly is,' said Mark as the two approached the table to take small honey cakes from the tray that had been laid there. 'But is that Merrill's Geographica Brittanorum I spy?'

The evening was well advanced by the time Sir Joseph and the prior had completed their survey of the adjacent regions, having made note of those fragmentary ruins deemed worthy of further investigation. At last, the prior set down his spectacles and tapped the spine of one of his books.

'Stephenson's Western Itineraries,' he said. 'Of little use to us tonight, I fear, but the name calls to mind the issue you raised with me earlier.'

'How so?' asked Sir Joseph, pretending interest in a faded print.

'The name calls to mind another Stephenson we once had here. Lived in the village. He was a revenant from this place but always stayed hereabouts, as many do. Leo Stephenson was his name, as I recall. He lived with some friends of his up by the millpond end. Dark, brooding kind of fellow but with an abiding interest in the abbey, it would appear, and a close confidant of Abbot Cole.

Certainly, he was always here to assist at the various events of the calendar, although I never took to the man myself. He moved away some six years ago, I suppose, a year or so before the fire.'

'I see,' said Sir Joseph in measured tones that laboured to conceal a rising interest. Edward, who was studying a wall map with Mark, also glanced across. 'And do you suppose we might discover the date of his awakening? This man, if he is indeed the same man, moved from one side of the nation to the other, establishing himself in the vicinity of Darkharrow, concealing his status as a revenant and marrying into the local gentry in defiance of all law and custom.'

'Darkharrow? I have heard of it. A most remarkable place by all accounts. Well, it would be irregular, of course,' said the prior with a smile, 'but I may feel minded to consult the archives tomorrow morning, now that you have stimulated my own curiosity.'

'It appears she was abducted by her own stepfather,' said Sir Joseph to Matthew Corvin, a week or so later when the pair met in London, 'although we have been unable to discover his present whereabouts.'

'I am sorry to hear it,' said Corvin, nodding gravely. 'Her proposal was an alluring one, fantastic though it seemed.'

'But we have found out sufficient information to mark this Jonah as a person of particular interest. It appears he is a revenant, one who emerged from Breasham Abbey, the place that they call "Whale Hall", some thirty years ago. We made extensive enquiries in the vicinity and were able to speak to several of his acquaintances. It appears that he kept very much to himself and to the society of a close group of friends. No one we spoke to was able to shed much light on the content of his character, although it is fair to say we came upon no one who spoke of him with warmth. He lived amongst them for a quarter of a century, having reawakened as a mere youth, and yet none could speak with confidence of his origins.'

'His origins?' asked Corvin. 'The time and manner of his first death, I suppose you mean.'

'You have it,' agreed Sir Joseph. 'I understand it is customary for such details to be recorded next to the body of the deceased, but no one could tell us these things. It appears that he maintained close links with the abbey throughout his time in that region but then departed abruptly rather more than five years ago.'

'Therefore, you have as yet discovered nothing that brings you any closer to locating Laura?'

'Well, quite,' conceded Sir Joseph, 'although I suspect the answer is connected with Breasham and there is more that may be discovered there, if only the right questions are to be asked.'

Corvin sniffed and pulled his coat more closely around him. The two men sat in an upstairs room of a public house in the docklands area of London. A small fire burned in the grate before them but did little to drive the chill from the damp air. Corvin was wreathed in his own breath as he reached for the poker and stirred the dull coals into a rosier glow.

'And there will be war, they say, when spring comes,' he observed. 'The king will stand for no more of the Spanish and their piratical ways. If the spice trade cannot be made secure the whole of Europe will be at daggers drawn once more.'

Sir Joseph nodded. 'The dons are resentful of the last treaty, forced upon them when their king was an imbecile and that plague in Iberia reduced their armies to mere shadows of their former selves,' he noted.

'Whereas, for his part, our noble monarch hopes to establish a martial reputation and re-gild his nation's military laurels,' observed Corvin ironically. 'His reputation is certainly in need of some form of rehabilitation, with half the nation on the verge of starvation. There have been riots in the northern cities, you know?'

'I have heard,' nodded Sir Joseph. 'I trust I may detect your hand in this matter.'

'You may certainly detect my approval,' said Corvin, 'as such expressions of popular discontent are distant rumbles of the rising storm that gathers in the realm, but as to my direct intervention, well there are many who claim to speak with my voice. At present the swell of rebellion somewhat outstrips the scale of my organisation.'

'And does His Majesty imagine that dispatching the better part of his army overseas at this time will contribute to the peace of the realm?' mused Sir Joseph.

'Perhaps he is ill-advised,' suggested Corvin with a wry smile.

'Perhaps he is,' agreed Sir Joseph. 'I daresay his enemies will seek to take advantage of the situation.'

'Of whom I count myself amongst the most implacable,' said Corvin. 'And I shall take what advantage I may, although it would be surprising if he didn't leave a body of troops sufficient to put down any uprising that he might predict.'

'That he might *predict*,' repeated Sir Joseph. 'Then I suppose you must endeavour to surpass his prediction.'

'Indeed. You are ready to assist me in preparing this, I collect?'

'With all my heart, and yet in truth I find myself distracted.'

'Distracted?' Corvin asked, furrowing his brow.

'As you know, I am first and foremost a natural philosopher. My guiding principles are reason and the dictates of intellect in the face of the evidence presented to them.'

'And yet?'

'And yet I seem strangely incapable of ignoring the urgings of my inner mind,' said Sir Joseph, stirring uneasily in his seat, 'those regions least accessible to reason, those regions we might assign to the location of the more primitive instincts, the more primal passions. Those urgings impress me with a powerful sense of certainty that our friend Laura is a person of the foremost importance and that the finding of her should likewise be amongst our foremost considerations.'

'So, you, Sir Joseph Finch, one of the leading intellectual lights of the nation, advocates that we should proceed according to a... hunch?' laughed Corvin. 'I never thought I should live to witness such a thing.'

'Certainly, I do not propose that you should direct any proportion of your resources to such a thing,' said Sir Joseph, whose discomfiture rose with a flush into his cheeks. 'I do, however, propose to concentrate my own attention on this issue, and I know that your son would wish to make his own contribution, should you permit it.'

'He loves her, then?' observed Corvin wryly. 'A young man's first and most heartfelt affliction, I suppose. I could see the way that wind was blowing even before the assault on our camp.'

'I think he does,' agreed Sir Joseph, 'although I would not claim any special authority in that field. I believe that my young friend Edward loves her, too. At present, in her absence, they seem quite capable of setting aside any rivalry, of working in perfect amity. How matters might transpire were we to succeed in bringing about her liberation is another issue entirely, of course.'

'Of course,' agreed Corvin. 'I trust they would not quarrel, would compose their differences like civilised men.'

Sir Joseph snorted with amusement. 'You think? I have seen enough of the mark of Eros on young men's passions to discount no contingency whatsoever. I suppose Edward is not the fighting sort, however. Any trial of arms between him and your son could necessarily conclude in only one outcome.'

'There are more ways than one to vanquish a rival in love,' observed Corvin.

'There most certainly are,' agreed Sir Joseph, 'and Edward must need have more recourse to wit than to arms, I suppose.'

'And I suppose the girl in question may have a say in this?' ventured Corvin. 'It appears we are dangerously neglectful of her own desires in this respect.'

'You are in the right of it,' nodded Sir Joseph, 'and the girl in question is no more than a notional concept at present, unless our enquiries shed any further light on her whereabouts.'

The girl in question, even as this conversation took place in distant London, looked out bleakly on the crowded streets of Tewkesbury. Most of the sleep halls she had thus far visited had been in rural settings or on the outskirts of larger settlements, but Tewkesbury's stood in the centre of the town. A considerable crowd had gathered to greet the arrival of her party, some motivated by religious zeal, others by mere idle curiosity or the desire to confront those who held views contrary to their own. Tewkesbury stood on the fringes of those regions which clung to the ancient faith, and sectarian differences had caused its inhabitants to hate each other with a lively enthusiasm in times past. Nowadays, such differences slumbered under the mantle of tolerant apathy that marked the nation's embrace of its faith, but a renascent passion for such issues seemed likely to imperil that social calm.

'How far to the abbey?' asked Jonah, twitching the curtain aside to look out of their carriage window.

"Couple o' streets,' grunted Blood, looking over his shoulder. 'But at this pace we'll be lucky to make it by nightfall.'

Laura regarded the sea of heads and faces beyond the glass with apprehension. Her companions had found it necessary to raise their voices above the hubbub in the narrow street around them. In front rode Mortlake and Boyle. Behind rode Maigret at the head of a column of the awakened dead that numbered rather more than a hundred. Each of them wore a white shirt and a strip of red cloth tied around their brows in celebration of the blood that flowed once more in their veins. Jonah had argued passionately against this accompanying procession but argued in vain. The abbots of the west in council had made their support conditional upon the measure, and Jonah had reluctantly been obliged to concede to it. Those whose Laura's touch had awakened were a heterodox band by any measure, but a proportion of them had insisted on following her and the man they were told was King Stephen's son. Many of them had lived and died in that king's time, and many of them marched again beneath the banner of his house, which had long lost the capacity to inspire the loyalty or hatred that once it had, hanging fading in the rafters of many a church or abbey. Now, stitched from newly bright fabric, the iron-collared black eagle on a field of gold made a curious spectacle for onlookers as it fluttered above the strange cavalcade that made its way through Tewkesbury.

'I told them this would never do,' said Jonah, shaking his head grimly. 'In the rural areas, perhaps, but in towns such as this? We are not ready to foment a general uprising – not yet. This will certainly attract unwanted attention.'

'And yet there is nothing demonstrably illegal in our demonstration,' noted Blood. 'We do not call for the overthrow of king and state, do we? It is long since the display of your father's banner was considered a treasonable act, after all.'

'True enough,' conceded Jonah, 'but this ostentatious display of enthusiasm can only attract the official eye upon us. And we are not yet ready. There are yet a dozen halls we must visit before our ranks may be considered complete. And then, of course,' he said with a glance in Laura's direction, 'my father must be summoned.'

Chapter Seventeen

Word had spread like ripples across a pond, with a speed that seemed entirely independent of the limitations of human travel. Already, as Laura prepared to undertake her second programme of awakenings, news of her extraordinary powers had spread throughout the western abbeys and through the surrounding lands. Already she was being treated with a respect that bordered upon veneration by all except he who was the chief of her captors. Those present with her now regarded each other with disquiet as a party of mounted constables pushed through the press, led by a severe middle-aged man with the staff of office that marked him as the chief magistrate of the town. With a clatter of steel on cobbles and the creak of leather the carriage jolted to a halt.

'Good day to you, sirs,' began the magistrate, leaning down from his mount once the window had been let down. 'I would be glad if you would state your names and your business in this town.'

'And a good day to you, sir,' said Jonah, with what vestigial bow could be accomplished within the confines of the carriage. 'My name is Jonah Stephenson, and these are my companions, Richard Blood and my daughter Laura. We are simply journeying to yonder abbey,' he said with a nod to the distant towers of the west end, visible beyond the rooftops. 'Our business is entirely lawful; I do assure you.'

'And these others?' asked the magistrate with a jerk of the head towards the crowd of white-clad revenants who shuffled behind.

'They have chosen to accompany us of their own free will,' answered Jonah. 'They have no official connection with my party.'

This answer did not satisfy the magistrate, and indeed a measure of jostling and shouting in the crowd suggested that others shared his concern. A conversation began in which Jonah was required to describe his intentions in more detail. During this time, Laura had opportunity to reflect upon her circumstances. She had passed much of the day's journey in the state of semi-stupor that had characterised her mental condition for the greater part of the previous week. She barely answered when addressed, and her voice, when raised above a whisper, could utter no more than a few words of assent or acknowledgment. She continued to perform her duties, as required, in the halls of the slumbering dead, but a state of exhaustion had settled upon her that suppressed her spirit to a remarkable degree. The world around her seemed robbed of colour and of meaning. Amidst the chill of winter and the grimness of her circumstances she had withdrawn to a place within herself, warmed by golden recollections of times past, her spirit sustained by thoughts of her friends, of Emily, of Edward and of Thomas. Now, the small part of her that remained alert to her material situation tugged at the edge of her consciousness and slowly she responded, regarding with wonder the sea of faces beyond her carriage window. Their voices, a low hum, seemed measurably more distant than the familiar voices of Jonah and of Blood. The focus of her mind sharpened to distinguish the meaning of their words, the significance of their context. She stiffened, completely alert now, and cast her eye first to the figures in conversation on the far side of the space in which she sat and then to the handle of the door next to her. She reached for it, depressed the lever and the door sprang open. Within a moment she was gone, stepping quickly down into the midst of the crowd. Faces turned to her as she squeezed through the press. In some eyes, those more alert, recognition dawned.

''Tis the holy woman!' went up the cry. 'She who has raised the dead.'

'Witch, more like!' accused another, a sentiment echoed elsewhere amongst the press, and suddenly there was a great deal of pushing and shouting as some sought to protect her, some to seize her. With a rising tide of panic in her breast and hot tears in her eyes she made her way towards the edge of the street, uncertain of her direction, only following the path of least resistance to her progress. And now there was fighting around her, cries of anguish and of rage as scuffling figures tumbled in her path. She stepped over them, dodging to avoid a figure that snatched at her sleeve, another whose lips murmured a prayer, whose eyes glowed with sudden adulation. At last, pushing at a door, she found herself in a roadside tavern and stumbled to a halt amidst a crowd of market-day drinkers seemingly unengaged with events outside. Some drew back, regarding her with varying degrees of surprise or suspicion.

'Good day to you,' she gasped wild-eyed, stroking her hair back from her face distractedly and glancing over her shoulder to see whether she was pursued.

'Good day, madam,' replied the barman, setting a foaming tankard on the bar. 'And what may I...?'

Before he could complete his enquiry, the door swung open and Jonah stepped through with Blood at his heels, offering a glimpse of the still surging crowd beyond, where constables were struggling to restore order, dragging miscreants away, beating about them with their staves.

'No!' screamed Laura, 'I will not come with you.'

'You will,' demanded Blood as the patrons of this place muttered and their complexions darkened.

'Let us see no fatal outbreak of chivalry,' warned Jonah, twitching his coat aside to reveal the pistol in his belt. 'This is my daughter, and she must submit to my authority as she is duty-bound. Let none interfere who values their hide.'

Blood strode forward as the drinkers drew away, seizing Laura by the arm as she shrank back against the wall.

'Come,' he grunted. 'Your protestations are in vain.'

'Are they now?' she cried defiantly, impulsively embracing him where he expected her to recoil, pressing her hand to the side of his neck. 'Are they indeed, Mr Blood? I could take your life in an instant.'

She found herself glaring into Blood's eyes and saw momentary fear flicker there, quickly suppressed as his whole body tensed.

Laura was conscious of others coming into the bar now; white-shirted revenants, blue-clad constables and Messrs Mortlake, Maigret and Boyle. Tears blurred her vision.

'But you will not,' said Jonah softly, his face filling her vision now as he approached closer, 'because it would accomplish nothing whatsoever, and because it is not in your nature. Yours is to give life, not to take it.'

'I did once,' gasped Laura desperately but with no great conviction. Already her hand was falling away from Blood's neck.

'In extremis,' admitted Jonah, 'but it will not answer here. Besides, you have forgotten, have you not?'

'Forgotten?'

'If you will not attend to your duty to myself, then I urge you to consider your duty to your sister. Her life – her second life – depends upon you, as you well know.'

His hand moved hers aside with a gentleness that seemed strange in him, and a bitter resignation settled upon her together with an overwhelming wave of fatigue that would have seen her drop insensible to the floor had Blood not caught her up.

'Damn you, Jonah!' she murmured as the party bore her away towards the carriage once more.

'The king's bastard!' exclaimed the bishop. 'Well, that explains a great deal, I must say.'

The bishop, now restored to his comfortable London residence, drummed his fingers on the desktop before him and regarded Lord Clarey through narrowed eyes.

'Indeed,' nodded Clarey. 'It appears Blanchflower is his natural son, although the connection is not publicly acknowledged on either side. Nevertheless, the man's intolerable arrogance is armoured by that circumstance. Clearly, he considers himself beyond reach of ordinary authority, answerable only to his royal parent.'

'And you discovered this, how?' Turnbull raised an eyebrow.

'I have my sources,' said Clarey with a wry smile. 'And you will gather I felt minded to devote some considerable energy to my enquiries.'

'And to his destruction,' supplied Turnbull.

'After our encounter in the Eastings,' continued Clarey smoothly. 'Where, you will recall, the man showed an unseemly neglect of protocol.'

'And offered to cut your noble throat.'

'Just so,' agreed Clarey with a shudder.

A contemplative silence settled upon them in which the patter of rain could be heard on the windowpanes, the rattle of coaches in the street outside.

'And you are well, I collect?' asked Clarey at length. 'Happy to be returned to the centre of things once more?'

'I am,' confirmed the bishop, stretching himself comfortably and reaching for the cupboard at his side where the brandy was kept. 'Too early for a drink, do you suppose?'

'Never in life,' said Clarey with a peremptory glance at the clock on the mantel, which told four of the afternoon, 'or too late. And you will see that no blame attaches to you for your handling of affairs in the Eastings.'

Turnbull poured two glasses and frowned, passing one across to his guest.

'Blame? When was there ever talk of blame?'

'None that mattered,' countered Clarey quickly. 'Not in quarters where opinions truly count, but you will understand that all of us have enemies and there are those who would make mischief for us however unblemished our reputations might be, however stellar our accomplishments.'

'Hmm,' conceded Turnbull doubtfully.

'And the Earl of Stanwick, that preening ninny they sent out in your place, can only cause your tenure to be seen, in retrospect, as a golden age. I trust you have securely re-established your position within the archbishop's confidence, by now. I hear his health was not improved by exposure to southern climes.'

'Nor indeed his moral standing,' laughed Turnbull, taking a sip from his glass. 'It appears that the church in Rome is likewise no stranger to sodomy and that he found much to amuse him there.'

'Amuse him?'

'He travelled in order to purge his soul of temptation and grow nearer to God,' supplied Turnbull. 'His exertions there have surely brought him measurably closer to departing this earthly realm – you only have to look at him – but nearer to judgment, too, and I suppose he must tremble at that prospect.'

'He looked frail last week at the abbey, I thought,' agreed Clarey. 'And do you still have his confidence? I know there was loose talk of Bishop Craddock rising high in his estimation.'

'Craddock?' Turnbull snorted dismissively. 'He is a windbag. Baseless self-confidence and fawning upon one's betters will only get one so far.'

'I'm sure you are in the right of it,' observed Clarey, carefully maintaining the neutrality of his expression. 'And how do you suppose you stand regarding the succession? I mean, if Lamb were to expire tomorrow?'

'I conceive I would be tolerably well-placed,' declared Turnbull, 'although naturally I would place some reliance on the support of friends and of connections in the position to advance my cause. May I pour you another glass?'

'Of course,' agreed Clarey, extending an elegant hand with his glass. 'But the Church faces great challenges, does it not? I take it you have heard of events unfolding in the north and west.'

'Events?' Turnbull asked quizzically.

'I imagine events here in London have occupied the greater part of your mind in recent weeks. No, reports suggest nascent rebellion gathering there.'

'I had not heard,' admitted Turnbull. 'Doubtless it will be suppressed in due course. But how does this tend towards the Church in particular?'

'There is no open rebellion at present, no descent into lawlessness that might be identified as a clear challenge to the king's authority, instead, we see a reawakening of old heresies. It appears that the Pharisees are on the rise, that the book of Romuald is borne aloft at many a gathering and religious enthusiasm stirred up in a manner unheard of since King Stephen's day, full three centuries ago.

'The Wytch King,' mused Turnbull. 'How curious... and the Pharisees have barely raised their heads in recent times, not since a great many of them were burned in the fourth King Richard's day, as I recall.'

'And yet they are renascent. The established faith has slumbered in complacency, has lost the fervour that once inspired its devotees to passionate action. Hardly has a head rolled for heresy for two hundred years and more. Indifference has bred tolerance. The vast mass of the populace has a comfortable attachment to the Church and its dogma in the way that they are attached to the bones of the land and the woven strands of tradition that sustain them. Our common faith is one strand in the fabric of their lives but not the dominant one, not the one that guides their thoughts and actions in every sphere of life... as once it did, perhaps.'

'Perhaps,' conceded Turnbull. 'And you regret this, this moderation in religious thought and practice?'

'I do not,' snorted Clarey. 'And I rather fear that we shall see it swept away. Hard-held faith may once more be on the rise. The Pharisees have always been great ones for prophecies, you will recall, and there is a rumour that their one king will rise once more. It is said that his followers are awakening in droves and emerging blinking from the sleep halls. It is said that they are being deliberately reawakened.'

'Impossible!' snorted the bishop. 'How can that be so?'

'I think you know,' said Clarey with a significant look.

'I do?'

'You do.'

'Oh, do you mean that girl? I suppose you do. I forget her name,' pondered Turnbull, light dawning.

'You condemned her as a witch, you will recall,' reminded Clarey. 'But I gather she eluded the noose or the pyre. It is no more than supposition, of course, but I remember reading your report.'

Turnbull's eyes clouded with the memory and his glass hung suspended for a moment in its journey to his lips. In truth, the girl had been a frequent presence in his thoughts ever since the day he had condemned her, ever since news of her escape had reached his ears. She was an enigma, and one that troubled him greatly. He well remembered his interview with her. Laura – the name swam towards clarity in the forefront of his mind.

Perhaps, then, I am not an ordinary girl, she had said, and there was a glint in the girl's eye when he passed sentence on her that haunted him to that day. There was despair there, of course, and resignation to the fate that had been decreed for her, but there was more besides, a flash of something that no words known to him could completely describe. He hesitated to use the word "divine" in any human context, and yet that word approached most closely to the spark he had glimpsed. He told himself that he was deceived, that the Devil's work could encompass myriad forms, but that nagging doubt remained, that he had condemned a saint and might himself by posterity be condemned someday. The news that she had escaped affected him in a manner than no other lapse in the custody of the condemned could possibly have provoked. Well he recalled the sleepless nights that had ensued, the bitter recriminations that had followed. But whereas the greater part of him longed to bring her case to its fiery and lawful conclusion, a stubborn and entirely uncharacteristic strand of self-doubt nagged at him with agonising persistence.

'She is the key,' he found himself saying. 'The true, the vital key.'

'Have you heard?' cried Thomas Corvin, erupting into the rear room where Edward, Sir Joseph and his friend Sir William Mallory were dissecting a beetle. Faces rose from their inspection of the subject, faces wearing expressions suggesting various degrees of disapproval. In each case this initial frostiness quickly warmed in the face of the transparent joy that shone in the intruder's eyes.

'Hmm?' said Sir Joseph mildly, his own eyes strangely magnified by the spectacles he wore when conducting such investigations. He swept them off now, blinking as his colleagues straightened themselves to face their visitor. Mould stepped silently into the room, with a nod of apology.

'Hear what?' said Edward.

'Why, that there are strange stirrings in the west,' said Thomas, throwing his coat onto the back of a chair. 'My father has received news. It is said an army of revenants has been summoned and they are led by a son of the Wytch King himself. What do you think of that?'

'I am astonished,' said Sir Joseph, setting down his scalpel. 'Sir William, may we perhaps resume our investigations at some later date? Please accept my earnest apologies but I have interests in those regions, and I fear my young friend's news may affect us directly.'

'Certainly,' Sir William, a man rather more elderly than Sir Joseph, nodded gravely.

With Mould in attendance Sir Joseph led his friend from the room, still speaking in animated tones of the curiously striated carapace.

'You are wounded, I see,' observed Edward, regarding the bandage on Thomas's hand.

'It is nothing, a scratch sustained in fencing practice this morning,' said Thomas, approaching the table. 'My friend George is a fierce fellow with a sabre. But what of my news? Do you think our Jonah is implicated? And what of Laura?'

'He calls himself "Stephenson",' agreed Edward, thrusting his hand into a pocket to conceal the small, inglorious nick that he had inflicted on himself with a scalpel, 'which I suppose qualifies as hiding in plain sight. And we both know Laura's apparent capacity for raising the dead. It would certainly explain Jonah's motivation in securing her.'

'You are right,' agreed Thomas, striding restlessly around the room and rubbing his hands together. 'Surely you are. I tell you I am afire to be away there, Edward. My heart burns for Laura, you know. I feel it here,' he paused to indicate the centre of his chest, 'like a warm and constant ache that now pains me more acutely than ever with this news.'

'Are you sure it is not indigestion?' suggested Edward. 'The two are sometimes mistook, I know. I daresay Sir Joseph would make you up a draught.'

'A draught?!' Thomas laughed out loud. 'There is no draught on earth that could salve this affliction. Only Laura can cure me of it. You would not know, a monkish fellow like yourself, with the Church your betrothed and so on.'

'I'm afraid that the Church and I have broken off our engagement,' said Edward a little stiffly as Sir Joseph returned, setting down the beetle that he had absentmindedly carried out with him.

'Stephen's son,' he said with emphasis, turning from the table. 'Stephenson. Now it all makes sense.'

'Indeed,' agreed Thomas. 'Edward and I were discussing it just now.'

'It appears that Jonah wishes to reinvigorate the Phariseean heresy and raise the west in revolt,' said Sir Joseph, reaching into a drawer and pulling out a battered map. He smoothed it out on the table and the three of them gathered round to inspect it.

'Tell me what you have heard,' instructed Sir Joseph, glancing sidelong at Thomas, 'tell me exactly. Mention the names of places.'

Thomas spoke of three abbeys he had heard named in his father's council and the town of Tewkesbury. Sir Joseph located these places on the map with pins, using a length of twine to connect them.

'If Jonah began his progress in the north-west, as he may well have done, he has journeyed southwards through those lands, which were, in ancient times, the heartlands of the Wytch King's support. I suppose we shall see that progress continue – it would be logical enough – terminating in the south-west, perhaps in Devon or even Cornwall.'

'What of this place,' asked Edward, tapping the tiny illustration that represented Whale Hall, 'where we were ourselves about the turn of the year? Surely, he must pass by Breasham, if he has not already done so.'

'He must,' agreed Sir Joseph. 'Certainly, he must. And I suppose we must go there, too.'

'Then there is not a moment to be lost!' announced Thomas vehemently. 'I suppose it is too late now, today, but we must surely ride out on the morrow, Sir Joseph. Shall I ask a few of my friends to accompany us?'

'Are you sure your father can spare you once more?' asked Edward as Sir Joseph nodded his assent. 'I know he considers you his rock, the anchor of his fortunes.'

'I salute your worthy concern,' said Thomas, 'and you do me a kindness in that estimation, but nothing shall stand in the way of my participation in this mission, not even should my father counsel against it, not even should he expressly forbid it. Filial devotion urges otherwise, but my mind is quite fixed on the issue.'

Sir Joseph exchanged a wry glance with Edward. His shrug went unnoticed by Thomas as the young man turned to recover his coat.

'I shall go at once to see to horses and provisions,' he said. 'Blakelock will certainly come with me, and perhaps I shall also ask Wiseman and Barrow.'

When Thomas had gone Sir Joseph called for tea, and he and Edward sat to consider the significance of Thomas's news.

'She is a person of wit and discernment,' said Sir Joseph, seeing that Edward's face wore the signs of despondency, 'and I know that she values you highly.'

'And do you suppose that we might locate them?' asked Edward, grateful for this assertion but keen to move on to a broader consideration of matters. 'I am amazed that Jonah might be the Wytch King's son. How curious. It seems incredible. What times we live in.'

He settled back in his chair after having uttered these platitudes and waved a hand vaguely, to indicate his dismay.

Sir Joseph stirred a little sugar into his tea and frowned.

'And have you given any thought to the more particular significance of Whale Hall? I fancy the legend of the seven might be rather more than a legend.'

'What do you mean?' asked Edward. 'Legends might evolve from some small kernel of truth, I suppose.'

'Somewhat more than a small kernel in this case, if my suspicions are correct,' said Sir Joseph, 'because I rather wonder if King Stephen himself is lying in the belly of that hill.'

'What?!' Edward stared at him, round-eyed now. 'Surely not!'

'Why not? It would undoubtedly explain Jonah's remaining in the vicinity for so many years, before his journeying to the Eastings. But there is much we do not know. We have no inkling as to his motivations for going there. How could he have known or suspected that Laura would be born in that region and that she would have the capacity to awaken the dead? And yet he must have done. It would certainly be interesting to question him.'

'It would,' agreed Edward, with a laugh. 'And I suppose he would be glad to oblige us, keen to ease our minds on this issue, freely furnishing us with whatever information we cared to solicit. I take it you propose that Laura's journey must necessarily conclude at Breasham, with the awakening of the seven?'

'It seems likely that such must be his intention,' concurred Sir Joseph, 'and we must assume that King Stephen's six companions are his barons and councillors. My knowledge of that period in our history is too sketchy to offer more precise identification. Nevertheless, if Laura were able to awaken King Stephen the consequences might be very severe. It would at the very least plunge the nation into chaos, reignite ancient hatreds and undo the work of generations in promoting enlightenment.'

'But perhaps he may not be awakened,' suggested Edward. 'Laura spoke of hearts of ice and stone. Perhaps his is of stone.'

'Jonah evidently believes otherwise. We would do well to proceed likewise according to that assumption.'

It was a party of eight that arrived once more at Breasham Abbey two days later. They had ridden hard through a landscape lashed with spring rains that had turned the roads to ribbons of cloud-reflecting mire. Even Edward had eventually been obliged to concede that Thomas's friends were a welcome addition to their party. Should recourse to arms be necessary their muscular self-confidence, their evident proficiency in the use of deadly weapons, might prove useful.

'And you think he might be coming here?' asked Prior Hardiman whilst the group saw to the stabling of their horses. 'The abbot may be with him, I think. There was much excited talk with his confidantes when he rode out yesterday. I am not amongst his confidantes, I'm afraid, despite my rank. There is much loose talk of revenants coming forth en masse, of Romuald's words on the lips of the populace once more.'

'I fear a storm is rising,' said Sir Joseph, handing his hat to the prior. 'And it may be this place is the eye of that storm.'

The prior conducted Sir Joseph and Edward to his study whilst the others were offered food in the kitchen adjacent to the stable yard. Thomas, recalling the tedious proceedings of their last meeting, declared that he would join them later, that he was duty-bound to remain with Mould and with his friends.

'We believe his true name to be Leo, son of the Stephen that was called the Wytch King and who departed this earthly realm three hundred years or so ago,' said Sir Joseph when the three of them were comfortably established and a very fine venison pie had been brought.

'That is the trouble with revenancy,' said the prior, tying a napkin around his neck. 'The past is never reliably the past. There is always the risk that it may obtrude itself upon the present. I have heard of other examples, but this would be the most remarkable. What do you suppose he hopes to achieve by this,' the prior groped for words, 'campaign?'

'He evidently hopes to stir the embers of Phariseeism in the north and west,' explained Sir Joseph, 'and is employing our young friend Laura to raise his contemporaries from the ranks of the dead. It is said that an army of such revenants marches with him now, that the Wytch King's banner flies once more and that these reawakened passions may ultimately result in rebellion.'

'Oh dear,' said Hardiman through a mouthful of pie. 'I had not realised. As I have said, the abbot does not confide in me.'

'And we have other suspicions,' confided Sir Joseph. 'Having given much consideration to the matter we have arrived at the following conclusion,' he gestured for Edward to supply this, but it was first necessary for his young friend to deal with a mouthful of crust.

'We believe Jonah – for I shall continue to call him that – intends to raise his father,' said Edward, his voice somewhat muffled, 'using our Laura for that purpose.'

'And likewise, we believe,' continued Sir Joseph, 'that the identity of the Seven Sleepers is no longer in doubt, that the legend is a fact and that the sleepers are the Wytch King and his barons.'

'Good Lord!' cried the prior, leaning suddenly back in his chair. 'You do amaze me!'

'But where are the seven?' asked Edward. 'Where indeed? We believe that the issue is now within reach of resolution. It makes perfect sense that they should be here in Whale Hall, lying somewhere within the belly of that great hill out yonder, just as your late friend Abbot Cole believed. Why else should Jonah have spent so many years in this vicinity? Perhaps throughout his time here he awaited the opportunity to awaken them.'

'And now Laura has provided him with that opportunity,' added Sir Joseph, 'and, as I have said, we believe Jonah's southward progress will eventually bring him to this place and that he will oblige her to summon his father from the ranks of the dead.'

'Imagine it,' said Hardiman with a shudder. 'I scarcely dare contemplate the results. That king had an evil reputation.'

'He did amongst his enemies,' agreed Sir Joseph, 'amongst those who vanquished him, but history is foremost amongst the victor's spoils, is it not? There are many in the west whose ancestors followed that king to his ruin at Todmorton and who nurture a very different memory of his reign.'

'There are brothers here who are said to mutter Romuald's prophecies amongst themselves, and a few of those were amongst the party who rode north from here yesterday,' said Hardiman. 'They are due to return by nightfall on Friday. Perhaps they will bring Jonah and his party with them.'

'Perhaps,' Sir Joseph pondered, rubbing his chin thoughtfully, 'which leaves us very little time, if we would accomplish our ends.'

'Your ends?'

'Which are first to discover the chamber in which the seven must lie, and second to set in place a plan to bring about the liberation of Laura from her captors.'

'And you assume that I will assist you in this?' asked the prior, his face suddenly grave. 'A bold presumption indeed, for to do so must place me at odds with my abbot and the greater part of the community here.'

'I do,' said Sir Joseph simply. 'Because you strike me as an honest man and because, by your own admission, you are a stranger here, ill at ease in this milieu.'

'And I would dearly love to look upon the seven,' admitted the prior with a smile after no more than a few moments of apparent contemplation but ones that provoked acute anxiety in his guests. 'There, you have me. Where shall we begin?'

'You have a plan of this place, I assume,' said a relieved Sir Joseph.

It seemed that the previous abbot had been a meticulous and learned man who had collected his research in bound notebooks filled with detailed notes and sketches. These contained a compilation of various accounts of the legend of the seven sleepers, with annotations of his own and a variety of etymological and geographical notes. There were eight notebooks in all.

'I'm sure there were originally nine,' observed Prior Hardiman. 'But after Cole's death only these could be found in his chambers.'

'And you say he mentioned to you that he was on the verge of making an important disclosure to you,' said Sir Joseph.

'Yes, he did,' agreed the prior, 'before events overtook him. It was unfortunate. I suppose we will never know.'

'Is it possible his misfortune was brought about by some external agency?' asked Sir Joseph, rubbing his chin pensively.

'What do you mean? Do you suggest foul play?' the abbot frowned. 'I had not thought…'

'If Jonah feared that the location of the seven might be about to be revealed,' said Edward. 'Do you think him capable?'

'Why not?' asked Sir Joseph. 'He is utterly ruthless and calculating, it would appear. I suppose Cole's body was badly burnt.'

'It was,' said Hardiman. 'Almost beyond recognition. I fear he will wait in vain for reawakening, should he lie down there a thousand years.'

'May I see the body?' asked Sir Joseph earnestly, pressing a hand to the prior's forearm. 'I think this may be important.'

'You may not enter the sleep hall,' said the prior, shaking his head. 'That would never do. Such things are forbidden to the uninitiated.'

'Then bring forth his body. I trust you have a gurney for such purposes. Let me have sight of him.'

'Sir Joseph is a physician and anatomist of wide repute,' said Edward. 'He has attended upon members of the king's court, indeed.'

'I am not proposing to cure him, only to examine his remains,' said Sir Joseph testily. 'But I urge you to assent to this, Prior Hardiman. I suspect that a crime may have been committed and you must consider whether you are duty-bound to assist in an investigation that may lead to the apprehension of the offender.'

'Well, it would be highly irregular,' murmured the prior, 'but if foul play is truly suspected, he was a dear friend of mine, you know. Perhaps, oh, I don't know,' the prior moaned, clasping his head in both hands. 'You place me in such a quandary. I'm not sure what the present abbot would say. I wonder if we should await his return.'

'No one else need know,' said Edward eagerly, 'except perhaps Mark. I'm sure you could trust to his discretion. The two of us could assist you, if you choose to propose a time.'

'Time presses urgently upon us,' said Sir Joseph, getting to his feet. 'Jonah undoubtedly approaches, and the opportunity may not present itself again. I implore you with all my heart. Certainly, I doubt that Abbot Cole would censure you for this action.'

'Very well!' cried the prior, casting up his hands. 'Enough! Once more you overwhelm me. You fellows seem determined on the utter destruction of my peace of mind. Nevertheless, I shall fetch Mark directly and we shall see what we shall see.'

Chapter Eighteen

Abbot Cole's body had been anointed and cared for with all the diligence and experience that many centuries had taught the Camoldolite order. Nevertheless, he was in a sorry state, heavily blackened, with much of the face burnt away and much of one leg reduced to the charred bone. The prevailing smell was of aromatic spices but with a tenacious whiff of burnt flesh. Edward had seen plenty of dead bodies during his training but none that brought the bile to his throat in quite this persistent manner. What remained of Abbot Cole lay face upward on a gurney in a gloomy antechamber that was just beyond the sacred precincts of the sleep hall. Sir Joseph shone a lantern upon the corpse, the yellow light glinting on white tooth exposed by blackened, shrivelled lips.

'And do you see anything? Any evidence of foul play, I mean?' asked Hardiman, whose furtive, anxious movements and querulous voice were more suggestive of a thief in the night than of a person in authority.

'I confess I do not,' admitted Sir Joseph, probing at flesh speculatively with a lancet. 'At least not in this presentation. Mark, perhaps you would assist me in turning him.'

The young man, whose face wore a pallor sharply in contrast with that of the departed abbot's, took hold of the corpse's shoulder and raised the body on its side whilst Sir Joseph examined the back.

'Aha,' said the surgeon after a moment, in tones of great satisfaction. 'Hold the body just so, if you would, Mark. Prior, perhaps you would care to step across. Edward, will you ply your own lamp here. There, you have it. Hold it there. Now, what do you see, sir?'

'Why nothing,' said the prior skeptically. 'The flesh is quite blackened, is it not?'

'Direct your gaze here, to the side of the scapula. Just there. Do you see the incision?'

'I do. A narrow slit.'

'Narrow but mortally deep, I would suggest,' said Sir Joseph with satisfaction. 'I put it to you that Abbot Cole sustained these grievous burns after his death and that his death was precipitated by a stab wound to the back, entering between the fourth and fifth ribs. Delivered with sufficient violence the wound would have been instantly fatal.'

'Good Lord!' the prior shrank back.

'Who was last to see the abbot alive?' asked Sir Joseph, lowering the corpse, his face grim now.

'Why, the present abbot, Abbot Clutterbrock,' said Hardiman. 'You don't think...?'

'He is an adherent of Jonah, it would seem,' said Edward glowering.

'It seems entirely possible that it was he who murdered your friend when it appeared that he seemed likely to discover the whereabouts of the seven,' deduced Sir Joseph. 'The fire would have offered the perfect opportunity to conceal the manner of his death. I take it there was an official investigation?'

'There was,' replied Hardiman, his hands trembling as he removed his spectacles. 'The Lord Lieutenant's men were here.'

'But it appears they were not permitted to inspect the body.'

'No. Clutterbrock was elected soon after, with indecent haste in my opinion, and he refused to sanction such a measure. The fire was declared to be an accident and the case closed forthwith.'

'Hmm,' muttered Sir Joseph, wiping his hands on his coat and replacing his lancet in the case he always carried in the inside pocket of that garment. 'I suppose you will let us search his room.'

'That would certainly exceed my authority, I should say,' said the prior but with no great conviction, no firmness of tone that would forbid it.

'You know it, do you not?' asked Sir Joseph, 'You have always known that Clutterbrock is a bad lot. If it salves your conscience, you may state that the intrusion took place without your knowledge by guests who took advantage of your hospitality, took the keys from your belt as you slept. Perhaps you would lead the way?'

'Do you mean to force the drawer?' asked Edward sometime later as Sir Joseph groped in his pocket, bending over the abbot's desk. The man's room had yielded up no information of value, being furnished in a manner sparing of comfort and variety. There were only a few books, bound religious tracts, that Hardiman leafed through disapprovingly and a wardrobe that contained nothing except underclothes, robes and the flute that was the abbot's only concession to the secular world. There was nothing at all to suggest avarice or the pursuit of luxury. It seemed that the abbot sought reward exclusively in the next world.

'I mean to try,' grunted Sir Joseph, inserting a probe carefully into the lock.

'I think I can open it,' suggested Hardiman.

'Really?' asked Sir Joseph, raising an eyebrow. 'You have skill in this field?'

'No, I have the key from on the windowsill,' said the prior helpfully, holding this in front of him.

The drawer proved to contain a small sum of money, various forms of correspondence which Sir Joseph perused with interest and a leather-bound notebook.

'I believe this is the ninth notebook,' said Hardiman, taking it up. 'The one that was missing from Cole's room.'

'May I see?' asked Sir Joseph, setting down the papers.

It was growing dark now and Sir Joseph crossed to the window, holding it up to the fading light, turning the pages with slow deliberation.

Returning to the prior's quarters, having first removed all obvious signs of their intrusion, the three men studied the notebook with interest. A clock ticked on the mantel, its sound impressing on each of them the urgency of their task. The abbot had left no exact indication of when his party would return. A week's absence had indeed been mentioned, but the abbot's well-known want of constancy preyed on the prior's mind and there was a risk that he might return at any time. On balance, the prior thought they should have at least a day's notice. He thought it likely that the abbot would send in advance with instructions to prepare for the entertainment and provisioning of a large party, should he desire to accommodate one. This somewhat reduced the risk of Jonah's sudden arrival in their midst but did little to bring forward the achievement of their ends.

'This old book – it contains all the answers, I collect,' said Thomas when it was close to midnight, peering over Edward's shoulder.

'It may,' conceded Sir Joseph, looking up. 'There are many sketch maps and annotations, but unfortunately the maps are fragmentary and difficult to interpret. In addition, it seems that several pages towards the end have been torn out.'

'And the late abbot, many fine qualities though he possessed, wrote with an execrable hand,' lamented the prior.

'Absolutely,' agreed Sir Joseph. 'At least a cipher benefits from a necessary regularity that may yield to intelligent analysis. Do you suppose this word says "wall"?'

'Let me see,' the prior adjusted his spectacles. 'Yes, I believe it does. Then this should represent an intervening space. I fancy this is the lowest level. I seem to recall a bend in the passage just so. Perhaps you would turn the paper a little. Yes.'

'And will it take you long, do you think?' pressed Thomas. 'I only mention it because we have also to evolve a plan for Laura's liberation, as I recall.'

'You are in the right of it,' affirmed Sir Joseph, his voice labouring to conceal a rising irritation. 'And you may be sure that we are giving the matter our urgent consideration. As you will be aware, there are several issues competing urgently for our attention just now.'

'I am glad of it,' said Thomas. 'I wish I could be of more assistance. The present abbot is aware of the location of the seven, I suppose. I imagine he would have checked to see that Cole's suspicions were correct.'

The others turned to him; the notebook momentarily forgotten.

'Why yes, I suppose he would,' agreed the prior.

'Indeed,' said Sir Joseph with a nod of warm approval. 'So perhaps we are in search of an area with signs of recent access after many, many years of neglect. Do you know of such a place, prior? Do these drawings suggest such a location to your mind?'

'Well, I suppose the north end of the uppermost level,' said the prior. 'The abbot arranged for building work there a few years ago to shore up one of the passages.'

'How long ago?' asked Edward. 'Exactly how long?'

'Why,' the prior scratched his head pensively, 'I suppose it was about five years ago. Shortly before the fire.'

'Shortly before or shortly afterwards?' pressed Sir Joseph with a glance for Edward. 'This may be important.'

'A few days before, as I recall. I may be wrong...'

'Could you take us to that place?' asked Sir Joseph with sudden urgency. 'I think we may have hit upon the trail.'

'But that is the top level,' objected the prior. 'Cole always believed that the seven lay beneath the lowest level.'

'He may long have believed so,' said Sir Joseph, 'but perhaps his mind turned otherwise in a manner that proved ultimately fatal to him. Perhaps the missing notebook pages described the course of those mental processes and the conclusions that resulted from them. Perhaps the sketch map we have been perusing makes better sense if interpreted as the upper level. Could that be so?'

The prior leant closer and adjusted his spectacles. 'Why yes, I suppose it does, and this area here, you see? It may indicate the area that Clutterbrock placed out of bounds.'

'How very interesting,' noted Sir Joseph, his eyes gleaming. He placed his hand on Hardiman's shoulder and looked earnestly into his face. 'Please, could you take us there? I believe this place may be about to give up its secret.'

'I cannot take you, Sir Joseph,' said the prior, shaking his head. 'You know that. You have already destroyed my peace of mind and caused me a deep uneasiness in my conscience. There are some boundaries that I will not cross.' There was a note of decided obstinacy in his voice that brooked of no opposition on this point at least. 'I will take Edward, however,' he added, 'and Mark.'

It was late at night as the prior led Edward and Mark deep into the belly of the hill. Some of the other brethren they encountered seemed surly to a point barely shy of insolence when addressed by their prior, but there could be no objection or opposition from them as the small party proceeded through the outer precincts of the sleep hall and into regions that were barely frequented. Outside, a squally wind whipped thin, chill rain about the humped green slopes, but inside all was quiet and still except for the echo of their voices and the sound of their footfalls. Lamplight flickered along the cool passages where the dead lay sleeping in their hollow halls to either side or in their stone-cut niches in the walls themselves. Edward was used to these things and gave them hardly a thought, except to remark that the quality of darkness was somehow more profound than that in Darkharrow, the air more still, more sparing of that vital unseen element that his lungs now craved.

'We are deep within the hill now,' explained the prior, holding up his lamp, 'and the air is stale here. It becomes staler still as we advance, and you will find that the dead have been removed to areas judged to be more secure. Observe,' he instructed, turning the lamp to illuminate some flakes and shards of stone that had fallen from the ceiling some way ahead.

'This region is judged unsound,' added Mark, 'and ordinarily we are forbidden to come this way. Not that our duties ever require it. I believe the ceiling is shored up with timbers around that corner yonder. Is that not right, uncle?'

'It is,' agreed Hardiman. 'And there is an area where there was a partial collapse, as I recall. Very dangerous indeed. Clutterbrock ruled it out of bounds.'

'And yet Abbot Cole's plan marked it out particularly,' said Edward, 'unless our reading was mistaken.'

'It was correct, alright,' grunted Hardiman, whose customary good humour seemed entirely to have deserted him and whose movements had acquired a nervous, bird-like quality. 'Nevertheless, I feel loathe to go further. Perhaps we should…'

'I share your trepidation,' ventured Edward, before the prior could give further voice to his anxiety, 'and yet I suppose we must go on. I should not care to admit to Sir Joseph that mere faintness of heart curtailed my exploration.'

'No,' said Hardiman, swallowing hard. 'No, indeed. We shall advance, but I urge you to step carefully, the footing is quite treacherous, and this area is unmapped in detail.'

Hardiman was correct. There were places where parts of the roof had collapsed, and the passage which once had been neatly rectangular in section became an irregular tunnel, varying in height and aspect, held up, here and there, by ancient timbers of uncertain temper. On occasion it was necessary to stoop and once to crawl across a scree of loose stone through a space no higher than the desk in the abbot's office. Edward was acutely conscious of the staleness of the air, of his breath rasping in his throat from his exertions and of the frail yellow flicker of the three lamps in the cloying dark.

'How stand you for oil?' he asked his companions, having checked his own and found it to be less than half full. It would surely be fatal to be without light in the labyrinthine bowels of this hill.

'About the same,' said Hardiman, having checked his own. 'I think we had best turn back.'

'There is a little breath of sweeter air here,' came Mark's voice, echoing from further ahead. 'I feel it on my cheek.'

'Then there must be a ventilation shaft,' said the prior, his face now streaked with dust, his eyes glinting in Edward's lamplight. 'Perhaps we shall go a very little further.'

Presently the passage became sounder, although narrow, and they came to a junction with another way, this one partially blocked with a doorway of long-decayed timber that they could push aside easily. Turning left, towards where a faint breath of air caressed their cheeks, they proceeded for some minutes until their progress was arrested by a further, stouter door.

'I fancy we have reached some point of access to the hill,' announced Hardiman, indicating a place where cobwebs stirred in the faintest of breezes above the door. 'I suppose it is locked and not merely jammed.'

No amount of heaving or cursing proved effective in dislodging the door, and after a while, conscious of the diminishing oil in their lamps, they retraced their footsteps to the junction with the first passage that had taken them there. The ceiling was higher in this area, so high that in places it was lost in darkness, and they appeared to be moving along a narrow cleft. A sharp cry indicated that Mark had stubbed his toe on a fallen stone and tripped, dropping his lamp, which was immediately extinguished. Hardiman and Edward advanced to help him to his feet, and Edward, stooping forward, felt an icy drop of water on his neck. Glancing upward, holding up his lamp, he observed a darker patch of gloom above him.

'I shall be fine, I assure you,' Mark was telling Hardiman. 'Although I thank you for your solicitations.'

'Look here,' said Edward urgently. 'Bring your light hither.'

'Hmm?' Hardiman and then Mark emerged from the darkness. Mark's lamp remained unlit but the prior's shed the strongest light, and by this it was possible to discern the edges and the first few feet of a vertical shaft above them.

'Do you suppose this is for ventilation?' asked Edward, craning his neck upwards and straining his eyes to pierce the gloom.

'I feel no air from it,' said Hardiman with a shrug. 'But I hesitate to suggest any other purpose. There is no access.'

'Not now there isn't,' noted Mark, stooping to examine the floor, 'but once there was, for sure. Bring your light down here.'

Scuffed upon the grime of the ancient flags was a set of parallel marks such that might have been made by the foot of a ladder.

'And this, what is this?' asked Edward, picking a strand of some ancient fabric from amongst the loose scatter of material at the base of the wall. 'Might it perhaps be a fragment of a winding sheet?'

'It might,' agreed Hardiman, lamplight glinting in eyes grown wide with wonder, eyes that stared upward into the yawning darkness above them. 'And there is the faintest whiff of spice down here, do you detect it? Take a deep breath, if you will.'

'There is,' agreed Mark eagerly. 'And we have not smelt it elsewhere for some way, for twenty minutes or so, I should think.'

'We must return with a ladder,' said Hardiman to Edward with a sniff. 'I wonder if we stand on the verge of a discovery that will amaze your friend Sir Joseph.'

Sir Joseph, in anticipation of this discovery, was more dismayed than amazed, driven to a frenzy of frustration that he might not be present as the ladder was taken through the sleep hall and along to the site of their investigation as a new day dawned outside. By this time Thomas and his friends had been acquainted with developments and it was all they could do to convey some semblance of normality as the brothers of the abbey moved around them, going about their duties or passing to and from the abbey for their prayers. There was an atmosphere of intense, but decently suppressed mutual suspicion. Some of the more senior brothers sensed that their guests were hiding something of importance from them. They, for their part, were hard pressed to conceal their unspoken sense that the west was in the grip of an awakening. The chosen one, she that was foretold in ancient prophecy, was approaching from the north to summon the faithful from the slumber of ages.

Edward's eyes were gritty with dust, as well as from want of sleep, as he ascended the ladder, but a mounting excitement gathered in his breast. Below, the pale faces of his companions could be discerned in the outer fringes of the lamplight, but his gaze was directed upward as his free hand groped at the edge of a smooth stone parapet and he pulled himself higher. The top of the ladder fell a little short of the parapet's upper extremity, but the gap was an inconsiderable one and by placing his lamp on its top surface Edward was able to heave himself over, finding himself at the edge of a wide semi-circular chamber. The voices of his companions, seeking assurance of his safety, nagged at the fringes of his consciousness, but the whole of Edward's attention was absorbed by the circumstances of his discovery. The glimmer of his lamp revealed a high vaulted ceiling, carved in a manner that called to his mind the corbelled vault of the chapter house in the abbey below. The walls from which this great vault sprang were carved with semi-engaged columns topped with capitals wrought to resemble the iron-collared heraldic eagles of King Stephen's house. Nevertheless, these things barely brushed against the surface of Edward's mind as he advanced, lamp held high, towards the largest of the carved stone biers with which the chamber was furnished and which formed a broad arc around the circumference of the place. The air was still with the silent peace of ages, and Edward was aware of his own breath harsh in his throat, of the blood surging in his veins as he approached the foot of the bier. He was used to the company of the dead and he liked to consider himself a rational creature, but despite the urgings of his upper mind a rising superstitious dread lapped at the lower fringes of his consciousness. He paused and swallowed hard, standing for a moment to calm his breathing and to fortify his resolve. Stepping forward once more, his gaze fell upon the simple stone-carved nameplate at the foot of the bier, and with his free hand he brushed a little dust aside, the better to read the shallow inscription.

"Stephen, Rex Britannicus", he read, his lips moving silently as he straightened to survey the gloomy chamber around him once more, but the bier was empty; all the biers were empty, and he was obliged to report that the seven sleepers were elsewhere.

Sir Joseph was afire to see the chamber once its situation had been described to him. The opaque expression in his face, when accepting his ineligibility for so doing in Hardiman's presence, spoke of a private resolve to do so regardless, should an opportunity present itself. There was much discussion of the seven and of the reasons for their absence, but none could propose an option that satisfactorily matched the available facts. By now the prior had returned to his duties in order to maintain the pretense that life proceeded on its normal course. His guests had retired to the lodgings that had been prepared for them, there to continue their fevered deliberations.

'Do you suppose that Jonah had the seven moved elsewhere within the hill?' asked Edward, sitting on the edge of his bed with his shoes kicked off. 'Perhaps he has concealed them amongst the ranks of the less illustrious dead, in order that they may be more readily accessible for Laura's visit here.'

'It is certainly possible,' mused Sir Joseph, lying on own bed and regarding the cracked ceiling above with a critical eye. 'But only Hardiman would be able to tell us whether such an arrangement has been made – and even he might be deceived if the abbot is complicit in the scheme.'

'As he may well be,' said Edward.

'As he may well be.'

Thomas, whose quarters were next door, knocked boldly and walked in, looking eagerly from face to face. He shared his companions' desire to establish the present location of the long-deceased king and his men, but the need to release Laura from her captivity occupied the forefront of his mind. Certain details within Edward's account of his explorations suggested to him a means by which this might be accomplished.

'You will pardon my intrusion, but did I hear you say that there was a door to the exterior of the hill, within a short distance of the chamber?' he asked. 'I have been pondering your story.'

'The prior believed so, yes,' agreed Edward, 'but it was a stoutly constructed door, and we had no means of unlocking or destroying it.'

'I see. Well, do you suppose that you and Mark could batter it down, if supplied with an axe or two?' asked Thomas. 'I regret that I am debarred from setting foot there myself, as I am quite sure I should make short work of it.'

'I am certain we should deal with it handily,' said Edward a little stiffly, detecting a slight upon his physique. 'But why do you ask?'

'I ask because if another point of access could be found to the hill it might equally well serve as a means of egress,' said Thomas, beaming in the manner of one who has shed sudden light into the darkness.

'That,' said Sir Joseph, raising his weary head from his pillow, 'is a suggestion of particular interest.' He rubbed his eyes. 'How fortunate that you can combine both brains and brawn within that single elegant frame. He is a revelation, is he not? Would you not agree, Edward?'

'Yes,' allowed Edward with an expression stretched into a form that conveyed some measure of approval.

Laura had never heard of Whale Hall until Jonah's account of his awakening. After this, the name of Breasham Hall became familiar enough to her ear. It seemed that the place featured large in the forefront of her captor's mind. Certainly, it was referred to frequently in his conversations with his companions as they continued their odyssey around the western fringes of the realm.

Laura had the sense that it was somehow pivotal to this project, that their arrival there would constitute some important waypoint on that journey. She knew that it would not be journey's end – that distinction belonged to a place in Cornwall, but the talk she had overheard suggested that it would thereafter be the gathering point for some great assembly of the faithful. Armed with this knowledge, it might be supposed that she would have regarded the great isolated hill with some interest as her carriage bore her towards it one showery day in March. Indeed, some small part of her consciousness directed her eye that way as the jolting carriage bore her party along the rutted track that led southward and westward from Holmbridge. The huge green shoulder of the hill thrust upward beyond woods where bare branches showed an array of unexpectedly vivid colours in the brilliant midday sun. The mere, whose reflection gave the hall its name, was on the far side of that great mass, and beyond, at no great distance, were the shores of the Bristol Channel. The occasional white fleck of a gull against the clear blue of the sky or the loom of an approaching grey cloud testified to that proximity.

'Will we stop at Dornock for a bite?' asked Blood, sitting opposite her, tapping the point of his knife absently against his palm.

'I would rather press on,' said Jonah, leaning across Laura to look out of the window on her side. 'I suppose your luncheon can wait a while. Doubtless that girth will sustain you a little longer.'

'I suppose his girth will sustain him for a drive as far as Muscovy,' laughed Maigret, who was the fourth occupant of their carriage, causing Blood to grin and utter an oath, pushing him roughly away until admonished by Jonah.

Such trivialities barely registered with Laura. She lived in the past, at least insofar as the present would allow, and the future held no meaning for her. She sang a little song almost inaudible to the others and cocked her head to one side as Emily approached. Emily was often with her now, a close companion in the cold of the night, a vital confidante when the lonely hours oppressed her.

'Will you brush my hair a little, sister?' she asked, and Laura smiled assent, brushing her own hair in long, slow movements, lips moving wordlessly in some private dialogue impervious to the understanding of her companions. These shared a glance of disquiet amongst themselves and Maigret raised a finger to tap his temple significantly.

'She has eaten, I collect,' said Blood, whose earlier enquiry had concerned the girl's welfare as much as his own.

'She broke her fast,' grunted Jonah, recalling the morsel of crust dipped in milk she had reluctantly been persuaded to consume. 'And will not starve, I warrant.' His fierce glare beat down the eyes of Blood and Maigret, who shrugged and returned to their own internal preoccupations as the carriage trundled onwards.

'And who is that you converse with?' he demanded of Laura, although he knew well enough by now.

'Why, 'tis Emily, of course,' said Laura, glancing at him sidelong, brush momentarily stilled. She smiled dreamily; eyes unfocused for a moment. 'She enquires as to your health.'

'Like hell she does,' snarled Jonah. 'I wish you would abandon this, this affectation, lest others conclude that your wits are astray.'

'Certainly, I shall mention it to her,' said Laura, the brush resuming its motion. 'Do you hear that, sweet sister? Our father doubts our sanity. That is surely very illiberal in him.'

'I doubt yours, surely I do,' muttered Jonah, turning aside to stare gloomily at the dark mass of cloud that was gathering behind the hill.

If Emily had been a constant and welcome companion to Laura, there were others whose presence was more troubling to her. Generally, the shades of the dead were timid in presenting themselves to her inner eye, lurking at the fringes of that vision where they exerted a moral force upon her that varied from wistful pleading to resentment. Likewise, any direct communication from them was received only through Emily.

'Mrs Shelby regrets that you passed her by yesterday,' she told her now. 'She reached out for you from her bier as you went by, and she smelt the scent of bread upon you. Such a smell, she says. It made her weep.'

'I cannot wake all the dead,' said Laura with a shrug. 'You must tell Mrs Shelby that I have not the strength. I am to wake only those I am obliged to wake. You may tell her that I regret it, however.'

'And then there is Sir Richard Cordingly,' said Emily, leaning her head on Laura's shoulder now and looking up into her eyes. 'He is a very angry fellow, wishes vengeance on the line of those who murdered him. I don't like him at all, but he is exceedingly importunate. He speaks against you most intemperately for declaring his heart a stone.'

'A stone is a stone is a stone,' declared Laura, shaking her head sadly. 'You must bid him press his suit elsewhere.'

'I wish she would desist from that,' said Maigret, regarding her with ill-concealed dismay. 'She chills me to the bone.'

'Do I?' asked Laura, her eyes lifted suddenly from Emily's. 'Do I really? There are shades who would pull you down once more.'

'Be quiet, daughter!' snapped Jonah. 'Enough of this. Would you rather travel alone?'

Laura cast her eyes down meekly once more after a glance that assured him that whatever silence she might be induced to keep, she would never travel alone.

Chapter Nineteen

'This is she, then? The one whose advent we have awaited so long?' asked Hardiman as Laura was helped down from the carriage.

He said this for the benefit of those passionate and open Pharisees around him, rather than through any sense of personal conviction. In the last few days, a mounting excitement had manifested itself at Breasham Abbey, even before their guests had ridden away, even before the message had been received to prepare for the arrival of a large party.

'Aye, it is she,' said Abbot Clutterbrock, stretching himself cautiously and handing his coat to a servant.

'I had imagined she was young,' said Hardiman, observing as Laura stood blinking around her, running a hand through hair that was streaked with grey now, 'barely more than a child.'

'She is young,' said Clutterbrock, regarding his subordinate disapprovingly, 'whatever appearances might prompt you to conclude. Now I hope you have all ready, as I required of you? As you see, we are a considerable party.'

Abbot Clutterbrock smoothed down his robe and waved his hand to where a procession of carts and carriages was entering the stable yard. He was a small, wiry man, much given to fasting and to self-denial that he endeavoured to impose on others, too. His regime favoured parsimony in material circumstances that Hardiman did his best to oppose for the sake of others as much as for himself. And yet a spiritual fervour that embraced such policies seemed to have taken hold in the community in recent weeks, and Hardiman found himself even more distanced from those around him. This, amongst other considerations, had strengthened his resolve to act decisively in face of this new challenge.

'I suppose the village is likewise a-heave,' ventured Hardiman as another carriage opened to decant a party of those whose clothing marked them as churchmen. One, with a red face full of peevish dissatisfaction, approached and became recognisable as the Bishop of Chester, an old friend of Clutterbrock's. He opened his mouth to speak, but before he could utter a word a tall, dark-haired figure came striding forward and the crowd fell back before him.

'It is good to be able to welcome you back here, sir,' said Clutterbrock in astonishingly servile tones, ones that Hardiman had never thought to hear from him. Indeed, he seemed barely able to give the newcomer eye contact.

'This is Prince Leo, son of Stephen, our once and future king,' added Clutterbrock reverently, making a bow and doing his best through the action of his eyes and through sheer moral force to enforce the same upon his subordinate.

'Prince Leo,' said Hardiman, 'your servant.' Laura came up behind him, with Blood and Maigret on either side of her. The prior made a vague dip that might, with a generous spirit, be acknowledged as a bow and looked full into Jonah's face. 'You are very welcome. All is prepared according to your instructions.'

'Good,' grunted Jonah, whose habitual dark clothing was now enlivened by a jewelled brooch with the emblem of his father's house. 'Perhaps you would show us to our quarters. I daresay you will tell me that we shall dine before long.'

'Of course,' nodded Hardiman with a glance at Laura. 'And this is she that legend foretold? May I hope to be introduced?'

'Aye, this is Laura, my daughter,' said Jonah, turning to her. 'The vessel of the Lord's Grace, no less. But you may not converse with her. She is fatigued from her journey, and she must prepare herself for tomorrow. I trust you have your list.'

'Of course, my Lord,' said Clutterbrock. 'The elect are made ready. That is certainly the case, is it not, Hardiman?'

The expression on Clutterbrock's face promised fierce retribution if the instructions in his letter had not been carried out precisely as directed.

'It is,' agreed Hardiman somewhat distractedly, his eyes following Laura as she was shown past him and into the reception hall.

There was much to be done. The abbey and its environs must suddenly feed and otherwise accommodate the multitude that now followed in Jonah's wake. There were by now more than a thousand of them, with scores of carriages for the better off, carts and conveyances of various types for the more humble. These already clogged the roads of the village beneath the abbey. And then there were those who travelled on foot, a slow-moving procession of white-shirted revenants and religious enthusiasts that straggled along the road for rather more than a mile, all looking to providence for shelter and food, all now Hardiman's responsibility as dusk gathered around the mere.

Laura's list consisted of twenty-two men and three women that had passed within the portals of the sleep hall during the last three centuries. They had been persons of note in the vicinity: landowners, civic dignitaries, clerics and religious luminaries of various kinds. An itinerary had been prepared that would allow for her to lay hands on each of these in turn in the most efficient manner, beginning with one Richard Castle and ending after a tour of the various halls and passages that should take rather less than an hour or so. Her final appointment was with the late distinguished judge George Armstrong, whose Phariseean tendencies had led to his dismissal from the bench during the last century. She had long ago argued that her work was no spectacle to be gawped at by the merely curious, had declared that it was intolerable that she should be expected to work her miracles with more than five or so in attendance. Jonah had once insisted on accompanying her during her progress, but now he preferred to stay away, occupying himself instead with the business of fermenting his nascent rebellion amongst the peoples of the north and west. In truth Laura's work had little to recommend it as a spectacle, as the onlooker had only her assurance of its success or failure. Even those corpses whose spirits she had rekindled remained apparently inert for some days thereafter, only gradually showing signs of life that the Camoldolites could nourish and urge towards eventual reawakening.

So it was with only Abbot Clutterbrock, Prior Hardiman and three of the abbot's closest associates to accompany her that Laura made her way into the gloom of the sleep hall on the morning of the following day. Mark followed the small party unobserved, for to him had fallen the important duty of closing and locking various doors once the party had moved on. On these occasions Laura was fully conscious, never more so, fully aware of the world around her and Emily stood back mutely in some recess of her mind as her sister went about her business. The first two corpses she visited were quite dead, beyond all hope of reanimation, but the third responded to her touch and so did the fourth, leaving her with the ominous sense of gathering fatigue that she was used to in these circumstances. It was not the healthy fatigue that comes from brisk exercise or honest labour; rather, she well knew, it derived from the unnatural draining of her spirit, the drawing off of a vital essence that might not be replenished. The small white hand that rested upon the brows of the dead had lost the litheness of youth, thickening now around the knuckles. The face that bent close in the flickering lamplight was hollow of cheek and sunken of eye. She felt especially drained now, with a deep ache in her bones that spoke of an exhaustion that was almost complete. Was this it? Had she no more to give? Would Jonah's ultimate aims be frustrated by the premature expenditure of the last remaining spark of her life-force? There was a certain bitter joy in her heart as this thought brushed against the surface of her mind. She stumbled on the threshold of one chamber, quickly supported by the monks on either side of her.

'Is it meant to be like this?' she heard one of them ask.

'Skin and bone,' muttered the other. 'Hardly more than a waif.'

'Be quiet,' snapped Clutterbrock behind them. 'Like all of us she is the servant of the Lord.'

When she was conveyed to the twelfth of her appointments, she became aware that something was wrong and that this something was external to the various physical and mental troubles that afflicted her. Scarcely had she placed her hand upon that dead skin than a gasp behind her made her twitch in sudden alarm, to look up from the wizened features of her subject. At the far side of the small chamber in which they stood another lamp had appeared abruptly.

'What is the meaning of this?' demanded Clutterbrock, peering at the intruder, who was soon joined by another. 'Who are you?'

'I am Laura's liberator,' said a voice that thrilled in Laura's heart and caused her to gasp, even as Clutterbrock grasped her by the forearm and pulled her roughly towards him. 'I am he that shall release her from the foul, demeaning servitude that you and those like you have imposed on her.'

Thomas Corvin, for it was he, advanced towards them with the blunt nose of a pistol directed at Clutterbrock's anguished face. Edward, Laura saw with delight, came after, his own trembling pistol wavering uncertainly between Clutterbrock's three companions.

'Thomas,' breathed Laura. 'You have come for me.'

'I have,' agreed Thomas, advancing close now, pistol held steady at the abbot's head, 'and I shall surely shoot this dog down where he stands unless he unhands you directly. Unhand her, sir, at once.'

'This is an outrage!' spat Clutterbrock as Hardiman edged out from behind him to circle around the chamber and position himself to the rear of the intruders. 'This is a sacred precinct. How dare you invade the peace of the departed? You will surely burn in hellfire for all eternity, for this.'

'Silence!' snapped Thomas, cocking his weapon so that the hammer stood poised to fall, 'or I shall spatter your brains in a very pretty pattern. Then let a thousand years reawaken you, if they may. Unhand her, I say.'

Laura felt the abbot's hand relent in its grip and she fell with a sob into Thomas's embrace.

'Now stand back. Do as I say. Against the wall, yonder,' ordered Thomas, gesturing with his pistol as the three monks fell back, faces sullen and resentful. 'Let none amongst you venture a sudden move.'

Mark slipped into the chamber, nodded with approval at what he saw and crossed to join Hardiman, who now stood anxiously at Edward's side. Clutterbrock's face registered this circumstance for the first time now.

'Hardiman! What is this... treachery?' roared Clutterbrock, stepping forward.

'It is what you see,' said Hardiman grimly, 'and I think it strange to be accused of betrayal by one who encompassed the murder of my good friend Abbot Cole, that worthy man.'

'What?!' Clutterbrock choked, eyes opened wide and his mouth moving wordlessly, but he uttered no more accusations, even as the other monks regarded him wonderingly.

The newly discovered door had indeed been broken down as Thomas had proposed, and it did give access to the flank of the hill, emerging into a high cleft on a cliff face quite invisible from below and almost inaccessible. A dense thicket of bramble, gorse and small trees had grown there since last the door was opened, and it had taken Sir Joseph and his party the best part of a day to clear a path through it. As the midday sun of a March day stood clear above them, Laura was helped down the steepest flank of the great hill to where a covered cart stood waiting in a lane below. Soon they were away. Within the sleep hall, Clutterbrock and his companions lay tied hand and foot amongst the dead, their plaintive cries echoing along the dark corridors. Eventually, when someone remarked upon the lateness of the hour, a party would be sent to find them, but by then Laura and her liberators would be far away. The small fishing village of Brissingham lay close at hand, and there, at the quay, a boat was waiting.

It was the first week in May, and three days of unseasonably warm weather had brought London an early foretaste of what the coming summer might hold. For more than a week after her liberation Laura had lain in bed whilst a slow recovery took hold in her and she began to regain some of the vitality that once had been her endowment. At first, Sir Joseph attended upon her every day, but in truth none of his learning or his experience equipped him to treat the malaise that afflicted her. He could only hope that the passage of time, rest, security and the company of friends would see the improvement of her condition. Perhaps, if she were no longer required to pour out the essence of her life into the bodies of the dead, she would in time see her own vital spirit replenished. Perhaps. Undeniably, as the weeks passed by and April passed into May her friends remarked a discernible plumping of her cheeks, a straightening of her back and a new sparkle in her eye. For herself, Laura's mood was far from the enjoyment of perfect felicity, although the living nightmare of those grim days past was beginning to recede, the dark tide ebbing within her. She dwelt now within the house of Sir George Pellew, through the kindness of his wife Elizabeth, an old friend of Sir Joseph's. Sir George was a wealthy gentleman whose house in the north of the city was equipped with observatories, libraries, collections and laboratories that testified to a passionate interest in natural philosophy that equalled that of his friend, Sir Joseph. Sir George's experimentation with the properties of materials had caused him to ingest a variety of substances that some had warned might be injurious to him. However, whilst his material being continued in rude good health the mind within had declined to a sad degree. Although he experienced periods of lucidity, for much of the time Sir George was troubled by delusions. There were times when he believed himself to be a bluebottle. In accordance with this notion he also believed, wrongly as it proved, that he could fly in time of need. In an attempt to demonstrate this capacity, he had leapt from the head of the staircase at his London home. The flight, as even he had been obliged to concede, had been but of brief duration, the trajectory mostly downward and the landing disappointingly heavy, resulting in the breaking of both his ankles. Despite this mental infirmity, he was an amiable and a generous host, who shuffled about his house wearing an old dressing gown, thanking the servants for their solicitations and distributing small gifts of buttons or blank pages torn from his jotter. Laura quickly conceived an affection for the old gentleman, who was indeed at least twenty years older than his wife and Sir Joseph.

'The view is a very splendid one, is it not?' he asked her as they stood at her window one afternoon, looking south across the city.

'I could not wish for a better one,' she told him, regarding the myriad small vessels that moved busily on the Thames with the childlike wonder that yet remained in her after weeks spent there. 'I confess I shall never cease to delight in the life of this place. There are so many, many people, all busily engaged in their interlocking lives, buying, selling, loving, studying, endlessly discoursing and labouring in a thousand different trades. It is so different from the Eastings that is my home, Sir George. On a different scale again even to Norwich.'

'Indubitably,' nodded her host, whose insanity manifested itself in no obvious fashion this morning, unless one were to remark upon the copper coal scuttle he cradled in his arms, stroking this gently as he spoke. 'And do you find your removal from that place a burden to your mind?' he continued.

'Not at all,' answered Laura. 'To be sure, I think of it often, but I well know that I am fortunate to enjoy your kind hospitality and I am resolved to welcome all the new experiences that this great city affords to me.'

'And you are recovering, I collect?' asked Sir George, turning his face upon her, this filled with a benevolent interest. 'Sir Joseph talks endlessly of your condition, sets great store in your growth in strength, day by day.'

'I thank you for your concern,' replied Laura with a warm smile. 'And I believe I am a little better than I was even this time last week. Sir Joseph is perfectly content with me, at least so far as he will admit.'

'And you do not entirely share his confidence?' probed Sir George, his face clouding somewhat.

'Pray, do not be alarmed,' assured Laura, placing a reassuring hand on Sir George's forearm. 'I only mean that there are many factors that bear upon my recovery – and not all of them are susceptible to Sir Joseph's intervention.'

'I see,' said Sir George, raising an eyebrow that brought this declaration immediately into question.

Mrs Harding, the nurse whose duty it was to see that Sir George adhered to his regime of medicines, came into the room at this point and Laura was left alone with her thoughts. With one part of her consciousness, she attended to Sir George's oddly wheedling voice as he engaged in a futile dispute with Mrs Harding about the efficacy, taste and odour of the draught that he must consume. On the other hand, the greater part of her was moved to consider her reflection in the mirror above the mantel. Her eyes filled with tears as they were wont to do on these occasions, wiped impatiently away with the back of her hand. There had been a time when the sight of her own reflection was a horror, a pain too sharp to bear, that she had avoided at all costs, refusing even to enter a room that contained a mirror. Now she had become inured to that pain, had hardened her heart to it, even though the sight of her thin grey locks still pierced her to the core and caused those bitter tears to rim her eyes once more.

Edward was a comfort to her, and Thomas, when he came. But he came infrequently now, caught up with his father's business as rebellion simmered beneath the city's placid surface. In truth, there were occasions when she was glad that such matters detained him. As she had changed, so had he. The glint of passion in his eye had gone. That well-remembered spark of amorous intent had been a precious treasure to her in the long days of her captivity, but now it had faded. Had it ever been there at all? Had it only ever been the confection of a wishful heart, one that yearned to see her own desire reciprocated? But now she saw pity in his eyes – and other things, besides. There was guilt, perhaps, and regret, too, possibly even a strand of superstitious disgust, a complex melange of emotions that made it hard for Thomas to be with her. A lithe sword arm and a body trained to a fine pitch of perfection was no protection from this assault against his inner mind. It had begun even as they stood in Whale Hall and his unwavering pistol commanded her release. Even then his eye had flickered to her face and a cold shadow of shock had passed across his own. There had been a discernible catch in his voice as they withdrew, and the arms that had embraced her as they stood upon the windy hillside betrayed a curious reticence. She had felt his kiss on her forehead then, but the finger that lifted her chin the better to behold her face was atremble and the eyes that regarded her were filled with naked, wondering dismay.

The sound of activity downstairs reminded Laura that Sir Joseph had promised to call. He visited once a week in general, ostensibly to minister to his old friend Sir George. Only a very small circle of people were aware of Laura's presence in his house. It was well that this was so. She shuddered, when she thought of it, to consider that Jonah's men must be searching the country very diligently to find her, must be enquiring in every street in London, in fact. But for now, she felt secure. Leaving Sir George and his reluctant acceptance of his medicine behind, she moved out onto the landing. From here she could see down into the hall, to where Sir Joseph was handing his hat and coat to Bristow, the butler. Sensing her presence, he glanced up and offered her a warm smile, touching his brow in a mock salute.

'And how are we this morning?" he asked when she had descended to the green drawing room that offered the best light in this season.

'I am very well,' she answered, having rushed into his arms and been warmly embraced and released. 'And I am glad to see you.'

Sir Joseph regarded her affectionately at arm's length, head cocked on one side, his keen eye traversing her for any evidence that might contradict her declaration of wellbeing. He found none and found, in fact, that he appeared to be looking at a moderately healthy woman in her late forties. He released his gentle hold on her forearms.

'Shall I call for tea?' she asked, once he had given account of his activities during the last week and she had asked after her friends.

'That would be delightful,' agreed Sir Joseph as she pulled the cord that would summon either Bristow or one of his underlings. 'I see that you are quite comfortable here now, quite at home in these surroundings.'

'Most certainly I am comfortable enough,' said Laura with a laugh. 'Who wouldn't be? This place is to Groomfield as Groomfield is to a pauper's hovel. No, in every material sense I could hardly be better provided for.'

'And how do you... feel, in yourself, that is?' asked Sir Joseph after recollections of Tithing Harrow had been exchanged.

The delicacy in his question and the tone of the voice in which he asked made it clear that it was her mental wellbeing that was the subject of his enquiry. They were seated now, and for a moment she looked down into her hands, folded neatly in her lap, before responding. It was hardly necessary for her to survey the content of her mind before making her answer, but she did so anyway, recognising that Sir Joseph required particular reassurance on this point. In truth, she was happy to admit that her mind had been as sick as the body that sustained it at the time of her rescue. But now she felt much recovered. Emily remained, as ever, on the fringes of her mind, but her sister seemed to have lost the capacity for independent speech and action that once she had, reverting instead to the dear creature of treasured memory that was her rightful status. Nor was she any more assailed by the shades of the dead, by night or by day. A calm had settled upon her, and in that calm both body and spirit grew a little stronger day by day.

'And will Thomas come to see me again soon, do you suppose?' asked Laura, when tea had been brought and she had heard his activities described, so far as Sir Joseph was able to recount. 'I have seen him only twice in these six weeks, and even then, he was in company.'

Sir Joseph looked out of the window as he raised his cup, the better to conceal the pity that momentarily clouded his eyes.

'He is heavily engaged, as you know, very regretful that his duties forbade him…'

'Of course,' agreed Laura, nodding sadly. 'I quite understand. And I well appreciate it would be indelicate to importune him in any way.'

'I shall, of course, mention my visit today, when next I see him,' soothed Sir Joseph, 'convey to him your compliments and good wishes.'

'I should be obliged,' replied Laura, catching sight of herself reflected in the windowpane as a sudden gleam of light marked the passing of a cloud. A bitter pang of regret pierced her heart once more as she was reminded of her stolen youth.

'And Edward? I gather he is a frequent visitor here,' continued Sir Joseph, remarking with concern the sudden sadness in her eyes. 'I trust you find consolation in his company.'

'I do,' said Laura warmly. 'I do indeed. He is such a friend to me.'

It had been transparently obvious to Laura that the young man had laboured to maintain his composure in her presence during the first few days after her release. Laura's prevailing emotion at that time had been a pleasurable relief that bordered on the ecstatic once the reality of her unexpected liberation had come within her comprehension. The trancelike state that she had dwelt in for the last weeks of her captivity yielded slowly to the evidence of her senses even as the cart bore her away.

Thomas, once he had helped her to her place and he had looked upon her in daylight, sat like stone, seemingly incapable of intelligent speech. Edward, however, had placed his arm around her shoulder and drawn her close to him, soothing her with kind words, even as Sir Joseph had taken her pulse and made the first and most elementary investigations of her health. Sir Joseph was well-used to maintaining a front of professional neutrality in these circumstances, but Edward's countenance betrayed the same shocked concern that she had witnessed earlier in that of Thomas. Edward's face remained turned resolutely to face her, nevertheless, and his hand had held hers gently as the cart bore them towards their waiting boat.

Recollection of what were becoming to seem distant events made her smile as they walked in Sir George's garden later that day. Edward had brought cakes from Cheapside Market, and the few that remained stood with their coffee cups on the little wrought iron table by the pond. Her own inclination would have been to sit there longer in the warm afternoon sun, but Edward insisted that she should take a few turns around the larger of the two lawns that occupied the greater part of the garden.

'Sir Joseph recommends that you should take frequent exercise,' he had said, taking her hand to help her from her chair. 'Even if it is only a very little – and I shall hold you to your duty. Surely those fat carp are sufficiently indulged.'

Brushing her hands to remove the cake crumbs that she had been feeding to those creatures, Laura had surrendered to her friend's good sense. There remained a dull ache in her right hip and her movements lacked the lithe grace that had distinguished her even a few months since. Nevertheless, Edward was pleased with her, and they spoke with such cheerful familiarity as they walked, it was hard to believe that those grim days with Jonah had ever happened. They had begun to seem like a dark dream. It was a dream that, once remembered, had the power to dim the brilliance of the brightest day, however, and this it did from time to time, even when her mood was at its most buoyant. The sight of a crow could provoke its recollection or the yawning mouth of a dark passage between two houses. Her eye clouded now as they stood beneath the blossom-bowed cherry that stood at the furthest extremity of the garden, and they turned to look back at the house. Edward regarded the sudden pallor in her cheeks and squeezed her hand in a way that he thought she might find comforting.

'It is a fine house, is it not?' he asked in the hope of offering distraction.

'It is very fine,' she murmured, 'and Sir George and Lady Elizabeth have been kindness itself.'

Then she turned suddenly upon him, and her face was full of concern.

'Oh, Edward. Do you think he will find me again? I swear I could not bear it.'

'Not whilst I live and breathe shall I allow it,' said Edward, swinging her hand, 'and I know there are many who would likewise lay down their lives to protect you from that foul toad of a man.'

'Because I am a tool that they would employ to unseat the king?' asked Laura, and then, before Edward could open his mouth to respond, raising her free hand. 'No, pray do not answer that, I beg you. It was a question that betrays a self-indulgence that is quite unworthy of me.'

'Surely he must search for you,' pondered Edward after a while. 'But Sir Joseph takes precautions to ensure that he is not followed when he attends here, and so do I. My journey here this afternoon was so circuitous I should have confused myself utterly had I not paused from time to time to assure myself of my location.' He laughed. 'I am far from confident in finding my way in this vast city, and you will not be surprised to hear that it took me the best part of an hour to make my way back to Sir Joseph's lodgings on my last visit here. I swear I passed by the same street hawker selling lavender on four separate occasions, and at last I was obliged to take a hansom cab for fear of missing my supper.'

They walked back to their place by the pond now, where a few small birds flew up from their preoccupation with the remaining crumbs. Laura was glad to ease her hip and she stretched her back carefully as she settled herself into her seat once more.

'And you will come again next week, I suppose,' she asked, when Edward drew out the pocket watch that Sir George had given him to find that it told four of the afternoon.

'I will, and I hope to have news for you. Corvin has summoned his confederates to an important meeting in a few days' time. Doubtless, his own plans must adapt to meet present realities.'

Chapter Twenty

'The public finances are in a parlous state, I collect,' said Sir Joseph.

'When were they ever not?' observed Matthew Corvin. 'But the recent harvests and the various economic difficulties have rendered them still worse. My contacts in the Treasury have furnished me with some most interesting information. Perhaps you would care...' He pushed a document across the table to Sir Joseph, who drew out his spectacles from his jacket. 'Even the headings make most stimulating reading.'

They sat in the small room above a printer's shop that Corvin had engaged as his London headquarters. A lazy fly buzzed at the window and a clock ticked quietly on the mantel.

'And you propose to share this with your confederates when you meet tomorrow?' asked Sir Joseph, having read for some moments.

'I do. As you know, delegates from most regions are already in the city, and most at great personal risk. There is only so much that can be accomplished by encoded message or by word of mouth.'

'There is considerable danger to the movement,' observed Sir Joseph, 'with so many of your adherents gathered in one place.'

'Of course,' agreed Corvin grimly. 'But needs must, and we must agree a course of action. I particularly wish to acquaint them with one particular statistic,' he said as he tapped the document in Sir Joseph's hand, 'which must surely stiffen even the frailest resolve.'

'This one, I assume,' said Sir Joseph, turning the paper.

'Indeed. Officials have always refused to confirm the figure, but there we have it plain. Between a quarter and a third of the nation's wealth is spent on the care of the dead, and this whilst the common folk starve in the streets. It cannot go on.'

'But it will so long as the bloated behemoth of the state sustains it,' said Sir Joseph, setting down the document with great care, as though it had the power to explode in his face, 'and the present monarch sets his face against change.'

'And there's the rub,' said Corvin, rubbing his chin pensively. 'How fare your plans for reanimating the late, dear queen?'

'Well, Laura is restored to us, as well you know,' said Sir Joseph, folding his spectacles.

'Of course,' said Corvin. 'Thomas has described events in detail. I take it the flame of his sudden passion is extinguished.'

'So it would appear. The poor girl presents the appearance of a much older person now. She is somewhat recovered but remains very weak. I fear her frame will sustain little in terms of physical affront. She may already have reached the limit of her endurance regarding the waking of the dead.'

'And yet you still propose to employ her as we have discussed?'

'She is resolved upon it herself,' said Sir Joseph regretfully, 'and wishes to play some part in the downfall of the vast mechanism we deplore. I cannot dissuade her; even should I wish to. If we would bring about change, we must all commit ourselves without reserve, whatever that resolve might cost us. Laura has made that choice.'

'A brave girl,' observed Corvin. 'A witch or a saint, depending on whom you ask, and one whose person is sought with the utmost zeal by the king's men and the Phariseeans, too. Where do you stand on that? On her status, that is?'

'Naturally I reject both labels,' said Sir Joseph, 'since they derive from irrationality and ignorance. Of course, she is a person of great interest, with powers seemingly beyond our comprehension, but I do not ascribe this to supernatural phenomena. Her powers lie beyond the means of science to comprehend just now but may yield at last to our understanding in some future age, when our knowledge is more advanced. Such is my faith, one that derives from the power of the human mind to unlock the secrets of the universe. Why, in the dawn of time even the clap of thunder was ascribed to the anger of the gods.'

'And science is your god?'

'It is not,' answered Sir Joseph carefully. 'Certainly, it is not. I only say that the Lord's creation is accessible to human understanding and that intelligent enquiry is what sets us apart from the savages.'

'Whose own irrational prejudices may be about to plunge us into another dark age,' stated Corvin with a sniff. 'Religious passions are rising, are they not? It seems an unpropitious time to provoke a revolution based on reason.'

'And yet it must be done,' said Sir Joseph, 'and I believe the circumstances may yet occur for us to play our strongest card.'

'Really? You regard her as our strongest card? I should have thought her more a desperate last hope. There is no guarantee that the old queen is susceptible to waking, even should we be able to place Laura at her side. It seems ironic that so fervent a proponent of reason should place such reliance on chance and on a power so far beyond the grasp of that reason.'

'Ironic it might be and yet there it is,' said Sir Joseph with a grim smile, 'and I believe I have the beginnings of a plan.'

The Duke of Cumberland, the late queen's cousin and once her Prime Minister, died in the last week of May. His physician, the eminent Sir James Baskerville, had predeceased him by several weeks, and Sir Joseph, almost equally eminent, had been prevailed upon to replace him. In fact, any apparent reluctance on Sir Joseph's part was no more than affectation, as the opportunity to minister to the ailing noble seemed to him to be a situation that might be exploited to great advantage. It was quite clear that the Duke was dying, quite clear that only palliative care was called for and that the administration of laudanum, in increasing quantities, was all that was required of Sir Joseph in the medical way. Whereas the Duke's last days offered no more than appropriate remuneration and the chance to say farewell to a thoroughly decent old man, his funeral arrangements brought with them numerous enticing opportunities. Sir Joseph went to visit Matthew Corvin on the afternoon of his first house call, taking Edward with him.

'Yes, I have contacts,' nodded Corvin, sitting across a plain table from his guests. 'You would be surprised at the extent of my web.'

'But we would need uninterrupted access to the Royal Mews, to the carriage house itself,' noted Sir Joseph. 'Are your contacts quite so extensive?'

'I must speak to Searle,' replied Corvin, naming one of his chiefs of staff. 'But I believe we have a sympathiser in that area, or at least one with the ability to wield influence there. I shall certainly enquire. And perhaps I might enquire as to the way your mind moves? There is a glint in your eye that speaks of a certain smug self-satisfaction.'

'How well you know me, Matthew,' said Sir Joseph with a smile. He beckoned to Edward, who had thus far held his silence, staring into a glass of watered wine with an expression of barely contained impatience. 'Edward, perhaps you would describe what we know of funereal customs in the royal house.'

'With pleasure,' said Edward, his face suddenly animated, his grip tightening on the glass.

'And how is Sir George today?' asked Edward, when news of the Duke's death had been conveyed to Laura and she had uttered appropriate sentiments of regret. The Duke's reputation had been well known, even in the distant Eastings. It was as though an era died with him, the late queen's era, and carried her reign further from the national consciousness towards the realm of history.

'He is well enough,' answered Laura, 'although he resisted taking his black draught with unusual force this morning, and he spoke most intemperately about Sir Joseph indeed. I blushed to hear him; I swear.'

She smiled at the recollection and nudged at a fallen twig with her toe. They sat, as so often, by the pond and listened in companionable silence for a while as a thrush sang its liquid paean of joy in a tree at the end of the garden.

'Lady Elizabeth is a handsome woman, is she not?' observed Laura after a while. 'And she has been kindness itself since my arrival here, shown me every sign of sympathy and indulgence. More than any poor supplicant could wish for, in fact. She gave me this necklace, certainly the loveliest thing I have ever worn.'

She held it away from the wrinkled skin of her neck for Edward to admire, a slender silver chain with pendants that diminished in size according to their distance from the central one. Each held a tiny, sparkling gem of some sort.

'Indeed, she is a fine woman,' agreed Edward.

'And she bears her misfortune in a very dignified and resolute fashion,' continued Laura. 'It cannot be easy to be wife to a celebrated lunatic, no matter how wealthy.'

'I suppose it must be a trial to her,' concurred Edward. 'But she is well-regarded in society, by all accounts. Perhaps her situation brings with it less of the social burden, less of the stigma that would attach to it in our own dear Eastings.'

'It could hardly be more onerous than that of being mother to a witch,' said Laura dryly, causing Edward to frown. 'My poor mama.'

'Well, the analogy is not exact,' he said.

They lapsed into silence once more, each lost in their own thoughts whilst the song thrush poured out his eloquence upon the world.

'Sir Joseph is very attentive upon his friend,' said Laura at last. 'Even before my own arrival here his visits were very frequent. Or so I understand.'

'Definitely,' said Edward gravely. 'Evidently, he feels a keen sense of duty to Sir George as his friend and mentor. I believe he held Sir George's intellect in the highest regard before the episodes that occasioned his eccentricity.'

'Or madness, as some would say,' observed Laura, 'although to see him discuss the content of the news sheets with the Reverend Pritchard after church this morning you would not have thought him unsound of mind. He is an inconsistent lunatic.'

'I don't suppose we should invite consistency in that respect,' said Edward, 'and you will recall that Sir George's mind was reputed to be amongst the keenest in the land at one time.'

'Have you noticed a particular reserve in Sir Joseph's relationship with Lady Elizabeth?' asked Laura, observing the flight of the thrush to a neighbouring garden. 'It is as though he measures his speech and his glances, the set of his features, with great exactitude when he calls upon her.'

'I confess I have not noticed,' admitted Edward.

'But then you are a man,' laughed Laura, the tilt of her chin, the sudden light in her eyes recalling the girl that once had been with such sudden clarity, that Edward's own responding smile took the place of a voice that for a moment he dared not trust.

'I suspect that same reticence is not apparent when they converse privately together,' she continued. 'Tell me, does Sir Joseph ever open his heart to you with regard to that heart's engagement with the female sex.'

'He does not,' confessed Edward. 'I presume you do not suggest he harbours a preference for his own?'

'Sir Joseph? Never in life,' said Laura, squeezing Edward's hand. 'No, I only suggest that for some men the world offers only one true abiding love and that these men are often the prisoners of their own constancy, their own devotion. They hold to that love regardless of the circumstances that fate imposes on them, whether that should entail the satisfaction of their desire or its frustration, and they will not look elsewhere for consolation.'

For a long moment Edward did not answer, could not answer, only casting his eyes downward whilst words jostled for attention within his inner mind.

'And you think that Sir Joseph is such a creature?' he asked at last.

'Perhaps he is,' agreed Laura. 'Perhaps he loves Lady Elizabeth. You know of no other liaisons, I presume?'

'And what of Lady Elizabeth?' asked Edward, shaking his head. 'Have you observed in her behaviour anything to suggest that this hypothetical attachment might be reciprocated?'

'Her behaviour exactly mirrors that of Sir Joseph, I should say,' said Laura thoughtfully, 'a public reticence and reserve that might be thought excessive in one who has known the man for so many years, a man who has preserved her husband from any number of episodes that might have brought about his premature death or indeed his committal to an asylum.'

'She must be very grateful,' said Edward ironically, provoking a wry smile in his companion.

'How she must rejoice,' she said. 'And yet each is governed by the iron hand of duty, at once their solace and their pain.'

'And which now prevails, do you think?' asked Edward, as the subjects of their discussion emerged from the house, advancing towards them across the terrace, apparently conversing about nothing more controversial that the dovecote which stood in clear need of restoration.

'I trust I find you well?' said Sir Joseph when they stood before them, when Edward and Laura had risen from their seats. 'There is a fine colour in your cheeks just now.'

Sir Joseph placed a chair for Lady Elizabeth, and soon tea was brought as they settled to discuss Laura's recovery, the likely temperament of Lady Elizabeth's new neighbours and various other subjects as the shadows lengthened across the path and the declining sun settled behind the distant bulk of Saint Paul's.

'It grows a little chilly,' observed Sir Joseph at length, 'and there are matters I should like to discuss with Laura indoors, if I may suggest our withdrawal there.'

Once inside, once the corridor had been checked to ensure that no servants lurked within earshot, Sir Joseph settled himself in a chair and leaned close to Laura.

'Are you still prepared to carry out the task you once proposed to us?' he asked.

Laura did not respond at once. Her eyes opened wide, and the slightest twitch of her head indicated her concern that Lady Elizabeth remained present.

'You need not concern yourself in that regard,' said Lady Elizabeth with a smile. 'I am long a Corvinite. I believe Sir Joseph trusts to my discretion.'

'None more,' said Sir Joseph with a private glance that escaped neither Edward's nor Laura's attention. 'I would not ask this of you were I not sensible of your desire to advance our cause and my belief that you are physically and mentally recovered to an extent that might render your participation possible.'

'I do feel much better,' said Laura, 'but what exactly do you require of me? If I must awaken the queen, I shall certainly make the attempt, but I always understood that a great many practical difficulties stood in the way.'

'And still they do,' confessed Sir Joseph. 'But the Duke of Cumberland's death and his approaching funeral have brought about an opportunity, a combination of circumstances, that may never occur again, and I believe we may be able to place you within the royal crypt.'

Laura regarded the grave faces of her friends, wide-eyed.

'How so?'

'The Raven has adherents in many places,' said Sir Joseph, 'and one of those is the master carpenter whose duties entail the maintenance of the various carriages within the Royal Mews.'

'I see,' said Laura doubtfully. 'And how does that assist us?'

Sir Joseph stood and crossed to regard a small landscape painting with apparent scorn, clasping his hands behind his back.

'In order for me to make that clear, I must first describe to you the proceedings of the funeral that will shortly be taking place,' he said, turning to face them once more.

It appeared that the Duke's body had already been attended by senior members of the Camoldolite order and anointed in the manner that would begin the process of its preservation. For now, it lay in state within the royal chapel attached to St James' Palace. On the day of the funeral the open casket would be conveyed to the Royal Mews and there placed upon the magnificent, gilded catafalque that was traditionally used on these occasions. Draped in black velvet embroidered with the Duke's heraldic arms, drawn by eight black horses with nodding black plumes on their heads, the catafalque would progress through the streets of the city. Its passage would be attended by regiments of horse and foot guards, followed on foot by civic and religious dignitaries, perhaps as many as a thousand strong. At the steps of Westminster Abbey, the casket would be carried in, to lie beneath the high altar whilst William Turnbull, the Bishop of London, delivered the service.

'Bishop Turnbull?' asked Laura, her eyes clouding with fear at the recollection of his heavy features, his pitiless gaze. 'The one who condemned me to be hanged?'

'The same,' agreed Edward. 'For now, he is returned to London.'

Laura nodded and swallowed hard as Sir Joseph continued his account.

After the funeral the casket would be returned to the catafalque and then drawn through the streets to St Dominic's Abbey, the sleep hall in which the bodies of the royal dead had lain for five hundred years or more, the Duke's casket vanishing within the portals of that place and from the sight of all except the Camoldolites. Once inside, the catafalque would be drawn within the vestibule of the crypt, the horses taken away, the great doors shut, and the vehicle left overnight for the Duke's last solitary vigil before the Lord's altar. Only with the coming of the new day would the body be taken from the casket and carried to the bier that had been prepared for it within the precincts of the crypt itself.

'And you are quite sure of this?' asked Laura. 'Your description sounds very exact.'

'It is as exact as we can make it,' said Sir Joseph, 'and it may surprise you to learn that we have a highly placed sympathiser within the order itself. Without his assistance we would have no understanding of the nature of proceedings or the layout of the crypt itself.'

'But you have not made it clear how I may be introduced into that crypt in the first place,' objected Laura. 'I suppose its custodians may take a dim view of my strolling in.'

'Indeed, they might,' agreed Sir Joseph, 'and you must listen some more.'

Chapter Twenty-One

The guards at the gate of the Royal Mews were unused to late-night visitors, but these were not ordinary circumstances: the palace had been the scene of purposeful activity throughout the day as preparations were made for the state funeral that would take place on the morrow. It was well after ten of the clock and all the workmen had long gone to their homes when Mitchell, the duty sergeant, peered through the gate to see who had summoned him from his desk. The urgent, importunate jangling of the bell obliged him to set down his newssheet, button his jacket and make his way to the great double gates that gave access to the yard.

'Well?' he demanded, peering into the gloom, adding, 'Oh, it's you, Hughes,' when the visitor approached closer to the gate, coming within the dim circle of light cast by a lamp on the far side of the yard. 'I'd have thought you'd have had your fill today.'

'I have so,' answered the visitor, who was the chief carpenter of the palace. 'But there's a shim on that forward axle that preys most cruelly on my mind. I knew I should ha' checked it earlier on, but that wretched greaser Colmore would bang on interminably about his mother and it quite went out o' my head. I'd be mortified if the damned wheel came off in the Strand.'

'So would we all,' laughed the sergeant, jingling his keys, squinting to find the right one and pulling open the gate a few moments later. 'Although it would surely make an occasion to remember.'

'Not one I care to contemplate,' said Hughes, standing back as Thomas Corvin, Edward and Laura filed through, dressed as the poorer type of artisans, carrying various toolboxes and a few lengths of wood.

'I hope you're paying overtime,' observed the sergeant, nodding to Hughes' 'artisans' and closing the gate behind them.

'Ha!' grunted Thomas, in a manner that he hoped suggested ironic scorn.

'You mind your lip now,' said the carpenter as the party crossed the yard and the sergeant scratched his rump before turning back to the guard house.

Once inside the great coach house, with the door shut behind them, Thomas, Edward and Laura embraced each other and slumped to the floor in relief. Hughes, having lit a lamp, regarded them disapprovingly. His face, unevenly lamp-lit, was unnaturally pale and flecked with beads of sweat.

'You did well,' said Thomas at last. 'Very well.'

'I thought the catch in my voice would surely betray me,' said the carpenter, shaking his head. 'I must be mad to do this. Whatever was I thinking?'

'I suppose we must light more lamps,' said Edward, looking around the cavernous coach house, where various of the royal house's gilded coaches and carriages stood about in shadowed bays, 'in case anyone should happen upon us, and we should need to seem to be at work.'

'Will you show us where we must hide?' asked Laura, crossing to the catafalque which occupied the centre of the space, ready to be drawn out into the yard beyond when morning came.

'Aye,' said Hughes, mopping at his brow with his sleeve.

The catafalque was essentially a tall rectangular box with two axles and four wheels, draped in embroidered black velvet, surmounted by an elaborate canopy with flags and feathered black plumes. The open casket was to lie beneath the canopy on its flat surface, surrounded by an ornate, gilt work structure carved with mourning angels and heraldic beasts. Since the casket needed to be raised high for the purposes of public display, the hollow box beneath was surprisingly capacious, transfixed by the axles but otherwise largely empty. Into this space, the carpenter had secretly installed four padded shelves, each large enough to accommodate a person lying down. These could be accessed simply by lifting the vehicle's hanging velvet skirts and crawling between the wheels.

'It is very dark in here,' called Laura when she had squeezed into place.

'Here,' said the carpenter stooping to pass a lamp to her. 'There is a hook, just so, above your shoulder.'

'This is excellent,' said Edward, joining Laura, holding up the velvet so that Thomas could complete the party. 'We shall be a little cramped, but I should think it will answer. What do you say?'

'I say this will be the strangest journey of my life,' noted Thomas with a grin, climbing onto his shelf and stretching himself out. 'How long do you suppose we shall be in here?'

'Sir Joseph calculates our confinement during the service and during the journey to St Dominic's should be no longer than four hours,' said Edward, whose height obliged him to stoop in the centre of the space.

'Oh dear,' said Laura, regarding a chamber pot that hung at one end of the space. 'I trust that there are occasions when a lady may be allowed some privacy.'

'The lamp may need to be dimmed on occasion,' conceded Edward, catching her drift, 'and it certainly would not do to upset the pot.'

The somewhat nervous hilarity occasioned by this remark was stilled when Hughes thrust his anxious, fractious face into the space.

'You'll need to be a damn sight quieter than that,' he snapped, 'unless the noble corpse be presumed to be rejoicing in some private joke...I trust all is to your satisfaction?'

'It is perfection itself,' said Thomas soothingly. 'I could only wish you had thought to install a card table. Four hours of confinement here may rather drag, I fear.'

'I should think boredom might be the least of your concerns,' observed the carpenter, whose frayed nerves made him impervious to humour, however broad, 'and you may wish to recall that you must still remain in there even in St Dominic's, at least until nightfall.'

The guard sergeant's duty was to end at midnight. His replacement, a corporal called Busby would doubtless have been notified that Hughes and his party were on the premises. It had been decided that Hughes would leave around one o'clock. If challenged as to the whereabouts of the rest of his party he would simply claim that they had left earlier, their passage unrecorded by the sergeant, whose duty might primarily be considered to control entry rather than exit. If necessary, the corporal might be advised to take this up with his superior on the morrow. For now, though, there was little to do except to lay out some of the carpenter's tools in case their subterfuge should be investigated. They had not long completed this when there came the sound of approaching conversation and the door swung open that gave access to the palace itself.

'The casket will proceed this way, then, and not across the yard?' asked Bishop Turnbull as he walked with Abel

Ward and a palace official along the corridor that led to the coach house. 'It is a shorter distance, I collect?'

'It is,' agreed the official, whose name was Dawkins. He was still somewhat dismayed at having been summoned at this hour. 'And it does not place us at the mercy of the elements, should the weather be inclement?' he continued. 'Once beneath the canopy of the catafalque, of course, such contingencies need not concern us.'

'Of course,' agreed the bishop, waiting as the official fumbled for a key as they approached another door.

'The distance from the chapel to this place is three hundred and twenty-two paces, by my calculation,' added Ward. His irritation at what he considered to be Turnbull's overly thorough attention to the details of tomorrow's proceedings had manifested itself in the provision of numerous such tedious statistics during the course of their tour, 'and it has taken us, allowing for pauses, let me see, five and a half minutes.'

'Thank you, Ward,' said Turnbull vaguely, as the door was opened, and they passed through into the coach house. Even at this hour, final preparations were being made to the catafalque, workmen paying close attention to the spokes of one of its great black wheels. He had been acutely anxious about the conduct of this funeral, ever since Lamb had placed it in his hands. It was a compliment, as all acknowledged, and with the succession to the archiepiscopacy very much in question much depended on everything running smoothly. For this reason, Turnbull had insisted on detailed oversight of every aspect of the proceedings, from the order of service to the details of the route. The inspection of the catafalque itself, very much an afterthought, was amongst the last of the checks on the extensive list that he had prepared.

'I had thought that this was all ready,' observed Dawkins irritably, as they approached the catafalque. 'You, sir! Was this not all prepared earlier?'

'Pardon me, s... s... sir,' stuttered the carpenter, his evident anxiety perfectly explained by the circumstances. 'I've been troubling myself about this here axle. Couldn't sleep 'cause of it and thought I should give it one last look over, see.'

'I applaud your concern,' grunted the bishop, noting that the man's assistants stood about, looking suitably shifty or cowed. One young man held a hammer with a trembling hand. A slight woman in her middle years, whose wispy grey hair strayed from her headscarf, averted her gaze abruptly when he looked at her, her hand frozen in the act of polishing the gilded lion at the front of the vehicle.

'Very well, carry on,' nodded Turnbull as Dawkins described the process by which the casket would be loaded onto the platform.

It was not until he was walking back along the corridor, the official's voice still droning in his ear, that a vague anxiety he had been experiencing swam within the focus of his inner mind. He stopped abruptly so that Ward came within a hand's breadth of colliding with his back.

'My Lord?' asked Dawkins, interrupted in his flow. 'Something troubles you? All is not to your satisfaction?'

'Wait,' the bishop snapped, raising his hand as he struggled to define the nature of the circumstance that had so abruptly pierced him. It was the woman's pale face that for the briefest of moments had registered within his vision. But whose face? And why was he afflicted by such sudden anguish? Why was that face so familiar to him and yet so strangely unfamiliar? He closed his eyes, and the answer, floating tantalisingly out of reach, came at last within his grasp, bringing a leap of satisfaction in his heart. It was the girl, Laura DeLacey, she that he had condemned to death, she that had escaped his justice, she that was called a witch or a saint.

'What is it?' asked Ward at his shoulder. 'You look as though you have seen a ghost.'

Not a ghost, but certainly a spectre that had haunted his dreams these last months. With recognition came surprise – somehow, she appeared aged, although the identification nevertheless became more certain with every passing second. He was also beset by an agonising irresolution. Certainly, he should turn back, summon guards, order the immediate arrest of that party and bring the girl before him. And yet he found that he could not. It was abundantly clear where his duty lay. A large part of his mind oppressed him with the consciousness of this turn of events. His lips moved wordlessly as Ward and Dawkins regarded him with wondering concern.

'You are unwell,' said Ward, eyes wide, and then, to the official, 'he is unwell. Perhaps there is somewhere at hand we could sit down, obtain a drink?'

'Why yes, of course,' said Dawkins. 'There is a room just here.'

'No, no,' Turnbull wagged a finger, trying to compose himself. 'That will not be necessary. I am fine. A momentary faintness, that is all. Doubtless some fresh air will revive me. I believe I have seen enough, sir.'

Ward paused for a moment to watch as the bishop stepped out once more, his considerable bulk regaining the swaying gait that distinguished him but somehow shorn of the confidence that was also its endowment. He frowned, scratched his chin pensively and glanced along the corridor behind them.

'That's me out of here, then,' said the carpenter some time later, having studied his pocket watch once more. 'I suppose that fool of a sergeant will have gone by now. I shall wish you Godspeed.'

He shook hands with each of them, murmured more about the desirability of divine intervention and withdrew to the yard. Listening at the door, the others could hear his receding footsteps, even the great gate creaking open to let him out. At last, there was silence once more.

'I suppose we had better put out these lamps,' said Thomas at last, 'saving just the one and being prepared to darken even that one at the least sign that anyone approaches.'

'Yes,' said Edward. 'I suppose we should.'

He regarded Laura anxiously. Seated on an upturned pail she had barely spoken since the bishop's departure.

'What if he knew me?' she asked, posing a question that she had asked in various forms during the last hour or so.

'Do you think we should still be at liberty?' replied Thomas a little shortly, his patience wearing thin after having previously made several soothingly emollient responses. A warning glance from Edward caused him to turn away and pace off into the enveloping darkness beyond the lamp's meagre circle of yellow light.

'We shall do what we shall do,' said Edward, taking her hand and looking into the strangely aged face that still, even now, had the capacity to shock him. 'You know it.'

'We shall,' she whispered, squeezing back. 'Surely we shall, but this night will be the longest of our lives.'

Even if it is not the last, was the response that came into Edward's mind, but remained unspoken as the night trickled slowly past them and the first signs of dawn lightened the sky beyond the coach house windows. When Edward's watch told five, they took their places within the body of the catafalque, sitting on the ground and waiting to move onto their narrow shelves at the first sign of movement beyond.

Bishop Turnbull had attended the late queen's state funeral, some years previously, and others of various exalted persons since then, but the Duke of Cumberland's most nearly approached the dignity of hers, representing a genuine outpouring of grief across the capital and the nation beyond. The streets along the route from St James' Palace to the abbey were crowded not only with the citizens of the great city, but also by peasantry from the surrounding country and by people of the middling sort, who might have travelled considerable distances to be present on this occasion. There was a respectful silence, no more than a susurration of doffed hats as the long procession came past, with splendid guardsmen trotting in front of the catafalque. Drawn by its eight coal black mares it made a splendid spectacle, great black plumes nodding in the breeze, gilt angels glinting in the morning sun as the aged duke, beneath his dark canopy, set out on his final journey. Behind the catafalque walked close members of his family, a footman with his favourite dog and then companies of guards with slow-cadenced steps and finally representatives of the Houses of Parliament, of the Church and of the city's many guilds. The procession was the best part of a mile long. Standing in the wide space that had been cleared before Westminster Abbey, the bishop awaited the duke.

A perceptive observer might have noticed the unusual pallor of the face beneath the ornate mitre that was the mark of his high office. He was dressed in all the extravagant pomp of that office, his considerable bulk swathed in embroidered silks. In his right hand he bore the spectacular jewelled crook that recalled to some minds the fact that a bishop represented the shepherd of a spiritual flock. Not that there was anything about Turnbull that suggested even the most tenuous connection with agriculture. Nor could his mind be said to occupy the spiritual plane as the procession drew into the square that was called the Sanctuary and approached his place at the west front of the abbey. Turnbull's brain was preoccupied with more earthly considerations, and its relentlessly fevered activity had allowed him no sleep at all.

'Why should she be there?' he had asked himself, the question nagging at the core of his rational mind whilst he had lain restlessly in bed. Myriad possibilities and contingencies had paraded themselves before his mind's jaundiced eye, in turn dismissed or retained according to their merit until by dawn this winnowing out had led him to a single irresistible conclusion: the girl was beneath the catafalque and this conveyance was intended to carry her into the presence of the dead queen.

'So why do I stand here so complacently?' he asked himself now, as the catafalque approached the gorgeously attired group of clergy of which he was the leader.

He made the sign and uttered the few necessary words of blessing as the wheels ceased to turn and the catafalque drew to a halt. A party of guardsmen stepped forward and slid the casket from its place, shouldering it with practised ease and standing ready to follow the bishop through into the abbey. Those who knew Turnbull well may have noticed a slight hesitancy in his turn and in his slow step through the great portal of the west front towards the high altar. Ward and Clarey, who certainly fell into this category, noted the somnambulistic pace of his progress, even amidst the crowd of attendants with staffs, candles and censers, and wondered as to the content of his mind. Certainly, Turnbull was rarely troubled by nerves, by self-doubt or by any want of confidence.

For his part, the bishop was barely conscious of his progress along the nave. The independent action of his legs, muscle memory, and an innate sense of the requirements of the occasion carried him automatically forward, whilst the greater part of his being surveyed the options that fate had placed before him.

'I know,' he told himself, 'I know that the girl is beneath that catafalque. No one else of consequence is privy to that knowledge. Therefore, I have in my hands the power to affect the outcome of their plan to awaken the queen. For that is surely their plan. Surely it is. I have long known it in my heart. The girl may not be able to accomplish it, however. She is said not to be successful in every case. But what if she were? How then might matters fall out? And where do my true interests lie? Does the present king command my loyalty? And if not? If not, indeed! Am I, William Turnbull, a rebel in my heart, a traitor to my king?'

The dignity of his status and the circumstances of his present activity rendered it impossible for him to mop his brow, although a trickle of sweat traversed his brow, causing him to blink the salt from his eye.

'But where do my true interests lie?' he asked once more, continuing this internal dialogue even as his slow progress carried him past serried ranks of lords and his fellow bishops. 'Where do the true interests of the nation lie? How may things turn out, were the queen to awaken? Would the king step willingly aside to accommodate his mother? The constitutional lawyers would surely be set to a frenzy. How may I profit from those circumstances, should they occur?'

The guardsmen set down their noble burden on the dais that had been prepared for it before the high altar, surrounded by flowers. Turning towards this lectern, a tiny part of Turnbull's mind reflected humorously that the late duke had hated flowers, had been a martyr to hay fever and that this quantity of pollen-heavy blooms would certainly have carried him off, had he not already been dead. This little sanguine gust dispelled some of the more feverish strands of thought that oppressed his consciousness and enabled him to think with clarity and singleness of purpose once more.

'What am I thinking of?' he demanded of himself. 'I am unwell. I have been working too hard and have permitted an illusion, a momentary phantasm to disturb the order of my mind. Perhaps the face I saw last night was not as I had imagined. Perhaps I have constructed a vast edifice of conjecture and wild imaginings upon foundations of the frailest kind. Surely, I must master myself now and proceed according to the order of service I have so diligently devised. All eyes are upon me now. There is Lamb. There is His Majesty; a very ill look in his face, brought about by the indulgence of excess rather than grief, I suppose. Now, where do I begin? Ah, yes.'

The bishop raised his arms, brought his hands together and began the bidding prayer.

It seemed to the occupants of the catafalque, or at least to those with breath in their lungs, that many hours had passed before the great doors shut in St Dominic's and silence reigned at last. In truth only three hours had been necessary for the funeral service and the sombre procession from Westminster to the abbey that had ensued from it. And now the catafalque stood at rest and the last soft footsteps of the attendants of this place had faded away, leaving only stillness and calm. A day of tedious inactivity ensued in which Laura, Edward and Thomas could do little but occasionally shift carefully in their positions to ward off cramp. There were occasional visitors to the chapel, individual monks paying their respects, but for the most part it remained a place of quiet and rest as the day passed and the shadows lengthened across the flagstones of the floor. At last, night came, and the hour of crisis approached. In his casket the pale features of the Duke of Cumberland were limned by the moonlight that crept in from the high windows and which would paint him vaguely with the colours of stained glass as the moon moved in its course across the night sky beyond. To be alone beneath the eye of the heavens for this one first night was the time-honoured privilege of the noble dead committed to this place, to feel the light of Heaven on their countenance before their final journey to the subterranean dark. But the duke was not alone. Chilled, cramped and easing aching limbs with the most cautious of movements, Laura, Edward and Thomas had passed a most disagreeable day. Now, long after the last footsteps had faded, Thomas extended a pole with a mirror at its end downwards beyond his shelf, peering out so that he could search the dim reflected view of the chapel beyond. There were no signs of movement, no evidence of human presence, only the complex pattern of light and shadow cast by the high gothic windows above. Cautiously, setting the pole aside, he let himself down to the floor and crept out between the wheels, rubbing his neck ruefully as he stood, searching the darkness of the shadows between the great piers with eyes that were sore and gritty.

'I believe we may speak,' he said in the softest of whispers.

A few moments later and his companions stood beside him, likewise, stretching complaining joints and muscles, likewise afflicted by the strangest sense of supernatural unease, for their sense of intrusion on the duke's communion with his God was not one that might be readily set aside. There were many other reasons to be uneasy, not least of which was the very real fear that their necessary passage to the royal crypt might be disturbed or detected.

'I ache so much. My body is afire,' grumbled Edward, 'and during that wretched interminable service I felt surely that my body would betray me and that I must lash out with my leg when cramp set in. The agony of it – unspeakable. The dull ache of it pains me still.'

'Most definitely,' said Thomas with a sniff. 'And now I suppose we shall inspect the plan. Bring it out, if you will.'

'You are survived, I collect,' said Edward to Laura, when his own ills had subsided from his mind, and he was groping in his pocket for the document in question.

'I believe so,' agreed Laura in a voice that was barely more than a croak. 'Unless this is Hell and the hours of torment my frame has endured just now, some form of purgatory.'

'Spread it out, just so,' said Thomas, indicating the edge of the mounting platform next to the catafalque. The steps of this would be used tomorrow to take down the duke's casket and remove him to that chamber in which his body would be treated in readiness for its committal to the royal crypt.

'We had best hope that these doors are unlocked,' said Thomas, tracing the route with his finger.

It was not a long route and in truth each of them had practised it in their minds so many times that they could easily have traversed it blindfold, should the need arise. But Thomas had insisted on an actual plan drawn on paper, in case of some unexpected contingency, and so a plan had been provided. The provider, a well-placed monk within this very community, was no great draughtsman, but the structure of the place was clear enough, the position of doors marked with a bold line, places of likely human habitation circled vigorously as though to command their confinement.

'Will I fetch the stretcher?' asked Edward at length, having observed Thomas's furrowed brows for some time.

'Aye, let's away, then,' said Thomas. 'Pass it down to me; softly, mind.'

Edward crawled beneath the catafalque once more and groped for the two stout lengths of canvas-bound timber that would serve as the late queen's royal conveyance.

'This way, I believe,' said Laura when all was ready, indicating the dark portal that led towards the crypt. 'I hope the duke will forgive us our trespass on his solitude.'

'I suppose he may rejoice in his cousin's reanimation, if you are able to bring it about,' observed Edward as they approached the great double doors.

The door, to their enormous relief, was unlocked, as they had been promised, but three hearts trembled nevertheless in three mouths as Thomas raised the latch with a huge complaining creak that must surely carry to every obscure and distant corner of this vast abbey. For a while, eyes wide, they stood in breathless silence until the echoes had died away and no other sounds had ensued from it, no sudden cries or footsteps, no metallic swish of swords from scabbards. And then the ancient door must be eased open, inch by agonising inch on hinges that had clearly known no oil this last age.

At last, a sufficient gap stood clear, and Thomas wiped the sweat from his brow, exhaling ostentatiously between pursed lips. 'Unmask the lamp,' he said.

The lamp, once the shutter had been drawn up, cast a yellow glow enough for them to make their way through into the passage beyond, the darkness yielding to reveal the carved likenesses of stern kings and princes on the walls on either side. It was only a short way to the royal crypt, and here at least the tall silver-bound doors opened with barely a complaint. They found themselves in a rectangular chamber of indeterminate extent. Although the plan assured them it was rather less than eighty yards in length the feeble light of their lamp barely reached to the far end of the space, revealing only a serried rank of royal corpses on wide-spaced biers that vanished by degrees into darkness. Laura was all too used to the company of the departed and Edward likewise no stranger to corpses, but Thomas, despite his previous intrusions into Darkharrow and Whale Hall, seemed afflicted by a form of paralysis. His lips moved wordlessly. His brow was as pale as those of the kings and queens before him, each draped in the simple white sheet that the Camoldolites had clothed them in.

'This is she,' said Edward, moving forward and shining the lamp upon the austere features of Queen Charlotte, who lay, as they had expected, on the last stone bier, the one that was furthest from the entrance.

'Come on, Thomas,' implored Laura, placing her hand on her friend's arm and looking up at his wan face anxiously. 'We have found her. What ails you, my dear?'

'Why, nothing,' said Thomas, trying to compose himself. It was hardly the moment to bring to utterance his overwhelming sensation of awe as he regarded the faces of these illustrious royal dead. To look upon these features was like surveying the breadth of five hundred years of the nation's history. Faces familiar to him from prints and paintings lay there pale beneath the lamplight's touch. Surely that was King Ambrose II, who had died of apoplexy upon hearing the news of the destruction of his treasure fleet, and there King Raymond, whose long reign had seen famous victories against the Turks, famous defeats at the hands of the Scots. Every face had a story to tell, stories that were ingrained in his being since boyhood.

'Come on,' urged Laura once more, shaking his arm. 'We must not delay.'

Laura's injunction was intended for herself as much as for her companion, since her own throat was congested now by a sense of overpowering dread and her legs were suddenly leaden. It was as though she moved through air the consistency of treacle as she approached the lamp-lit queen. The great weight of her responsibility bore down upon her like something physical, something that draped itself immovably around her shoulders and sapped the very strength from her. Beneath her now were the waxen, pale features of the aged woman she must awaken, for there was nothing in her apparel or in her features to distinguish her as a queen. In death all were equal beneath the ministration of the Camoldolites. Laura had seen many portraits of Queen Charlotte, and there could be no mistaking her identity. The prominent nose, the high cheekbones and the broad, intelligent brow were familiar enough, but the thin hair, scraped back around her head, was nothing like the glossy mane that spilled from her crown in the painting that thrust itself now into the forefront of her mind. In that picture she had stood next to Richard, her Prince Consort, he who had pre-deceased her by a full twenty years, and their children had played at their feet: Prince Henry, who now sat uneasily upon her throne, and his little sisters, Alice and Margaret. The queen had stood upon an artfully placed dais in order that her head might be at the pinnacle of the composition, with velvet curtains and marble columns framing the family behind.

'And now we are here,' said Laura to herself, 'and my hand is upon your brow and the hopes of the nation rest with me. I do not think I can bear it. What if I fail? What then?'

She bit her lip and the cool of the queen's brow was in her palm and the eyes of her friends were upon her, anxious, expectant.

'Well?' asked Thomas after a while, when Laura had closed her eyes and swayed with some internal process that was mysterious to him.

Hush,' hissed Edward, finger to lips.

Seconds trickled past Laura like hours, and she could not bring herself to reach down through that dead flesh to the heart within. In this limbo there was no failure and no success, only the thick darkness beyond this small empire of light, only the thudding of her own heart in her breast. But she must. She must. She screwed her eyes tight shut and bowed her head at last, reaching down, down through the chill tissues to the royal heart, to place her finger there and feel – ice. Her head snapped back, and she moaned as that vital spark of life departed her and surged into the queen's heart, spreading already like tiny wildfire through those stilled cells and fibres.

'Laura,' gasped Edward, moving forward to support her as she stumbled away from the bier.

'It is done,' she breathed.

'She lives?' demanded Thomas, his face swinging from Edward to Laura and back.

The faintest twitch of a nod was all that Laura could offer in return, as Edward lowered her gently to the floor, propping her back against the wall of the chamber. Even so, her head lay slumped on her chest. Edward and Thomas exchanged anxious glances.

'What ails her?' asked Thomas, placing the lamp close to her face.

'You know what ails her,' replied Edward grimly. 'She has given too much.'

'Too much?! You don't mean…' cried Thomas aghast.

'No,' Edward shook his head. 'I don't think so. She needs a little time to recover, that is all.'

'How much time?' asked Thomas anxiously. 'We must bear the queen away.'

Edward could only shrug. Together they regarded their companion despairingly as the minutes passed.

'We should bear her back to the catafalque,' said Thomas at last. 'And then return for Her Majesty.'

'You are right,' Edward began to say, but at that moment Laura stirred and raised her head, brushing away the loose hair that had fallen like a curtain around her face.

'I am recovered now,' she said in a voice that was no more than a whisper. 'Help me to my feet, if you will. I shall walk by your side.'

Bearing the queen's body on their stretcher the party made their way back to the catafalque. Here, the process of sliding her between the wheels and lifting her up into the shelf that had been prepared for her proved to be exceedingly awkward and entirely unsuited to the maintenance of royal dignity. Thomas feared that those moments would remain permanently imprinted on the surface of his mind. Placing hands on the dead queen in order to move her onto the stretcher had seemed offence enough, but that of awkwardly manhandling the stiff limbs into her hiding place brought the bile to his throat and left him gasping for breath.

'It's just a body,' he told himself. 'Just dead flesh and bone.' But this hardly seemed to help.

Leaving Laura sitting wearily on the steps of the mounting platform, he and Edward returned to the crypt, making their way to one of the lower levels where the eighth Duchess of Exeter's body lay. She had been chosen for her resemblance to Queen Charlotte, and her body was to be placed on the royal bier in the queen's place. It was hoped that the resemblance would be sufficient to deceive the casual observer. If any close examination were to be made the substitution would surely be detected, but perhaps by then it would be too late.

At last, it was done. The duchess lay in unwitting enjoyment of her new royal status and the three intruders were restored to their places beneath the catafalque, even as the first light of dawn began to leaven the darkness in the skies above London.

'How are you, Laura?' whispered Edward as he shifted his position once more in his vain search for respite from intolerable discomfort.

There came no reply at first from the inky darkness of the niche within which she lay, but at last, as Edward reached out for her across the void between them, he heard a vague reassuring murmur. He remained un-reassured.

'She has given too much,' he told himself. 'And perhaps she will never recover now. Perhaps, when next I see her in daylight, her youth will have fled still further from her.

Perhaps she will present the appearance of a truly aged woman now.'

He bit his lip and drew his knees up under his chin.

'But then surely one more single spark of life should not have depleted her resources so extensively,' he continued. 'And surely Jonah has overseen the pouring out of hundreds, perhaps thousands. Could it be that her vital essence stands at such a low ebb that she is on the brink of death herself?' Truly, the hollowness in Laura's cheeks when first he had set eyes on her in Whale Hall had shocked him to the core. It was as though only a gossamer thread of life connected her with this earthly realm, and that its severance would consign her to oblivion.

'Never again,' he muttered. 'I shall never permit it again, whatever the circumstance.' A strange congestion came into his throat as, with his mind's eye, he surveyed the years of their growing up together, images of her youth swimming before that vision. Her beauty, her heavy golden tresses and the wonderful clarity of her complexion in those days, pierced his heart with grief and regret. But these things were of the flesh, of course, doomed to decay in the way of all flesh and come to dust at last. He consoled himself with a vision of her soul, the sweet, noble soul that remained un-withered within her, the indomitable spirit that yet looked out through those dark-rimmed eyes.

'I love her,' he told himself. 'I truly do. I love the soul of her that abides within that untimely-aged frame, and nothing shall diminish it.'

The notion of declaring this love had come often to his mind in the days and weeks before they were reunited and before he saw what had become of her. To be sure, there were many occasions when he had considered what it might be like to be married to Laura, visualising their walk to the altar, their emergence from church into a shower of rose petals and the cheers of the congregation. In his more fevered imaginings, he had dwelt upon the union of their flesh, the necessary carnal conclusion of that blessed day. But now his mind shrank from such contemplation and hunched in darkness, he hugged his knees more tightly as he strove to drive it from his thoughts.

On the shelf beneath Edward lay Thomas, whose own mind moved restlessly in the consideration of the past few weeks as the hour approached when the Camoldolites should return. Laura dwelt likewise in his thoughts. He was not much given to the examination of his own conscience, or indeed the analysis of his own emotions, so the importunate urgings of these had caused him considerable anguish. It was true that he had never actually declared his love for Laura, despite having rehearsed the framing of these words a thousand times, but still he felt a bitter sense of having betrayed her. Such thoughts had oppressed him ever since the day of her rescue, but now, as she lay silent in the darkness so close to him, they assailed him with force.

'I am a shallow creature indeed,' he admonished himself, as he had told himself so many times, 'to find my love for her so abruptly extinguished. But surely pity is no substitute for passion. My heart lies like a stone within me and the fierce fire that once burned there is snuffed out. My love is turned to ashes. That same wilful, ungovernable heart stands in bitter opposition to my conscience, but surely it may not be induced to lie. That is why it pains me so. That is why I can barely bring myself to look upon her face and her presence is torment to me now. How I wish I could bring about an encounter with that fiend, Jonah.' He clenched his fists and screwed his eyes tightly shut. 'Then I should surely send that callous bastard screaming back to the pits of Hell.'

Laura's own thoughts were of Emily. She was barely conscious of her material circumstances, barely conscious of her companions in the thick darkness around her. Emily's sweet face was lit by the clear sunlight of some distant day, her hair twined with the flowers of spring as in the paintings of Primavera she had seen in books.

'Take my hand, sister,' offered Emily, 'and come into the light. Surely, it is dark where you lie. I can barely see you.'

'I may not, sweet Emily,' Laura replied, her lips moving silently. 'For I am not what I was. I fear you would be shocked. Everyone is shocked and hardly can they meet my eye. Poor Thomas is mortally afflicted. How I feel for him. How I feel for myself. All my dreams are brought to nothing.'

'Come and gather flowers with me,' urged Emily. 'See, I shall make you a garland like this.'

'Your fingers were ever nimbler than mine,' said Laura. 'And now my hands are loath and stiff.'

'Give me your hand,' said Emily, reaching out to her. 'Come into the light where I may see you.'

'No,' said Laura. 'I may not. It is not time. Not quite, I think, and there are things that I must do.'

'What things, my dear?' smiled Emily. 'Do you not wish to be with me?'

'I cannot say,' murmured Laura. 'I only know…'

Edward's hand upon her shoulder recalled her from her dream, and Emily, placing her finger to her lips, withdrew.

'Hush,' hissed Edward softly. 'Thomas heard a door. I think they come.'

Chapter Twenty-Two

It was time. The disk of the sun was risen above the eastern horizon and the duke's vigil was complete. To the accompaniment of chanting and of the swinging of censers, his casket was lowered from his high platform and taken through to the place that had been prepared for him in the crypt below. The great doors to the vestibule were eased open to admit a broad path of bright morning light and the horses brought in that would draw the catafalque away. Soon the wheels were in motion once more and the vehicle made its way through streets that were barely waking to resume its place in the Royal Mews. Now there was no ceremony. The black mares bore no feathered crests and barely a street sweeper or baker's boy stood to doff their caps instinctively as the cortege rumbled past. It was still some way from its destination, in a quiet narrow thoroughfare, when a high-walled wagon pulled out from an intersecting street and blocked its way entirely. The driver, seemingly the victim of some form of fit, tumbled from his perch and lay twitching, groaning in the road.

Cursing, the driver of the catafalque and his mate dismounted and crossed to see what ailed the man. It was clear that they could make no further progress until the vehicle was moved on. Already the street behind them was filling gradually with other vehicles and with curious pedestrians, moving forward to see what incident had occurred. Whilst all attention was focused on the blockage and on the apparent medical needs of the wagon driver, a group of men converged on the rear of the catafalque. With practised speed they accomplished the unloading of its precious cargo, masking with their backs its transfer to a waiting cart. Within moments Thomas, Edward and Laura were aboard and the cart lurched away along the congested road in the opposite direction. Observing this, the driver of the blocking wagon sat up, brushing aside the ministrations of those who had come to his aid.

'A momentary dizziness, that is all,' he said, getting to his feet and brushing off his clothes. 'I thank you for your concern.'

'Now, perhaps we can get this here wagon out of the road,' said the catafalque driver, handing him his hat. 'Some of us have duties to attend to.'

It was not long before the cart had placed three streets between its occupants and any possibility of pursuit. The driver cast back his hood and grinned.

'Father!' gasped Thomas.

'Aye,' said Matthew Corvin wryly. 'I thought I should see to this myself and be amongst the first to congratulate you on your success, for success it is! I presume that bundle back there is Her Late Majesty.'

'So it is,' Thomas assured him, his eyes bright with delight now. 'And we have spirited her away even beneath the noses of the Camoldolites, even as we dared hope. It was a long and awkward confinement in the belly of that great hearse, but surely it has served its purpose. And now we have our queen. I give you joy!'

'And does she live? Or at least will she live once more?' asked Corvin, glancing behind them to where Laura and Edward sat with their backs to the canvas canopy that enclosed the vehicle.

'Laura assures us that she does. I suppose we must trust to her judgment.'

'I hardly dare believe it,' laughed Corvin. 'Such a bold stroke – the stuff of legends indeed.' His eyes narrowed. 'And what of Laura? How does she fare?'

'She yet breathes, as you see,' said Thomas gravely. 'But she is grievously stricken. I fear for her.'

'She deserves our gratitude, the nation's gratitude,' said Corvin. 'And yet she made this sacrifice of her own volition.'

'Let us hope it was not the ultimate sacrifice,' observed Thomas, turning to meet Edward's gaze and finding his expression to be one of concern rather than triumph or relief. Laura's head was on his shoulder and his arm around hers. Her eyes were fast shut and her face deathly pale.

'We must get her to Sir Joseph,' he said.

'Without delay, Sir Joseph awaits us.'

'We have it on good authority,' said Sir Richard Cranshaw, the head of His Majesty's intelligence services.

'But to deliberately raise my mother from the dead,' said King Henry incredulously. 'How can such a thing be possible?'

'I do not claim to know how it is possible,' said Sir Richard patiently. 'Such things lie beyond my remit. I only know that there are those amongst your enemies who consider it to be possible and are making plans to encompass it.'

The king frowned and shifted uncomfortably in his seat. He was a tall, bulky man with a weak chin that he attempted to disguise with an irregular growth of beard.

'Incredible,' he said. 'And what are you doing to frustrate the ambitions of these… fantasists?'

'Well, you may be sure that the guard at St Dominic's has been doubled,' said Sir Richard, regarding his king with the closed expression that he habitually wore in this company.

'Good,' grunted the king, and then, waving his hand vaguely, 'What authority? How do you know this fantastic plan is being evolved? There has never been a royal reawakening... not in hundreds of years. Not that I ever heard of, and I do not think I am an ignorant man, hmm?'

Sir Richard, who held exactly that opinion, held it with fixed and immovable conviction, placed a file on the table at the king's side, a table that held an open bottle of cognac, much depleted. The stench of it was on the king's breath as he coughed while regarding the file without enthusiasm.

'It's all in there,' said Sir Richard.

'I don't doubt it is,' replied King Henry. 'And I shall give it my full attention later, you may be sure. But you are fabulously paid to keep me informed, as I recall, and I would be obliged if you would apprise me of the essentials of its contents.'

'Of course,' said Sir Richard levelly. 'You will recall that there are troublemakers at large in the west of your realm, preachers of sedition who hope to raise a rabble in support of antiquated and heretical religious practices.'

'Go on,' said the king, reaching for some candied nuts from the bowl that stood beside his glass and placing these in his mouth, muffling his voice somewhat. 'I have heard these things. I am told that a commission of enquiry is being established, that militia are being raised to stamp it out.'

'Indeed, well the leader of this group claims to be the son of King Stephen.'

'Really? The Wytch King's son?' King Henry's eyes were suddenly wide.

'The same, awoken from the dead himself and proposing to raise his late, unlamented father, too.'

'What is this melancholy obsession with raising the dead all of a sudden?' demanded the king petulantly. 'I never heard of such a thing. May not the dead be left in peace? It seems an imposition on the realm.'

'The reawakening of the dead is not uncommon, of course,' explained Sir Richard, clasping his hands behind his back now. 'Our faith acknowledges it, although, as you rightly point out, your late-departed ancestors have thus far remained…'

'Dead,' snapped King Henry. 'And long may they continue in it. I tremble to consider what troubles might afflict the realm if my ancestors were to start strolling forth demanding their crowns. I suppose the lawyers might be fantastically enriched.'

'Well perhaps,' agreed Sir Richard. 'Although the letter of the law is clear enough. Natural justice might seem to require that a king's reign ends irrevocably with his death, but I'm afraid the statute book stipulates that the next king rules simply as steward for his dead father.'

'Or mother,' supplied King Henry, his brows knitting.

'Truly.'

'What are you saying?' demanded the king, leaning forward in his seat now, eyes staring. 'Do you propose to tell me that my late mother could resume her reign as though her death were no more than a temporary inconvenience, as if she were no longer "late"? And what of me? Am I meant to step cheerfully aside to accommodate her?'

'I imagine you would wish to form your own policy in those circumstances, and it is not for me to advise you,' said Sir Richard smoothly.

'Well, what are you advising me? What are you doing, in actuality?' demanded the king, whose face had achieved a very dangerous shade of red. One of many flying particles of spittle landed on Sir Richard's lapel. He was reminded of the persistent rumours that the monarch had conspired in the murder of his mother. It was said that the Duke of Westmoreland, a particularly unscrupulous, ambitious and malevolent man had encouraged him in this regard. Sir Richard shuddered to think of him. But then a providential cancer had carried him into the certain embrace of Satan some years previously and the truth died with him. Unless the queen awoke, that is. What a story she might have to tell. There were doubtless many, many reasons for His Majesty to be alarmed.

'You may be sure that we are trying to locate the chief conspirators,' informed Sir Richard, resisting the impulse to step back, 'and the girl that is the focus of the various plots. She is the one who is said to have the power to raise the dead. She is the key. Without her it is likely their schemes would come to nothing.'

'This is outrageous!' growled King Henry, rubbing his chin anxiously. 'Clearly she needs to be removed from this… this…,' his lips moved wordlessly for a moment as he sought a suitable description, '…equation. I mean, have her killed. Certainly, have her killed. Get rid of her. Do whatever is necessary, for God's sake. Where is she, hmm? Where on earth is this wretched girl?'

'It appears she is in the hands of the Corvinites,' said Sir Richard, having weathered this storm, 'but she is urgently sought by the followers of this Leo as well as ourselves. It is said that she has already reanimated hundreds of dead heretics in the west of the realm but was taken away from them before they could achieve their ultimate end.'

'I repeat,' drawled the king, speaking with exaggerated slowness, as though addressing a child. 'Where… is… she… now?'

'We do not know,' admitted Sir Richard with an expression that approached regret. 'There is a limit to our intelligence. The likelihood is that she is in London, however, because if their aim is to reawaken Queen Charlotte she must necessarily be in this city.'

'Thank God for the intelligence services,' scoffed the king, shifting uneasily in his seat and rolling his eyes. 'However else should we manage? And doubtless your minions are knocking on every door, searching every cellar, yard and attic to find this girl.'

'As you suggest, all available resources are devoted to it, sir.'

'Hmm.'

'Are you ever coming back to bed, Harry?' came a sleepy voice from the king's adjoining bedchamber.

The king's face betrayed irritation and his glance seemed to defy his distinguished subject to venture any indication of amusement or disapproval. Sir Richard's features remained impassive, although a tiny glint in his eye hinted at the storage of a humorous memory for later enjoyment.

'Well?' a plump blonde young woman appeared, framed in the doorway with a sheet clasped to her ample bosom in a manner that might be supposed to preserve her modesty. 'Oh, it is Sir Dicky. You should have said it was Sir Dicky, dear. How do you do, Sir Dicky?' She brushed back some of the loose strands of hair from her face.

Sir Richard inclined his head gravely towards the Countess of Graveney, whose elevation to the peerage she owed to her elevation of His Majesty. He was said to be besotted with her.

'I am very well, my lady,' he said, favouring her with a tight smile. 'I trust…'

Sir Richard's polite enquiry after the countess' mother, who was a milkmaid but now one in possession of a house in Belgrave Square, was abruptly curtailed by a sharp glance from King Henry and the raising of his hand.

'Business, my dear,' he said to his bed mate, in remarkably indulgent tones. 'I don't suppose we will be long now, but I trust you will allow us to proceed.'

'Of course, sugar plum,' cooed the countess. 'I trust you will call upon us again, Sir Dicky, when there is less business to attend to. Perhaps we may go to the races again… oh!' she perceived the knitting of her lover's eyebrows and withdrew with a giggle, allowing Sir Richard a glimpse of her fine pink rump as she turned.

'Ahem,' said the king when she had gone. 'Now, where were we?'

'The girl,' suggested Sir Richard, whose cheeks now ached from the muscular discipline that had been required of them.

'Ah, yes. The girl.. Well, I suggest you catch her as soon as you can.'

'Indeed, sir,' said Sir Richard. 'Our thoughts exactly. We shall do our utmost to do so.'

'Well, that will be all, then,' said King Henry, rising from his seat somewhat unsteadily and glancing towards the bedchamber. 'Keep me informed, will you?'

'Of course, Your Majesty,' replied Sir Richard, stepping backwards towards the door in the manner that protocol required.

Sir Richard had barely emerged from the royal apartments when he became conscious of several officials advancing towards him across a quadrangle. The leader of this cohort was immediately recognisable to him as Bentley, his Chief of Staff, but his two companions wore the robes of the Camoldolite order. All of them approached with an urgency and agitation that filled him with concern.

'Sir Richard, I must speak with you immediately,' called Bentley, even before he was within normal hailing distance. Bentley's usually pallid features were flushed, and beads of sweat stood out on his narrow forehead. 'If we may just…' Bentley glanced around to see that various servants and palace dignitaries were within earshot and, taking Sir Richard's arm, propelled him purposefully into an empty passage that opened onto the quadrangle.

'Bentley, what on earth?' asked Sir Richard, thoroughly concerned by now.

'It is the queen. She is gone!' Bentley panted, his grip on Sir Richard's arm showing no sign of relenting.

'Dear Lord,' gasped Sir Richard, absent-mindedly brushing away Bentley's hand. 'How so? Are you sure?'

Sir Richard's extreme agitation had caused his habitually closed expression to register unseemly alarm as he looked up to find the Camoldolites regarding him anxiously.

'You had better tell me,' he said, composing his features once more.

The Camoldolites, who proved to be the Abbot of St Dominic's and his prior, spilled out their story, recounted it once more, provided the additional details demanded by Sir Richard and then waited as he stood regarding the quadrangle beyond with apparent stony displeasure. A soft rain was beginning to fall. Fleeting shadows marked the passage of a flight of doves above.

'It is as we had feared,' observed Bentley, contributing nothing of use to the circumstances, a contribution all too typical of him.

It appeared that the queen's body had been substituted with that of another, that the substitution had not been remarked for several days, that the Camoldolites had no idea how the dead monarch could have been stolen from under their noses. An enquiry was already underway. Or so the abbot assured Sir Richard.

'Yes, yes, and doubtless someone will eventually pay a high price for this incompetence,' snapped Sir Richard with a glance of malignance the significance of which was not lost on the abbot, who swallowed hard and bowed his head. 'But that is hardly the most pressing issue just now.'

Sir Richard frowned and squeezed the bridge of his nose as though focusing his thoughts there.

'I suppose we must tell the king,' Bentley sighed, after some moments of silence had passed.

'I think you may find him indisposed just now,' said Sir Richard, glancing up. 'But surely, I shall inform him in due course. For now, you must gather all the departmental heads and require them to assemble in my office one hour from now. Who is it that best knows the girl? Turnbull, was it? Yes? Fetch him, too.'

Bishop Turnbull, summoned from an excellent luncheon with indecent haste, soon found himself in a room crowded with intelligence officials and with those members of the government with a particular interest in that field. Clarey was there, as were various other exalted figures he knew in some degree. The Intelligence Committee was one of the more potent organs of government, and some of the noblest lords in the realm served upon it, as well as many who owed their presence more to the sharpness of their wits than the glory of their escutcheon. Several, emboldened by their exalted rank, showed evidence of impatience at the circumstances of this gathering, the peremptory nature of their summons. Sir Richard was not even a peer of the realm, and he had refused the offer of one on several occasions, thereby securing a well-deserved reputation for incorruptibility. Those whose consciences were less easy in this respect regarded the king's head of intelligence with a snobbish resentment and suspicion that had hardly abated after thirty years of loyal service. There was an air of tense expectancy in the air as Sir Richard came into the room, and a hubbub of conversation stilled the instant the door closed behind him.

'Forgive me, Lords, Gentlemen. I would not have summoned you here at such short notice were it not necessary,' he began, 'had not a crisis of the gravest magnitude forced my hand. Believe me, I do not exaggerate.'

William Turnbull was amongst those least surprised by the startling news soon to be imparted to the gathering, having suspected its content the moment Ward appeared at his elbow, note in hand. Now, he did his utmost to arrange his features into some semblance of shock and surprise that would not seem out of place in the circumstances. The late queen's body was missing; he had foreseen it the moment he had recognised Laura DeLacey in the coach house, he told himself. He had nursed that suspicion in his breast and told no one. A taint of treachery clung to such behaviour, and consciousness of this notion left him drained of energy, momentarily queasy in his ample midriff He found that Clarey was looking at him intently and averted his gaze, glancing down at hands that fidgeted restlessly now in his lap.

'Turnbull,' Sir Richard's face was turned towards him, his face grave.

'Hmm? Yes? How may I assist?' answered the bishop in a voice that, even in his own ears, sounded like the bleating of a sheep.

'You have met this girl, I believe. Pray describe the circumstances of this encounter and tell us your impressions of her.'

Turnbull gave an account as required, rambling and disconnected in a manner quite unexpected from him. He prayed that this might be ascribed simply to shock, although with no confidence that Clarey at least would be deceived. He dared not meet his eye.

'It seems that there can be no doubt of Miss DeLacey's capabilities,' said Sir Richard, naming her for the first time, 'regardless of its apparent improbability. The most distinguished scientific minds are at a loss to explain it.'

'And I have heard that the most distinguished religious minds are apt to ascribe it to the Devil's work,' observed Lord Harvey in his cracked old voice, high rank and advanced age enabling him to interrupt Sir Richard without fear of censure.

'That may be the case,' allowed Sir Richard patiently, 'but such questions need not detain us now. We must ask ourselves how we should best proceed, if we are to defend the nation's interests. I invite your contributions.'

There was a lengthy silence as those present dwelt upon the content of Sir Richard's question. All had heard that Laura was able to raise only a proportion of the dead. It was not unlikely that Queen Charlotte would prove incapable of reanimation. But if she was, what then? What if she were to appear at the doors of parliament, or at the head of a regiment of guards, or even at the forefront of a vast mass of the common people such as the Raven was said to command? And then the late queen had been beloved of the nation in a way that her son was demonstrably not. The fifteen years of his reign had done little to enhance a reputation already mired in controversy when he was merely Crown Prince.

'What do the lawyers say?' grunted the Duke of Albany, who was one of the queen's oldest surviving councillors.

'What do you think?' huffed Sir Richard. 'The letter of the law seems clear enough on the face of it. The king is officially steward of the realm, that is all, so long as the body of his predecessor remains theoretically capable of resurrection. But doubtless the finest legal minds can be prevailed upon to muddy the waters and to demonstrate beyond all reasonable doubt that white is black and black, white. Their opinions on any given case are hardly more constant than those of physicians when considering a malaise or proposing a remedy. All that we are sure of is uncertainty.'

Sir Richard's career had been a long and distinguished one. He too had served Queen Charlotte. He might also be deeply troubled in his conscience by the choices that may soon need to be made.

'I suppose Lord Ogilvy will know very soon,' said Lord Clarey, naming the Prime Minister. 'And he will agree that this issue merits discussion at the highest level. I imagine that he will wish to convene his cabinet immediately.'

'Most certainly,' said Sir Richard with a nod. 'And if parliament were to be summoned it might be invited in emergency to pass legislation appropriate to the circumstances.'

'It might,' cackled Lord Harvey. 'But we all know it'll be a cold day in Hell before His Majesty summons parliament.'

There was a murmur of agreement and other practical matters were discussed, the policing of the streets, the interrogation of informants.

'We shall leave no stone unturned in our efforts to recover the body of Her Late Majesty and bring the perpetrators of this crime to justice,' said Sir Richard at length. 'I look forward to your wholehearted support in this. You may be sure I shall inform you of any fresh developments.'

'You knew, didn't you?' said Clarey as he and Turnbull walked away from the meeting, regarding the bishop sidelong with a penetrating stare. 'Go on, admit it. You knew.'

Turnbull shook his head. 'What would lead you to such an extraordinary conclusion, Clarey?'

'The fact that I have known you since we were both small boys,' said Clarey. 'The fact that you have absolutely no talent for hiding your inner mind from me. The fact that I am a person of insight and perspicacity.'

'Matched only by your surpassing humility and want of pretension,' scoffed Turnbull.

'Tell me,' Clarey urged, catching Turnbull by his forearm and obliging him to stop, turning the bishop towards him. 'Look me in the eye and tell me you did not know.'

For a long moment, the two stood eye to eye. At last, the bishop sighed and the tension drained from his shoulders.

'You have me,' he said simply, feeling a warm sense of relief that was as welcome as it was unexpected.

'Then why on earth did you not disclose it?'

'You had best come back to my house,' muttered Turnbull wearily, 'unless you propose to hand me over to the constables this instant.'

'It was easier not to,' admitted Turnbull with a sigh, when he had completed his account.

'Easier... not... to,' repeated Clarey, regarding him over steepled fingers from the other side of the table at which they sat.

'Yes.'

'Aye, well,' said Clarey after a moment. 'I suppose inertia is a force much overlooked in the affairs of men.'

'I suppose it is. And now I am a traitor,' said Turnbull glumly, 'by my own inactions condemned.'

'Condemned by no one more than by yourself,' observed Clarey, 'if I read your expressions right.'

'You always read my expressions right,' sighed Turnbull. 'I am as a crystal vessel to you, in which all my thoughts and sentiments are laid bare.'

'I think a crystal vessel may be pitching it a little high,' laughed Clarey. 'A net of walnuts may be a more precise analogy, and I consider myself a fair judge of walnuts. But tell me, Turnbull, what on earth induced you to keep your suspicions to yourself? What vast credit you could have garnered to yourself had your intelligence led to the discovery of the plot, the arrest of the conspirators. You do amaze me. Nothing could have contributed more to the likelihood of your succeeding to the archbishopric.'

Clarey shook his noble head wistfully and Turnbull bit his lip.

'And you suppose these things have not occurred to me?' he asked bitterly. 'You may be sure they will occur to me with baleful regularity as far ahead as I can predict. There are some who say that in each man's life there comes but a single crisis, the outcome of which will direct the future course of that life. Perhaps I have encountered that crisis and my conduct in the face of it has been found wanting.'

'This girl, then,' pressed Clarey, declining to pass judgement on Turnbull's musings. 'She exercises some melancholy influence over you, some power to impede the execution of your will? You have conceived some affection for her, perhaps?'

'Far from it,' grunted Turnbull. 'I condemned her to be hanged, did I not? And if she has repaid me by the frustration of my ambitions you may be sure it does nothing further to commend her to me.'

'Then why?'

'I do not know why,' acknowledged the bishop irritably.

The two men held each other's gaze for some time, and then Clarey turned slowly away.

'Well,' he said. 'When you do know, perhaps you would be so good as to share it with me. Friends share such things, do they not?'

The bishop's confidence in the friendship that existed between he and Clarey varied in its intensity. There were times when he doubted the sincerity of the noble lord's attachment to him, times when he wondered whether Clarey truly cared about anything that did not advance his own interests. Turnbull felt no sense of resentment, though. He was, after all, as selfish as any living creature and it would have been hypocritical of him to deny this to others. Still, his desire to draw on Clarey's friendship came sharply into focus when the new day dawned, and a second handwritten note arrived from Sir Richard.

'He desires me to appear before him at noon,' he said to Ward, setting down his spectacles and glancing at the clock on the mantel, which told ten past ten.

'We shall have plenty of time, then,' Ward assured him, noting with interest the unusual pallor in his superior's features. 'I daresay we may continue with these papers a while yet.'

'We may not,' said Turnbull testily. 'Certainly, we may not. Summon a cab, if you will. We must get ourselves to Clarey's at once. He will wish to accompany me, no doubt.'

'Of course,' conceded Ward, judging correctly that the wishing was all on Turnbull's side.

Within twenty minutes they stood on Clarey's doorstep in the Strand, where Graves, Clarey's butler, accepted the bishop's card and conducted them through into his drawing room, it being explained that His Lordship was presently taking his bath.

'You will wait, I take it?' said Graves, noting the bishop's state of transparent agitation.

'Certainly, we will,' snapped Turnbull, 'and perhaps you would be so good as to convey to His Lordship the urgency of our situation.'

'Of course, My Lord,' answered Graves unctuously, inclining his head and withdrawing.

Half an hour passed during which Turnbull divided his time between anxious pacing and repeated inspections of his pocket watch. This was thought to be a little slow, and so Ward's own watch had to be brought out on occasion for the purpose of comparison. Graves, when he returned with tea, was also asked what time the long case clock told in the hall.

'It really will not do to be late for Sir Richard,' said Turnbull when Graves had gone, causing Ward further private amusement.

'He wishes to be reminded of your impressions of Laura DeLacey, I suppose,' remarked Ward.

'I imagine he does,' replied Turnbull, deeply uneasy in a mind troubled with more fevered imaginings, 'although heaven knows my acquaintance with her was brief enough.'

'More extensive than any others he can rely on, I suppose,' said Ward.

Turnbull opened his mouth to reply to this, but at that moment Lord Clarey walked in, pink, perfumed and resplendent in a mustard-coloured waistcoat and breeches of a fine sky blue.

'Turnbull,' he said, crossing to shake his hand with a nod of acknowledgement in Ward's direction. 'An unlooked-for pleasure, indeed. How you must thirst for my company. Why, we only parted at dinner last night. I had wondered if I might see you at Blake's, later,' he added, mentioning the club of which they were both members. 'But here you are hauling me from the depths of my tub like some importunate trawler man, and the sun barely over the horizon.'

'A curious catch, indeed,' said Turnbull, wrinkling his nose. 'And one that stinks like a whore's parlour. What one earth have you on you?'

'What, this?' beamed Clarey, showing no evidence of offence. 'Well, this is simply…'

'Never mind,' snapped Turnbull, rolling his eyes. 'I am not come to discuss scent, with you. Sir Richard has summoned me.'

'So I gathered…'

'And I would be glad if you would attend with me.'

'Because?'

'Because I would value your support,' said Turnbull, somewhat plaintively. The private glance that accompanied this assertion was intended to convey his extreme anxiety that Sir Richard might draw from him some involuntary confession of his culpable inaction in the present case, 'and I know that you stand high in his favour.'

'But he has not invited me,' protested Clarey, albeit with a playful smile on his lips that promised future assent.

'Clarey,' rumbled Turnbull, knitting his brows, the merest twitch of his head in Ward's direction indicating his reluctance to plead, to abase himself in these circumstances.

'Oh, very well,' said Clarey, noticing his friend's squirming. 'I suppose I have time to break my fast?'

'You do not.'

Lord Clarey was an old friend of Sir Richard's, having studied at the same Oxford college, and so Sir Richard expressed no objection to the attendance of Turnbull's noble companion. The party established themselves at a plain table in an austerely furnished office and Bentley joined them to take notes.

'And you say the girl gave no indication that might lead to her confederates?' said Bentley.

'I'm not at all sure that she had confederates at that stage,' said Turnbull. 'I received the impression that she was a simple thing, taken from the bosom of a respectable family.'

'And condemned by you to death,' observed Sir Richard.

'Well, yes. Although I trust you will not expect me to make apology for it,' said Turnbull a little stiffly. 'Had her sentence been carried out according to my orders I doubt we would be sitting here now. Clearly, she was a person with capabilities that might pose a danger to the peace of the realm. My conscience is clear. I acted decisively to snuff out that threat before it could evolve.'

'I see,' said Sir Richard, 'but did you not think to inform us of this threat that you sought so earnestly to preserve us from? Did you not think to present to us a person with abilities so remarkable they might be unique in the history of the nation, if not the globe? You resolved instead simply to have them hanged. Correct me if I am wrong.'

'Er, yes,' said Turnbull, feeling a prickle of heat traverse his scalp. 'Although I believe I had the necessary authority and that the appropriate authorities were notified. That is so, is it not, Ward? Word was conveyed to London, was it not?'

'Buried amongst a sheaf of inconsequential notices,' observed Sir Richard acidly, before Ward could open his mouth.

'But notification nevertheless,' protested the bishop. 'It may be that...'

'Really, Turnbull, I do wonder if this advances our investigation,' said Lord Clarey, causing the bishop to feel a surge of affection for him. 'Perhaps this aspect of things can be deferred to a later stage, given the urgency of the situation. You mentioned that the girl appeared initially to have no suspicious connections of any kind?'

'Indeed,' agreed Turnbull, seizing upon this lifeline with relief. 'Although I imagine that after having made good her escape, she was quickly taken in by our enemies, persuaded by them to contribute to their pernicious schemes.'

'And what do we know of these conspirators?' asked Sir Richard after a long, considering glance in Clarey's direction. 'I understand there was a raid on a rebel encampment in the marshes and that certain intelligence was gleaned from this.'

'There was,' said Turnbull, hoping that the circumstances of this raid may not be subject to too close a scrutiny.

'And was any light shed on the identities of the leading conspirators, other than Corvin, of course, who lamentably was allowed to slip through the net?' asked Sir Richard.

Turnbull felt a renewed sense of despondency. 'We have the reports there, I believe,' he said to Ward. 'And I'm sure you must have copies in your own files.'

A discussion took place regarding the various names yielded up by those captured in the raid, those whose flesh had been cruelly mortified during the investigation, many of whom had perished from it, even before the formalities of a trial.

'Always we face the same frustrations,' observed Bentley, demonstrating his particular talent for pointing out the obvious. 'Each of these names is a nom de guerre, an alias. Unless we are able to establish their true identities, we have nothing.'

'Thank you, Bentley,' said Sir Richard heavily, and then, 'something amuses you, Ward? I am surprised that you should consider this the time for levity.'

'I'm sorry,' answered Ward, blushing furiously. 'It's just that I was studying the list of names and a humorous conjunction occurred to me.'

'Go on,' instructed Sir Richard, 'let us see if we share your appreciation.'

'It's just that Corvin is known as the Raven, is he not? And the fifth on the list here has the name John Cordwell, which also suggests a bird to my mind. I have an interest in ornithology, you see, and Corduelis is the Latin name for the finch, you see. Raven, Finch, do you see? That was…'

'Hush!' ordered Sir Richard abruptly, raising his hand.

'I'm s… s… sorry,' stammered Ward.

'You need not apologise,' Sir Richard told him after a long moment in which he seemed distracted by some internal preoccupation. 'In fact, you may bask in our congratulations, if my suspicions are correct. Remind us of what we know of Sir Joseph Finch, who, I believe, has a house in that vicinity and a wide circle of associates in London, too.'

'He is a distinguished physician and a natural philosopher,' said Clarey. 'Very highly thought of, I should say. I have encountered him on numerous occasions. You will recall that he attended to the Duke of Cumberland during his last days.'

'He did,' agreed Sir Richard. 'And so, he will have been well-placed to gain intelligence pertaining to royal burial arrangements, of the layout of the royal crypt.'

'I believe no taint of suspicion attaches to him,' observed Bentley. 'There are no previous records, to my knowledge.'

'Indeed,' said Sir Richard with a frown. 'And we are snatching at straws, but it seems we have few alternatives at present. Perhaps you would care to invite him here to speak with us. He is a man of rare intelligence, it is said. Doubtless, it would be interesting to hear him give account of himself and to solicit his views on the security situation that we face.'

'Will I contact the constabulary?' asked Bentley.

'Good Lord, no,' said Sir Richard. 'Why ever would we do that? Sir Joseph is a perfectly respectable gentleman, and a certain circumspection may be necessary, at least initially. I do not say the constabulary are dim-witted; far from it. I only say that large brains are not foremost amongst their endowment and that a love for procedure, a devotion to precedent are not necessarily best suited to our interests on this occasion. Pray, send some of our own gentlemen, some who may be trusted to respond with decorum in any circumstance.'

'Certainly, I shall attend to it this afternoon.'

'Do it now, Bentley,' demanded Sir Richard.

It was said that instinct was a vital component of intelligence work and that Sir Richard's instincts were honed to a very fine edge. In truth, he would have resented the accusation that he placed reliance on such a nebulous, supernatural concept and would have defined it instead as a shifting melange of indicators based on half a century of hard-won experience. Nevertheless, various such indicators, some that escaped precise definition, warned him that Sir Joseph's was a significant name.

Chapter Twenty-Three

Later that afternoon, at Sir Joseph's house on Carlton Square, Mould opened the door to find two gentlemen standing on the doorstep. These were dressed smartly but, in a manner, so unremarkable as to defy recollection; itself a cause for suspicion, at least in Mould's acutely suspicious mind. In addition, there was a suavity, a confidence about them that immediately set his nerves on edge.

'Pray, is Sir Joseph at leisure to receive us?' asked the larger of the two, once they had given their names and announced themselves as colleagues from the Society.

'May I beg enquire as to your business with him?' asked Mould, having glanced at their cards and stowed them in his pocket. 'Is he expecting you?'

'Indeed not,' said the smaller man, 'but we have an issue of particular importance to discuss with him, a confidential matter that he will certainly thank us for bringing to his attention and would certainly resent if there was any appreciable delay.'

'Uh huh,' said Mould, noting the veiled threat that any servant must acknowledge. 'Well, he isn't in at present, sirs.' He gestured through to the hall where various items of furniture could be seen, swathed in dust sheets. 'We have the decorators in, see? Hellish mess. Interminable delay. Sir Joseph has taken lodgings in Worthington Street, temporary, like. Perhaps you would care for his direction?'

Mould took a card from the hallstand and passed it to his visitors. These declared their gratitude, tipped their hats and presently withdrew, leaving Mould standing in the hall with a thoughtful expression on his face.

'Intelligence fellows,' he said to himself. 'Written all over 'em.'

Then he made his way upstairs and closed the curtains in the room that looked out through the last of the four windows there, his private prearranged signal to Sir Joseph that all was not well. Having done this he collected the bag that was already made ready, let himself out through the back door and made his way through the garden to the gate that gave access to the lane.

Benbow and Lafferty, Sir Richard's two agents, stood watching from the end of the street as the curtains swept across. Benbow nodded sagely and made an entry in a small book, having first drawn out his watch and noted the time.

'That'll be a signal, then,' said Lafferty, who was inferior to him both in size and status.

'It most certainly will,' agreed Benbow, putting the book in the pocket of his coat. 'And I daresay this here direction is of small use to us.'

'What do we do, then? Are we to come back later and break in at the back?'

'Perhaps, if we are directed to,' conceded Benbow. 'But I recall no such instruction in our briefing. Perhaps you were at a different one.'

'So, what, then?' asked Lafferty, having shaken his head vigorously and shuffled his feet.

'Well, Lafferty, a signal presupposes the presence of a person to be signalled at, does it not?'

'Ah,' said Lafferty. 'Now I see.'

'And we have only to look out for him.'

'People say that you exceeded your brief in the Eastings,' said King Henry, arms folded over his paunch, looking up disapprovingly at his natural child's bearded features.

Colonel Danny Blanchflower's notion of standing to attention might have invited the criticism of many of the army's drill sergeants, but it was far from the casual slouch that was his usual manner. It reflected his understanding that his father's approval, or at least tolerance, was unusually important to one whose conduct strayed so far beyond the confines of law or morality. For this reason, his uniform was immaculately clean, and his back was moderately straight as the monarch walked slowly around him, regarding him rather as though he were a prize bull at a county fair, splendid, powerful but harbouring potential menace.

'I have heard it said, Father,' agreed Blanchflower, staring straight ahead and regarding his military bearing complacently in the mirror above the mantel. 'I have heard it said by your enemies, by the enemies of the realm. Do you propose to censure me? Is that why you have summoned me?'

'No, indeed,' said the king with a sniff. 'Although there are many who would applaud it. No, rather I wish to draw upon your, shall we say, propensities to address a serious issue that has troubled me these last few days.' He frowned, clasping his hands behind his back now. 'You have heard of this girl, I suppose?'

'The one who is reputed to be able to raise the dead? Yes, I have heard of her.'

'Well, would it surprise you to hear that my mother's body has been stolen from St Dominic's? Stolen, I say!' A flush appeared in the king's cheeks and spread darkly across his features. 'What do you think of that?'

'I am surprised, nay, alarmed to hear it,' said Blanchflower, finding no need to dissemble. 'And has she brought her back to life?'

'We do not know,' answered the king. 'And we do not know where they have hidden her. I suppose I do not need to spell out for you the possible consequences if she were indeed resuscitated?'

'No,' said Blanchflower after a moment for consideration. 'You do not.'

'And then there is this other band of traitors and heretics making mischief in the west. I may be sending you that way in due course. I am told they hope to secure this girl's services in reawakening King Stephen. The Wytch King, no less. Can you imagine then what travails might afflict this unhappy realm?'

'Yes,' grunted Blanchflower. 'I imagine chaos might prevail.'

'It might,' agreed the king. 'It very well might, which is why I am determined that this threat must be snuffed out before it can develop further. This girl must die.'

'I suppose Sir Richard is engaged upon it,' said Blanchflower. 'I suppose he may secure her person in due course.'

'I suppose he will,' conceded the king. 'But I want you in on it, Daniel. There must be no mistake. I do not care about arrests, charges, days in court and the whole sorry, tedious, longwinded process of the law. I want her dead and I want her dead with all possible dispatch. Do I make myself clear?'

'You do,' said Blanchflower with the faintest of nods. 'Will I approach Sir Richard?'

'No, no, no,' muttered the king, shaking his head. 'Sir Richard is a stickler for due process.'

'And you do not trust him to execute your will?'

'Of course, I trust him,' said the king. 'If I did not trust him, he would not occupy such a vital post, would he? No, I simply wish to override his instincts in this case, as is my prerogative.'

'Indeed.'

'I want you to find out how the investigation fares.'

'And you think that Sir Richard will share this with me.'

'Not at all, but Bentley is a weakling and doubtless he will succumb to whatever moral or physical force you can apply to him. Find out what they are doing, find out where the girl is and then have her killed. Kill her yourself, if need be. Do I make myself clear?'

'Yes, Father.'

'And do not call me "Father". It is not common knowledge, and I would not wish it to be. One day you will forget yourself and refer to me thus in public.'

'Yes, Your Majesty.'

'Good, then you are dismissed.'

Blanchflower saluted, swept his hat to his head, clicked his heels together and withdrew, leaving his royal parent looking abstractedly out of the window and chewing his nails.

Sir Joseph's professional duties occasionally required him to attend to Lady Erskine, who dwelt on the opposite side of the square. Lady Erskine, an elderly widow, was troubled by a few largely imaginary conditions and chronically fearful that one of these would be fatal to her. Naturally, her fears grew in intensity and in legitimacy with every passing year, and so Sir Joseph found himself increasingly in attendance upon her. On this occasion, as on many others, his visit concluded with his prescribing the sizeable and disagreeable-tasting black tablets that his patient found most effective in settling her palpitations. She professed herself much recovered almost immediately upon having consumed one of these harmless sugar pills, sat up straight in bed and demanded tea and crumpets. Having exchanged pleasantries for half an hour or so, she thanked him for his solicitations and the consultation ended. It was as he was descending the staircase from her room, reflecting upon the unconscious power of the mind over the body, that he glanced out of the window and saw that the significant pair of curtains had been drawn in his own house across the square.

'You were saying, Sir Joseph?' prompted Lady Erskine's youngest son, Sir Adam, himself in his early seventies, noticing that the physician had abruptly halted, both in movement and in speech.

'Hmm? Oh, yes. The street cleaners are indeed shockingly neglectful of their duties,' agreed Sir Joseph at length, resuming his step and his train of thought. 'I wonder if you would be so good as to summon me a cab?'

'A cab, sir?' frowned Sir Adam, plainly wondering why Sir Joseph should require to be conveyed the fifty paces across the square in this manner.

'I have an engagement at my club,' explained Sir Joseph, 'or I should certainly be guilty of a scandalous indolence.'

'Of course, I shall ask Titchmarsh to attend to it directly,' said Sir Adam replied with a chuckle, naming their butler.

When the cab arrived, together with a fortuitous shower of rain, Sir Joseph hurried to it, his person partly shrouded by a servant bearing an umbrella. Looking surreptitiously from the window as the vehicle drew away, he noticed two dark-clad men standing at the corner of the square with apparent nonchalance. Surely these were representatives of the state.

'Oh dear,' he said, settling back into his seat. 'I do not care for this at all.'

Once clear of the square he gave instructions to the driver, and some minutes later was set down not at the Albany, his club, but at the Black Bull, an inn that stood at the corner of Milton Lane and Frogmore Street. Here, as was their prior arrangement, he found Mould nursing a quart of ale and looking even more than usually glum.

'Do you think you were followed?' he asked, glancing around through the smoke-hazed space, taking off his hat to avoid the lowest of the ceiling beams.

'Don't think so,' grunted Mould, wiping his mouth with the back of his hand. ''Least I ain't seen any'un.'

'Two dark-clad gentlemen in the square, one markedly taller than the other,' observed Sir Joseph. 'I trust they came calling.'

'Those'll be the ones, sir,' nodded Mould. 'Intelligencers by the looks of it.'

'Well, now they await me in the square,' said Sir Joseph, shrugging off his overcoat. 'And they may wait as long as they wish.'

'We shall not return there?'

'We shall not. At least not for the present.'

'Then what?'

'First we shall await darkness.'

At nightfall, with the Thames a sky-reflecting ribbon beneath the darkening silhouettes of the city, the two men slipped from the inn and made their way along the narrow lane that led towards the river. Two figures immediately detached themselves from the wall further up towards Frogmore Street and came after them, their pace apparently casual but nevertheless allowing of no innocent interpretation.

'I believe we are pursued,' said Sir Joseph out of the side of his mouth, having spared a momentary glance over his shoulder.

'Indeed, sir,' said Mould, cracking his knuckles. 'Would you care for me to engage them?'

'No, we should certainly avoid confrontation at this point,' murmured Sir Joseph. 'I trust the boat is in its place?'

''Was earlier on, sir,' grunted Mould.

Milton Lane was a dead end that gave access to a short length of river wharf, hemmed in on either side by warehouses. Here, a small rowing skiff was habitually moored, ready for just such an emergency. But when they arrived on the wharf's edge a few moments later, it was to find their boat missing.

'It were definitely here earlier, sir,' assured Mould, scratching his head. 'Some bastards must have thieved it.'

'An untimely crime,' said Sir Joseph despairingly, looking back to where their pursuers were approaching, a perceptible confidence in their step as their quarry's situation dawned upon them. 'And now we are trapped.'

'Not quite, sir,' announced Mould, indicating with a nod the fisherman mounting the ladder from his own boat, almost lost in the shadow of the warehouse to their left. 'Not if we're quick.'

The fisherman, a man of advanced years, had barely reached the wharf and reeled in surprise when the fugitives were suddenly upon him.

'I'll give you five guineas for your boat, sir,' cried Sir Joseph, pressing this sum into the man's hand, waving his objections aside. 'Much more than what it's worth, I don't doubt, but our need is very great.'

'Eh! What the…?'

The fisherman's mouth was wide in incomprehension, his arms likewise cast wide as Sir Joseph and Mould threw themselves into his boat, struggling to free the painter, reaching for the oars and pushing off out into the stream even as their pursuers came running to the wharf's edge. His cries were lost in theirs as the current carried them away into the great river, almost a third of a mile wide at this point.

'Ha!' said Sir Joseph triumphantly after a few minutes of grateful exertion, leaning on his oar. 'Let them pursue us now.'

'I wonder what that-there fellow was trying to tell us, sir,' said Mould, wiping sweat from his brow. 'I ain't sure he wasn't trying to warn us o' somethin.' Not that we gave him half a chance.'

'I doubt he will report us to the constabulary,' said Sir Joseph complacently, rowing more gently now. 'I suppose I gave him twice the value of this tub. Three times, even. Now, perhaps if we let the stream carry us down a little, we may come ashore by Maynard Street.'

'Perhaps,' said Mould with a sniff, 'and perhaps not, sir. I think I knows what our friend was trying to tell us.'

'Oh dear,' said Sir Joseph, following Mould's grim glance to see that the bottom of the boat was already awash. 'Do you think she will swim?'

'I think we shall, sir,' said Mould, unlacing a boot.

'I see,' said Sir Joseph. 'I take it you can swim, then?'

'Not yet,' said Mould glumly. 'Never 'ad the need.'

'Necessity will be the spur, I suppose,' said Joseph as the chilly waters rose around his calves.

'Daresay it will, sir. Daresay it will,' muttered Mould, surveying the dark waters bleakly.

Turnbull was in an exceedingly ill humour as the archbishop's barge conveyed him homeward across the Thames. A message had reached him that afternoon to say that Lamb lay dying and wished to see him urgently. Turnbull, rejoicing in every aspect of this news, was filled with a sense of pleasurable anticipation as he hurried to his superior's bedside. Surely, the old man meant to indicate his preference that Turnbull should succeed him, a very weighty endorsement to be placed in the balance when such matters were decided. His satisfaction was enhanced still further when enquiry revealed that no other prelates had been summoned, that Turnbull alone had dwelt in the ailing archbishop's thoughts. His hopes were dashed, however, his mood abruptly darkened, when Canon Geoffrey Wakeman, the head of the archbishop's household, met him at the head of the stairs and began uttering apologies.

'I c... c... cannot tell you how much I regret...' he began, glancing over his shoulder in the direction of Lamb's bedchamber.

'Hmm? What?' wheezed Turnbull, breathless after his unusually purposeful ascent of four flights.

'He n... n... no longer wishes to see y... you,' stammered Wakeman, whose inaugural sermon before the new king some years ago had brought the congregation in St Paul's twenty minutes of excruciating awkwardness.

'What do you mean he no longer wants to see me?' snapped Turnbull incredulously. 'He summoned me, did he not? I don't suppose it was any idle whim of your own.'

'He did, but n... n... n... now he has thought better of it, or perhaps he has f... oooor... got it,' said Wakeman, quailing before Turnbull's furious gaze.

'Nonsense,' snarled Turnbull. 'I shall see him myself.'

But when Turnbull stood before Lamb and Lamb, ancient and shrunken amongst the white sheets, opened his eyes, there remained an undiminished fire in them.

'What are you doing here?' he demanded, his voice faint, but the tone offering no evidence of affection or positive intent regarding Turnbull's future prospects.

'Why, your worship, I was told that you had summoned me,' said Turnbull in a voice adjusted to the soothing of those whose ends were near.

'Well, I didn't,' snapped Lamb shortly. 'And whoever told you that's a damned liar.'

'Oh, I see,' said Turnbull with a sharp glance at Wakeman, who stood wringing his hands by the door.

'Now get out!' ordered Lamb, spittle flying. 'Can't a man get some rest?'

'Of course, I'm so sorry to have disturbed you,' murmured Turnbull, beating a hasty retreat.

And so, as he looked out upon the benighted Thames, Turnbull had cause to reflect bleakly that Lamb's addled wits might yet come between him and the consummation of his desires. By now it was quite dark, with myriad lights shining from the north shore and a chill breeze rippling the reflections on the black waters. The ornate canopy above him offered some protection from the elements, but despite this the night air was cool and he pulled his coat more tightly around him. Recalled from his private thoughts, he became aware that the oarsmen had ceased rowing, that some of them were peering away northwards and their bosun rising to his feet.

'Where away?' he heard the man ask, and one of the oarsmen pointed out into the darkness.

With the oars stilled, piteous cries could be heard from some way away across the waters.

'Folks in the swim,' said the bosun, looking along the vessel towards where the bishop sat. 'Shall we pick 'em up, sir?'

'Of course, it is no more than our Christian duty,' nodded Turnbull, thinking that his supper had receded still further from him now. At once the crew sprang into renewed motion and the barge surged forwards towards the northern bank, oars rising and falling briskly. Moments later and two dark figures were being heaved wetly over the gunwales by strong arms, slapped on the shoulders by their cheerful rescuers and wrapped in dry coats.

'Will I bring them aft?' called the bosun.

'Aye, let me have sight of them,' grunted Turnbull.

There was a small lamp beneath the canopy, and into the circle of dim light cast by this, two figures presently emerged, dry coats wrapped tightly around them, hair plastered wetly to their heads.

'I hardly dare hope adequately to convey our gratitude for your timely intervention,' said the smaller of the two humbly, 'for surely we were moments from succumbing to the waters.'

'Ah,' said Turnbull, recognition dawning. 'Sir Joseph Finch, is it not?'

'Why yes,' said Sir Joseph. 'And this is my man, Mould. And you must be…'

'Bishop William Turnbull,' supplied Turnbull, noting with satisfaction the dismay that momentarily visited his guest's face.

'Of course,' said Sir Joseph, recovering his composure, 'and I am glad to make your acquaintance once more. Your reputation grows apace, your noble work in the east country the talk of the nation in recent times. Delighted though I am to be able to offer you my sincere congratulations I could wish that our meeting had been under more propitious circumstances. Certainly, you have me at a significant disadvantage, I wonder if you would be so kind as to…'

'I do indeed have you at a disadvantage,' said Turnbull, 'and the disadvantage is more severe than you appreciate, given that I am fully aware that orders have been given that you should be taken in for questioning.'

'Oh,' said Sir Joseph slowly. 'I see.' The briefest of sideward glances betrayed his dalliance with the notion of taking once more to the chill embrace of Father Thames.

'I urge you not to do anything foolish,' said Turnbull, noticing Sir Joseph eyeing the cold, dark waters. He patted the leather-upholstered bench at his side. 'I urge you rather to sit here with me and place some notion in my head as to why I should not convey you immediately to the Tower, where the king's men would doubtless be delighted to entertain you. Perhaps your man would go forward with the oarsmen so that we can speak in private.'

With a sigh, Sir Joseph settled himself at Turnbull's side and Mould withdrew shivering forward, regarding the bishop balefully over his shoulder. Sir Joseph's mind had been oppressed by a sense of gathering gloom ever since he had seen Mould's fateful signal earlier that day. It was one thing to conspire with the king's enemy under an assumed name, to dwell in two worlds necessarily separate, but it was quite another to find those worlds suddenly collide, his wealth, his reputation and his person suddenly under immediate threat. Naturally, he had long considered exactly that contingency, but to see it vividly brought into being was still deeply shocking. There was much to think about but little that his inner being could contemplate with any sense of complacency. If his first appearance before Sir Richard's men failed to give satisfaction, he might undergo investigation of a more rigorous nature. Sir Joseph's bowel twitched liquidly within him at this prospect. He had never yet been required to test the limits of his physical courage. In extremis, he wondered whether his flesh would betray him, whether the horrors of the torture chamber would draw forth his confession at last.

'Yes, an interview with the authorities lies in store for you, if I command it,' said Turnbull, 'but I'm sure we are both reasonable men.'

His own feelings were ones of frustration that he had again been placed in a position that obliged him to make a potentially crucial choice. On the last occasion he had acted against his better judgement and found himself forced to conceal potentially vital knowledge from the authorities. On this occasion he resolved to act in accordance with the dictates of expediency. A brief word with the bosun would be sufficient to make the Tower their destination.

'I should like to think so,' said Sir Joseph warily, 'and I can think of nothing immediately that might dissuade you from that course, except to say that my conscience is entirely clear, that I have done nothing contrary to the interests of the people and the future felicity of the nation.'

'Or contrary to the interests of His Majesty?' pressed Turnbull.

'You may be sure that my devotion to the throne is second to none,' answered Sir Joseph awkwardly.

'But not, perhaps, to its present incumbent,' said Turnbull wryly. 'Pray tell me, Sir Joseph, are you part of a plot to unseat His Majesty and replace him with his late-lamented mother, Queen Charlotte? Speak plainly now.'

'That is an extraordinary accusation for one gentleman to make to another and one that I absolutely decline to respond to,' said Sir Joseph, a haunted look entering his eyes whilst shifting awkwardly in his seat.

Turnbull nodded slowly.

'Extraordinary it may be, but we live in extraordinary times, do we not? I know a great deal about this plot,' he said. 'Would it surprise you to know that I recognised Laura DeLacey in the royal coach house on the eve of the theft of Her Late Majesty's body? Yes, Sir Joseph, unlike many in authority I have a fair idea of how that feat was accomplished.'

Turnbull quailed inwardly at having ventured this unlooked-for confession of his own. He had certainly not planned this disclosure, had not intended to open himself in this way. He found that Sir Joseph was regarding him intently, undoubtedly wondering whether to believe him.

'But you did not intervene,' he said.

'I did not,' agreed Turnbull, 'and you may interpret that as you will.' *And I wish you better luck than I have had*, he added silently, cursing his own inconstancy.

'I see,' said Sir Joseph, whose mind was likewise presently in a state of confusion that allowed of no more complex response.

'And tell me,' continued Turnbull, a gathering grim excitement in his breast. 'Was she successful in her attempt? Is the queen to be resuscitated?

'We may be frank with each other, I assure you,' pressed Turnbull, when Sir Joseph hesitated and looked away. 'For we are effectively alone, and each may confidently deny the content of this conversation.'

'Why do you press me so?' asked Sir Joseph. 'When you could simply deliver me up to the Tower?'

For a long moment Turnbull appeared to regard the dark dome of St Paul's with stony indifference whilst his heart strove for supremacy over the dictates of his brain.

'Because I wish to see the girl,' he said at last.

'You wish to arrest her?'

'I wish to speak to her,' corrected Turnbull with a shake of his head.

'And you expect me to trust you? You, who sentenced her to be hanged?' asked Sir Joseph incredulously.

'I do,' said Turnbull simply.

'Assuming that I knew where the girl is presently located, and assuming that I was willing to conduct you into her presence, why on earth should I place any trust in your discretion?' asked Sir Joseph, peering sidelong at the bishop. 'Surely, I should anticipate our immediate arrest.'

'Indeed,' agreed Turnbull. 'But when we are set ashore in a few minutes' time, I shall be alone and I shall be at your mercy, should you choose to overpower me. I speak theoretically, of course. Likewise, once at your mercy, you may then convey me to the place where you have hidden her. Doubtless you will thereafter soon wish to find a new refuge, but I conceive such thoughts are already in your mind, given that all your known contacts will certainly be under investigation. If you wish, you may tie me up and leave me there until Sir Richard's men come looking. My own reputation will be secure, since surely no one would conceive that I would willingly place myself in the custody of conspirators?'

'You will not convey me to the Tower?' asked Sir Joseph, regarding the bishop with a piercing gaze.

Turnbull shrugged. 'I have indicated as much. You have not heard me to issue such instructions.'

'I do not understand what you hope to gain from this,' said Sir Joseph. 'I know you for a cruel, vain, rapacious creature.'

'I am shocked that you should think so,' said Turnbull, raising an eyebrow, 'and you may leave my own motivation for the scrutiny of my conscience.'

'I had no idea you were in possession of such an object,' said Sir Joseph wonderingly.

'I ask again, if you have finished insulting me,' said Turnbull, 'will you convey me into Laura's presence?'

'I will,' said Sir Joseph, making his decision and looking straight into the bishop's eyes. 'I believe I will.'

Chapter Twenty-Four

Edward and Laura had been playing cards, but now it was late, and it was clear that she was fatigued. Edward gathered the pack and stooped to collect the two cards that she had let slip from her hand.

'Must you treat me like an invalid?' she protested. 'Am I so inflexible that I may not pick up my own cards? Or do you suspect me of cheating you?'

'My luck allows of no opportunity for you to cheat me,' grinned Edward, replacing them in their box. 'To feel the need to cheat requires some want of success, some adversity to oppose, and my luck with cards is so pitiful I seldom invite it in those I play. I console myself that I am a force for moral probity in the game.' He glanced at the clock. 'But now you must be a-bed. Surely Sir Joseph would disapprove of you. Bed by ten, he says, and now it is almost eleven.'

'Well, I was barely awake before noon,' she said, as Edward pulled back her chair from the table at which they sat and observed with an agony of pity as she struggled to stand, 'and I am already in my night clothes, as you see. I shall surely be asleep even before you set foot in the street. Perhaps you would call Amelie to turn down my bed.'

'Of course.'

Edward took Laura's arm gently and accompanied her in her slow progress from the room. Tonight, she seemed a little recovered, a little of the old Laura had crept back into her. For the first forty-eight hours after their trespass in the royal crypt her friends had despaired of her recovery. Confined to bed she had trodden an uncertain path between delirium and sleep. It was clear that Emily was often in her thoughts, but her murmurings were of her mother and of her school friends, too. Sir Joseph found her pulse to be faint, her heartbeat irregular and her prospects for recovery bleak.

'Surely she may rebuild her strength,' Edward had protested when this prognosis had been disclosed to him, 'given time and rest. No one could want for better care.'

'And yet it may not be sufficient,' Sir Joseph had told him regretfully, 'and you must prepare yourself for...'

'How shall I prepare myself for that?' Edward had asked bitterly.

'I regret that I can offer you no guidance on that point,' Sir Joseph had replied. 'I wish that I could find some guidance for myself. But you have only to look upon her to see that her days are numbered.'

It was true. Laura's cheeks were more sunken than ever since her encounter with the queen, her skin now pitifully slack and wrinkled around the mouth and eyes. To see her so reduced was like a knife to Edward's heart. To hear Thomas's name upon her lips as she slept or maundered between sleep and waking was more painful still. Edward was often at her bedside in those few days, there to hold her hand or to assist with her nursing. But today she had seemed somewhat recovered, had been more wakeful and had eaten a little dry toast. A resurgent spirit had refused her confinement to bed, and her thoughts had seemed more ordered. It was possible to feel that there was some hope after all.

'And will I see you tomorrow?' she asked now, turning to him as they crossed the threshold of her bedchamber. 'You are very dear to me, you know.'

'And you to me,' he said, patting her arm and blinking tears from his eyes. 'Of course, you shall.'

Amelie, Laura's servant and appointed nursemaid, appeared at their side, having arrived with the self-effacing stealth that was one of her more remarkable characteristics.

'Beggin' your pardon, sir, Sir Joseph has returned,' she said to Edward. 'Begs to see Miss Laura, if she is at liberty to receive him.'

The glint in Amelie's eye hinted that there was more to this request than presently disclosed. Having descended the staircase two steps at a time Edward was able to confirm this for himself, finding a rather damp Sir Joseph waiting with Mould in the library. Standing with him was a portly cleric of middling years, whose florid features presently held an expression of extreme anxiety.

'This is Edward, my assistant,' said Sir Joseph with a nod. 'Edward, may I beg to introduce to you the Bishop of London?'

'Turnbull!' said Edward, surprise driving out etiquette.

'Yes,' said Sir Joseph carefully, with a look that invited trust and patience, that enjoined on the young man a particular circumspection and restraint. 'He wishes to see Laura.'

'He does?' Edward swallowed hard and his eye darted towards the door.

'He is alone,' said Sir Joseph, noticing his young stead's nervousness, 'and we stand in no immediate peril, although I must speak with you privately just now. She is awake, I take it?'

'Laura, you must attend to me,' said Edward a few minutes later, finding her sitting up in bed and having her thin hair brushed by Amelie. 'You must not be alarmed if I tell you that Bishop Turnbull stands outside your door. He wishes to speak with you, that is all, and Sir Joseph has said that he may ask. You may say no, if you prefer. He is prepared for that.'

'Why should I not be alarmed?' said Laura, swallowing hard. 'And why should he desire this? The last time we conversed it was only to condemn me to be hanged.'

'I do not know,' admitted Edward. 'I only know that he has made this request and has undertaken not to impede our escape, for surely events are moving quickly and we must get you away very soon in case we are discovered.'

'And you trust him?' asked Laura, eyes agape.

'Sir Joseph trusts him,' said Edward.

'Then I must trust him, too, I suppose, although this will be a very strange encounter. What on earth can he want with me?'

A few moments later William Turnbull, Bishop of London, advanced cautiously into the room. He was not a man used to humility or the consideration of the feelings of others, so his present state of mind, his present behaviour, caused him to feel as though he had entered some strange foreign land. In ordinary circumstances an escaped fugitive might quail before a peer of the realm, but now it seemed that those roles were reversed. Turnbull felt a dryness in his mouth as he looked upon her and found that his hands were trembling. She appeared so old, so frail, but a curious serenity was upon her and the eye that met his was steady.

'Miss DeLacey,' he said, unable to meet that eye for more than a moment.

'Bishop Turnbull,' said she in soft voice, barely audible. 'I had not expected to see you again in this world.'

'Indeed,' he said with a slow nod.

'You wished to speak with me?' she enquired. 'What was it you wished to say, for many might consider our encounter an unlikely one? I take it you have not come to carry out my sentence with your own hand.'

'I have not,' said the bishop.

'Then why?'

'You are changed,' said Turnbull, approaching a little closer. 'You are changed so much since first I saw you.'

'You don't have to tell me that,' said Laura with a wry smile. 'You may be assured that I am the first to know. I have poured out my youth into other bodies and they walk the earth again because of me.'

'I have heard,' said Turnbull. 'And I conceive you are a very remarkable person, as others have assured me.'

'So, I ask again, Bishop Turnbull, why are you here?'

'She is fatigued,' murmured Edward, who stood at Turnbull's shoulder. 'Say what you will and be gone.'

Turnbull licked his lips. He had assured himself that his motivation in coming to this place had been to gather intelligence on the rebels and traitors that plotted against the king. Once his supposed custody in the hands of Sir Joseph and his confederates was ended, he would have much to report to Sir Richard and the authorities. Doubtless, this would do something to bolster his position. Faced with Laura, however, these worldly considerations receded from his mind, and he was brought abruptly into the presence of less comfortable thoughts, ones that had troubled him persistently since the day he had condemned her. Turnbull was not a religious man, except in the most conventional sense, and the faith served merely to encompass his ambition and embody his will. He had never experienced any sense of the divine, never felt the presence of anything beyond human understanding – anything that might be supposed immeasurably greater than himself. Until now. With surprise, as shifting veils of self-interest and self-deception moved aside, Turnbull realised why he had desired to come before her. He wished to make his apology, to beg her forgiveness and so to be at peace with himself.

He looked up, his eyes cleared, and he opened his mouth. At that moment there was a sudden great commotion downstairs. He span round and exchanged an anxious glance with Edward, even as the young man recovered from his initial surprise and dashed from the room. There were shouts, a shot, the sounds of running feet in corridors and on stairs, and suddenly Edward was back, slamming the door shut and pressing his shoulder to it.

'What is it?' cried Laura, her small voice hoarse. 'Are we discovered?'

'Uh, huh!' nodded Edward, his eyes wide with alarm. 'And we are trapped in here.'

It was true – the room was on the third storey and offered no means of escape. Already, the doorknob was rattling, and a heavy shoulder rebounded from the other side. There was cursing, another great thud and suddenly Edward, an inconsiderable weight, was flung backward as the door burst open. Two troopers of the Scarlet Band stood framed in it, breathing hard, surveying the occupants of the room as Edward scrambled to his feet, panting with fear.

'Here!' shouted one of them along the corridor outside, and within instants the two moved apart to admit another, a burly giant in a feathered hat with an expression of grim satisfaction on his face.

'Blanchflower!' cried the bishop. 'What are you doing here?'

'This,' grunted the soldier, raising his pistol, levelling it at Laura.

'No!' wailed Turnbull, throwing himself in front of the startled girl even as Blanchflower pulled the trigger. There was a loud report, acrid smoke and the bishop fell back, clutching his chest, turning, lurching sideways, collapsing with a thud to the floor and knocking over a bedside table as he fell. Even as these events occurred Edward was roaring with insensate fury, hurling himself at Blanchflower's legs at knee level. Edward was no athlete, but his point of impact was well judged and his impetus sufficient to topple Blanchflower like some great tree, the discharged pistol flying from his hand. A moment later and strong hands were dragging him away, voices roaring in his head. All was confusion. There were more shouts and screams, more gunshots, the sound of clashing steel on steel. Edward, suddenly released, rolled away and scrambled to his feet as Thomas Corvin lunged into the room, his sword darting at one of Edward's assailants. The man stepped back, tumbled over Blanchflower's half-sprawled figure and received the blade full in his belly. The man screamed, head thrown back and clutching at his abdomen even as Corvin tugged the blade free. The other soldier was bringing his own sword round in a whirling arc, parried by Thomas and dashed aside, his face a snarling mask of fury. There were more clashes of steel. Blanchflower, entangled with the writhing body of the fallen man, cursed and pulled free another pistol from his belt. Edward hurled himself upon him, grappling with him for the weapon, whimpering, cursing, his heart pounding heavily in his chest. There was another shot and Blanchflower gasped. His body spasmed beneath Edward's and then lay still. Edward whipped round and found Sir Joseph standing in the threshold with a smoking pistol in hand and two strangers at his shoulder. The third soldier, seeing that two more pistols were trained upon his head, dropped his weapon.

'Out!' ordered one of the two strangers, seizing him by the collar and ejecting him roughly from the room with an encouraging kick. 'Simon, watch this one. What about the others?'

Various exchanges of a practical nature took place, during which it was established that Blanchflower was dead and his companion shortly to be so, making a deal of noise about it. Edward barely noticed this melee and crossed to where Laura was cowering against the bed head, her face ashen.

'You are unharmed, I take it?' he asked, pressing her hands in his.

'I believe so,' gasped Laura. 'But...' her glance encompassed the scene of carnage around them.

'What about this one?' asked Thomas, referring to the bishop, after having likewise received assurance of her wellbeing. 'Is that a bishop?'

'It is... was...' said Edward, looking over his shoulder to where Turnbull lay in a pool of his own blood.

'Is,' gasped the bishop, wiping blood from his mouth and then, with emphasis, '*is*.'

Exchanging a wary glance with Edward, Sir Joseph stepped forward to attend to the stricken cleric, turning him gently onto his back and pulling his clothing aside to come to the wound. He looked up, frowned and shook his head.

'I saw that,' croaked the bishop. 'Don't you shake your head so, sir.'

'We must get you out of here,' said Thomas to Laura, wiping his sword on a corpse's coat. 'Doubtless more will be coming. Our numbers are too few. Edward, take her down the servant's stairs and out through the kitchen, then...'

'I know,' said Edward impatiently, helping Laura to swing her legs out of bed. 'We have practised the route. Come, my dear. We must be away.'

There was no time for farewells. Even as Sir Joseph barked instructions that the door should be lifted from its hinges, that Sir George's medical bag be fetched, Edward was hurrying with Laura towards the servants' quarters and Thomas rushing downstairs to see if there were any further intruders to be dealt with. He found Lady Elizabeth cradling a fallen Sir George in her lap. The old gentleman had heard the commotion when first Blanchflower and his men had burst through the front door and come shuffling along to intervene. Sir Joseph had been in the company of Lady Elizabeth in the library and emerged to find Bristow and two footmen grappling with the intruders. Sir George, roaring defiance, had snatched up an old fishing rod, thinking to catch them with it, and this, being mistaken in the confusion for a long gun, had resulted in his being shot down. Within moments Thomas Corvin had arrived in their midst with four of his companions, and the running skirmish had ensued that left three of the Scarlet Band dead, one in custody and an unknown number making good their escape. Danny Blanchflower, the king's bastard, lay upstairs with his brains spread across a Turkish rug. Sir George, shot in the throat, had likewise breathed his last, his blood making a great spreading stain on Lady Elizabeth's dress as she wept over him. Thomas took all this in – the toppled tables and vases, the corpse of a trooper in the threshold of the library, the grim-faced cluster of his own men as they reloaded their pistols or bound torn strips of fabric around flesh wounds.

'Sir Joseph, what are you doing? We must be away!' he cried as Sir Joseph came in view with the bishop, borne carefully down the stairs on the door by Mould and a group of perspiring servants.

'I must treat this man first,' said Sir Joseph grimly, and then to the servants, 'clear the table in the library, place him there.'

'But sir!' objected Thomas. 'The king's men may be upon us within minutes.'

'He took a bullet that was intended for Laura,' snapped Sir Joseph. 'And I will have that bullet out this minute or it will surely be the death of him.'

'And what if you are caught?' objected Thomas as the physician strode past him. 'What then of our plans?'

'I will not leave this man to die,' grunted Sir Joseph, opening Sir George's medical case and withdrawing a pair of long-nosed retractors. 'You do as you will. Take Lady Elizabeth, I beg.'

'Will I strap him down?' asked Mould, nodding at the groaning bishop while slipping off his belt.

'You will need to,' agreed Sir Joseph, stripping aside the bishop's upper garments to reveal the gaping wound as Thomas stood watching aghast.

'I warn you, sir, this will pain you extremely,' he told Turnbull. 'But I shall trade considerations of comfort for speed as necessity dictates. We must have that ball out of you, if you are to have any chance at all.'

Turnbull, unnaturally pale of face by now, might have uttered some reply but at that moment Mould's thick belt was pulled between his jaws and he found his limbs bound tight by various cords pulled hastily from curtains.

'Well, I shall leave you to it,' said Thomas after a moment, 'though surely you have taken leave of your senses. Lady Elizabeth, you must come with me now. Your husband is beyond help, as you see.'

'I shall stay with Sir Joseph,' said Lady Elizabeth, kissing her dead husband's brow. 'But surely you must go and your friends with you. I do not fear Sir Richard's men.'

'Then you are a fool and so is he,' muttered Thomas, but he beckoned to his men and strode from the house.

Emerging from the kitchen door, Edward led Laura limping through the kitchen garden and out to the small orchard that occupied one part of the rear of the grounds. Here there was a door into the garden of the adjacent house, a property that had long stood empty. Their escape plan, one that had been practised on several occasions, envisaged that they should make their way out onto the street unobserved around the corner from Sir George's house. Progress was slow since Edward, out of necessity, had to place his arm around Laura's shoulder and support much of her weight. At last, he had the orchard door open, having groped in the darkness for the handle and rattled the key ineffectually in the lock before engaging the mechanism. Swinging the door shut behind them, he turned, made to re-establish his grip beneath Laura's arm and felt a sudden sickening impact on the back of his head. There was a momentary explosion of light, pain and then... oblivion.

'Laura, my sweet,' said Jonah's gloating voice in the darkness. 'We have been waiting for you.'

Her first cry of despair was stifled by the rough hand clamped over her mouth. More strong hands were upon her, urging her away along the path that led past the empty house towards the street, where a coach and four horses waited, snorting and stamping as the whiff of gun smoke drifted along the street.

Even as she was hurried away it became apparent that it was Blood and Maigret that confined her in their brutal grip, Jonah striding in front.

'Home sweet home for you now, daughter of mine,' said Jonah, pausing to swing open the gate. Crossing to the coach and glancing warily along the empty street, he exchanged a few terse words with those in the driver's position. There was an instant, as the door was pulled open, when Laura felt the grip on her upper arm relent. Immediately, as she had been considering for some moments, she jerked free from that grip and tore at the necklace that Lady Elizabeth had given her, snapping the fine chain and clutching it in her hand. At the same time, she twisted and fell away, the curses of her captors ringing in her ears. The brutal hardness of the street surface was suddenly on her cheek, her body pressed against a wheel that began gradually to move. Reaching out amongst the filth and ordure in the gutter she released the necklace and made two swift movements with her finger, even as strong arms heaved her to her feet.

'No more of your little tricks, miss!' hissed Maigret in her ear.

'Done,' said Sir Joseph ten minutes later, dropping a gory pistol ball next to the motionless bishop's body. 'Someone else may close him up properly. At least the chief cause of mischief is removed, and he has some small chance of survival.'

The bishop, who had passed out some time ago, carried away by the unbearable agony of Sir Joseph's intervention and through want of blood, lay insensible of his condition. The physician wiped his bloodied hands on a towel brought from the kitchens, gave instructions that his friend Dr Mendelssohn be summoned from his house three streets away and turned to where Lady Elizabeth stood watching from the threshold, a handkerchief pressed to her mouth.

'I shall go now,' he said. 'Will you accompany me, Lady Elizabeth?'

'I will not,' she answered, her eyes already red-rimmed from weeping. 'My duty to my husband forbids it. But you must certainly go.'

'They may mistreat you,' said Sir Joseph grimly, pulling on his coat. 'I do not doubt Sir Richard's men will call upon you soon enough. I am amazed we have remained undisturbed so long, although it may be Blanchflower acted independently in this outrage.'

'I think not,' she said. 'And I suppose I know little that they have not already gleaned. I know not where the queen is kept. And I have friends in high places who may be prevailed upon to protect me.'

'Let us hope so,' said Sir Joseph, glancing at the clock on the mantel, which told nearly midnight. 'Mould, perhaps we shall follow Edward's route. Doubtless he will be well away by now and will have Laura safely at Mrs Coles'.

Mrs Cole, who kept a small inn at the rear of St James' Park, was an old friend of Sir Joseph and had been briefed to be prepared for unexpected visitors at any time of day or night, taking them in without fuss or question. On this occasion her night was to remain undisturbed. It was Mould who stumbled over Edward's unconscious form as they made their way through the connecting garden door.

'Sir,' he grunted, stooping to investigate, and then, ''tis Master Edward, sir.'

'What?!' Sir Joseph whipped round, turning back and joining Mould at the young man's side. 'Curse this darkness. He yet lives, however,' he said, fingers groping for a pulse and finding one. 'We must carry him out into the street, where there is a little light.'

'Miss Laura,' said Mould grimly, looking up and catching an answering glint in Sir Joseph's eye.

'Yes. The swine have her, it would appear.'

Between them, they half-carried, half-dragged Edward down a passage that led past the neighbouring house and emerged onto the street, through a gate that swung open now. Edward was stirring and groaning, even as Sir Joseph propped him against a wall and ran probing fingers around the back of his scalp, finding a bruise the size of hen's egg but coming away with no blood.

'There is no depression, I think,' he muttered. 'I suppose he will live, although I daresay his head will ache mightily.'

'He wakes, sir,' said Mould as Edward's eyes eased open and he began to twitch and stretch his limbs cautiously.

'What happened, Edward?' demanded Sir Joseph, bending close to his face.

'I know not,' groaned Edward. 'They jumped us, I suppose. Oh, my head. My poor head.'

He groped gingerly amongst his hair.

'You will survive,' assured Sir Joseph, 'but the same may not be true of Laura. I wonder who has taken her?'

'If 'tis the king's men there is some hope of due process,' observed Mould. 'They'll have 'er banged up somewhere by now.'

'But if it was Jonah's people,' said Sir Joseph grimly, 'I imagine they will wish to convey her back to the west, where they will oblige her to awaken his father.'

'If he can be awakened,' said Mould.

'And if she yet has the strength in her to do so,' said Sir Joseph. 'I fear for her.'

He crossed to the kerb, where fresh marks made by some wheeled vehicle could vaguely be discerned in the darkness, and he stroked his chin, looking anxiously along the street. As he turned back a tiny glint caught his eye and glancing down, he saw Laura's necklace in the gutter.

'Observe,' he said, stooping down. 'This is Laura's, I believe.'

'And these marks next to it?' asked Mould at his shoulder. 'They seem natural to you, sir?'

'No, indeed not. Step back, if you will, you are shading the streetlight.'

The two men peered into the gloom at their feet and then regarded each other thoughtfully.

'Edward,' called Sir Joseph to where Edward yet sat ruefully nursing his head. 'Come and see this, if you will. I believe Laura has left us a message.'

'What message?' asked Edward, climbing painfully to his feet.

'Only a single letter,' said Sir Joseph, 'unless we are deceived. What might she hope to convey with a single letter T?'

'I sent Thomas along as soon as I heard,' said Corvin. 'One of the bishop's bargemen was in our pay. He recognised Sir Joseph and sent word to me. It seemed to me that something decidedly odd was underway.'

'I'm glad that you did,' said Sir Joseph. 'I suppose Blanchflower would otherwise have achieved his ends.'

'I am surprised that you should have risked your life to save Bishop Turnbull's' observed Corvin, taking a sip from his glass and leaning forward to refill Sir Joseph's.

It was almost two of the morning, but neither felt in the least bit sleepy. Each felt the powerful sense that events were approaching a crescendo, that the next hours and days might determine the future courses of their lives.

'I am surprised, too, when I consider it,' admitted Sir Joseph. 'I was not in my habitual mind just then. My body was awash with humours inimical to rational thought. Edward had told me that the bishop threw himself before Laura, in order to spare her from Blanchflower's bullet.'

'But his was a reign of terror in the Eastings.'

'It was,' sighed Sir Joseph, 'and I suppose he deserved to die. But I am a physician, dedicated to the preservation of life, and established habits are hard to shake. Besides, I felt there was something strange about him, even as we spoke on his barge.'

'Strange?' Corvin asked quizzically.

'More than anything he wanted to meet Laura,' said Sir Joseph, savouring a noble claret on his palette, holding the glass up to regard candlelight through the clear red breadth of it. 'Perhaps in some subtle way he is changed by her. I believe he is under her spell.'

'An unfortunate form of words, when discussing one accused of witchcraft,' observed Corvin.

'I know not how else to explain it,' said Sir Joseph, 'although we both know there is no substance in any such superstitious allegation.'

'Uh huh. And where is she now, do you suppose?' asked Corvin. 'My son is eager to pursue her, although not, I think, with the same passion that once motivated him. Rather, I think, he feels a powerful sense of duty to her that derives from the extinction of that passion.'

'I'm sure it does,' said Sir Joseph. 'And we are not sure where they have taken her. I think we may assume that Jonah has reclaimed her. It would make perfect sense for them to head west to re-join Jonah's followers and for her to be brought eventually into the presence of King Stephen's corpse.'

'And yet? You are not convinced of this, I surmise.'

Sir Joseph described to Corvin the circumstances of Laura's abduction, the sign that she had left, if indeed it was a sign.

'And there is nowhere in the south-west that satisfactorily explains this T?' asked Corvin. 'There is Taunton, perhaps, or Tiverton or even Tavistock.'

'Of course, there are,' agreed Sir Joseph. 'And yet I am uneasy in my mind.'

'And this, I suppose, explains your presence here, your absence from the saddle of some horse traversing the western highway,' said Corvin, regarding his friend with a wry smile.

'It does. Laura was trying to convey some vital message to us, and I know not what it was. You may be sure I shall devote the whole of my resources to discovering what she meant.'

'Of course, for you are likewise under her spell,' observed Corvin.

'Rather because I know that Laura will lead us to the Wytch King,' said Sir Joseph, ignoring this jibe, 'and because I know that the frustration of Jonah's desires is as important as the advancement of our own. How fares Her Majesty, incidentally?'

'I am told that it is too early to tell,' said Corvin, pursing his lips, 'but you may be sure that arrangements are in place for a general uprising in her support, should she awake. Hardiman and his nephew have her in a place, a cellar, where the conditions best match those of the crypt from whence she was taken. If she does awaken you will soon know.'

'How so?'

'Because the signal to all our followers is the ringing of church bells,' explained Corvin. 'You will hear them ring out from one side of the nation to the other.'

Chapter Twenty-Five

For a long time, Laura sat slumped in the corner of the carriage seat and watched out of the window glumly as the dark streets of London passed her by. Soon the buildings were more widely spaced, giving way to the larger houses, the parks, orchards and market gardens of the northern suburbs. She was returning to the Eastings, the place that she once had called home, and yet this brought little consolation to her heart. Across from her sat Jonah and Blood, and next to her was Maigret, puffing at a pipe that filled the space with smoke that stung her eyes. There was no conversation to speak of once they had put a mile or so between them and the site of her abduction. Jonah continued to regard her with the grim satisfaction of one who has recovered some artefact of value. She drifted in and out of an uneasy sleep, her mind oppressed by a sense of bleak despair, her eyes sore from the shedding of bitter tears.

'Yes, weep, daughter,' Jonah told her at one point. 'For what good it may do you. There is no escaping your appointment with destiny now.'

'Should've done it sooner,' grunted Maigret around his pipe. 'Instead of wastin' her on wakin' all those others.'

'You know my thinking,' snapped Jonah, 'and there was no knowing the doing of it might take their toll of her.'

'There wasn't, was there?' laughed Maigret, sparing a glance for Laura's hunched figure at his side. 'There might have been for those with eyes in their heads.'

'And you had better curb the tongue in yours,' warned Jonah, slapping the pipe from his mouth and grasping him by the collar, hauling the man half across the carriage towards him, 'if you desire to retain it.'

'You know my feelings, that is all,' said Maigret calmly, resuming his place once released and groping at Laura's feet for his pipe.

'And I have heard them expressed until I am sick to the heart,' said Jonah, cracking his knuckles. 'There is enough left in her for one last great awakening, I swear. I have seen it. Three hundred years we have waited, but tomorrow will bring an end to it. My father will begin to travel the road that will bring him amongst us at last.'

'And what if his heart is of stone?' murmured Laura. 'What then will you do?'

'It is not,' said Jonah with grim certainty. 'I know it. We all know it. Faith in this one certainty has sustained us for all these long years. Tomorrow you will know.'

By dawn they were on the outskirts of Chelmsford, where they took a change of horses and some refreshments. Laura was permitted to step down here, to stretch her legs and drink a little, although she would not eat. She glanced into the west along the road that they had travelled, to see if there was any sign of pursuit, but she saw only a few slow wagons and a lone horseman with a satchel of post. She wondered if her necklace was already discovered, the significance of her quick, crude message in the gutter understood. There was surely no prospect of escape. Jonah's four companions watched her closely, and in any case her legs seemed barely capable of supporting her weight. There was a fatigue in her, bone deep, that allowed of no physical exertion of any kind. Even to raise her arms was to feel the ache of wasted muscles that had no more to give, and she knew in her heart that she was dying. In London, hope, rest and the company of friends had sustained what spirit remained to her, but now she felt it ebbing away hour by hour, even as the carriage ate up the miles between her and her appointment with the Wytch King. There was a freedom to be sought in letting go, in surrendering her spirit to the darkness that summoned her. In addition, denied any other means of striking back, there was a fierce victory in prospect if, by giving up what life remained to her, she could frustrate Jonah's ambitions.

'I suppose you have him in Darkharrow,' she ventured at one point, having turned the matter in her mind for some hours. 'Although how you placed him there, I cannot tell.'

'You may suppose what you like,' grunted Jonah, staring out at the passing fields and villages, 'and you will find out soon enough.'

Edward awoke with a start, having slept for a few hours on a hard bed in the small room next to Sir Joseph's. He rubbed his hands over his face, swung his legs out of bed and splashed some water onto his face from the jug and bowl by the fireplace whilst the disconnected thoughts that had troubled his sleep swam into focus at last. Then, drawing on stockings and breeches and reaching for his coat, he made his way onto the landing and knocked softly on Sir Joseph's door. When there was no immediate response he knocked more firmly, finally opening the door a little and venturing in.

'Sir Joseph,' he said.

'Hmm, what?' There were sounds of sudden movement and the cocking of a pistol.

'Don't shoot! 'Tis I,' gasped Edward, raising his hands.

'Oh, Edward, it is you,' said Sir Joseph, carefully letting down the hammer and putting aside the pistol. 'You startled me. I shall have to get used to life as a fugitive.

Open the curtains a little, if you would. What ails you? What time is it?'

'It is a little after four,' Edward told him. 'And I would not have disturbed you, but I think I know where they have taken Laura.'

'You do?' Sir Joseph sat up in bed, reaching for his spectacles.

'I do. They have taken her to Tithing Harrow. That is the T Laura made.'

'The Eastings?' asked Sir Joseph, frowning. 'But why on earth would Jonah take her there? The whole of his support lies on the opposite side of the country.'

'Because of Darkharrow,' said Edward, his eyes gleaming. 'The Wytch King lies in Darkharrow.'

'A ridiculous notion, Edward. I am surprised that you should embrace it,' chided Sir Joseph. 'I suppose your uncle and the abbot might have something to say about accommodating such an infamous corpse, unless you suggest that they are part of Jonah's conspiracy, too.'

'They may be,' agreed Edward, 'and you will recall that there was a great fire in Darkharrow some years ago, soon after Jonah's arrival in the Eastings. We well know that Jonah has a penchant for setting fires.'

'Hmm. he does…'

'And in the chaotic circumstances of a fire, when the dead are being hastily removed to spare them from the flames…'

'Yes,' agreed Sir Joseph, casting off the covers in one decisive, sweeping movement. 'You are right! And the dead brought out from there in haste would doubtless be disassociated from the name plaques that identify them in that place. There must have been great confusion.'

'Absolutely,' said Edward excitedly, 'and in that confusion it would have been easy enough to introduce corpses from outside, take them into Darkharrow and find places for them after the fire was extinguished and all set to rights.'

'I suppose he must have had them carried across from Whale Hall,' said Sir Joseph, rubbing his stubbled chin, 'when he had established in his mind that Margaret DeLacey might be the one who could awaken the king. But this could surely not have been accomplished without connivance or assistance from within. Jonah would need to be sure that the Wytch King was in safe hands, would be attended to in the proper manner in order to safeguard his flesh.'

'He must,' agreed Edward. 'And if old Noah were his accomplice, it would scarcely amaze me, I confess. He is a sour enough old man, to be sure, a close, secretive fellow and one who never showed me a single kindness beyond the bare minimum that his duty to my mother required of him.'

He handed Sir Joseph his coat as the physician stepped out of bed.

'To think that I may, myself, have unknowingly gazed upon the Wytch King's face,' he said, with a shudder.

'I must get word to Corvin,' said Sir Joseph, inspecting his watch. 'They have a very substantial head start on us and we must get ourselves to Darkharrow with all possible speed. Doubtless Thomas would wish to accompany us, and I suppose a party of his muscular bravoes would also be to our advantage.'

'Blanchflower is dead, I hear,' said Sir Richard, drumming his fingers on his desktop as Bentley stood before him the next morning.

'He is,' said Bentley, whose long, mournful face seemed longer even than usual. It was a face well adapted to the

443

expression of regret, and now it set forth all its very considerable powers in this regard.

'I see. And how did this come about? I understand the house was one of a dozen or so we had under observation, ones known to be frequented by Sir Joseph's friends and associates. I understand this house was known to contain a person answering the description of the girl we seek and that the premises were being observed in case we might be led to Sir Joseph's associates in this conspiracy or to the hiding place of Her Majesty's body.'

'Yes,' said Bentley.

'So, what happened, Bentley? Hmm? How did Blanchflower come by this information?' continued Sir Richard, although he had a shrewd idea exactly how this had come about. Bentley's fleshy mouth worked silently for a few moments, a string of saliva briefly connecting upper and lower lip.

'He came to see me, sir, when you were with Lord Ogilvy, and he had a written commission from His Majesty, no less, commanding me to share our intelligence with him. I had no choice.'

'You could have refused, Bentley,' snapped Sir Richard. 'You could have dissembled, delayed, charmed him with your silver tongue, anything to buy sufficient time to see me back here.'

'And would you have refused?' asked Bentley, showing a little fight. 'Had you been in my place? You know what he is like... was like.'

'Yes, he was a very intimidating presence,' conceded Sir Richard, 'to those ready to be intimidated. Evidently, His Majesty sought to enforce his own priority on our investigation and Blanchflower was sent to destroy the girl.'

'Evidently he failed,' said Bentley.

'And paid the ultimate price for it, it would appear,' said Sir Richard. 'The domestic staff will be interrogated in due course, but I doubt they will add much to what we know already. I suspect Lady Elizabeth may have more to contribute, but then of course she is too well connected to subject to the full range of investigative procedures available to us.'

'Indeed,' agreed Bentley cautiously, wondering whether he had weathered the storm.

'And time is against us,' continued Sir Richard, studying his fingernails.

'Quite.'

'I must see Ogilvy again,' announced Sir Richard, his gimlet eye resting upon Bentley's pale features once more. He smiled a thin smile. 'Perhaps you would be so good as to inform His Majesty as to the fate of his assassin.'

It was late in the afternoon by the time the coach arrived in the vicinity of Market Lavenshall. Here, in the road outside the King's Head, they were stopped by a party of the Lord Lieutenant's constables, searching passing vehicles for an escaped prisoner. There was no way of avoiding them, and Jonah, having peered out of the window, threw himself back into his seat with a curse, his eyes momentarily glazed with confusion.

'Pistols,' he grunted to his companions, fetching his out and placing it ready in his lap, covered by his coat.

'What if I were to alert this constable?' said Laura, watching as a burly, red-faced man approached their side of the carriage.

'Then I would shoot him down and you will be complicit in his death,' growled Jonah. 'I suppose his widow and children would curse you in all eternity.'

Laura shrank back in her seat, wide-eyed as the constable rapped on the window with his cane and Jonah lowered it.

'I'm sorry to trouble you, sir…' began the man, but then his voice died away and the light of recognition entered his eyes. 'Jonah Stephenson,' he said.

What he might have gone on to say would remain forever unknown as Jonah swiftly raised his pistol and discharged it full in the constable's face. The noise, in the narrow confines of the carriage was tremendous and Laura winced, closing her eyes even as the vehicle lurched forward, horses lashed into furious movement. Maigret and Blood had their window open, firing their pistols, too, as the carriage gained speed, leaving the constables milling in confusion behind them.

'We won't have long,' warned Blood, settling back into his seat. 'They'll be after us soon enough.'

'Long enough,' said Jonah, looking up from where he was engaged in pouring more powder carefully into his pistol. His glance met Laura's. 'Destiny awaits you.'

Laura looked out of the window bleakly as the coach swept past Cottersley Park. There, conversing with a neighbour at the gate, was Becky Marchmayne, a basket of cut flowers on her arm. She looked up as the coach moved onward and for a moment Laura met her eye. There was no spark of recognition there. Why would there be? Laura bore no resemblance now to the girl that she had known; that girl from another life so long ago. She mused wistfully on the brevity of life, the high value to be set on memory, as the coach trundled onward, and the first cottages of Tithing Harrow came in view.

Groomfield, when they drew into the gravelled courtyard, was closed and silent. There was no sign of human habitation and the windows stared emptily over weed-grown grounds. The roses that were once her mother's delight blew wild along the borders and the lawns were turned to meadows.

'And where is Mama?' asked Laura, peering out. 'Does she not dwell here anymore?'

'I know not,' grunted Jonah. 'Like you I have not been here for many a month. Come now.'

He extended a hand to her as the coach drew to a halt before the handsome grey stone steps at the front of the house. The front door proved to be unlocked but there was no sign of life within, and the premises bore signs of neglect as pronounced as those outside. Here a picture had fallen from the wall, shards of glass scattered across the parquet, there, in Jonah's study, an irregular slew of correspondence drifted from desk to the floor. Laura was almost too weak to walk now, supported on either side by Boyle and by Mortlake, who had come down from their place at the front of the coach.

'Watch the gates,' said Jonah to his men. 'I suppose we shall have company soon enough and be ready to leave the moment I return. You,' he jerked his head at Laura, 'come with me.'

It was futile to issue such a command, necessary only to grasp her beneath the arm and urge her forward towards the stairs that led to the cellar. Here, Jonah jangled keys for a moment and having unlocked the door, led her down the steps into the cool darkness below. He left her propped against the wall here, lost in the consideration of her life in this house and returning presently with a lamp. By its light he unlocked another door, the one that gave access to his wine cellar, one that Laura had never known anyone else to enter. Jonah was famously abstemious in nature and extremely sparing in his distribution of wine, but he let it be known that he had been laying down a collection of the more distinguished Bordeaux vintages in a long-time investment.

'I have laid down a few dozen cases of Pauillac and Margeux, but Saint-Estephe is my particular delight,' Laura remembered him saying once, with an unaccustomed sparkle in his eye.

Now she saw why, as the door creaked open, and she was admitted to a space rather larger than she had anticipated. The first part, that visible from the door, was taken up with wine racks from floor to ceiling. Behind these was another section, with a low-vaulted ceiling dominated by a great stone bench. There were other narrow benches against the walls on which six white-shrouded corpses lay, but Laura's attention was immediately drawn to that in the centre of the space. On this bench lay two bodies, side by side. One of these was certainly King Stephen. Even in death his sunken-cheeked features recalled to Laura's mind the picture she had seen in Jonah's book. The other, lying beyond the dead king, was the small form of her sister.

'Emily!' she cried, a hot prickle of shock traversing her scalp.

Her sister was unnaturally pale of face, but time had yet to shrink her tissues and it was possible to conceive that she fallen asleep only a moment ago. Laura moaned and lurched forward. She might have swooned, her consciousness reeling beneath this shock, but Jonah swept her up and placed her before the bench.

'Now,' he said as her head lifted once more. 'Look around you. You behold the seven sleepers of ancient legend, my father and his councillors. They have slept here beneath your feet this last five years even as the household lived its life unknowingly above, even as you grew from childhood to maturity. Do you remember a day, long ago, when Darkharrow burned? That was when we brought them here, secreted amongst all those other displaced corpses.' He laughed. 'A bold stroke, indeed, and one that placed the seven conveniently at hand, within my own protection.'

'I remember,' murmured Laura, as the events of that long-distant night came once more to her mind. The scent of burning was in her nostrils, and she had a vivid recollection of standing next to Emily, watching the flames against the night sky. 'So, it was you who set that fire, you who ensured that my father's body was burned.'

'It was – a blaze that encompassed two ends. But now the hour has come, the hour for which I have awaited three hundred years. Three hundred summers, Laura, three hundred long winters, but now my father shall shoulder those years aside. Do your work, daughter. Rekindle the fire in my father's heart and open the door into a new age. If you do as you are bid then you may perhaps summon your sister, too.'

Laura glanced from the king to her sister and panic gripped her. Her eyes filled with tears and the moisture fled from her mouth.

'But I do not think I am strong enough,' she moaned.

'Yes, you are,' snarled Jonah. 'Do it, I command you.'

'No,' Laura shook her head, 'let me try first with Emily.'

'Ha, you are insane if you think I will wear that. Wake my father first, or I swear...' he drew a large knife from his belt, 'I will cut off her head and then none shall wake her, ever.'

'NO!' screamed Laura, lashing out with such unexpected speed that the knife was knocked from his hand and went spinning across the floor.

'Do it,' he snarled, 'or I swear I shall throw her head down the well outside,' he repeated.

Laura closed her eyes tight, tears splashing at the dead king's feet. A picture of Emily's lovely dead face drifting down through dark water came into her mind with irresistible force.

'It will kill me,' she said in a small voice. 'I know it.'

'Do it,' said Jonah a third time, taking her hand and placing it firmly on the king's cold brow. 'Now is the moment. It is your immutable destiny.'

Bowing her head and sighing in despair, Laura focused her mind and stooped through the king's dead tissues, down and down to the cold hard heart and found it… a stone. She looked up as though from the ocean depths, and to the distant surface she rose, but it was too far, too far, and she was conscious of her lungs bursting, her heart faltering within her. She would never reach it.

And then there were noises. A part of her was aware of a sudden scream, of a movement from the shadows, of her mother rushing furiously at Jonah with knife in hand.

'Leave her alone, you demon!' her mother shrieked. 'I shall send you to Hell.'

Jonah span round, seized the wrist in his iron grip and snatched the knife away, plunging it into her breast with a single brutal movement just as Laura surfaced behind him, eyes springing open. The dreadful panorama seared her consciousness. There was her mother, mouth wide, toppling away and clutching at her breast. A rattling gasp issued from her throat, and for an instant her eyes met Laura's. There was despair written in that final glance but rage and overwhelming heart-bursting sadness, too. And there was love in one forlorn glimmer that died as the focus faded from those shadow-wide pupils. An answering flame erupted in Laura's own breast – and with it a fierce resolution sparked. In one blinding, blissful moment of clarity all things were laid out before her and her course absolute. Jonah was breathing hard, his back to her now. With a smooth, decisive gesture she placed her hand to the side of his neck and pressed hard, reaching down suddenly through his pulsing flesh to the living, leaping heart within. She squeezed with a grasp of such passion, such furious conviction, that her own heart swelled within her, even as Jonah's instantly burst beneath her iron-clawed fingers like some rotten fruit. That organ gave one last juddering spasm, and a great flash of life transfixed her even as it leapt from Jonah. He gasped, threw back his head and was instantly dead, toppling sideways like some fallen tree. Letting go, subsiding backward onto the bench, Laura twisted and found her face next to Emily's. Raising a hand that felt leaden now, she groped for that pale brow. She felt once more like a diver, plunging into the cool embrace of the ink-dark sea, swimming hard for Emily's heart, enfolding it in the warmth of her infinitely loving embrace, relinquishing the single great spark she bore into that cold organ and seeing the blue fire of life race through those tissues. It was done. The gift was given. Laura felt her own heart stilled now, a stifling constriction and pain as the great darkness of death rushed up to enfold her. Yet even as the light of her spirit was extinguished, she became fleetingly aware of one last joyous sensation, distant but clear, a sound on the fringes of that departing consciousness – the ringing of church bells.

Epilogue

'I never saw anything like it, Sir Joseph,' said the sergeant, holding up his lantern. 'An' I seen a few choice things; I can tell you.'

'Indeed,' said Sir Joseph, surveying the cellar bleakly and stooping at Laura's side.

'All dead as a doornail,' said the sergeant, 'and Dr Henderson sent for to give them the once over. There are four dead upstairs stopped a bullet or took a blade after we followed 'em up from Lavenshall. Put up quite a fight, too. We've got three dead of our own, you know, and another half dozen shot up or carved up to varying degrees. Quite a little battle it was... and then this.' He gestured at Margaret DeLacey's body in its dark pool of blood. 'Easy to see how that one copped it. That's the lady of the house, if I'm not mistaken, and 'im... he's – rather, 'e was – her husband, Jonah Stephenson. We were chasing after 'im after 'e shot poor John Potts full in the mouth, out by the King's Head. Not sure about these others on the slabs, though, or the little old lady lying dead there. Not a mark on 'em that I can see. I daresay you'll shed some light on it, pardon the pun,' laughed the sergeant, setting down his lantern. 'Shall I have them brought forth? I don't suppose Dr Henderson will mind, what with you being a famous physician and all.'

'Yes, bring them forth,' confirmed Sir Joseph after taking a moment to gaze into Laura's face, finding a certain serenity there. 'But these two on the slab and the other shrouded corpses you may leave to me. There are people coming up from London to look after them, and they will certainly take them away in due course.

'I suppose the Lord Lieutenant will need to be informed,' said the sergeant with a frown. 'Otherwise, that might be exceeding my authority, begging your pardon, sir.'

'The Lord Lieutenant is Sir Peter Marchmayne, I collect?'

'He is sir.'

'I shall speak to him, then. I don't suppose he will object.'

Edward and Thomas were waiting outside, sitting on the steps, whilst a party of constables dragged away the bodies of Jonah's companions. Edward had his face sunk in his hands whilst Thomas stared abstractedly across the courtyard to where the weathercock swung gently atop the stables.

'I think we must look after Emily,' said Sir Joseph, kicking thoughtfully at a step with his toe. 'I suspect that Laura may have bought her a new life at the expense of Jonah's and of her own.'

'And what of her mother?' asked Edward, raising his head so that the puffy redness around his eyes was clearly apparent. 'What happened there?'

'I suppose we will never know exactly what transpired,' said Sir Joseph. 'Although I think it is reasonable to suppose that she came upon Jonah unawares and made some effort to intervene. The place seems uninhabited, does it not? But the sergeant told me that Mrs Stephenson lived here alone in a single room next to the scullery. Certainly, she paid a high price for her attempt.'

'She did,' agreed Edward, his voice somewhat hoarse, 'although it seemed to me, she thought her life already over when last we called upon her. Will we take Emily with us now? And what about the dead king?'

'I should like to consign him to the pyre,' said Sir Joseph, 'but I suppose that should be for others to decide. I shall send word to Sir Richard. As for Emily, well doubtless we must entrust her to the care of Hardiman and Mark. If she begins to awaken, they will know what to do.'

'Do you not fear arrest, Sir Joseph?' asked Thomas, recalled from his own thoughts. 'I daresay there is a warrant with your name on it in London.'

'But not yet here, as you have seen,' said Sir Joseph, indicating the sergeant's back as he opened the door to the empty coach some way away. 'Here my reputation is intact, at least until word reaches those in whose duty might be to detain me, and besides, you heard the bells a pealing. The queen is returned. Who knows what will happen now? There will be some uncomfortable choices to be made by many in present authority, you may be sure.'

Turnbull lay in bed, his habitually ruddy features oddly pale and flaccid, as Lord Clarey sat beside him and bestowed upon him the benefits of companionship, the diversion of conversation, although the conversation was decidedly one-sided.

'How I envy you your present indisposition,' said Clarey, patting his friend's hand soothingly. 'Here you lie, pleasantly insensible of the trauma afflicting the realm whilst I must endure an agony of indecision. How should I place my support? Which party is most likely to prevail?'

The bishop, had he been able, would certainly have retorted that he had not had himself shot as an act of political expediency. Instead, he merely grunted and rolled his eyes.

'Her Majesty is awakened, you know? I suppose you heard the bells,' continued Clarey, 'and all is changed within a heartbeat. Parliament is summoned and the lawyers are fairly frothing at the mouth. The nation is embroiled in a state of turbulence such as I never thought I should live to see. And here you lie, Turnbull, whilst the world hurries on around you. Oh, and the archbishop has died. That is the other thing I had meant to tell you. I thought you would want to know.'

Turnbull blinked. The doctors had assured him that he was likely to survive if the wound remained free of corruption. Undoubtedly, Sir Joseph's decisive action had saved his life, just as his own intervention had saved Laura. But for what? Did she yet live? Clarey's voice droned in his head. His wound pained him, despite the laudanum that was prescribed him, and he knew full well it would be weeks before he was the man he once had been. If ever. Clarey's news about the archbishop left him strangely unmoved, and part of him stood aside to regard this with wonder. He was changed. He knew this. His eyes flickered to the window, where rain pattered on the glass and an image of the girl came into his mind – as it often did. "Hearts of ice and stone" she had mentioned to him once, when describing the extent of her dominion over the dead. He closed his eyes, the better to exclude Clarey from his reverie, and wondered whether one still-beating heart had felt her power, too.

If you enjoyed Heart of Ice and Stone, you may also enjoy its sequel, Well of Souls, coming later in 2023.

Before then, you may wish to check out other fantasy books by Martin Dukes, written under his pen-name of RJ Wheldrake.

That Which The Deep Heart Knows
1st in the Chronicles of Toxandria
Romantic Fantasy

An ancient empire, a prince unexpectedly thrown into the maelstrom of politics - and a tavern girl. Love, loss and a conflict of gods.

A Trick of the Light
2nd in the Chronicles of Toxandria
Fantasy

When your destiny was death but you're not going down without a fight. Born in a land where a cruel god holds sway, Stilli Zandravo makes a grim discovry about her past which changes her life forever.

Printed in Great Britain
by Amazon